Advance praise for *Th*

"An exquisite exploration of motherh[...] withholding the truth from generatio[...] ers are bursting with life, and the sly way [...] [h]eart of the story is sure to surprise. Haunti[...]

—Fiona Davis, *New York Times* bestselling author
of *The Lions of Fifth Avenue*

"A thrilling story, remarkably told, Nathan Gower's debut *The Act of Disappearing* is as propulsive as it is moving. A mystery lies at the heart of this novel, but Gower also never loses sight of the humanity of his characters in his honest portrayal of parenthood, family, and mental health."

—Lara Prescott, *New York Times* bestselling author
of *The Secrets We Kept*

"*The Act of Disappearing* is a perfectly calibrated balance of propulsive suspense and elegant prose, resulting in a complex and beautifully written debut. The novel introduces readers to compelling characters and conjures different time periods and places so vividly that they will feel the real world is falling away as they disappear into its pages."

—Silas House, author of *Lark Ascending*

"Set in rural Kentucky and Brooklyn, Nathan Gower's *The Act of Disappearing* is a cinematic, suspenseful literary page-turner rich with memorable and lively characters. A remarkable novel about a community's secrets and silences, familial inheritances and myths, and the power of sharing hidden stories."

—Carter Sickels, author of *The Prettiest Star*

"*The Act of Disappearing* broods on identity, small-town secrets, multigenerational legacies, and the claims we have to our own and others' stories. Indelible, charismatic characters—Julia White and Kate Fairchild chief among them—propel Nathan Gower's intricately plotted cold-case mystery. A beautifully imagined, splendid debut."

—K. L. Cook, author of *Marrying Kind*

"Nathan Gower's *The Act of Disappearing* masterfully alternates two suspenseful storylines that will keep you up turning pages straight to the stunning end. This is a remarkable debut!"

—Jessica Anya Blau, author of *Mary Jane*

The

Act

of

Disappearing

Nathan Gower

mira

Recycling programs for this product may not exist in your area.

ISBN-13: 978-0-7783-6954-7

The Act of Disappearing

Copyright © 2024 by Nathan Gower

For questions and comments about the quality of this book, please contact us at CustomerService@Harlequin.com.

TM is a trademark of Harlequin Enterprises ULC.

Mira
22 Adelaide St. West, 41st Floor
Toronto, Ontario M5H 4E3, Canada
BookClubbish.com

Printed in U.S.A.

For Rochelle, always

THE PHOTOGRAPH

All cameras capture the dead.

The shutter opens, consumes the light, creates the image: an illusion, the ghost of some former self, what *was* but can never again *be*. The same person is never photographed twice.

That's where we start—with a photograph, the end of one life, the beginning of another.

The date printed on the back is July 4, 1964.

See the glossy surface of the front, the train bridge stretched across the Ohio River. Notice the brilliant bursts of fireworks against the fallen dusk, curtains of light threatening to drape the truss of the bridge. Now look down to the bottom-right corner: see the tiny figure of a woman suspended in air—captured in the liminal space between life and death—falling to the black waters below.

If you squint, you may even see what she holds in her arms, crushed against her chest with the shattering force of a mother's love: a swaddled baby.

My name is Julia White. This is not my story.

PART ONE:

THE RABBIT NEST

1

A dead body is a haunting thing. Every time I close my eyes, the onslaught of memory: blue-white skin and twisted limbs, bulbous eyes, and purple lips—my mom's corpse lying stiff in her Poughkeepsie apartment, an empty pill bottle atop the note on her nightstand. Most days I can forget. But today, on the three-year anniversary of her death, the swell of grief crushes my ribs, an inflating balloon that refuses to burst.

Right now, I need my mom more than ever. I've been on mental health leave from work for the past few weeks, but now I'm back at the Sundowner bar in Brooklyn. Inside, the blue-black darkness is a salve against the hard light of the city. An hour into my shift I have stirred myself into negronis and Manhattans, shaken my regrets into gimlets and margaritas. Then some guy sporting an ironic fedora orders a dirty martini—Ryan's drink. I reach for the olive brine, but it's too much. Pinprick sweat gathers at my temples. I rush to the closet-sized bathroom behind the bar before my knees give out. Kneeling on the filthy terracotta floor tiles, I retch out the remnants of a blackberry smoothie, seedy and blood-purple. I wipe the seat of the toilet with a paper towel, rinse my mouth, check my mascara. As soon as I get back to the bar, Myra pulls me aside, tucks my hair behind my ear.

"Jules, honey, you don't have to be here," she says. Her voice holds the authority of a bar manager and the concern of a roommate. She's both, so it works.

"Of course I do." I can barely afford to eat, let alone help Myra pay the rent. Sure, our little Crown Heights studio is *Brooklyn cheap*, but it's still Brooklyn.

"Look at me, babe." Myra tilts my chin, catches my eyes. "It's okay if you're not ready. Give yourself time." The jaundice glow of the bar cuts across her skin, splitting her into shadow and light. The silhouetted hook of her nose, the curvature of her ear—my brain morphs her face into a mirage of Ryan. I try to edge past her, but she won't budge.

"I can't—" I start, but I don't know what comes next.

Myra pulls me into her, kisses my forehead. "We'll talk about it later. If you insist on staying, then get that guy another old-fashioned." She nods toward an old man sitting alone in my favorite corner of the bar—the dead zone where you can drink in the shadows, hiding from the incessant hum of electric light.

I serve the old-fashioned but don't say anything—nobody chooses to sit in the dead zone if they want to make small talk. By the time I come back to the other side of the counter, two emo-looking dudes are whisper-yelling about something.

"I swear to God, that has to be him," one of them says. His lip piercing is infected—cherry red, encrusted. My stomach lurches.

"Twenty bucks says it isn't," says the guy next to him. I try to ignore them, but I have to grab a jar of Luxardo cherries from under the counter, so I come into their orbit.

"Hey, help us settle something," says Mr. Infection. It isn't a question, but a demand. "That guy over there," he says, stealing a glance at the man in the corner sipping his old-fashioned. "Is that who I think it is?" I want to tell them both that I'm not in the mood to referee their little boy battle. But I need tips, so—

"It would help if you tell me who you think he is," I say. He looks back one last time, then leans in close.

"Jonathan Aster," he says, just above a whisper.

I have no idea who Jonathan Aster is. Well, that's not entirely true. His name floats in the ether of my consciousness the same way it does in most New Yorkers'. The idea of him—his fame, his mythos—these things I know. But I couldn't pick him out of a lineup, and I certainly don't know why he would be ordering drinks in our seedy little hipster bar. Jonathan Aster probably has *SoHo penthouse* money. I'm sure he could find a nice top-shelf bourbon in Manhattan without needing to cross the bridge.

"Okay, so I'm totally sorry about this," I say, serving the old man another drink. I gesture to the guys at the counter. "But those two goth wannabes over there think you're Jonathan Aster, and they're not going to leave me alone until I find out." He eyes the two dudes on the other side of the bar, stirs his drink.

I wait for him to answer. He doesn't.

"So, I mean—are you? Jonathan Aster?" The man studies my face, tilts his head. He leans forward out of the shadows, giving me the best look at him I've had all night. His iron gray hair curls at his ears, frames his angular face. His emerald eyes pop against his black suit, his silver tie. He looks to be pushing seventy, maybe even older—but he's controlled, assured. He stands slowly, moves to the other side of the table, pulls out a chair.

"Care to sit with me?" he says. He moves back to the other side, slides into his seat, takes a drink. Saliva rushes against my tongue the way it does just before I puke. The scorch of vomit threatens my throat, but I'm able to choke it back down. Whether he's Jonathan Aster is no matter—I know the type of man he is. I slide the chair back under the table, the legs hitting the metal pole underneath with a *clank*.

"And then what?" I say.

"Pardon?"

"I sit with you, and then what? You buy me a drink?"

"If you'd like."

"So I just walk off my job and have a drink with you. And then—what's next? You tell me about your job? Your money? Your power? Maybe I reach across the table, brush my fingers over your knuckles." I cock my head, study his face. "And then we have another drink, and another, and another. Pretty soon you're hoping I forget that you're old enough to be my grandfather. Maybe I go home with you. Am I on the right track here?"

"You have quite an imagination," he says.

"Maybe." I lean across the table, get right in his face. "But look me in the eye and tell me you don't think you're three steps away from buying access to my body like it's just another cocktail." His eyes widen, an animal caught in a snare. He sips the dregs of his bourbon. The liquor shimmers on his upper lip.

I start to leave, but no—I won't give him the satisfaction. I won't be made to feel crazy. Not tonight.

"Here's the thing," I say, locking eyes with the old man. "I don't care who you are. I'm paid to serve you drinks, not to stroke your fragile masculinity. You want to impress someone with your mystery and intrigue? Try those two fanboys at the bar."

"Fair enough." He holds a hand in front of him—a flag of surrender. I collect his empty rocks glass and turn to leave. "But could I ask you to do me one small favor?" I would ignore him, but then he adds one word, one that sends pinpricks down my spine: "Julia."

I freeze. Slowly, I turn back to him.

"How do you know my name? Who are you?" He reaches into the leather messenger bag at his feet, pulls out a paperback book. When I see the cover, my face catches fire. I pull back the chair, take a seat.

"I am Jonathan Aster," he says, placing a pen atop the book. "And if I've found the right woman, you're Julia White." He flashes a smile, crinkling the skin around his eyes. "Would you do me the honor? Please?" He extends the pen to me, opens my book to the cover page.

I can't say anything for an eternity—maybe two full minutes— so I sit, stunned, listening to one of the world's most famous art photographer drone on about how much he loves my little book.

"It's remarkable, really—the blending of genres. I've never seen anything like it." He thumbs through the dog-eared pages, then flips back to the note before the prologue. He raises a finger with a dramatic flair, reads my words back to me: *"What follows is both real and imagined, history and myth, fact and fiction. The truth of this story belongs to me—and hopefully to my mother. Beyond that, I make no promises."*

He looks at me with wonder in his eyes. "Simply marvelous," he says. I'm lost in the moment when I feel a hand against my shoulder. I flinch.

"Sorry, love," says Myra. "Didn't mean to scare you. Just checking to see if we need anything over here." She smiles at Aster, but then looks to me, cocks her eyebrow in a way that asks, *Is this creepy old man threatening you?*

"We're good," I say, placing my hand on top of Myra's. "Just give me a sec and I'll be back at the bar." The two goth fanboys are gawking, but I avoid their eyes. Myra waves me off.

"Take your time." She regards the book on the table. "Who am I to keep you from your fans?" She nudges my shoulder, walks away. I look back to Aster, but I don't know how to proceed.

"Listen, Mr. Aster—" I start.

"Jonathan. Please."

"I'm sorry about earlier. I just—" I stop, gesture around the room as if it holds an explanation. A man walks through the front of the bar, and for a split second, I think it's Ryan.

"You're a woman who works in a dark room full of men," he says. "No apologies needed." Tears threaten my eyes. Grief pools inside me, an inkblot spreading through the chest.

"So, how about that drink?" asks Aster. "Is that allowed?"

"I don't drink," I say reflexively. I realize only after I say the words that I am telling a half-truth.

"A bartender who doesn't drink? Seems like a story waiting to be told." I grab a cocktail napkin from the table, dab my eyes.

"Why are you really here?" I ask. "I mean, I'm flattered you've read my book—really, I am. To be honest, I'm not even sure how you found it."

"You can find anything if you know where to look."

"Sure. But it's not exactly topping any Google searches. My little indie publisher says I've sold an astounding 376 copies." Instantly, I'm transported back to the night of the book launch last month, memories skipping across my mind's reel like jump cuts in a movie: my slackened face in the dirty bathroom mirror. Ryan's greedy hands across my chest, my hands pawing at his shirt. My bare back pressed against the cold concrete wall. Hot breath against my ear. The tug and pull of dry skin. I try not to blink. My throat constricts. "The fact that you've found a copy can't be a coincidence," I say, willing myself back to the present moment.

Aster pushes the book in front of me, extends the pen in my direction once again. It's clear he isn't going to talk until I comply. I take the pen, swoop my signature below my printed name on the title page. Aster studies the signature and smiles.

"I'm here because I need your help," he says. "With a job."

"A job?"

"Or an assignment, if you prefer."

"I don't prefer anything. I'm just trying to figure out—"

"I want you to write a book for me." He says this without

a sliver of irony, which is enough to make me laugh out loud, despite everything. Aster holds his glass in the air, gestures toward the bar for another drink. I must be making an incredulous face because he adds, "Is the idea really that absurd? That I would ask a writer to write a book?"

I'm forced to gather myself. "Look, Mr. Aster, you seem to be a sincere person."

"I like to think so."

"But you've got the wrong woman."

"How is that?"

"You're in New York City. Writers are like weeds around here. We grow from every crack in the asphalt."

"And?"

"And I'm thrilled that you like my work, but that book in your hands wasn't good enough to get a single offer from any of the big publishers, let alone the medium ones."

"So, they were wrong," he says, shrugging.

"Were they? Besides I'm not even a biographer, so—"

"To hell with the biographers," he says, swishing his hand through the air like he's swatting a fly. "They've already written everything there is to know about my life, and frankly, none of it is very interesting." He reaches into his bag, emerges with a manila envelope. He carefully unwinds the threaded clasp at the top, pulls out an eight-by-ten photograph.

"I don't need you to tell my story." His voice pulls taut at the edges by some invisible thread of pain. "I need you to tell hers." He pushes the picture into the light. As I study it, a breath catches in my throat. My eyes flick over the glossy surface. I see the woman, the baby. I can't bear to look longer than a second or two.

"You took this picture?" I ask.

"That's right. But I've never shown it. It's not a part of my public work."

"And you want me to—what, exactly?"

"Find the story," he says. "And then tell it." As he says this, I'm hit with the sudden realization of what I hold in my hands: an original *Jonathan Aster*—and one of his earliest works. It's likely worth high six figures, maybe more. "You write the story, Julia," he says, as if reading my thoughts, "and that photograph is yours to keep."

"Or sell?" I say, testing him. He winces, but then nods.

"If you must."

"Why?" I say. "Why me?"

"Because it's a story that must be told," he says. "But it's not my story to tell."

2

1947

It wasn't but ten minutes after Norman Fairchild opened the store there on the north end of Main Street when the phone rang.

"Fairchild Shoes," he said.

"Norman," started the woman on the phone. He couldn't quite place her voice at first, but after a moment or two it settled into him. Mrs. Eubank—the neighbor woman. "I don't mean to pry, you know I don't. But that baby is at it again. Been screaming for over an hour. It's coming straight through that front window."

"Well, that's what babies do, Janice."

"I know what babies do, thank you very much. And I know that they don't go on like this. It's carrying all the way up Poplar Street."

The welcome chime clanked against the door, and Norman looked up to see his young clerk, George Caldwell, swing into the store. The boy hurried behind the counter to punch in on his time sheet, smelling of hair oil and aftershave. Norman looked beyond him, through the glass of the storefront, watched as Dennis Ashby clicked on the lights at the jewelry store across the street. On a nice day like this in May, all of downtown Gray Station would be humming with business soon.

"Okay, Janice," said Norman.

"You want me to go check?" said the woman. "Make sure everything's okay?"

"No, don't bother yourself." Mrs. Eubank pushed a sigh through the receiver.

"Now listen, Norman. We all know about Edith, it's no secret. If you need me to go check—"

"I said don't bother yourself," repeated Norman. He thumped the phone back on its base, maybe a little too hard.

Norman hurried the five blocks back home. George would be fine by himself—he was only eighteen, but he was a good, honest clerk. Talked about going into the ministry, maybe even a seminary education. Perhaps not the best salesman, but the numbers always came out right when he was left in charge, and that was the main thing. Besides, George had lost his old man in the war, and that would always count for something.

A cool spring breeze propped Norman up as he made his way south down Main Street past Dreyer Brothers Furniture and Riverview Bakery. Then he turned east onto Poplar, squinting against the bright sun. The baby's howls echoed against the folk Victorian brick houses, hurrying him along past the Eubank place and toward his own yard. By the time he reached the front door, a ring of sweat had gathered around his starched collar.

He pushed through the door, crossed from the foyer into the living room, and closed the bay window. The baby was lying on a blanket in the middle of the floor in nothing but a cloth diaper. Norman scooped her up.

"Okay now," he whispered, bouncing the child in just the right way, rubbing his hand in a counterclockwise circle against her back. A spoiled smell hung thick in the room. The bottom of the girl's diaper was soaked through, wetting Norman's palm. He held the baby against his chest, moved into the hallway, climbed the stairs. He paused in front of the closed bedroom door, but did not push it open, didn't knock, didn't even call her name. He went to the nursery down the hall and changed the soiled diaper, powdering the child's red bottom with careful hands. When the baby was clean, Norman got her dressed and lay her in the crib. He went back into the hallway, planting his feet outside the closed door. The baby began to fuss back in the nursery.

"Edith," he said. "Kathryn needs to eat." She didn't answer, so he gripped the door handle, found it was locked. "Listen now. I'm going to need you to open this door. We can figure this out, but the baby's got to eat." He stood silently for a while, though he knew it wasn't much use. He had half a mind to kick in the door, but then thought better of it.

He went down to the kitchen to check the refrigerator for a bottle, but no such luck. He pulled a can of evaporated milk and some Karo from the pantry—he knew to do that, at least—but he could never quite remember how much to mix. The baby was working herself into a fit upstairs. Norman wiped the sweat from his forehead, went to the console table out in the hallway where they kept the telephone, and called Edith's sister.

"I'm sorry about this, Clara," he started, "but I can't seem to figure out how to make up this bottle." He pulled on the cord, just something to do with his hands.

"So it's happened again," said Clara.

"She'll be alright. It's just that the baby needs—"

"I'm coming over."

"No, there's no need—" he started, but she had already hung up.

It took Clara half an hour to come in from the little farmhouse she and Raymond kept out there in the country off

Highway 41. Norman bounced the crying baby and watched through the bay window as she pulled the Chevrolet pickup into the front drive. Clara pushed herself through the front door, suitcase trailing behind.

"Where is she?" said Clara. Norman looked up, angled his eyes toward the locked bedroom beyond the ceiling. Clara nodded, touched the baby's red cheek, and then went straight to the kitchen. She fixed up a quart of formula, poured ten ounces of the mixture into a glass bottle. Norman watched her as she worked—controlled, precise. At thirty-eight, she was ten years older than both he and Edith. He hoped it was somewhere in those ten years that a person learned how to manage this life.

When Clara finished with the bottle, she handed it to him, then smoothed the white collar on her green-checkered dress and made her way up the stairs. After Norman fed and burped the baby, the two of them fell asleep right there in the rocker beside the bay window in the living room.

For the next three days, Norman came and went from the shoe store on Main Street, walking the five blocks each way. He braced himself each time the phone rang, but it was never Mrs. Eubank. Clara was there at the house to look after the baby, to tend to Edith in the locked room upstairs. At the store, George stayed on the register or took measurements for customers, so Norman was left to the solitude of the repair shop in the back—the work he loved, quiet and restorative, not just for the shoes mounted on the cobbler anvil.

On the fourth day, the sky closed in on him while he was walking home. The rain came in sheets, so by the time he reached the front door to the house on Poplar, he was soaked through to his undershirt. The thunderheads roared around him, darkening the stoop of the house. He never even noticed that Clara's Chevy was gone from the driveway.

He tried to shake the water from his feet on the porch, but

no matter—he still dripped puddles in the foyer, dampened the carpet as he walked from the living room to the kitchen. And then all at once, there she was—balancing the baby on her hip, flipping burgers on the cast-iron skillet, humming along to Bing Crosby's "Beautiful Dreamer" on the radio.

"Edith," he said. She swung around, her ivory A-line dress swishing across her knees. She looked at him and then at the baby—really studied the child as if she was just then seeing her for the first time.

"My goodness," she said. "Isn't she just perfect?"

3

The dark always helps.

With the city lights pinched from the room by blackout curtains, I lie in my loft bed in the studio, unable to see the texturized ceiling twelve inches from my nose. This has been my salve for the past month—floating into the *nothingness* of black space, a waking dream, listening to the steady drone of the box fan as it chops away the outside world.

"Okay, but what does that even mean?" says Myra, tucked into her bed four feet below me. In my pool of grief, this oil-slick of joy: listening to Myra's voice in the small hours of morning. We trade the darkness of the bar for the blackness of this apartment, our bodies swallowed by the night, nothing left but voices in the void.

"I don't know exactly," I say, "but that was his answer." Aster's words have played in loop inside me for the last six hours: *It's a story that must be told, but it's not my story to tell.*

"And that's it?" says Myra. "Dude didn't give you anything else to go on?"

"Not really, no."

"Like, he didn't tell you where he took the picture? Not even the name of the woman?"

"He just said that the photo is all I need. That the story will tell itself." As I say this, I'm haunted by the image once again, a beautiful horror: the woman jumping to certain death in the turbid water below, the burst of fireworks celebrating her final act.

But the baby—oh, God, the baby.

At four thirty, I wake up with a crush of panic on my chest. I climb down from the bed and grab my phone, throw on an old Vassar hooded sweatshirt—the one with the frayed pull strings and worn elastic that Myra and I always fight over in the winter. Out on our little balcony, sitting in the punchy October wind, I start with a Google search based on the only information I have: the back of the photo says July 4, 1964. I type in: *woman jumps from train bridge 1964*—but the results don't yield anything helpful. Then I run a series of searches for the bridge itself—*train bridge over river/famous railway bridges/ train bridge+fireworks*—this gets me nowhere. Then it hits me: *the photograph is all you need.*

I scroll through the camera roll on my phone, find the pic I snapped of Aster's photograph just before he left the bar last night. I do a reverse image search. No perfect matches, but close enough: the same train bridge, stretched across the same river, almost at the same exact angle. I click on the image, which leads me to some tourism website managed by a small city government— some place called Gray Station.

"Seriously, Aster?" I say to no one in particular. "You want me to go to Kentucky?"

An hour later, the city still sleeps. Delirious from exhaustion, I'm caught in the liminal space at the edge of consciousness. I slip back in time, discover some version of myself sitting with Myra in the Sundowner's tiny backyard, waiting for my book signing to begin. Amber light from the setting sun peeks between the buildings, gleams off empty shot glasses on the table. Myra settles my jittering knee with a careful hand, offers a toast. A smattering of friends clink champagne glasses.

Later—I down another shot of vodka while Myra introduces me to the mostly empty room. I stand on the wooden stage and read passages from my book, voice halting, speech stuttering. The room swells with impatience: clanking of silverware, a cleared throat, the scuff of wooden chairs across concrete. In the corner, a pyramid of unsold books mocks me. Empty seats line the perimeter of the room.

And that's when I see him. Ryan Alman—my college boyfriend, my almost-fiancé.

"Buy you a drink?" he asks after the reading. I'm just drunk enough to say yes. Images of the next two hours flit across the reel of my mind: more drinks. A hand against Ryan's biceps. The scruff of his beard against my neck. The rest of the night fades into darkness, and then memory restarts with a shock of light in the morning.

A cool breeze whips against my face, pulling me back into the present. I wonder if Ryan is lying awake like I have most nights the past month. I scan back through my texts since that night, all unanswered. A few of them catch my eye as I scroll.

Fri, Sept 3
Wow, what a night. Was great to see you but that was probably not the best idea?
(4:30 AM)
—

Can u talk?
(7:18 PM)

Sat, Sept 4
is everything okay?
(1:12 AM)
—

are u just going to ignore me?
(2:15 AM)

Mon, Sept 6
Look, I'm sorry for all the late texts but I'm really not in a good place right now.
(3:47 PM)
—

just trying to make sense of this.
(6:50 PM)

Sat, Sept 11
god, after all these years you really haven't changed
(2:17 AM)

i can totally remember why we broke up
(2:18 AM)

Wed, Sept 14
look I'm sorry. Don't know why, but I am. Can't we just talk about this?
(6:48 PM)

Sun, Sept 18
whatever Ryan. Have a great life i guess
(7:16 PM)

Reading back through the texts again wrecks me like it does every time, but I can't help myself. I always think I must have missed it: some clue that would help me understand why he's ghosted me. But no—I'm always left with the scattered pieces of a jigsaw puzzle.

I flick my thumb hard across the length of the screen, flying down to the last text.

Mon, Oct 3
Okay, I really don't know what's going on. We hadn't seen each other in years, spend one night together which to be fair we probably shouldn't have but whatever, that's no reason to completely ghost me. U can hate me if u want, I don't get that but fine but we really really need to talk. I'm serious. This isn't okay, you have to call me. Please.
(8:42 PM)

I want to throw the phone off the balcony, but I think twice and toss it on the cushioned chair beside me instead. I tuck my knees up into the sweatshirt, watching the morning sun fight to push through the darkness.

Two days later, Myra and I take the train from Grand Central to Poughkeepsie. After a quick Lyft to the outskirts of town, we stand in the middle of the rural cemetery I haven't visited since last year. Marigold sunlight pours over the tombstones of my mom and my grandma Margaret—the only earthly remnants of the two fiercest women who ever lived. I linger in silence for over thirty minutes, remembering, thinking. I will myself to be here in this moment—not to be distracted by thoughts of Ryan Alman.

"I'd stand out here all day with you, Jules—you know I would," says Myra, checking her watch. "But I need to fill this belly." She thwacks her stomach with an open palm, sounding off a hollow *thud.* "Let me put some brunch in this gut and then we'll sit our booties out here until they close the gates."

The thought of eating makes my insides lurch, but I don't tell Myra this. Instead, I smile, lean my head on her shoulder. A heart can only swell so much before it bursts. Myra's warm body is a buoy in my sea of grief. I enter into a prayer—one not uttered in words, but through my pulsing fingers and thrumming heart.

At a café on the Hudson, we help ourselves to a seat at one of the open cast-iron tables outside. I order a small plate of fresh fruit just so I'll have something bright to look at, and Myra stuffs her face with a Greek omelet, chasing it with a blood orange mimosa.

"I think I'm going to do it," I say, mostly to myself.

"Write the book?"

"Well, at least go down to Kentucky. See if there's a book worth writing." Myra takes a sloppy bite of the omelet, wilted spinach clinging to her bottom lip.

"You don't have to rush into anything, Jules." I poke at a piece of watermelon.

"I need to get away from myself," I say. After the words are out of my mouth, I realize they don't really make sense. Whatever. Myra understands. She always does.

"And Aster is paying for this?"

"He gave me a check. Called it an advance. Told me to cash it if I decide to do the research." Myra raises an eyebrow, and I know exactly what she wants to know. "Ten thousand," I say. She drops her fork, clanking it against the metal table.

"Get it, girl!" she says. She reaches out, gives me a high five over the table. I can't help it: I smile, maybe for the first time in over a month. "But let me be clear about something— you're buying this mimosa." She takes a long swig, draining half the glass.

"It's only a drop in the bucket, love." The numbers swirl through my mind. Credit card bills. Medical expenses. Back rent. If I didn't have Myra, I don't know how I'd survive. "I'll take care of the rent this month. It's the least I can do." Myra waves me off.

"So, Kentucky?" she says. "Honey, you are going to be so lost down there. Bluegrass and horses and—what else?"

"Bourbon," I say.

"And KFC," adds Myra. I smile, but then I think of fried chicken, the pull of the skin, the grease against my fingers. I look away, see a woman next to me slicing through an egg, the yolk running into the blood of a rare steak. Then Myra dabs her finger against bits of fallen feta on her plate, and it's all too much. I barely make it to the trash can ten feet away before I puke. Myra hurries to me, puts her hand on my back, shields me from the crowd.

"I'm so sorry," I say, wiping my mouth. But sorry for what? A viscous trail of spit clings to my fingers. Myra rubs my shoulders, and we sit there on the sidewalk next to the trash can. She tilts my chin toward her, studies my eyes. A change comes over her face, and I know she's figured it out. I can lie to myself, but there's no fooling Myra.

"Jules, are you—" she says, gesturing to my stomach. "Any chance you could be—"

"Don't tell anyone," I say. Hot tears flood my eyes. Myra pulls me into her, cradles me against her chest.

"Oh, sweet girl," she says.

4

When they finished the procedure that first time, Edith came
back to herself in pieces. First, the hands resting in her lap—the
dead ones, sitting there like they belonged to someone else—
became her own once again. She flexed her wrists, lifted a finger to her lips. Yes, she still existed. She had a hand, a finger,
a face. The rest of her would be alive again soon.

How much time had passed? An hour? A week? When she
tried to stand, the room twisted around her, dazzling pinwheels
of light. She collapsed back onto the stiff bed behind her.

"Woah, there," said a voice from somebody, somewhere.
Then he was beside the bed, touching her elbow.

She had an elbow, an arm.

"Easy does it now, Mrs. Fairchild," he said. He was a big man,
friendly looking. He had a mustache. He was not Norman. Norman was at home.

"What am I—" she started. It wasn't the question she meant
to ask, but it was all she could think to say.

Later, she swallowed pills from a paper cup. They wouldn't
tell her what they were for, but still—she rolled them against

her tongue, felt the texture like tiny horehound drops. The pills might help. Or they could kill her. Either way, she swallowed.

She didn't have to sweep the hallways that day—first timers got the day off. They said it would get easier. In a few weeks, she might get the treatment in the morning and feel well enough to play bridge in the common room that same afternoon.

"How are we feeling today?" said one of the nurses—the one with the kind eyes and crooked teeth.

"I don't feel—" started Edith, but then the words stopped. She was nothing but fragments and sharp edges. The nurse tilted her head, placed a careful hand on Edith's knee.

"That's okay now, honey," she said. "That will do just fine."

Three days later, the nurse with the kind eyes guided her down the hallway, fingers brushing against her shoulder. Edith didn't resist. Back in the treatment room, she looked at the stiff bed with indifference. There were three men in the room—big men, the one with the mustache. They would hold her down. This was the worst part.

"I won't fight it," she said to nobody in particular. The nurse with the kind eyes helped her get settled onto the bed, eased her head back onto the pillow.

"That's it," said the nurse. "Open up wide for me now, honey." She worked the rubber guard into Edith's mouth. She gagged, but then remembered:

Breathe through the nose.

In (one-two-three).

Out (one-two-three).

The nurse dabbed her temples with the fluid. Edith closed her eyes, her lids glowing pink against the sharp fluorescent light.

Then came the moment of euphoria, just before they cranked the machine: she saw Kathryn running through the grass in the backyard on Poplar Street, the frills of her too-long dress brushing against her toes. The girl crunched through fallen magnolia leaves, her outstretched arms spinning around her tiny body, cupped palms capturing the honeysuckle air. Norman wasn't there—he didn't need to be. Just the perfect two-year-old beauty, fierce and alive.

Then the electrodes fired against her temples, and her sweet girl disappeared into the black of night.

5

The next day, I call the number Jonathan Aster gave me at the bar. After it rings what feels like twenty times without going to voicemail, I realize that it must be a landline. *This guy is old-school*, I think, but then I remember: he's a solid seven decades, so no, *he's just old*. When he finally answers, I blurt it out.

"I can't do it." I'm sitting on a bench outside of my ob-gyn's office in Crown Heights, reading the label on a bottle of prenatal vitamins.

"That's unfortunate," says Aster. "Thank you for considering." Without another word, he hangs up. I hit Redial because—well, I don't really know. But I expected more pushback from him, and now I feel like I've made a mistake I can't take back. He answers on the third ring.

"Don't you even want to know why I'm turning you down?" I stand, pace in front of the bench.

"You don't need to explain yourself, Julia." I can't understand why, but his answer chokes me up. I can't speak for a moment, but I don't want to hang up either. "However, if you'd like to discuss this further," he says, "why don't we meet in person?" I nod, but then there's more silence, and I remember he can't see me.

"Okay," I say. Off in the distance, starlings swirl, flecks of black against the bright blue sky.

An hour later, I'm sitting in front of the fountain at the Brooklyn Museum, trying to scarf down the rest of a chef's salad I picked up on my walk over. On my phone, I scan through one of those pregnancy websites where they compare your growing fetus to fruit. *Six weeks: your baby is now the size of a pomegranate seed.*

I spot Aster ten yards away as he approaches, a leather messenger bag slung across his chest—the same one he had at the bar. He's wearing mirrored sunglasses and a newsboy cap, probably to keep a low profile.

"Really, I could have come to you," I say, rising to greet him. "I feel terrible that you had to come all this way." I hear an apology pulling at the edges of my voice, and I hate myself for it. I don't owe this man anything. This must become my mantra.

"How about a walk?" says Aster, and then he's off, leading down the sidewalk along the perimeter of Prospect Park. In the daylight, I expect him to look frail, but no: he's fit, vibrant—the type of guy you see on infomercials drinking organic green smoothies.

"So, let's get this out of the way," I say. With some angst, I hold the ten thousand dollar check out in his direction, but he keeps his hands clasped behind his back like he's waiting for handcuffs.

"Shall we discuss your decision first?"

"It's just bad timing. My life is a dumpster fire right now."

"I see. And writing this book would somehow make it worse?"

"Maybe. Probably. I don't know."

"Sounds convincing." He turns to me and smiles. I stop walking, look him in the eye. Then the words just pour out, water from a burst hydrant:

"Last week was the anniversary of my mother's death, and

my book isn't off to a great start, and I'm a twenty-eight-year-old bartender bumming off her roommate's kindness because I make barely enough money to eat and am drowning in my mother's medical bills, and I'm pregnant, and my ex-boyfriend, who knocked me up, is an unbelievable jerk." I expect some look of surprise—a raised eyebrow, widened eyes—but nothing.

"I'm sorry to hear that," he says.

"Which part?"

"Well—" He pauses, searching for words. "The boyfriend and the roommate and the— Well, all of it." He loops his hand through the air as if trying to draw a neat little circle around everything.

"*Ex*-boyfriend," I say. "We broke up, like, six years ago during undergrad."

"You've been pregnant for six years?" he says. I try not to smile, but I can't help it. I love a good dad joke.

"He was at my book launch. Myra told me not to invite him, but—"

"Myra is?"

"My roommate—sorry. So anyway, the whole night was super depressing because there were only, like, fifteen people there. And afterward Ryan and I talked and had drinks and—"

"And here we are."

"Yes, here we are," I say, wishing it was really that simple. We walk farther west along Eastern Parkway, passing the main branch of the library on the left. Aster stops and regards me, studying my face like he's trying to work out a puzzle.

"I intend to ask you a deeply personal question, Julia. Whether you choose to answer is, of course, your prerogative."

"Um, okay?"

"Do you plan to keep this child? To see this pregnancy through?"

"Those are two different questions."

"I suppose so," says Aster. "Either way—if you do keep the baby, wouldn't the money I'm offering you make things easier? That check is just to get you started—travel expenses and whatnot. I can provide more as you need it."

"But see—that's the other thing," I say. "To be honest, the whole money situation is just bizarre. You float me ten grand because—what? You like my writing?"

"No," he says, "I gave you ten thousand dollars because this is a very important project. And I believe you are the best person to complete that project."

"But you don't even know me!"

"Ah," he replies, removing his mirrored glasses. "But what if I do?"

"What are you talking about?"

"I don't like to make assumptions," he says, "but I'd like to think you know that I'm fairly well established in the world of photography."

"I mean, that's a bit of an understatement. But yeah. So?"

"So, the art world is a fairly small place." He leads me to a bench in Grand Army Plaza. "Those of us on the inside of that world have to look out for each other. Exchange favors, that sort of thing. Without that community, none of us could make it."

"I'm a writer. I know all about that." Aster smiles, nods.

"Well, years ago, before I gave up public speaking, I'd frequently give talks at universities. NYU, Columbia, Cornell." He turns to me, raises an eyebrow. "Vassar."

"Wait—you knew my mom?"

"Mary White was a fantastic art historian," he says. "One of the finest in the world." I plant my feet on the sidewalk, coming to a sudden epiphany.

"You sought me out because of my mom. It had nothing to do with my book."

"It has *everything* to do with your book," says Aster. "Reading your work made the life of your mother real to me—far beyond the little bit I already knew. The way you told her story was piercing, haunting even." Aster reaches into his messenger bag, pulls out the familiar manila envelope. "When I reached the end of the book, I couldn't help but think that this photograph would have thrilled your mother." He takes my hand, places the envelope into my grasp.

I pause for a moment, thinking. "You have to know you could be throwing your money away here, right?" So many questions roll around in my head, but this is the only one I can manage to ask. Aster shrugs.

"Money is nice to have," he says, "but it's never been the currency of art."

"Then what's the point?"

"The story is the point. The woman in that photograph is the point." He smiles, but there's some seed of regret buried in the squint of his eyes, in the slope of his posture. "She was very important to me. And I very much believe she will become important to you, too."

"This would be so much easier if you just told me who she was. If you gave some context." He places his hands on my arms—it feels fatherly, maybe, but I've never had the reference point for that.

"Easier, yes. But nothing about this can be easy. That's not how this story works."

"I don't understand."

"You will, dear," he says, and then he steps away. "The choice is yours. Take a few days to consider and let me know." As he turns to leave, I feel the weight of the envelope in my hand.

"Mr. Aster," I say, holding it out to him.

"You keep it. I've had it all to myself for over fifty years. It's time to share that burden."

6

1952

From the looks of things, just about all of Gray Station had come down to the riverfront. There'd been a buzz about town all week since the announcement in the paper, and now that the day had come, it seemed the whole city had shut down for the afternoon. Picnic blankets were stretched across Riverview Lawn and down toward the bank of the Ohio. Norman found a good spot for the four of them—him and the girl, plus his sister-in-law, Clara, and her husband, Raymond—and set up the folding chairs he'd bought for just this occasion. They were smart-looking things—aluminum frames stretched with a bright mesh of green and blue fabric. Edith sure would like them.

"Now, look here, Kathryn," said Clara. She held the girl's hand and pointed out over the river, gesturing to the towering steel stretched between Kentucky and Indiana. "They've been building this bridge for three years now, and it's finally ready for a big ol' train to come across it. What do you think of that?" The girl squinted against the sunlight to study the structure, trying to figure out just what was so special about it. Clara made a *choo-choo* noise and chugged her arms back and forth, and at least that made the child laugh. "It'll be a sight to see," said Clara, looking back at Norman and Raymond with a pitiful smile.

Raymond dug a penny from his pocket, cupping the coin in his palm, hidden from view.

"Miss Kate," he said, "what is it you have sticking out from behind your ear?" The girl turned to her uncle, swooped a hand up to her right ear and then her left. "Naw, you ain't going to be able to get it like that. Come over here and let Uncle Raymond get it for you." She ran to him, and he made a show of pulling the penny from behind her ear. "Well, then, I guess this belongs to you," he said.

Norman watched his daughter from behind and noticed the canary-yellow bow he had tied into her hair that morning was crooked. He sure wished he could do a better job of all this.

The announcement in the paper had said the first train should cross right at 4:25 in the afternoon, but here it was a quarter to five and still nothing. Folks across the lawn busied themselves by snacking on buttered popcorn and lemon shakeups, bought from the vendors along River Road who had set up shop for the occasion. Clara fanned herself with an advertisement that Dennis Ashby had printed up earlier in the week—10 percent off those new Kodak Brownies he was selling over there at his jewelry store on Main Street. It was a fine idea, Norman thought. He surveyed the crowd, and sure enough, those new cameras were peppered all over the lawn, everyone waiting for the perfect shot of that first train. Even Mayor Jennings had one strapped around his neck. Norman watched him shaking hands down there close to the river's edge, sweat shimmering on his bald head in the wavy August heat.

The girl had gotten restless, so Norman sent her along between the blankets and lawn chairs to collect dandelions. She captured a smile from every person she passed. She just had a way about her.

"She sure is a charmer," said Raymond. He pulled a Coke from the cooler he had lugged from the truck. He cracked open the can, sucked down a healthy gulp. "I'd like to get her into the show one of these days." Norman turned his head, clenched his jaw. The man was always going on about that silly little magic show he put on at the community hall every month. A grown man waving a wand, pulling rabbits out of his hat. The whole mess was embarrassing. "I always loved making her momma disappear," he said.

"You hush now," said Clara. "No need to bring that up. This is a happy occasion."

"Well now, did I say something wrong?" asked Raymond. He slipped a flask from his vest pocket, splashed some bourbon into his Coke. He offered the flask to Norman, who waved it off. He had to be careful about drinking in this hot sun, especially with the girl to worry about.

"No, I guess not," said Clara, softening. "It's just—" She broke off, gathered the words. "It doesn't feel right talking about her when she's not here." A moment passed between them. Norman caught himself looking at the empty chair beside Clara. He'd brought it for Kathryn to use, but still, it looked awfully vacant.

"I suppose I can understand that," said Raymond. "But look, Clara, it ain't as if the woman's dead and gone. This thing with her—" he said, shaking his head. "They'll get her fixed up down there and she'll be back with us again, right as rain. The real Edith. Just like last time." Clara and Raymond both looked at Norman to see what he thought. But he didn't have much to say about that, truth be told. He decided just a little drink might not hurt, so he reached out for the flask after all.

He had closed his eyes there in the warmth of the sun just for a minute or two, and when he opened them back up again, the girl was gone. Clara was thumbing through the summer Sears catalog she brought with her, and Raymond was having himself another drink, forgoing the Coke now and sucking straight from the flask.

"Where's Kathryn?" said Norman. He sat upright and craned his head around, looking. Clara flopped the catalog down in her lap.

"Well now, she was right here a minute ago," she said. Norman stood to get a better look. He could see down to the shoreline to the north and back to the string of brick-front buildings along the roundabout to the south. A trail of sweat dripped from his armpit down the length of his side. Clara stood now, too, kicked off her flats and climbed atop the fabric of the lawn chair.

"Easy now," said Raymond, fiddling with the flask, trying to work himself to his feet. "You're liable to put a foot right through that fabric, Clara."

"Kate!" she shouted. "Kathryn Marie!" She garnered some looks from a few folks nearby, but her voice didn't carry far with all the activity going on around them. Norman made his way through the maze of blankets, trying to be careful not to step on anyone but keep his eyes up at the same time.

"Y'all see a little girl come through here?" he asked. "Five years old. Got a big bright yellow bow on her head." No, sorry, they hadn't seen her they said, so he went on and tried some folks down a ways toward the river. He heard Clara yelling out the girl's name again, and now Raymond was headed in the other direction up toward the east side of the lawn. And then all at once there was a commotion from all sides.

"There she comes!" shouted a man up ahead. For a split second, Norman thought he might be talking about Kathryn, but no, of course not. The man shielded his eyes from the sun and pointed off south down the train tracks where you could just barely see the locomotive coming into view. The crowd hooted and hollered, everybody standing at once, making it impossible for Norman to see farther than ten feet in any direction.

They raised their cameras up to eye level, aiming through the viewfinders.

Norman pushed his way to the sidewalk, hurried back to where Clara was still standing atop the mesh lawn chair, her hand cupped to her mouth. She screamed the child's name again and again, but even ten yards away, Norman couldn't hear her voice above the yells of everyone else. The train was almost on them now, the engineer blasting the whistle as it approached the first truss of the bridge. The sound was nearly deafening. Norman caught eyes with Clara, but he could only shake his head. Then, when he turned back up the sidewalk and looked toward downtown, he saw Raymond standing at the cross section of Main Street and River Road.

Dangling at his side, gripped loosely between his fingers, was a canary-yellow hair ribbon.

The caboose of the coal train was halfway across the river when Norman made it over to where Raymond stood. Clara hurried to catch up, leaving the folding chairs on the lawn. She was out of breath when she reached the men.

"Listen to me now," said Raymond, bracing Clara by the elbow. "There's no need to panic here." He'd found the ribbon caught in one of the shrubs hedging in the sidewalk along the lawn. "At least now we know she went this way," he said. With the train across the bridge now and trailing out of sight into Indiana, the crowd erupted into applause.

"We need to hurry," said Norman. People began to disperse, and the streets would be filling up soon with cars and pedestrians every which way. They split up again, with Raymond heading east farther down River Road, Clara walking the roundabout in the town square, and Norman going south along Main Street. She wasn't in front of his shoe store. He pushed on, walking faster than the gridlocked cars could make it down the street.

"Hey there, Norman," called someone from an Oldsmobile stalled in the parade of traffic. "Everything alright?" Mrs. Eubank was leaning out of the passenger window now, gawking at him. She was such a nosy woman, but no matter—Norman needed the help.

"Y'all seen Kate around here anywhere?" he asked, skipping the pleasantries. He leaned down, looked through to the driver's side of the car, saw Pete behind the steering wheel. Janice looked at her husband, but he just shrugged.

"No, I'm awfully sorry, Norman," she said. She put a hand to her chest as if she'd just realized. "Is she—"

"She just took off on us," said Norman. "She couldn't have got too far though."

Before he could say anything else, Mrs. Eubank was swinging herself out of the car. She marched right up to the next vehicle in line, a baby blue Chrysler Newport. She tapped on the windshield.

"The Fairchild girl is missing," she said matter-of-factly. "Cute little thing with bright red hair. Answers to Kate or Kathryn." She paused, turned toward the sidewalk. "What was she wearing?"

"Checkered green dress," said Norman. He touched up around his throat. "With a little white collar." The woman got out of the car, and just like that, she and Mrs. Eubank were tapping on windshields in both directions. Pretty soon they had a nice little hunting party. Some of the husbands got out, too, abandoning their cars. "Traffic ain't going nowhere anyways," said Clark Bridwell, one of deacons over at First Baptist. Like so many other folks, he hadn't been able to look Norman in the eye since Edith went back down to the state hospital. But here he was, doing his best. "Now, where'd you see her last?" he said.

Twenty minutes later, there must have been fifty people spread out around the river and downtown, including two police officers. They'd walked the downtown loop three times over, checking every alley and crevice along the way. If it had been some other child, Norman might have had the frame of mind to consider the generosity of this little town. But there was no time for that. His little girl was still gone. He'd heard of these things on the radio, read about them in the newspaper. Sometimes they didn't turn out too good.

Most of the search party had turned back down toward the river. Norman overheard one of the police officers say they might want to start thinking about getting a boat out on the water.

"Why would we want to do that?" asked Norman, a shake in his voice. His legs felt like rubber. He stumbled a bit.

"Take it easy there, Fairchild," the officer said. "Why don't you just have you a seat right here on the grass and rest for a minute or two."

"I'm okay," said Norman. "It's just this hot sun." But he sat down anyway because he just couldn't seem to get his legs under him right. He thought about Edith, how he'd talked to her on the phone just two days before. She sounded good. Hopeful. Said she wanted to build a campfire in the backyard, sleep with Kathryn out under the night sky. They used to do that before the girl was born, before Edith's mind turned—just the two of them in sleeping bags, counting the blinks of fireflies overhead.

His head felt light, so he closed his eyes. And then he thought of something else: Edith, on her good days, used to walk Kathryn all over these downtown streets, sometimes coming down to the river and circling the roundabout loop two times over before walking the six blocks back to the house on Poplar. On an unseasonably warm day back in November, they stopped in at the shoe store on their walk. The day had been slow and George said he was good, so Norman joined them to walk back home.

"Go on now, Kate," said Edith, smiling. "Show your daddy

what you've been learning." Kathryn skipped up ahead of them, leading the way. Edith reached for Norman's hand, and they strolled the length of Main Street and over to Poplar, following the girl, letting her guide them all the way home. "It's an awful thing to feel lost," Edith said, looking away. "My girl's never going to feel that way if I can help it." When they made it to the house, Kathryn hurried to the flower bed out front, lifting the stone they hid the spare key beneath.

"I know where she is," said Norman, loud enough for the police officer to hear. He pushed himself up onto his feet, and the officer led him to the police car parked at the edge of the lawn. When they pulled up to the house on Poplar, Norman was sure she was there. She had wandered off, couldn't see her way back to the lawn chairs where they were sitting. She'd found the sidewalk, and the only thing she knew to do was to go home, just like her momma had taught her. This had to be true. Because if not—well, he didn't want to think about that just yet.

He asked if it would be okay if he went in alone to check for the girl, if the officer wouldn't mind staying outside. He didn't want to startle her if he could help it. The house was quiet, even after he called the girl's name. Still, he took a quick look in the living room and the kitchen, and then he headed up the staircase. The door at the landing—the one that stayed shut most of the time—was pushed ajar. When he went in, for just a second, he thought it was Edith curled up on the bed, her red hair draped across the white pillow. He touched the girl's face, careful not to startle her awake. Her cheeks were pink from the hot sun, but otherwise she was just perfect.

7

I've spent my whole life on the east coast, hemmed in by trees and rivers, so the space between things in rural Kentucky feels daunting. After renting a car at the nearest airport an hour away from Gray Station, I drive along an expanse of interstate, the Western Kentucky hills undulating like waves for as far as I can see. My phone says I have thirty miles of asphalt in front of me before I make my next turn, and the radio is all crackle and static. As soon as I mute the volume, the hum of tires over pavement coaxes me into memory: weekend drives with my mom upstate—past Albany and Saratoga Springs, then through unspoiled land into the foothills of the Adirondacks.

When I was a little girl, we'd take these drives every few months. I always knew when they were coming. Mom would sink into herself for days before, cocooned inside an unnamed sadness I recognized but couldn't comprehend. Then she would do the only thing she could: drive, running away from a blackness she could never really see coming. The first chapter of my book recounts one such drive—the pervasive stillness inside the car, the physical closeness but emotional distance of my mom, a pocket of silence bubbling between us like a third person. Sometimes she would reach across the armrest, touch my hand, remind me she was still there even when I knew she wasn't. That's the conceit of the whole book, really: a journey with a woman I never understood, right up until the moment I did. When I was in high school, that same unnamed sadness blossomed inside me for the first time—a genetic connection that had lain dormant since birth, tethering me to my mom like mycelium under the soil of our family tree.

A week before my book launch, I got a phone call from an editor at the *Miscellany News*, the student newspaper at Vassar. She wanted to interview me to accompany a book review, which was flattering in the saddest possible way. I mean, nobody reads the student paper—but still: this was the moment I finally realized my story would exist out in the real world, outside of my head, outside of my control. People were going to read the words that I wrote. They would know about my mom, her depression, the way she died. They would know my most private thoughts— unfiltered, raw, naked. Maybe that's why I didn't try harder to get more press for the book. Maybe I wanted it to fail all along.

And now I'm the one driving—into *Nowhere, Kentucky*—to research another woman's suicide three years after my mother's. The parallels are too painful to ignore. Sure, if I write this book for Aster, I'll have more distance from the story, less personal stake in the narrative. But every time I think about the photograph, I can't help being swept into memories of my own past. The woman in the picture is too far off to make out any distinguishing features, so my brain morphs her into my mom— crushing me against her chest as she plunges into blackness.

The thought of the baby is too much. I swerve onto the shoulder of the road, swing open the door, puke my morning oatmeal onto the gravel. I sit on the hood of the car, let the October wind cool my face. My stomach churns, and I realize the only thing I've eaten all day is now splattered on the side of the highway, as my mind flicks back to the baby tracker site: *Your baby is the size of a sweet pea.*

8

Two days after she got settled in back at home, Edith decided the backyard could use some color. She went outside and readied a patch of dirt, then she asked Norman to take the truck to the Whitfield nursery out there on Route 60 to pick up some nice big fall mums. He stood in the frame of the open door, looking at her with her knees sunken into the soil. He shuffled his feet atop one another.

"Why don't I take her with me?" he said, nodding out toward Kathryn. She was playing with her doll in the back corner of the yard.

"She's not a bother," said Edith.

"Oh, I know," said Norman. "Just figured I'd get her out of your hair for a bit." She stood, brushed the dirt from her knees. A breeze came by and claimed some leaves from the sugar maple in the center of the yard.

"I want her in my hair, Norman. I want every part of her. Her smell, her laugh."

"Yes, I guess you would," he said. "But I just—"

"You know, I was studying the calendar the other day," said

Edith. "I went back through the last five years. And the best that I can figure it, I've missed out on around nine solid months of that child's life."

"Okay," said Norman.

"Two-hundred and eighty-seven days if I counted them all right." She watched her husband there with his hand against the doorknob. She'd missed nine months of life with him, too, but she couldn't think of the right way to say it.

"Well, then, why don't we all go?" Norman looked at the sky, at the ground, everywhere but at Edith. "It's a nice day for a drive anyway, don't you think?" Edith couldn't respond to what he was really saying. She watched her daughter out by the edge of the fence, digging through the earth with a little shovel, looking for worms. A curl of her hair swooped across the freckled bridge of her nose. "Look, I'm not trying to keep you from—" started Norman, scratching at the stubble on the underside of his chin. "It's just that the doctors said—"

"A drive sounds just fine," said Edith. She removed her gardening gloves and forced a smile. She scooted past Norman into the house and started up the stairs, thinking she might freshen up, maybe put on a clean dress. But when she reached the second-floor landing, she found herself pushing into the spare bedroom, locking the door behind her. A rest might do her some good, she thought. She just needed a little rest.

9

I could say a lot about Gray Station, Kentucky, but I'll start with what I find to be the most remarkable: this little river town of twenty thousand people somehow feels *bigger* than Brooklyn. I don't mean it feels more dense—just the opposite, actually. Everything is so spread out, so open. Back home I can hop onto the 4 train in Crown Heights, make a few changes, and emerge onto the surface almost anywhere across the three hundred square miles of New York City. Being underground on the subway is like being on a *really slow* elevator: you start in one place and—*poof!*—you end up in another. It's easy to forget that the places in between even exist.

But when you travel through Gray Station, you drive right through the in-between. All of it. On the outskirts of town, you see cornstalks and soybeans—bursting fields of crops hedging in the winding highway. You smell the acrid-sweet musk of drying tobacco hanging in open barns. When you reach the city limits, you pass the dilapidated shacks and trailers of the south side of town, watch them give way to the folk Victorian mansions to the north. You see the connecting brick-front buildings on the picture-book downtown streets. You bump over the cobbled walking paths along the roundabout circling the old city square. And then—if it so happens you're visiting to research the woman who jumped to her death into the Ohio River in 1964—you end up where the land recedes into the murky river water beneath the shadows of a rusted train bridge.

I park my rented Corolla in an open lot along River Road and walk down the winding stony hillside to the shore. I let the frigid October water lap against my shoes as I regard the bridge, lifting my phone from my purse so I can compare the real world to Aster's photograph.

After I scroll through the camera roll and click on the picture, I'm surprised by two things:

1. The bridge is longer than I thought it would be, joining Kentucky and Indiana across a wide expanse of the Ohio River. Aster's picture is framed by trusses of the bridge, so the entire photograph is all water and metal and sky. In real life, the world feels wide open here at the river's edge, my line of sight stretching in panorama for miles in every direction.

2. More importantly, the bridge is also shorter than I thought it would be. I try to imagine a ten-story building sliding between the bridge deck and the water below—120 feet in my mind—and I think it might just fit.

And then I'm struck by this: What if she survived? Surely not the baby, but this woman—could it be? I study the photograph, see her body angling away from the camera. It's hard to tell just how vertical she is. The bottom of her skirt lifts into the air, her legs just beginning to flail out behind her. But could she have had time to correct herself, to pencil-dive into the water feetfirst? It suddenly occurs to me that Aster never said the woman died. Sure, he never said she lived, but—is it possible?

I ring the doorbell of the little bed-and-breakfast Myra helped me find. I can still hear her voice when she found it on the internet—*Jules, this place is straight-up Norman Rockwell.* She's not wrong. A hip-high white picket fence hems in a small grass yard. Brilliant orange-and-red mums line a freshly mulched flowerbed against the backdrop of yellow siding. Completing the picture is a wraparound veranda with an honest-to-God wooden porch swing. I fully expect the door will be answered by a Mr. Rogers doppelganger.

When the door actually swings open, standing in the frame is a girl who looks like she just raided Harley Quinn's closet. I'd guess she's sixteen or seventeen.

"Yeah?" she says, and honestly, I don't know how to respond. I look at her fishnet sleeves, the leather choker stretched around her neck, her pink-and-blue-dyed hair. A girl after my own heart.

"I'm looking for—" I start, but I'm so surprised that I lose my words. I check the notes on my phone and try again. "Is this the, um—Little Yellow House on the River? I think I have a reservation to stay here, but—"

"Sign the thing," she says, opening the door wider so that I can see a registry book on a table. "Your room is upstairs at the end of the hall." She smacks on a glob of gum, blows a bubble. It bursts across her nose and lips. She tongues it back in.

"So, I just—I mean, do you need to see my ID or anything?"

"You paid online, right?"

"Yeah."

"We're good, then." She starts to walk away.

"I'm sorry," I say, "but are you—the owner?" She looks at me like I just spoke to her in Mandarin.

"Uh, no," she says. "I just graduated high school, like, four months ago, bro." I think she might say something else. She doesn't.

"Right. Of course." All of a sudden, I feel older than I have in my entire life.

"My grandma's in the big room at the end of the hall if you need more towels and shit." She turns to leave, but then snaps back, like she suddenly remembers something. "Oh, right. Do you have any questions?" She asks this in monotone, as if reading from a script. I shake my head at first, but then reconsider.

"Actually, yes. What do you know about the woman who jumped off the train bridge in 1964?" She stops chewing her gum, looks at me like I just hit a puppy with a baseball bat.

"Um, okay—I meant like questions about the house, but whatever." She turns her head, yells down the hallway. "Hey, Mamaw!" she says, and I hear a fit of coughing from the room down the hall.

"Oh, that's okay," I say, holding up a hand. "You don't need—"

"Yeah?" shouts Mamaw.

"You know anything about a woman killing herself in 1964?" shouts little Harley Quinn.

"Killed herself?"

"Yeah," says the girl, "jumped off the train bridge!" The house goes silent for a beat, and I would trade my whole existence to just rewind to before I asked the question. I hear the creak of a chair down the hall, and then labored breathing. I start to tell the girl again that it's really okay, I don't mean to be a bother, but it's too late: Mamaw is rounding the corner, making her way straight toward me.

"I'm sorry," I say, though I don't really know what I'm apologizing for. Mamaw labors herself down the hallway with a walker. She wears a flannel nightgown printed with Siamese cats.

"You mean the Fairchild woman?" she says, and just like that, I might have a name to work with.

"Yes? Maybe? I'm honestly just getting started, so I don't really know." Mamaw has nearly made it to me now, so Harley Quinn gives me a look and ducks out.

"Just getting started with what now, darling?" she says. Her voice has the rattle of a forty-year smoker.

"Well, that's a long story. I'm working on a project. Doing some research."

"Research. Huh. Well, then, you must be the woman from

New York." I give her a look, but then remember: of course she knows where I'm from. My contact info was on my reservation.

"That's me," I say. "I'm writing a book."

"Is that right." She smiles with her mouth, but not her eyes. She's within three feet of me now, squeezing out the space between us. "Well, look here, honey," she says. "I'm just tickled to death to take your New York money. But let me tell you just one thing." She takes a moment to work out a cough, and then goes on. "People around here don't take too kindly to outsiders poking around in their business. You'd best be careful."

10

Edith had been on those new pills—chlorpromazine—for a couple of months. When she started to level out, the doctors told Norman it would be fine to leave the girl at home with her. He went to call Clara to tell her she didn't need to bother coming over the next day to watch Kathryn, but Edith said she wanted to make the call herself. Norman said that would be fine. He sat in the recliner and pretended to read the paper while she went to the console table out in the hallway where they kept the telephone. He couldn't hear Clara on the other end, but it was easy enough to follow the contours of the conversation. When they'd nearly gotten through with it, he heard Edith's voice go sharp.

"Why do you need to speak with Norman?" she asked. "I'm telling you plain and simple what the doctor said." She handed the telephone to Norman anyway, but she stood there in the hallway, watching him.

"Hey there, Clara," Norman said. "Yes, that's right. You need to trust your sister now. Yes. Those were his words. Okay, then, we'll talk soon. Tell Raymond that we—okay now. Bye, then." When he settled the phone back on the receiver and turned around, Edith was waiting for him.

That night, she slept in the same room with him, in the very same bed. Sometime in the small hours of the morning, he felt her toes rubbing down the length of his calf.

Before he left for the shoe store the next morning, Norman waited until Edith was in the bathroom fixing herself up, and then he pulled a chair close to the child as she ate her Sugar Frosted Flakes at the kitchen table.

"Alright now, Kate," he said, leaning close to the girl. "I want you to say it to me again."

"Daddy, I already know it."

"I know you do, honey. But I need you to do this for me." He listened for sounds from the bathroom, but the door was still closed. Kathryn chewed a bite of her soggy cereal for what seemed like minutes. She swallowed, wiped her mouth, took a long drink of her orange juice. Then she recited the phone number for the shoe store, enunciating each number slowly and clearly.

"Good girl," said Norman. He kissed her forehead, breathing in the scent of her honeysuckle skin.

He could hardly think of anything else all day while he was back in the repair shop, gluing in a new heel counter or working support into an insole. Every now and again he'd take a break and pop his head into the showroom out front.

"Everything going okay out here?" he'd ask George, and yeah, everything was *peachy keen* George would say back. Then Norman would add, trying to sound casual, "Any calls?" and George knew what he meant. No calls, he'd tell him, but he'd be sure to let him know if there were any.

Norman didn't call home all day, and he was right proud of it.

★ ★ ★

There were no customers out in the showroom thirty minutes before closing time, and George had already restocked the inventory. Norman checked his watch a couple times over, and then he figured he'd just get on with it.

"Let's go ahead and close it up," he said. He flipped the sign on the front door and told George not to worry about the time, that he'd pay him for the extra half hour. He walked home faster than usual, didn't take the same joy as he usually did in feeling the crunch of magnolia leaves beneath his feet on the sidewalk. When he got home, Kathryn was sitting in the middle of the living room floor, the plastic parts of a Mr. Potato Head set splayed out around her.

"How's my girl?" said Norman, hanging his hat on the rack. Kathryn was working hard at getting a plastic nose pushed into the hard flesh of a raw potato. Norman crouched down to help her, but no, she didn't want help. He watched the strain of her fingers, and when the nose was flush with the skin, she held it up for him to see, her lips curling into a smile. He picked up another potato on the ground next to her.

"Now what are you going to do with this one?" he said. He scooped up a funny-looking mouth and went to work it in, but the girl swiped the potato from his hands.

"That one's for Lucy!" she said, her eyes going big and serious.

"Is that right? And who exactly is *Lucy*?"

"She's a girl." She went back to playing as if that settled the matter.

"Oh, I see. And where is this girl Lucy?" asked Norman.

"She ran away when she saw you coming," said Kathryn. Her bright red bangs had grown long, nearly covering her eyes. Sometimes she looked so much like her mother it was haunting. "Lucy doesn't like anyone but me," she said. Norman watched the girl go back to her play. It was normal for a child to have an imaginary friend. It was perfectly okay. But then he thought back to just before Edith had gone to the state hospital this last time, how he had found her pulling out parts of the drywall in the spare bedroom, *trying to get to the voices.*

"I thought I heard you come in," said Edith, walking in from the kitchen. She had an apron cinched around her waist, and when she undid the string in the back, Norman caught sight of where the bottom hem of her skirt touched her thigh. "I sure hope you're hungry," she said.

Edith had fixed a nice big roast and served it up with mashed potatoes and glazed carrots. There was even a fresh basket of homemade yeast rolls in the center of the table.

"Well, would you look at this," said Norman. "What's the occasion?"

"Nothing specific," said Edith. "It's just that today felt special." Norman went to grab a beer from the refrigerator, but Edith told him to sit himself down. "You're up there working hard all day at the store," she said. "This here is my work. You leave me to it." She poured the beer and got herself some ice water.

"How about this, Kate?" she said, pouring the girl her very own glass of Coca-Cola. Kathryn was setting silverware on the table. She studied the glass with longing, and then shot a look over to Norman.

"Daddy?" she said. Norman nodded, began to say it was okay, but he couldn't get the words out before—

"You don't need to go and ask your father about every little thing, Kathryn Marie," said Edith. "I'm your mother. You hear me?" The girl placed the last knife down on the table and took her seat. "You answer me when I'm talking to you!"

"Okay, now," said Norman. He placed a hand on Edith's wrist. "She's just unsure, that's all."

"Unsure about what, exactly?"

"Just about—I don't know. About how things should work.

We're all doing our best here. That's all we can do." Norman went to serve the girl some meat and potatoes, but Edith took hold of the plate.

"I told you to let me do this, Norman," she said, but then her wrist bumped into the glass of Coca-Cola, spilling the drink onto the table and into Kathryn's lap. Edith put a hand to her mouth, and the girl cried.

"Everything's okay," said Norman, but by the time he got a washcloth from beside the sink, Edith was already out of the kitchen and halfway up the stairs. He started to call after her, but no—that would only make things worse. He cleaned up the mess and got Kathryn settled down, and then there was nothing to do but eat their dinner, just the two of them. Norman watched the girl poke at her carrots. He cut his roast over and again until his plate was lined with perfect cubes of meat, but he couldn't bring himself to take a bite. They went on that way in silence for ten minutes.

"Tell you what," said Norman. "Why don't you go change out of that wet dress and come back downstairs. I have a surprise for you." Kate did as she was told, scooting away from the table without a word. When she was gone, Norman covered the roast and vegetables with foil, then pulled a cold bottle of root beer from the refrigerator. He opened a fresh pint of vanilla ice cream and dolloped out a fat scoop into a tall glass. He poured too much root beer, spilling the foam over the sides like a baking-soda volcano. He wished Kate was still in the kitchen to see it. It would've made her laugh.

Norman wiped the glass clean and then looked at the wall clock. He figured he'd better go check to see if Kate was getting along okay. When he reached the landing, he saw the door to the spare bedroom—the one that was nearly always locked shut—was flung wide-open. He peered in and saw Kathryn in her frilly nightgown, curled up against her mother in bed.

Edith was stroking the child's head, humming a lullaby into the curvature of the girl's ear.

Without a word, Norman backed down the stairs, careful to zigzag in just the right way to keep the steps from creaking underfoot. He grabbed the root beer float from the kitchen counter, crossed into the living room, settled himself into the recliner beside the bay window. He thought about turning on the television so he could catch the end of the evening news, but no: he wanted to sit in the quiet, to try to listen for the soft whispers of his wife and child floating down from up above.

11

Never in my entire twenty-eight-year existence on this planet have I felt dumber than I do right now, trying to figure out the microfilm machine at the Gray Station Public Library. Sure, I could ask for help—but I just marched up to the circulation desk, all confidence and swagger, and announced to *Linda the Librarian* that I am a writer researching a local story from the 1960s. She pointed me in the direction of the small microforms room in the back of the building and said—and I quote—"Just holler if you need anything." My ego is too fragile for *hollering* at the moment, so I decide to fumble my way through.

It's easy enough to search the library catalog and find the call number for the box I need, but now I can't figure out how to load the roll of film onto the machine. I look up and see a teenage girl enter the room, and that is fortuitous because (1) like me, she clearly has no clue what she's doing, and (2) unlike me, she isn't embarrassed to ask for help. So I do what any reasonable person would do when she wants to maintain a persona of expertise but, you know, don't actually have any: I pretend to search for something important on my phone while I watch the librarian help the girl. And then I *expertly* mimic her actions without any help at all. Because I'm an expert.

Once the film is loaded, it doesn't take me long to figure out how to work the knobs—one for scrolling and one for rotating the image. I play around for a minute, mesmerized by the spinning of the film through the machine, and then I get down to business. The date on the photograph takes the guesswork out of it, and I assume the news would break the next day, so I scroll through the *Gray Station Gazette* until I find the archives for July 5 of the same year—and there it is, right on the front page:

Woman Jumps from Bridge, Killing Herself, Baby
By Gene Bartlett

GRAY STATION—A local woman, Edith Fairchild, 45, was pronounced dead after jumping from the Gray Station Railway Bridge late last night. A young child of uncertain identity and age is also presumed dead, though the search for the body in the Ohio River continues at time of press.

Near the end of the annual Independence Day fireworks celebration, several eyewitnesses saw Fairchild fall approximately 130 feet from the base of the train bridge into the water. Eyewitnesses say she was holding a young child in her arms.

The fireworks continued to launch from a barge on the river until enough of the crowd realized what had happened. "Nobody could hardly believe it," said John Richards, of Gray Station. "Some folks even thought it might be some strange part of the show."

Local authorities say Fairchild must have gained entry to the bridge by climbing the access ladder at the intersection of Poplar Street and Third Street, though no eyewitnesses can confirm.

The Gray Station Police Department is calling the act a suicide, and Police Chief Reynolds added that, "if the child is dead, as we suspect, we will investigate the matter as a homicide." Fairchild is known to have a history of paranoia and exhibiting ner-

vous behaviors. She had recently been rereleased from Western
State Hospital in Christian County.

When I reach the end of the article, I take photos of it
with my phone. At least I have a confirmed name now—Edith
Fairchild—but the article does nothing for my curiosity about
the baby. *A child of uncertain age or identity.* So much to unpack
there—but how? I mean, despite my newfound expertise in
using the microfilm machine, I honestly don't know what I'm
doing here.

But then I read the article again, and the last line catches my
eye. I know absolutely nothing about Western State Hospital,
but I'm a bona fide expert in *exhibiting nervous behaviors.* It looks
like it's time for a road trip.

12

Three days after the failed roast dinner they all went to church together—the first time in over a year. Kathryn sat between them in a pew toward the back, and Edith wore a smile the whole service, even when it was awfully hard to do so: just after they had settled in, Carolyn Adams came right up and shook Norman's hand, said she'd been praying for Edith every single day. But she said this only to Norman—as if Edith herself wasn't sitting right there, two feet away. Still, Edith smiled. It was the only thing she could do that wouldn't make things worse. She had learned this the hard way over the years.

Something else she had learned: other people were simply not capable of understanding. This included Clara and Raymond. Most of the time it included Norman. It wasn't that they didn't try; Norman especially tried, sometimes so much she wished he'd stop. It was just that—how could she put it? People couldn't feel the depth of the blackness inside her. Sure, they could feel sadness, of course they could. But what they felt had a bottom to it, something to stop you from falling into the full well of the thing. A bottom meant you didn't have to try to claw yourself back up against the slippery walls.

And then there were the voices. That was what the doctors called them—*voices*—but that word never felt quite right. More like *perceptions*. Like she was attuned to some frequency the radios couldn't pick up, like she could see and feel and hear every little thing there was, all at once. They came and went, and they made sense just right up until they didn't. And that was when she fell into the well again—black and deep and endless.

In the hospital, the nurse with the kind eyes had once brought her a poem, said it reminded her of Edith. *Pain has an element of Blank*, said the poet, though she couldn't remember their name. Maybe that was the only useful word: *blank*ness. But how can you make people understand something that isn't there?

When the hymns were through and the offering plate had been handed around, Reverend Blackstone stood before the congregation with his Bible laid out across the pulpit. He went into his sermon, but truth be told, Edith didn't pay him much mind. She placed an arm around Kathryn, scooted the girl as close as could be until she felt the warmth of her legs against her own, the points of her elbows and hips. She listened to the steady breath of the child, in and out, in and out, and she knew—just *knew*—that this was as close to God as she could get.

This girl, this perfect child, would be the one to understand her someday. She was sure of that much, if nothing else.

13

A quick Google search tells me that Western State Hospital is two counties south of Gray Station. And other than talking to random people on the street, I don't really have any other leads to follow, so—road trip. In the past four years, I haven't driven more than twenty miles at any one time without Myra in the car with me, and I suddenly crave her like a morning coffee. I call her on the way to the hospital, tell her about the newspaper article.

"So, like, she was in a mental institution?" she says.

"Apparently. I looked it up, and—get this. The place used to be called the *Western Kentucky Lunatic Asylum*."

"Gross," she says. Then I hear her chomping into something obnoxiously crunchy.

"You enjoying that?"

"What?"

"That effing apple. It sounds so delicious."

"I mean, it's a carrot, but—" She chomps down again right into my ear. I pull the phone away for a second, but then I gather myself. You have to take the good with the bad when it comes to Myra.

"Anyway, the article says this Edith Fairchild woman was

being treated for—and I quote—'*paranoia and exhibiting nervous behaviors.*'"

"Woah, Jules. They wrote a description of you."

"Right? But today they'd just call it *anxiety* or something equally vague."

"Of course. The term that means nothing and everything."

The line goes quiet then for a minute as I think about Edith Fairchild and the hospital she was in, how her diagnosis is so familiar to me, so relatable. Myra knows all about my mental health—something I'm grateful for. She's always there to listen without judgment. Did Edith Fairchild have anyone like that in her life?

I pull into the parking lot, and despite the brazen confidence of my GPS that *the destination is on my left*, I wonder for a moment if I'm in the right place. I expect something gray and boxy—you know, something that really gives an old-school *lunatic asylum* vibe, or at least like what you see in movies. But this place has a sense of—what's the word? *Grandeur*, maybe? The manicured lawn and groomed shrubbery make me feel like I'm driving onto the campus of some prestigious liberal arts university. After I park, I ascend the stairs leading to the main entrance—flanked with enormous columns like an old courthouse.

But that's where the facade crumbles. Once I step inside, the bursts of color from the greenery and fall leaves give way to off-white walls and glass barriers, to sterility and steel doors. There's a smell I can't quite place—sharp and metallic—and the quiet of the corridor is eerie. I head to the reception desk and scan the three faces behind the plexiglass, trying to decide which one looks the least like they want to break something. I choose window number three—mostly because the woman has big soft eyes that remind me of my mom's.

"Hi there—Sharon," I say, reading the woman's name tag.

I wait for her to respond. She doesn't. "Um...okay. Where do I start?" I pause again. Sharon adjusts her glasses, stares at me. "I'm wondering if you can help me with some research for a project I'm working on."

"History of the facility is on the website," she says. Then she slaps a "Next Window Please" sign on the counter.

"That's very helpful. But I'm looking for information pertaining to a specific patient. She was here sometime in the early 1960s. Maybe earlier."

"Honey, you ever heard of HIPAA?" she says, peering now over her bifocals. "There are laws for this sort of thing."

"I don't need much—nothing invasive or anything. I'm just trying to get some dates really. For when Edith Fairchild was at the facility."

"You got a court order, sweetheart?" She shifts her weight, leans across the counter.

"Well, no. I didn't think that would be necessary, seeing as she was my...aunt." As soon as the words come out, I realize I may have just broken the law. Oddly, I feel okay about it.

"Is that right? Your aunt?"

"Well, great-aunt," I say, but then I wonder if I should have said *great-great-aunt*. I try to run the numbers in my head before she can reply.

"You still need a court order," she says. "Family or not."

"Look, Sharon," I say, leaning in close. I remove my sunglasses so she can see my eyes. "I've come all the way from New York. I don't need much here. I'm just asking for an itty-bitty favor. Just some dates. We're not breaking any rules, right? Just bending them a bit. This information is just for my benefit, and nobody in the entire world is going to know. Can't we just pretend that I have that court order?" Sharon scans the room to see if anyone is looking.

"I might be persuaded," she says, eyeing my purse. "I reckon a big shot from New York could be pretty convincing."

★ ★ ★

Twenty minutes later, after I've driven to a gas station and withdrawn five hundred dollars of my advance from Aster, I return to Sharon's window, slide an envelope through the opening.

"Edith Fairchild," I say. My heart races as she studies the envelope. She looks at me, her eyes big and wild. I have the impulse to turn and run, thinking I may have completely misread her, but then—

"Please have a seat," she says, pointing to the cushioned chairs in the waiting area behind me. I sit like I'm told. When Sharon disappears into a room I can't see, I realize that she's either (1) illicitly getting the information for me, or (2) calling the cops.

When Sharon comes back into view, she motions for me to come to the window. She hesitates, and then slides a folded piece of paper across the counter.

"Here are some random numbers that don't mean anything," she says. "Will there be anything else today, Miss Great-Niece Fairchild?"

When I get back to the car and unfold the paper, I see a string of handwritten dates stretching down the left side of an otherwise blank page. The first date range is all the way back fourteen years before she jumped from the bridge: *June 14, 1949–September 3, 1949.*

I scan down the rest of the page, my heart sinking for this poor woman—her life reduced to a column of numbers. She was committed to the facility off and on for the better part of her adult life. But then, something catches my eye, something that breaks everything wide open: I expect the last date to end sometime before July 4, 1964. But they go on for years—decades even, stretching all the way to 1997.

Apparently, Edith Fairchild was mentally ill for more than thirty years after she died.

14

The truth was, Edith didn't much like taking those pills. They dried her mouth out something awful, and most of the time she stayed dizzy for nearly an hour after she swallowed one down. Three times a day—that's what was prescribed. Three times the nausea, the lethargy. And then there was Norman, always *watching*. She couldn't manage to get out from under him. He watched in the morning before he left for work, at noontime when he came home during his lunch break, in the evening just before bed. On Sundays he would pour all those orange-and-white capsules out on the kitchen table and count them with a butter knife—scraping away five at a time like a pharmacist.

The easiest time to fake it was in the evening. When they were in the bedroom getting ready to turn in for the night, she'd climb into bed without taking the pill—pretending that she'd forgotten again so that Norman would get to play his role. That's all he wanted, really: to be the protector, to feel like he was helping her in some way, any way. There was nothing wrong with that.

So he'd bring her the bottle and place it on the nightstand

without a word about it. Then he'd go to brush his teeth. She'd wait until he would peek out from the cracked bathroom door, and then she'd pop the pill into her mouth, roll it against the side of her cheek, take a long gulp of water. When he'd go to spit his toothpaste, she'd take the pill from her mouth and shove it between the mattress and the box spring. Every morning after breakfast she would retrieve the pill under the mattress, mix it into the spent coffee grounds, and throw it away in the kitchen trash.

Every now and again she'd think how funny it was: this meticulous process, carried out by a crazy woman. The thought made her laugh right up to the point that it didn't. Then she'd sit at the kitchen table, staring at a piece of dry toast, listening to the *tick tick tick* of the clock hanging on the wall.

15

"She didn't die," I say. Aster and I agreed that I would check in every few days with an update. Our first call isn't supposed to be until tomorrow, but this can't wait. I'm met with silence on the other end, so I have a brief freak-out moment where I wonder if I somehow saved the wrong number to my contacts list.

"This is Julia, I presume?" he finally says.

"Um, you presume correctly."

"Good. How is Kentucky? Are you settling in okay?"

"Jesus, did you not hear me? She didn't die."

"Who didn't die?" says Aster. I nearly throw my phone out the car window. He's just messing with me. He must be.

"You know who I'm talking about. Edith Fairchild. She jumped, but she didn't die."

"Edith Fairchild."

"Oh my God, yes, Edith Fairchild! Who else could we possibly be talking about?" I pull the phone away and breathe, trying to collect myself. "Okay, so I found an archived article in the Gray Station newspaper that clearly says she died."

"Okay."

"But she didn't. Unless a dead woman was admitted to a mental hospital."

"I see."

"And not just admitted once. We're talking at least nine times over thirty years."

"That does seem excessive."

"*Excessive?* This isn't like some *Weekend at Bernie's* crap we're talking about here. The woman lived for thirty years—*after she committed suicide.*"

"Sounds unlikely to me," he says, and I can't help it: I hang up on him.

All at once, hot tears rush into my eyes. I'm lost and alone. I think about my mom, her twisted face on the pillow next to the blooming peace lily on her nightstand. I think about the life growing inside me. I think about Ryan. My life is exploding, and I'm in Kentucky playing some rich narcissist's fantasy game of *Clue.*

I hit Redial, and when he answers, I waste no time. "Look, Mr. Aster," I say. "You sent me here with nothing but a picture and some cash. If this is all just some big joke to you, tell me now so I can get on a plane back home."

"It's not a joke, Julia." It may just be the poor phone connection, but his voice sounds brittle. "This matters more to me than perhaps anything I've done in my life."

"Then why didn't you tell me that she didn't die? Why not give me more to go on?"

"You have to trust me here," he says. "If you aren't able to do that, I completely understand. I'll pay for your ticket back to New York, and that will be the end of it. But if you're willing to continue—and I sincerely hope you are—I cannot interfere. The story must find itself. It's truly the only way."

16

1957

The gummy heat of August hung thick over Gray Station. With schools headed back in session in just over a week, Kathryn had been champing at the bit to head out to the county line and stay with Aunt Clara and Uncle Raymond for a few more days. She yearned for the open country sky, the blinking of lightning bugs at dusk, the cool mud of the pond squishing between her toes. Just as soon as Norman dropped her off, she threw her bag into the screened-in porch at the back of the farmhouse where she would sleep, doled out hugs and kisses to her aunt and uncle, and asked them if she could *pretty, pretty please* go down to the pond.

"You're ten years old, child," said Aunt Clara. "I reckon you don't need me to hold your hand." So she took off lickety-split down through the acre of woods and across the field to the little fishing pond at the back of the property. The neighbor boy was already there, waiting.

"Hey, Jack!" she said, panting a bit from the run. He was wading in the pond trying to catch frogs, the legs of his overalls hiked up past his knees.

"C'mon," he said, wasting no time with pleasantries. "I found something." He led her the other way across the field, shushing her as they passed his own house in case his dad had been drinking. The coast was clear, so they hurried down to the barbed wire fence at the edge of the yard. Jack put a hand across her chest to stop her. He kneeled, pointing to a rabbit's nest.

Kathryn watched him pull back the loose leaves and cotton-candy fur to show her the hole in the ground—maybe big enough for both of her closed fists. She bumped her head into Jack's as they both tried to get an angle to see down inside. Kathryn counted seven baby bunnies, their naked pink bodies pressed into one another like they were still in the womb. She wanted to poke them with a stick, but she knew Jack wouldn't like that.

"Don't touch them," he whispered. "Their momma won't come back if you do." One of his friends in Sunday school had told him rabbits hate the smell of humans like humans hate the smell of horseshit. That didn't seem right to Kathryn, but she was only ten and Jack was eleven, so he was a whole year smarter than she was. They squinted against the sun, watched a chicken hawk circle overhead. "We got to cover them back up," said Jack. "Or that hawk will get them." They folded the dead leaves back over the top, but Jack didn't think that looked like enough, so he went to get a few twigs. When he wasn't looking, Kathryn reached in the hole, ran her finger across their doughy little bodies.

That afternoon, they sat down at Jack's kitchen table while his mom fixed them some fried bologna. Kathryn wanted to keep the rabbit's nest a secret just for the two of them, but Jack went and blabbed to his momma about it. He always told her every little thing. Kathryn wondered what that would be like— to just talk to your momma, tell her about school or friends or even secrets. Mrs. Chandler had her back turned, auburn hair brushing the slopes of her slender shoulders, the bow of an apron hugged around her waist. When Jack stopped talking for a second, Kathryn edged in, asked Mrs. Chandler if she thought the momma bunny would come back to take care of her babies.

"I reckon she will," she said. She flipped the bologna with a heavy spatula, the grease popping above the cast-iron skillet. "So long as God gave her them maternal instincts." Kathryn smelled the frying meat, thought about the squish of rabbit flesh beneath her touch.

"But what if she smells the human on them and don't come back?" Kathryn asked. She didn't tell her what Jack said about horseshit. They didn't use curse words in front of the grown-ups. Mrs. Chandler plunked a can of green beans into a pan, turned on the burner.

"Well, she'll just do the best she knows how to do, Kate," she said. "Same as the rest of us." Then she turned, catching a shallow breath in her throat as the porch door swung open. Mr. Chandler came in, dragging his oil-sweet scent and heavy footsteps along with him. Kathryn watched him plunk his wooden leg across the kitchen floor, swinging his whole body forward with each step. He'd lost his leg in the war—she wasn't supposed to ask about it or even look too hard. Uncle Raymond said that every soldier gave up a part of himself for his country, and for Mr. Chandler, that part just happened to be his leg.

Kathryn wanted to talk about the hawk, but she couldn't ever think how to speak right with Mr. Chandler filling up the room like he did. The man appraised Kathryn sitting there at the table. He gave a little wink, then moved to Mrs. Chandler, putting his hands on her waist. It was only two o'clock, but the bourbon twinkled in his eyes—black diamonds, hard and sharp.

"Sure smells good in here," he said, burying his nose into Mrs. Chandler's neck, pressing himself into her body. She went stiff as a dead kitten, her hand gripped around the spatula.

"It'll be ready in about ten minutes," she said. She tried to pull out of his arms, but Mr. Chandler had ahold of her real good. Kathryn tried to catch eyes with Jack, thinking it might be a good idea if they left. But he was staring down at the table, rubbing his thumb over the back of a spoon like a worry stone.

"That ain't what I'm talking about and you know it," said

Mr. Chandler. He had a fistful of the woman's skirt. When he pulled on it just right, the skirt flipped up. Kathryn saw the bottom hem of her panties, but she looked away. Mr. Chandler nudged her from the stove, back toward the hallway.

"I've got to finish this dinner," said Jack's momma, leaning away. Mr. Chandler stepped back but never let go of the skirt, wadded into his grip like the nape of a puppy's neck.

"Let the boy flip the meat," he said, a warning in his voice. He caught eyes with Jack, held him in his stare. Jack's momma wiped her hands on her apron, followed Mr. Chandler back to the bedroom, and Jack went to the stove.

The next day, Kathryn begged Jack to go with her to check on the rabbits, so they went back down to the barbed wire fence. The leaves were scattered from the hole, and down inside were the pulpy remains of two half-eaten carcasses. All the other bunnies had disappeared.

"Oh, God," said Jack, a hand to his mouth. The way he said it sounded like he was caught between a curse and a prayer.

"That hawk must have got them," Kathryn said. She searched the empty sky.

"Naw," said Jack, studying the tiny stumps of flesh. "I think their momma ate them. I think she smelled the human on them and ate them right up." He went ahead and let his tears fall, never even wiped them away as they streaked his cheeks. Boys weren't supposed to do that.

Thunderheads gathered above, and the rain came all at once. As Kathryn looked at the mangled bunnies one more time, something opened up inside her, dark and viscous, an inkblot through the chest. She trudged back across the field and through the woods, leaving Jack behind in the pouring rain.

17

On the drive back from the hospital, I've nearly made up my mind to give up and go back to New York when my phone rings. *Myra*.

"I'm not sure I want to do this anymore."

"Jules." Her voice is serious, much more serious than I was expecting. "Don't freak out, okay?"

"Um, how am I supposed to not freak out when you say *don't freak out*? That's literally the only thing I can do."

"Okay, I know. But just— I need to tell you something, and I don't really know how to tell you without it sounding, like…horrible."

"Will it *sound* horrible, or is it actually horrible?"

"I mean, it's not…*unhorrible*."

"Do not make up words at me right now, Myra. Should I pull over? Seriously?" I go through the checklist of all the things she could tell me.

1. Aster is not who he says he is.
2. The photograph is a fake.
3. Someone just died.

When I get to that third possibility, I realize I'm talking to Myra and my mom is already dead so that only leaves—

"Oh my God," I say. "Is it Ryan? Is Ryan dead?"

"What? No, Jules, Ryan is not dead. Nobody is dead. But actually, now that I think about it, you might wish—"

"Just say it, Myra."

"Okay, but just so you know, I had no idea."

"Had no idea about what?"

"And I wasn't, like, *looking* for drama or anything, I just sort of stumbled onto it and—"

"Babe, just rip off the Band-Aid. Clean and quick." Myra goes silent, gathering herself.

"So I was scrolling online or whatever and came across this woman," she says breathlessly, "and I had a bunch of mutuals with her so I stopped and looked at her profile."

"And?"

"And her profile pic is—"

"Yeah?"

"Of her getting married."

"Okay?"

"To Ryan."

Back in my bedroom at the Little Yellow House, I collapse onto my bed. I slip the phone from my back pocket and stare at a string of new texts from Myra. She keeps saying she's *so so so so sorry*—as if she's the one who's done something wrong here. At the bottom is a final text with the woman's name.

So, okay, I do the perfectly rational thing and spend the next twenty minutes scouring every social media platform in the history of ever, looking for profiles for *Morgan Springer-Alman*. Nearly everything is privacy-locked, but eventually I stumble onto a public profile pic: a nauseatingly gorgeous brunette in a matte wedding gown—her shoulders angled away from the camera just enough to show a triangle of flawless skin peeping through the gap of the backless dress. And sure enough, there's Ryan right beside her, fingers intertwined with hers in a way that gets me *this close* to puking my afternoon granola bar onto the carpet of my rented room.

I feel dizzy. Beads of cold sweat gather on my forehead. There are so many things I don't remember about the night of my book launch, but this much I know for sure: Ryan wasn't wearing a wedding ring. I hate to admit it, but it was the first thing I checked for when I was close enough to see his hands.

I click around on Morgan's profile until I'm sure I can't access any more photos, and then I start googling Ryan himself. I know even before I start I'm not going to yield anything useful. He never once had any social media profiles while we were dating—not even Facebook, when everyone in the world not named *Ryan Alman* was on Facebook. And after ten minutes of searching, I realize his philosophy must be pretty similar these days. No profiles for Ryan Alman anywhere.

I take a deep breath and try to calm myself. Okay, so he got married, but maybe he also got divorced. He's just not married anymore—he can't be. But then why wouldn't *Morgan* have changed her profile picture? Whatever, I don't know who this woman is. Maybe she hasn't logged onto Facebook since they were married? Maybe this pic is the only remaining proof of their time as husband and wife? But whatever this is, I can't deal with it right now—with Ryan or his potential *wife*—so I throw my phone onto the pillow beside me. Just like that, with one phone call from Myra, my resolve to leave Gray Station and go back home has vanished. I don't want to face my life in New York. So I do the only thing I can manage to do: suck myself back into the vacuum of the Fairchild story.

I lie back on the bed, cup my open palms across my belly and think: Okay, so Edith Fairchild didn't die—but surely the baby did. Time to get back to work.

18

On her second day in fifth grade, Kathryn couldn't help but let her mind wander while Mrs. Anderson was up at the chalk board giving the math lesson. The easy problems bored her half to death, and the hard ones made her head feel bubbly like she'd been holding her breath under water. In any case, she just couldn't seem to make herself care about all those numbers and lines and decimals. She liked reading stories and poems—something she could disappear into, like one of Uncle Raymond's magic tricks.

She liked to doodle, too. And here she was sitting at her desk thinking about those poor dead bunnies out at Jack's house, so she decided she might draw some of them. She was sitting between her friend Bonnie Douglas and some boy named Steve. She didn't know the boy much because he had a different home-room teacher the year before. All of a sudden, he raised his hand and yelled out to the teacher before she had even called on him.

"Mrs. Anderson," he said, "Kate's drawing nasty things."

Kathryn looked down at her paper and saw the sketch as if someone else had done it. There were little stumps of rabbit bodies with blood spurting from where the heads might be. On the other side of the paper was a big momma rabbit gnawing on a severed bunny ear. All her classmates were looking at her now, the closest ones trying to angle themselves to get a good look at what she'd been drawing. Kathryn tried to cover it up, but then Mrs. Anderson made her way down the aisle of desks, her heels clicking against the vinyl floor tiles. When she got to Kathryn's desk, Mrs. Anderson looked over the paper and pruned her lips up like she'd been sucking on a lemon.

Near the back of the room, Janet Gardner stood up like she had an announcement for the whole class. "My daddy said to stay away from Kate Fairchild," she said. Most everybody turned to look at the girl, but Kathryn stared straight ahead.

"Miss Gardner, please take your seat," said Mrs. Anderson. Kathryn hoped that would be the end of it, but then—

"Her momma is plumb crazy," said Janet. "And daddy says the apple don't fall far from the tree." The whole room fell silent then, even Mrs. Anderson. Kathryn's face burned red like she'd been out in the hot sun. She studied her pencil sitting on the desk, and just for a second she thought it might feel nice to put the sharp lead tip of it right through her own hand.

At recess time, Mrs. Anderson marched Kathryn down the hall to Principal Newcomb's office, the picture of the dead bunnies pinched between her thumb and forefinger like a dirty tissue.

"Well, Miss Fairchild," said Principal Newcomb as he lingered over the picture. "I sure hope you have a word or two of explanation for this...artwork of yours." Kathryn tried to respond, but she was distracted by the way his little beady eyes were sunken into his big fat face, like marbles pressed into a lump of dough. "Kathryn," he said, softer now, "I'm trying to give you a way out of this. But you're making it awfully hard."

Kathryn eyed Mrs. Anderson standing by the door, the wooden paddle gripped in her angry fist.

"I didn't kill them or nothing," she said. "We just found them like that." It was all she could think to say, but it didn't seem to satisfy Principal Newcomb much.

"You mean to say you saw some rabbits that looked like this?" he asked. "In real life?"

"The hawk might have got them," said Kathryn. "But Jack says the momma rabbit ate them right up." She thought about how she had reached into the nest and touched the bunnies. She clenched her eyes, pretended she was hidden in the darkness of Uncle Raymond's magic box, waiting to disappear.

"And what about your own momma, Miss Kate?" said Principal Newcomb. "You ever think about her doing bad things to you? Like that momma rabbit did to her baby bunnies?" Kathryn heard his words, but she couldn't quite put them all together. Her vision blurred at the edges, and there was a sharp ringing in her ears. She felt something bubbling up inside her, a firestorm coursing through her belly and out toward her hands. Before she knew what she was doing, it was too late: she picked up the metal Swingline stapler on the edge of Principal Newcomb's desk and hurled it right at his forehead.

After a weeklong home suspension, Kathryn came back to school. On the day of her return, she sat alone on the hard gym bleachers at morning assembly. When Principal Newcomb took the floor to lead the students through the Pledge of Allegiance, the kids did the same thing they had done every morning since it happened: pointed to the man's swollen face, gawking as they counted the twelve stitches pulled taut over his gashed cheek. But now, Kathryn was there among them, her presence charging the humid gymnasium like a live wire. "Kate Fairchild did that," someone whispered. They stole glances at the girl herself, their looks lost somewhere between admiration and fear.

19

I've been astonished a lot these past few days, but maybe nothing has surprised me more than this: in a drawer in my bedroom at the Little Yellow House is an honest-to-God phone book. In print. For the current year.

At first, I think *how quaint* and shut the drawer, but then I reconsider. I just finished searching online for the existence of any remaining Fairchilds in the area, but it wasn't much help. The last name is more common than I would have thought. I found lots of social media profiles, and I came across more than one shady website promising *contact information, job history, and CRIMINAL RECORDS* in exchange for a credit card number. But I didn't see evidence that any of these digital Fairchilds are connected to Gray Station or even Western Kentucky, so I gave up.

But now I have a real live phone book. Hope springs eternal!

Then: I look, and there are no Fairchilds listed.

With nothing else to go on, I walk out of my room and down to the little common area on the first floor of the house. Mamaw calls it the *sitting parlor* and keeps a big mahogany server stacked high with fresh chocolate chip cookies. I grab a cookie and then notice Miss Harley Quinn curled up on the couch reading a book. I geek out a bit when I see the cover.

"Is that *Hangsaman*?" I ask. She checks the cover like she isn't sure what she's reading. "I love Shirley Jackson! She's one of the reasons I'm a writer." As I say this last part, my face flushes red. Telling people you're a writer is always met with one of two reactions: skepticism or pity. And when you're an author who has only written one failed book, either reaction feels earned.

"Yeah, I saw you wrote a book."

"How did you—" I start, but I can't put it together. First Aster reads my book, and now some random teenage girl in Nowhere, Kentucky, is talking about it.

"I googled you," she says. She must see my face go all weird because she quickly adds, "You're not special or anything. I google everybody when the reservations come in. It's part of my job. Mamaw has a strict *no murderers* policy, so—"

"Ah," I say. "More people should adopt that policy. The world would be much safer." She makes a face like she's not sure if I'm serious or not.

"Yeah, anyway. I had to go to the second page of results to find it, which I seriously never have to do. You should get a publicist or something."

"Sure, I'll get right on that." I take a big bite of the cookie.

"So, is that why you're here?" she says. "To write another novel?"

"Maybe. My first book wasn't technically a novel, and to be honest, I'm really not sure what kind of book this will be—if I ever even get enough information to write it." I spend the next thirty minutes telling her all the pertinent details—though I say nothing about Aster or his photograph, per our agreement. I get all the way to the weird part about the newspaper article where the reporter says Edith Fairchild died, but clearly she didn't.

"Why don't you just ask him about it?" says the girl.

"Ask who about what?"

"The dude who wrote the article. Gene Bartlett."

"I mean—I assumed he was dead, Quinn. That article was written in 1964."

"Bro. Did you just call me *Quinn?*"

"What? Oh, yeah, sorry," I say. "You just remind me of Harley Quinn. In a totally good way." She looks away, but smiles, despite herself. "Anyway, you think he's still alive? The Bartlett guy?"

"I mean, he was alive last year. I dated his grandson Tyler for, like, two weeks."

"Two whole weeks, huh?"

"Okay, so maybe *dated* is a strong word," she says. "But I gave him a hand job in that room you're staying in upstairs, so—"

We stare at each other in silence for a solid ten seconds, and then she bursts out laughing. I study Quinn—the salmon pink blush of her cheeks, the shy downturn of her chin as she becomes aware of her own laughter. I wish I could be eighteen again for a single day. That I could have memories grounded in this little Western Kentucky world and be best friends with Harley Quinn. A world where my mom isn't dead. A world where I never met Ryan Alman.

"Anyway," says Quinn, "his number is probably in the phone book."

Sure enough, Gene Bartlett's info is listed right there in black and white. I think about calling him, but this seems like a conversation to have in person. So, I thank Quinn with an awkward side-hug and enter Barlett's address in my GPS—ignoring Myra's new texts asking me if I've looked up Ryan's theoretical wife.

Ten minutes later, I pull into the driveway of a sixties-style A-frame house right at the edge of the Gray Station city limits. A stooped old man is raking dead leaves from a flowerbed in front of the house. I'm not even sure he notices that I've pulled into his driveway until I make my way up close to him. I move slowly, trying not to startle him, but he beats me to it.

"Toyota, huh?" he says, turning to me. He gestures out to the Corolla in the driveway.

"Uh, yeah. It's a rental." I think for a second this old man from Kentucky is going to rip into me for not driving an American vehicle, so I go in for a little proactive damage control. "It was basically the only thing they had on the lot. Smart folks around here already scooped up all the Fords and Chevys."

"Is that right?"

"You just can't beat a car made right here in the US, that's what I always say."

"Huh," he says, wiping a trail of sweat from his temple. "Well, I was aiming to tell you how much I love my little Prius hybrid parked over yonder in the garage. But I reckon we don't have so much in common as I imagined."

Well, crap.

I mumble a string of words that amount to a whole lot of nothing, but he just smiles and says, "So what can I do for you, Miss American-Made?"

"Right. Well, first things first, are you Gene Bartlett?"

"The last time I checked."

"Excellent. So, I'm hoping you can help me out on a story I'm tracking down."

"What paper?" he says. "I don't believe you're with the *Gazette*."

"No. Actually, it's a freelance thing. Might turn into a book if there is enough to it. I'm just running down some leads for now."

"Well, I'm just an eighty-four-year-old retired staff writer for a little country paper," he says with a wink. "I'm not sure I can help, but I'm pleased as punch to try." I pull my phone from my purse.

"I assume you're the same Gene Bartlett who wrote this article?" I show him the picture I took of the Fairchild clip.

"Afraid so," he says. A change comes over him. "What a terrible thing that was."

"And you reported here that the Fairchild woman died? That the fall from the bridge killed her?"

"Well, yeah."

"But why?" I say, and I'm met with a confused look.

"Well, I figure it's pretty self-evident, don't you?" he says. "I reported her dead because—well, the woman was dead."

"But that doesn't make any sense. According to her medical records, Edith Fairchild lived for another thirty-plus years."

"Aw, honey," he says, giving me a pitying look. "You're not much better of an investigator than I was."

"What do you mean?"

"The woman who jumped from that bridge was one hundred percent, stone-cold dead. But she wasn't Edith Fairchild." I look at the article on my phone. I couldn't possibly have misread the name.

"But you report right here in your own article—"

"Yes, I sure did. Because that's what the police told us at first. It was nearly ten o'clock at night, and we were already late to press. Somebody heard the name *Fairchild* and so we ran with it. Didn't you see the correction we ran the next day?" I think back to my day in the microfiche room and deflate. I'm so stupid. "It was a terrible error to make, I'll admit that much. But you have to understand—this here is a small town. Heck, it was even smaller back in the sixties. We all knew Edith Fairchild's history. She'd been in and out of that state hospital for years. It wasn't hard for us to believe that she—" He pauses, collecting himself. "Well, that she would have been the one in the river."

"But she wasn't," I say, trying to work it out.

"No, she wasn't." He takes a breath, scuffs his boot across the dirt. "It wasn't Edith. But it was a Fairchild just the same. The daughter. They called her Kathryn."

PART TWO:

THE FAIRCHILD GIRL
1962–1963

20

1962

Kathryn Fairchild had been called *crazy* her entire life. But the word took on a different meaning the day she stole Sam Sawyer's sweaty T-shirt right out of his duffel bag. She thought of the headlines plastered on the covers of the teen magazines she peeked at while waiting for her mother's prescriptions at Blakely's Drugs—*Boy Crazy, Crazy in Love.* She had no idea how it happened, but here she was: fifteen years old, and losing her mind over some boy.

Everyone knew Sam Sawyer, the dreamy senior at Gray Station High who ran track. And everyone knew Kathryn, the *crazy Fairchild girl.* Sam wasn't one of the boys who teased her at school—he would brush right by her in the cafeteria or the library without a word, and otherwise, there was no real reason for their paths to cross. But one day the stars aligned, and Sam Sawyer had no choice but to notice her. It wasn't at school, but at Fairchild Shoes up on Main Street.

Kate had a habit of stopping in at the shoe store after school, sometimes staying long enough to help poor George Caldwell do inventory. He'd been working at Fairchild's for longer than Kate had been alive, but he always seemed so frazzled. He could hardly keep up with the customers, much less worry about stocking shelves. Kate felt bad for the man. He and his wife, Margot, had just lost another baby, her dad told her. And these days her father just flat refused to come from the repair shop in the back to help out in the showroom.

When she walked into the store that afternoon, there were four customers lined up waiting for help, plus an enervated mother who needed shoe fittings for her three-year-old twins. The shelves looked a mess, and George wasn't fairing much better: his shirt was halfway untucked and his hair was matted with sweat. Kathryn took one look at him and marched back into the repair shop.

"Daddy, you just have to get poor George some help," she said, watching her father hammer a new heel onto a wingtip shoe. "It's a circus out there."

"Well, I suppose it's a good thing you stopped by," he said. "Help George clear the room out before you go, would you?"

"But what about tomorrow? And the day after? I've got school, and then I have to be home—you know that." Norman didn't answer, but he didn't have to. The doctors had gotten Edith leveled out by adjusting her medications, kept her out of Western State for the past year. But you just never could know for sure.

They stared at each other for a good long while. Then, with a heavy sigh, Norman pulled the wingtip from the anvil, took off his repair apron, and walked with Kathryn back out front. When they got to the showroom, George was measuring one of the twin boys over beside the children's rack. The customers had thinned out, but there in the corner, regarding a pair of Chuck Taylors, was Sam Sawyer—tall, sinewy, delicious. He wore a sleeveless shirt and Gray Station High track shorts. One good look at his muscled calves made Kathryn's mouth run dry.

"Hey there, young man," said Norman. When Sam turned around, Kate looked down at her hands as if she was just discovering them for the first time.

"Sir?" he said. He still had a grip on the sneakers.

"You want a job?" asked Norman. "Just a couple of hours after school each day. That's when it gets busy."

"Uh, well—" Sam started, clearly caught off guard.

"A dollar and a quarter an hour, plus a good employee discount." Norman nodded toward the shoes. "Kate here can show you the ropes." Kathryn suddenly felt her father's hand across her shoulder. She would have traded her soul to be able to disappear right into the floor. But since that didn't seem to be an option, she looked up—just in time to catch eyes with him. "What do you say?" asked Norman. Sam considered for just a moment, then shrugged.

"I've got track practice for an hour right after school," he said.

"No matter," said Norman. "Come in after practice and work a couple hours. We close at 6:30, so you'll make it home for dinner."

"Okay, then," said Sam. "Sounds groovy." He walked to the counter and shook hands with Norman—his movements smooth, his hard body pulled taut with the confidence of a man who's never been told no. Then he smiled at Kate, extended a hand right to her. "Hi there, boss," he said. "I'm Sammy." She tried to reply with her own name, and at first she thought she had. But no, she was too busy looking at the edge of his lips, the curvature of his ear.

That night in bed, she stared at the ceiling and mouthed his name over and again—*Sammy Sawyer, Sammy Sawyer*—all those soft consonants melting against her tongue like a warm piece of saltwater taffy.

Norman told Kate to come by after school every day for the next week to train the new kid. Kathryn didn't argue. That first morning she got up early so she could get her hair set in the curlers and have extra time to get herself made up with blush and mascara. She had swiped a tube of velvet Tangee lipstick from her mother's vanity the night before—sharp lines of candy apple red, glossy and dangerous.

Once the rollers were out, she propped the May issue of *Seventeen* magazine beside her dresser mirror, trying to tease her curls into *the absolutely perfect hairdo for the shape of her face* as directed by the cover. When she was as satisfied as she was going to be, she stepped back from the mirror and surveyed herself, standing tall on her tiptoes so she could just barely see where the bottom hem of her olive-green tunic dress met her freckled thighs. Every once in a while, she didn't hate the way she looked.

She hurried from school in the afternoon, wanting to beat Sam to the store so she could check herself before he arrived. When she swung into the showroom, George was sitting on the stool behind the register reading the *Gazette*, his feet propped atop the glass counter. At the sound of the welcome chimes, he glanced over the paper and eyed her as she came in. He let out a low whistle.

"Oh, you stop that, George," she said, feeling exposed. She'd known the man her whole life, but sometimes she just couldn't quite figure out George Caldwell. One minute he would be going on about his dream of working in church ministry, and the next she'd catch him looking just a little too hard at some pretty girl in the showroom, trying on pumps. Today, though, she didn't dwell on any of that. She wouldn't admit it, but the attention was nice—even if it did come from a married man who was going on thirty-three—it felt good when a man saw her as something other than the poor little Fairchild girl. She was becoming a woman now.

And she knew what women could do—the power they wielded in their bodies, in the curl of their lips, the curve of their necks. She'd seen it on big screens at the drive-in movies, read about it on the glossy pages of New York magazines.

They could turn men inside out—like Jayne Mansfield with a low-cut blouse or Marilyn Monroe with a flipped skirt. But it wasn't just fame that gave women this power. No, they all had it. Even her own mother—*crazy Edith Fairchild*—could work her dad into a soft lump of clay, pliant and powerless in her grip. Kate had seen it herself. And so she must have it, too—the seed of this power deep inside, waiting to be watered.

Just after she checked her makeup in the bathroom mirror and made it back out front, Sam pushed into the store, a garment bag draped over his shoulder. She had half a mind to run back to the bathroom.

"Hey there," he said. He studied Kate, his eyes roving the length of her body. "Sorry about this." He motioned to his shorts, his sweaty T-shirt. "Didn't want to be late. Is there somewhere I can get changed?" Kate instinctively looked to where George had been sitting behind the register, but then she remembered he'd gone back to the repair shop to show Norman the latest sales numbers.

"There's a bathroom," she said, motioning for Sam to follow her. He had to walk the length of the whole store. It was just the two of them in the showroom now, and the silence got to be too much. "So, you go by Sammy?" she asked.

"Or Sam. Whatever," he said. "My friends usually call me Sammy." She wasn't sure what that meant for her, but the day before, that's how he had introduced himself—*Sammy*—and the thought of this made her smile. He noticed.

"What?" he said, smiling back. They stood there that way, just smiling, and then she turned and led him to the back of the store. The bathroom was through an open door at the end of the narrow hallway, so she had to step inside—it was the only place to turn around.

He followed her into the closet-sized room—hardly big enough for the commode and a small pedestal sink. When she went to turn around, she found herself pressed right up against Sam Sawyer's chest. Her head came to just under his chin.

"Oh," she said, "I didn't mean— I'm sorry." If her mind had been clear, she might have realized that it was Sam who had pushed into the bathroom on her—not the other way around. But in the moment, she could only think of the musk of his skin, the feeling of his hard body pressed up against her own. When she tried to slip around him to make her way out the door, she felt the brush of his fingers against her waist.

"I ain't scared of you," he said, just above a whisper. "It don't matter to me what they say." His shallow breath floated against her neck. She looked up at his parted lips, the bridge of his nose, dirty-blond hair around his ears. His green eyes were the shimmering scales of a bluegill, flashing wild with light. She edged around him and went out the door, keeping just clear of his greedy hands.

She showed him how to use the register, how to fill out the receipts, where to store the carbon copies. Before she left, she went back to the little bathroom where Sam had changed his clothes just an hour before. His duffel bag lay open in the corner, his gym shorts and T-shirt on top like an offering. She lifted the shirt with careful hands and breathed him in—sweat and hair oil and Old Spice. Then she folded the shirt into a neat square and tucked it away inside her purse.

She waved to him on her way out the door, but she didn't give him the satisfaction of her smile. The moment between them in the bathroom was a flash of lighting, and she knew all at once that this—*this!*—was the power that women held: to withhold themselves. Yes, this power was buried deep inside her, lodged beneath her heart. Watered by Sammy Sawyer's animal yearning in the bathroom of the shoe store, she felt it begin to blossom for the first time.

21

It was the middle of May, only a few weeks before graduation, which meant one thing: the hallways of Gray Station High were swirling with ideas for senior prank day. Younger students didn't usually have a thing to do with the pranks—but when Kathryn heard Sammy Sawyer was scheming up a plan, she could hardly think of anything else.

Her stomach fluttered when she saw him standing with two other senior boys beside a row of lockers—Tommy Ashby on his right and William Carlisle on his left. Normally just the thought of being near a group of older boys would make her feel like she had swallowed a piece of hot metal. But after spending every afternoon with Sammy for the past week, she had half a mind to walk right up into the middle of the group, to brush her hand against his waist the way he had done to her in the bathroom at the store. When she made her approach, they were talking about the senior prank.

"Hey, Sammy," she said. When the other guys turned to look her over, she clutched her geometry book tight against her lime-green cardigan. Despite all her newfound confidence, she suddenly felt like she was walking on the pool deck in her bathing suit.

"Oh—hey," he said. Kathryn watched his eyes flick back and forth between her and his friends like he was trying to figure a way out. "Um, guys—this is Kate," he said. They stood in silence, watching her as if she might cast a spell on them. "We were just headed to class, so—"

"I have an idea," she said. "For the prank." William and Tommy exchanged a wry smile, but she didn't care. She kept her eyes locked into Sam's.

"Yeah?" he said. She nodded.

"Look, doll," said William. "It's called a *senior* prank for a reason."

"And we don't need a skirt planning our business," added Tommy. Kathryn shrugged.

"Your choice," she said. "But it's big. Something people would remember for a long time." She raised an eyebrow at Sam. When she turned to leave, he touched her shoulder.

"You've got my attention," he said. "Let's hear it." She narrowed her gaze.

"Oh, I don't know if you deserve it, considering the company you keep."

"Now, look here—" said Tommy, stepping forward. Sam put a firm hand on his chest, pushed him away. Kathryn closed the space between them, her chest mere inches from his.

"Walk me to class," she said, "And if you're lucky, I'll tell you about it." In one clean motion, she turned, her fire-red hair flipping in front of Sam's face, barely missing his nose. Her cheeks burned as she walked away. She had to fight the temptation to look back. After she'd made it halfway down the hall and Sam still wasn't there, she had all but given up. But then: a hand on the small of her back.

"Little Kate Fairchild," he said. "Who knew you were such a badass?"

★ ★ ★

Once the plan was laid out, they settled on a day. The Monday before graduation, right at the beginning of the week—before Principal Tucker would have time to suspect anything. Now it was up to Kathryn to get the supplies. It was easy enough to get the red paint, but for the most important part, she needed Jack.

She arranged to stay out in the country with Aunt Clara and Uncle Raymond the weekend before, and on Sunday afternoon, she took Jack out to the fishing pond to explain the plan. He cocked his head to the side, squinting at her in the afternoon sun.

"Now, why would you want to go and do something like that?" he said. Kathryn didn't expect Jack to understand. High school pranks were lost on him. He'd been homeschooled out here in the country his whole life.

"I reckon that's my business, not yours," she said. She could talk like this with Jack—open, free. It was their way. He wasn't like the other boys. They'd grown up together, laid a claim to one another from their earliest years. He didn't see her as *the crazy Fairchild girl*. She was just Kate—or Freckles, as he so often called her. He was her best friend in this whole wide world, now and forever. "Well," she said, "you gonna do it or not?"

At four thirty the next morning, Kathryn left a thank-you note for Aunt Clara on the kitchen counter, and then she tip-toed out of the house before the sun came up. Jack was already waiting for her on the road out past the winding gravel drive-way, the burning tip of his cigarette glowing red through the open window of his truck.

"You owe me for this one, Freckles," he said. "Big-time." She looked into the bed of the truck, just to make sure. They were all there, just as promised: four beautiful miniature donkeys.

Sam and the other boys had raised money from the rest of the senior class all throughout the previous week, and when

Monday came around, they had a handsome sum they could use to bribe Mr. Billings, the old janitor who worked the morning shift. Jack and Kate pulled into the school lot at the back of the building just as the sun was breaking on the plane of the horizon. Sam was waiting for them at the open back door, the key to the school dangling in his hand. Jack took one look at him, shook his head toward Kate.

"Well, I guess that clears it up," said Jack. He lit another cigarette, took a hard drag.

"What are you talking about?" said Kathryn. Jack nodded toward Sam.

"I should've known this whole thing was about a guy." Kate looked at him with pitying eyes. Sometimes figuring out Jack Chandler was like trying to read hieroglyphics. She had been in love with the boy for as long as she could remember, but he had never returned the interest. Was he really getting jealous now that she had taken a liking to Sammy Sawyer?

"I really appreciate this, Jack," she said. She placed a hand on his knee, but he pulled away, gripped the door handle.

"Well, let's get on with it," he said, swinging out of the truck. As they approached, Kate watched the way Sam surveyed Jack: studying his overalls, his peach-fuzz beard, his muddy boots. She flicked her gaze from Jack to Sam and then back again. She felt embarrassed for one of them but couldn't quite figure out which one.

The three of them worked fast to paint the big red numbers on the donkeys: *1, 2, 3, and 5.* Then they lugged the animals one at a time to the janitor's storage room by the back entrance, and Kathryn took a moment to make sure the bleach and other cleaning supplies were moved to a shelf out of reach. The last donkey wouldn't stay clear of the door, so Sam slapped it on the backside, sending it *hee-hawing* into the corner by the brooms and mops. He slammed the door behind it and then doubled over laughing.

As they walked back outside toward the truck, Sam slung an arm around Kathryn's shoulders. "This is going to be too much fun, Kate," he said. "Principal Tucker's gonna throw a hissy." Kathryn turned to look at Jack, watched the beat of his pulse thumping in his temple.

"Well, we couldn't have done it without Jack," she said. She reached for his hand, but he pulled away just as she brushed his pinky.

"Just make sure I get those donkeys back," he said, studying the dirt under his fingernails. "All four of them." He got in the truck and pulled away, leaving Kathryn there with Sammy in the door frame, their dark figures silhouetted by the blinding fluorescent light inside.

At seven forty-five, during the last part of morning assembly, Kathryn, Sam, William, and Tommy slipped out of the gymnasium and went to work. William and Tommy gathered the four buckets of donkey feed that they had stored in the first-floor student bathroom that morning. They split up, flinging carrots, half-eaten cucumbers, watermelon rinds, and all kinds of other goodies up and down the hallways. Kathryn waited beside the janitor's closet, but she didn't open it until she got the signal from Sam. He had been doing arguably the most important part: sneaking into Principal Tucker's office and affixing a mirror to the back of his door. When everything was in place, Sam gave the *thumbs-up* to Kate, and she released the animals. They scattered around the building, following the trails of treats in every direction.

When the gym doors opened at the end of morning assembly, students flooded the hall to go to first period, the commotion sending the donkeys into a frenzy. Number 1 ran toward the cafeteria, Number 2 was corralled into the library, Number 3 ran against the current straight back into the gymnasium, and Number 5 stayed right outside of Principal Tucker's office—

his head stuffed into one of the food buckets that William had conveniently left beside the office door.

But where was donkey Number 4? That's precisely what Principal Tucker was searching for during the next three hours of the school day. He gathered all available staff for the search, leaving the front offices unstaffed for most of the day. When that failed, he called in the authorities, having two deputies from the sheriff's office shine flashlights into every nook and cranny in the school building. Finally, citing a public health concern with sending kids into a cafeteria to eat lunch *with a dadgum donkey on the loose*, Principal Tucker dismissed the students early: a first in the storied history of Gray Station High prank day.

On their way out of the school, every member of the senior class flung paper flyers into the air, scattering them all over the hallways. Printed on the flyers was a clue for poor Principal Tucker, written by none other than Kate Fairchild, leading him to the mirror on his office door:

A Limerick for Principal Tucker
Here's a gift from the whole senior class,
One no future prank will surpass.
To find "Donkey Four"
Just close your own door
And there you will see the last jackass!

22

For the first time in her life, Kathryn Fairchild was notorious in Gray Station for something other than being the daughter of *the crazy woman on Poplar Street*. Students gawked at her as she walked the halls of the high school—that hadn't changed—but now they smiled, slapped her high fives in passing, pumped their fists and cheered. She still heard the popular girls whisper her name from the back of classrooms or in front of the long bathroom mirrors, but now they did so with a sense of awe. Same words, different context: *Kathryn Fairchild is crazy!* It's amazing what a few jackasses can do for one's reputation.

Of course, the whole thing did have a downside: if *everyone* knew what she had done, then that must also include Principal Tucker. She wasn't worried though. When she was called out of second period to his office the next morning, her classmates cheered. She walked with the strut of a proud peacock down to the front of the school. There would be a punishment—no doubt about that. Maybe Principal Tucker would put her on kitchen duty in the cafeteria or have her stay late scraping gum off classroom desks. Perhaps he would even suspend her for the rest of the school year—*a whole four days*. But she figured whatever punishment he could dole out would never match the shame she had carried around with her for the better part of her life. She had been reborn. Nobody could take that away from her.

But when Kathryn pushed into the office, she didn't expect to see her father sitting in a chair opposite from Principal Tucker's desk, bent over, his head in his hands.

"Daddy?" she said.

"Please have a seat," said Principal Tucker, motioning to the empty chair beside her father. His voice held no malice. "I'm sorry to pull you out of class like this, Miss Fairchild. But your father came to us this morning and asked if he could see you. There's been...an incident." She looked at her father—his puffy eyes and disheveled hair. The top button of his starched color was undone.

"It's your mother," he said, his lips pulling taut. He shook his head and then said it again, as if no other words were necessary: "It's your mother."

Earlier that day, Edith simply couldn't get herself clean. There in the house on Poplar Street, she scrubbed herself red in the shower, but the filth would not relent, clinging all over her body, biting her flesh like summer mosquitoes. So she got back under the water, moved the dial hotter, hotter still—pinprick heat turning to blistering needles. Even then, as she patted dry her scorched skin, she could feel the vileness coming back into her. She must bathe again. She must be clean.

She went to turn the water back on, but a wind swept over her naked body. It was coming to her again—the great expanse of every little thing. And all at once, she knew: they were watching. The man with the mustache, the nurse with the kind eyes and crooked teeth. They knew she'd been hiding her pills again, and now they were here—behind the mirror, under the floor vents, *watching, watching, watching.*

She covered herself with careful hands, turning her breasts from the mirror while she slipped on a bathrobe. But the water! Oh, how she needed the water. She ran to the bathroom downstairs, but before she even stepped into the room she could feel their presence. Did Norman know they were here? No—he couldn't possibly. They must have come in while she slept, tucking themselves under the baseboards like mice.

Her skin crawled with filth. She must have water—but how? They were everywhere—up, down, sideways. She swung out of the front door with abandon, running down Poplar Street in her robe. She crossed the intersection at Willow Street, her legs nearly clipped by a honking car.

When she reached Town Square Park, she scanned the faces in every direction—kids, mothers, fathers. This is where she would be safe. How could they find her here, among all the others? So she approached the fountain in the middle of the park, the iron cherubs on the perimeter beckoning her to the water, clear as blown glass. On a pedestal in the center was the figure of an angel, surrounded by open-mouthed fish. But no—it wasn't just any angel. *How had she not seen her before*—the tightly braided hair, the perfect curve of the hips, the freckled face.

"Oh, Kathryn Marie," she said. Then she let the robe fall to the concrete and stepped into the cold water, the ripples around her ankles like shiny manacles shimmering in the sun.

Back in Principal Tucker's office, Norman told Kathryn that the police had to subdue her mother right there in the middle of the park, with all those people just standing there watching her.

"They gave her a tranquilizer shot, like—" he said, breaking off "—like some kind of animal." Kathryn wanted to embrace her father, but she was frozen still. Principal Tucker adjusted himself in his chair, the leather complaining under his weight.

"News travels fast in this little town," he said, looking at Kathryn now. "I just thought you should hear about it privately before...well, you know." Yes, she certainly did know. Surely the rumors had already made their way around town. Soon they would hit the school. By lunchtime, everyone would know.

"Yes, thank you," said Kathryn, staring straight ahead. Her father was weeping now, and it seemed Principal Tucker simply could not abide so much emotion. He cleared his throat.

"I think it's best if the two of you go on home," he said. "I'll excuse Kathryn here for the day." On her way out the door, he touched her elbow. "And about that other thing," he said. "The donkeys." Kathryn blinked through wet eyes.

"I'm so sorry about that," she said, and she truly was. "Especially about that awful poem." This business with her mother was her fault—she was sure of it. What a fool she had been, strutting around like she was someone else, someone normal. She was a Fairchild. She was her mother's daughter. These past few days she had been a zebra hiding among horses, but she knew now she could never cover her stripes.

For the last three days of school, Kathryn sat in the back corner of all her classes, scraping the tender parts of her wrists with the sharp edge of an unwound paper clip.

23

1962

On his lunch break, Norman stepped onto the sidewalk out in front of the shoe store on Main Street, looking up at the bruised afternoon sky. Billowy clouds choked out the sunlight on the horizon, their underbellies charred black like a big burnt marshmallow. The rain was still a ways off, but he didn't want to risk it—so he drove the Oldsmobile the five blocks home. When he swung through the front door, the silence of the house was as thick as cold peanut butter. Sometimes it got like that when Edith was down there at the hospital. The quiet—the *stillness* of everything—was so full and heavy that you could feel the weight of it in your open palms.

He was fixing himself a ham sandwich with dill pickles when the phone rang. It might be nice just to let it go this one time, but on the fifth ring he thought better of it. He licked a bit of mayonnaise from his thumb, walked to the console table out in the hallway, cleared his throat.

"Fairchild residence," he said.

"Hello there, Norman," said the man on the phone. "This is Dr. Jenkins."

"Yes?" said Norman. Most of the time it was one of the la-
dies at reception who called. Norman leaned himself against
the wall so he could feel something sturdy, just in case.

"I wondered if you might be able to come down this afternoon," said the doctor. "Have a bit of a consultation."

"Well," said Norman, thinking. He'd have to leave George
alone for a few hours at the store until the new boy made it in.
Plus, there was this weather. "They're calling for storms," he
said. "Can't we go through with it on the phone?" He shifted
his weight, the floorboards moaning under his feet. The doctor was quiet for a bit too long.

"I think it might be best to do this one in person," he said.

The storm followed him like a shadow, the green sky pulsing
in the rearview mirror as he drove out of Gray Station. He left
instructions for George at the store: if Kate came by, he should
just tell her that Norman had gone out for a drive. There was no
need in giving the girl anything to worry over. She had more
on her plate than she could handle as it was. Ever since they
found Edith in the park fountain like they did, Kate seemed
like she was hallowed out. Just a shell of herself—like somebody
had opened her up and scooped out her insides. And in that
void, it was almost as if Edith had climbed right up inside her.
Sometimes she'd go quiet at dinnertime, pushing her vegetables across her plate, and Norman wouldn't know what to say.

The real shame of it was that things had been looking up
for all of them. Sure, he could have done without seeing Kate
fawn over the Sawyer boy so much, but there was no harm in
it. And Edith had been better. Not happy exactly—he couldn't
say that much. But they were managing the best they could,
the best they had in years. They'd been sleeping in the same
room for going on six months. Just last week she had pulled him
up from the chair after dinner, leaned into him. They danced
in circles right across the kitchen floor and into the hallway,

lost in each other. They used to do that before Kate was born. Seemed like these days every part of his life was marked by a *before* and *after*. Every now and again the *before* would show up in the distance ahead of him like a puddle in the wavy summer heat. But no, it was always a mirage. After all these years, he should've known better.

When he parked the car and walked toward the hospital, the first raindrops fell, round and heavy, plunking across the sidewalk like liquid pennies. The old woman at reception saw him coming, her eyes going big. She picked up the phone to page the doctor. Norman was used to sitting in the waiting room out front for long stretches of time, but even before he had a chance to sit down and flip through the new *Popular Mechanics*, Dr. Jenkins was there right on top of him.

"Thanks for coming down, Norman," he said, extending a meaty hand. Norman shook it, and then they were off down the administrative hallway and into a little ornate office. Just as the doctor was closing the door, Norman heard a shrill cry from somewhere deeper in the building. A clap of thunder boomed outside, rattling the windows. It was like something out of a Hitchcock picture. Norman startled, but the doctor didn't even seem to notice.

"I reckon you can get used to just about anything," said Norman. Dr. Jenkins looked puzzled. "The screaming, I mean."

"Oh, yes," said the doctor, sliding behind a mahogany desk. "It's an occupational hazard, I'm afraid." He shuffled some papers across his desk and then leaned back in his chair—far enough to where Norman thought he might tip over backward. "Let's not drag it out," he said. "We ran some blood work. Edith's pregnant."

Norman nodded, but he couldn't make sense of the words.

"All this time, I've thought of you as a sensible man," said the doctor, scolding him. "But you need to know that this is as much your fault as it is hers. We need to figure out how the two of you are going to deal with having another baby." A flash of lightning strobed through the window outside. Norman realized he'd stopped breathing.

"Do you understand what I'm telling you, Norman?" said Dr. Jenkins. He talked slowly, as if lecturing a child.

"I understand," said Norman calmly. He sat there in the chair with his hands gripped around the armrest. He counted the silent beats between the lightning and rumbles of thunder. The doctor shook his head.

"Well, I'll be damned," he said. "You're taking this thing better than I would have thought." Norman considered this for a moment, but he didn't think he had much to say in response. "Hell, even without her other complications, your wife is forty-three years old," he said. "You have anything to say for yourself here?"

Now there was a question worth considering—*did he have anything to say?* Well, if he had been in a better position to put his words together, he might have said that with all the time Edith had spent under the doctor's care here in this hellhole of steel doors and screaming lunatics, he hardly knew his own wife anymore. He also might have said that when she was at home on Poplar Street, she spent 80 percent of her time locked away in the spare bedroom upstairs, a prisoner in her own damn house, and all anybody could do was give her more shock therapy or stuff her full of pills. He may have even said that over the last decade, he could count on one hand the number of times he had made love to his wife—this woman who he still found so precious and life-giving and terrifyingly beautiful after all these years. And yes, he might have said that when she came to him last month with a hunger in her eyes, pushed him onto the kitchen table and rode him until they came together, their animal groans echoing through the open windows up and down Poplar Street—well, in that moment, he didn't have much to say at all. And above all else, he would have said he would do it again every night and twice on Sunday, no matter how many babies they threatened to bring into this cruel world.

But Norman didn't have those words, so he only shrugged and listened to the howls of the storm outside—one that wouldn't be satisfied until it had turned the day black.

24

Kathryn sat in the passenger seat of the Oldsmobile, holding her baby brother. She'd gotten used to this over the past few months—the feel of his bird-bone weight against her chest, the pull of his curious fingers across her skin. Every now and again it was nice to feel so needed—to know that some other human being depended on you so much that he just might die if you weren't around to feed him and dress him and sing him lullabies in the small hours of the night. But then there were days when the pressure threatened to crush her. Edith had only been home for the first few weeks with the baby, then she was back down at the hospital, the weight of it all suffocating her— something that Kathryn now understood, too. It was never a question whether she would have to help. Norman pulled her out of school shortly after the baby was born. Kate would have to homeschool, at least for a while. There was no other way.

Norman pulled the car into the empty gravel lot on the south side of Riverside Baptist Church, about twenty yards from the little yellow parsonage, parking under the drooping foliage of a weeping willow—the long, sad strips of leaves tickling the hood of the car. After he killed the engine, he kept his hands gripped around the steering wheel as if he wasn't quite sure what to do next. Sometimes Kathryn felt like he needed as much care as her baby brother—and that fell to her these days, too.

"Daddy," she said, jiggling the baby so he wouldn't fuss. She gave her father a chance to gather himself, watched as a change finally came over his face. He forced a smile.

They pushed themselves out of the car and made their way across the lot. The moving truck was already there in the black-top driveway of the little parsonage. Just as they approached, Kate saw George Caldwell backing down the steel ramp of the truck, wrestling with a furniture dolly under the weight of a big walnut dresser. Sammy Sawyer was on the other end, tip-toeing down the ramp to keep the whole load from veering off the edge. "Alright, there," said George. "Slow her down a bit." When Sammy looked over and saw Kate, he lost his footing, nearly sending the dresser off the side of the ramp. She couldn't help but smile.

She knew Sammy would be here. Her dad had closed the shoe store for the whole afternoon, paying Sammy his normal wage so they could all help George and Margot move from their little duplex on the south side of town over here to the church parsonage. Kate had picked out a yellow A-line dress with a cute little paisley pattern—mostly because it was shorter than her other dresses, the bottom hem swishing halfway up her thighs. Being occupied with the baby so much these days, she didn't have much occasion to see Sammy. She figured she'd make the most of it. But when her father saw her wearing the dress back at the house on Poplar Street that morning, he put up a fuss.

"Now, how do you expect to lug around boxes wearing a thing like that?" he had said. He was sitting at the kitchen table eating a steaming bowl of oatmeal—one that Kathryn had fixed for him just the way he liked, topped with a thick pad of sweet cream butter and a handful of raisins. She didn't miss a beat.

"Well, how do you expect me to lug around boxes with a baby on my hip?" she said, raising an eyebrow. That seemed to shut him up. He'd asked her the night before to come along to the parsonage and keep Margot company, maybe help her organize a few things in the new kitchen. He knew as well as she did that she'd have to take baby Danny along with her.

Just after the men got the dresser righted and rolled through the propped screen door of the house, Margot Caldwell popped out on the front porch. She had her curly black hair tied up in a green handkerchief, and with those long calves of hers poking out from under tight black capri pants, she looked like Audrey Hepburn in *Roman Holiday*.

"Oh my word!" said Margot, taking two big steps down the porch stairs out toward Kathryn. "Would you look at how big and strong that baby is getting." She reached out for the child, but Kate instinctively pulled away, tucking Danny's outstretched hands into her chest. The baby howled, and Margot stepped back as if she'd been shoved. "I'm sorry," she said, looking at her hands as if they were razor blades. "I didn't mean—"

"No—there's no need," said Kate, shifting the boy to her other hip. She shook her head, mostly at herself. It was like her body had reacted without consulting her mind. Still, she didn't want to hand over her brother, not just yet. "It's just that he needs a diaper change." She was thinking on her feet now, trying to figure out how not to hurt the poor woman any further. "I'll get him cleaned up, and then he's all yours."

Margot led Kate to a little bedroom at the back of the house to change the dirty diaper, and then she went to the kitchen to fix a pitcher of lemonade. Kate spread out a blanket for Danny and then went about the work of changing his soiled diaper, humming "You Are My Sunshine" to keep the boy from squirming. When she was finished, she let the baby rest on his back for a few minutes, taking a break herself and studying the little room. There were a couple of big boxes in the corner, but otherwise there was nothing to it but worn carpet and empty space.

A fresh start—that's what this house must mean for the Caldwells, especially Margot. This little bedroom, with the walls papered like they were in vertical yellow stripes, sure would make a handsome little nursery. It was a shame George and Margot hadn't been able to have a child yet. Kate felt a lump in her throat as she remembered how George looked when he came into the shoe store one morning—he returned the un-opened crib sheets that her dad had bought them for the baby shower, plunked them on a table in the workroom in the back without a single word. Weeks later, George and Margot came over for dinner. Kate was washing up the dishes with Margot in the kitchen when she let it slip that her mother was going to have another baby. Later that night they each cried, for very different reasons.

But the Caldwells still had time. They were young enough— Margot wasn't but twenty-nine years old. And she might need a baby to keep her company out here. Kathryn imagined how quiet and lonely life might be for a pastor's wife—her husband's attention always spent over there at the church house, fussing over the congregation. Plus, George would still be working part-time at the shoe store. The tiny church didn't bring in enough tithes to pay him a living wage, so he'd have to be bi-vocational for at least a while longer.

Danny was dozing off on the blanket now, so Kate stroked the wild little curls on his head, trying to nudge him over the edge of sleep. Everything about this baby boy amazed her. The wrinkles on his inchworm fingers. The peach-fuzz hair strewn across his shoulders. The way his forehead crinkled just before he worked himself into a fit. It was a wonder how the presence of someone so tiny could change the way you know this world, even the way you know yourself. She thought briefly about her

own mother—how she must have felt when Kate was born—
but she pushed the thought from her mind as quickly as it came.

The baby was breathing heavy now, so Kate thought she
might let him take a little nap. She edged out of the room,
closing the door softly behind her. When she made it back to
the living room, the men were taking a break. Her father and
George were sitting atop two kitchen stools they had dragged
into the middle of the carpeted floor, and Sammy had made a
makeshift seat out of a couple of boxes. The room smelled like
nothing but cardboard and sweat. Just as Kate cleared the hallway, Margot came in from the other direction carrying a tray
full of lemonades from the kitchen.

"Okay, then," said Norman, clapping his hands one big time
as he stood. He grabbed the mason jars of lemonade from the
tray one at a time, passing them around. "Since we're all here,
how about a little toast?"

"Oh, stop that nonsense, Norman," said George. "There ain't
any need for ceremony here. I just appreciate you all came out
to help." Kate watched her dad swing his arm across George's
shoulder. Then he guided him to the middle of the room to
stand next to Margot.

"Well, *Reverend* Caldwell," said Norman, drawing out the
words, "this new position of yours calls for ceremony whether
you like it or not." They all had a little laugh about that. George
shook his head, but Kate could tell that he was just as proud
as could be. After all these years, he'd finally been called as a
minister—working his way into a pastorate, even without ever
finishing that seminary degree he was always going on about.

As Norman went on telling stories, Kathryn regarded
George, trying to picture him giving a Sunday sermon or coun-
seling someone through the scriptures in his church office.
She couldn't quite look past the man she had come to know
all these years—quiet, small, a little aloof. Something about

George Caldwell was just a bit… How could she put it? Off-center? Sure, he had always been nice enough, and it was certainly true that the man was nothing but loyal to the Fairchild business. But she had trouble seeing him as a leader of any kind. He was awfully fragile—always too anxious about pleasing her father or Margot, like the wrong word from either one of them might just break him in two.

She looked out the window at the chipped wood siding of the white sanctuary building across the way, with its proud little steeple and tarnished church bell. Just past the Gray Station city limits, there was something distinctly *country* about being in this parsonage out here at the edge of River Road. The whole place was simple and quiet—and maybe just a bit spooky under the shadows of the towering black oaks out front.

"Seriously, now," said Norman, working into his finale. Kathryn shifted her gaze back to her father, his ramrod posture—despite his dreaminess. "Some other folks might look out here at this old church, at this little house and think, *So what? What's the big deal?* Well, I'll tell you what the big deal is." He looked away for a moment, his voice choking out in an unexpected sob. Margot took George's hand in hers, squeezing it tight. "You've worked your whole life for this, George. And by God, you deserve every bit of it."

"Well, I appreciate—" started George, but Norman cut him off.

"Who said I was done speaking?" he said, getting another laugh. He raised his lemonade high in the air, the cold jar sweating with condensation. "Here's to George and Margot. May God bless their new home—and that lucky little church across that parking lot." They took turns clinking their mason jars all around, and then drank. Kathryn only took a sip, but she watched from the corner of her eye as Sammy Sawyer drained his entire glass in three big gulps, his Adam's apple bobbing in his throat—something that might have struck her as grotesque in another man. A ring of sweat had soaked through his collar, and an inexplicable craving opened up inside her.

"So I guess this is what the American Dream looks like," said Sammy, pressing his cold mason jar to his forehead. "New house. New job. Same beautiful wife." Sammy winked at nobody in particular. George whimpered out a nervous laugh, but Margot didn't even blush. Kate's stomach churned with a flutter of jealousy. "I guess you've got just about everything you've ever hoped for," said Sammy. Just as the room fell silent, a shrill cry echoed from down the hallway. Baby Danny.

"Let me get him," Margot said, her voice small and unsure. "Please." She hurried down the hallway, leaving the rest of them holding their lemonades in the pulsing stillness of the empty living room.

25

One Friday afternoon—when Edith had been down at the hospital for going on two months—Aunt Clara and Uncle Raymond showed up at the house on Poplar Street, suitcases in hand. Norman made a show of putting up a fight, but no matter—they were coming to stay for a long weekend to look after Danny, to give Kathryn an overdue break. They'd been doing this every so often since the baby came along, trying to ease the burden on everyone. Even when Edith was home things were difficult, at best.

That afternoon before dinner, Kate went up in her bedroom for two hours with nothing to do but write in her diary. She had to be careful. It was in these moments, alone with the echo of her own thoughts, when she could sink down, down, down—into that familiar dark place, her chest contracting in on itself with the incessant worry of every little thing. To keep her mind in a good place, she decided she'd plot out a new magic trick she could perform with Uncle Ray. She wasn't much interested in any of the silly gags he did to please the kids: pulling scarves from his sleeves, blooming a bouquet of flowers from thin air—all that clown stuff. She only cared about the show-stoppers. The illusions that make you forget how to breathe right. Mostly, she just wanted to disappear.

Uncle Ray got her started when she was just a little thing. When the auto shop was closed for the weekend, he would take her into the empty bay and let her practice sleight of hand, body control, how to direct the eye of the audience. "Show them where to focus," said Uncle Ray, fluttering his left hand in the air like a turtle dove, "and then—*hocus-pocus!*" She mouthed the mantra back to him, trying to move in just the same way he did. But she wasn't satisfied.

"Where's the magic?" she said, fingering a piece of purple tulle fabric. Uncle Raymond laughed, and Kate felt as small as her eight-year-old body.

"Magic isn't for the magician. It's for everyone else."

"So, it's all just a lie?"

"No," said Uncle Ray. "Magic is a type of make-believe. The best kind there is." Kate still didn't understand. She gave Uncle Ray a look, and he smiled. "People create the truth they want to believe," he said. "The magician just helps them to see that truth."

After a few weeks of learning the basics, Uncle Ray wheeled out a huge black box into the middle of the garage. He told her he was going to make her disappear. *Abracadabra!* She was terrified and enraptured all at once—right up to the moment he showed her how it worked.

"That's not magic," she said, the swell of her heart deflating like a popped balloon. She regarded the rickety trap door in the back of the box, poked her head into the hidden compartment where she was supposed to crawl.

"No, girl—you're missing the point," said Uncle Ray, stooping down to be eye level. "The magic is in the illusion. Letting folks believe the impossible—there's real wonder in that."

"But I want to feel the magic myself," she said. Just imagine:

the black box swallowed your body into darkness, and then— *poof!* Gone. Blank. Nothing. No thoughts. No dreams. No sadness. "I want to disappear for real."

"Well, there's only one way to do that," said Uncle Raymond.

"Tell me," said Kate, eyes wide.

"You have to know the magic word."

"Abracadabra?"

"No," said Uncle Ray. "That's make-believe. You need the real magic word."

"What is it?"

"Ah, that's the problem, isn't it?" said Uncle Raymond. "Nobody's figured it out."

"I'll find it," she said. Uncle Raymond let out a belly laugh, but Kathryn meant it with every fiber of her being. She would find the magic word. She would find a way to disappear. You just wait.

The smell of roasted garlic and onions wafted into Kathryn's bedroom, pulling her out of the dreamworld and down to the kitchen. Uncle Raymond and her father were at the table drinking Pabst Blue Ribbon and going on about the war over in Vietnam. Aunt Clara was stirring some crushed tomatoes into a sizzling pan at the stove.

"What can I help you with," said Kathryn, pulling an apron from the nail beside the refrigerator.

"Oh, no, you don't," said Aunt Clara. "You don't have any business playing little *Momma Fairchild* today. Go sit yourself down and relax."

"With them?" said Kate, gesturing to her dad and Uncle Raymond. As much as she didn't feel like doing any work, she *really* didn't want to sit with the men and listen to them yap about war or President Kennedy. "You know good and well there's nothing relaxing about that." Aunt Clara gave her a knowing smile, but she wouldn't relent.

"Oh, they're just going on about a whole lot of nothing—just like always," she said. "You sit yourself right there between them. Girl like you will turn them into gentlemen in no time." Aunt Clara had a way of filling up the room with her booming voice and big laugh—swooping her hands through the air when she talked, sometimes making the men look small by comparison. There was nowhere in this world she didn't belong on account of her gender. Sometimes Kate felt like she had some of that gumption inside her—a different kind of power that she hadn't pulled out of herself just yet. One that wasn't bound up in making food or caring for babies or even sex appeal. She examined Uncle Raymond and her father, legs splayed, shoulders back. How would it feel to take up so much space for yourself and not be even a bit sorry for it?

The men hadn't so much as acknowledged her presence since she came into the kitchen. But now Aunt Clara had gotten her feeling all feisty, so she thought she might try a little experiment. She grabbed a can of the Pabst from the refrigerator and plunked herself down at the table. It wasn't until she cracked open the beer that the men finally stopped their jabbering and paid her some attention. She lifted the can to her nose and took a whiff—floral and sour, just on the edge of spoiled, like bread yeast. She expected her dad to tell her to put it down, but he just leaned back in his chair and crossed his arms—almost as if he were daring her to take a sip.

"Well, you aiming to drink that beer or just sniff at it?" said Uncle Raymond. He elbowed Norman and let out a throaty cackle—phlegmy and thick on account of his two-pack-a-day habit. Kathryn flicked her eyes back and forth between the men. Okay then—she figured she could call a bluff as well as anyone else. She closed her eyes and took a huge swig of the cold beer, filling her cheeks and then gulping it down fast so she wouldn't have to taste much. The residue lingered against her tongue, but her insides didn't burn like they did the time she and Jack snuck a pull of his dad's Jim Beam out in the country.

"Well, I guess you earned it," said Norman. "I reckon you've been grown-up for a while now. A little beer won't hurt nothing." Kathryn felt proud of herself just long enough to take another gulp of the beer. She let herself taste it a bit more this time. Just then she noticed the blue long-stem vase in the center of the table. She pulled it over, smelled the little bunch of white daisies it held.

"These for me?" she said, already knowing full well that Jack had sent them for her—same as always. She also knew what he had hidden for her at the bottom of the vase, but that would have to wait until later.

"Well, of course they are," said Uncle Raymond. Kathryn fingered the petals of the flowers—delicate and tensile at the same time, like flax paper.

"How is he?" said Kathryn. It had been nearly a month since she was out in the country. Things hadn't felt right between them for some time—really ever since the day she brought Jack and Sammy together for the prank at the high school nearly a year ago. Still, staying away from Jack for so long made her feel like she was missing a part of herself.

"Oh, you know," said Uncle Raymond. "Working as hard as ever. Zipping through his schoolwork in the morning, working in the garage all afternoon. That boy is something else."

"And not bad to look at either," said Aunt Clara, peering over her shoulder.

"Oh, hush," said Kathryn, smiling.

"I just don't know when the two of you are going to quit doing this little dance and just get on with it," said Aunt Clara. Norman plunked his beer down on the table.

"Get on with what, exactly?" he said, raising an eyebrow. Clara laughed.

"You know what I mean," she said. "Those two would make the most handsome couple you've ever seen."

"Stop that," said Kathryn. "We've been friends since we were in diapers. That's all there is to it."

Over dinner, Kathryn finished her beer. She felt light and good and just on the edge of happy. So when Aunt Clara went to check on Danny in the nursery, she grabbed herself a second can. Maybe her dad would have noticed if he wasn't already five beers into the evening. By the time they had dessert—strawberry shortcake with a fat scoop of vanilla ice cream—she was swimming through clouds, her head wonderfully light and bubbly. She decided she liked beer quite a lot.

After the plates were cleared, Aunt Clara shooed Kathryn out of the kitchen before she had a chance to do the dishes, so she took the blue vase up to her room, holding on to the handrail the whole way up to steady herself. When she lifted the little bunch of flowers, she found exactly what she expected at the bottom of the vase: a small black canister and a few coins bundled up in Saran wrap. She looked at the Betty Boop clock hanging on her bedroom wall. It took her a few seconds to get her eyes to focus, but when she finally saw it was nearly half-past six, she didn't figure she'd have enough time to make it to the drugstore before they closed. Besides, she had more important things to do. She'd been working herself up to it ever since Aunt Clara said she was coming for the weekend.

She checked her face in the vanity, touching up her mascara, putting on fresh lipstick—a tube of Flash Pink. She slipped into a yellow summer dress and grabbed her purse. On her way out of the house, she ran into Uncle Raymond burning through a Pall Mall on the front porch.

"Now, where are you running off to?" he said, flicking ash. She tried to think of a quick lie, but she found that the beer had slowed her down.

"That's for me to know and you to find out," she finally said. She stuck out her tongue, teasing her uncle. That was their way, ever since she was a little girl. Uncle Raymond took a hard pull on the cigarette. "You staying over this weekend, too?" she asked.

"I reckon I'll stay the night," said Uncle Raymond. "But then I gotta get back in the morning to look after the garage."

"Jack can handle it," she said. She thought about the little canister up in the bedroom. She'd be sure to make it out to the country in a few days.

"Sure he can. But that ain't the point. Neither of you have any business working yourself to death. You're still teenagers. You should be out racing cars and smoking cigarettes." He smiled, held out the pack like she should take one. She thought about it, but no—she didn't want to smell like she licked an ashtray. Not tonight. All at once, a change came over Uncle Raymond, like he was sitting in church and was just struck by the holy spirit.

"You're such a good girl, Kate," he said, his voice choking out at the end, giving him away. He'd had another beer after dinner, and now the alcohol twinkled in his wet eyes. "Go have yourself a good time." She turned to leave, stumbling just a bit on the porch step.

A coal train chugged across the rail bridge just as Kathryn approached the edge of the downtown loop. With the sun settling onto the river, the black train was silhouetted against the azure sky—a picture worthy of a postcard. Most of the storefronts were closed now, so Main Street was awfully quiet. And she figured that was a good thing. The alcohol was making her legs heavy, and she didn't want lots of folks seeing her clunk down the sidewalk like she was working through a bog at the river bottoms.

She made it to the shoe store right as Sammy Sawyer flipped

the sign on the glass over to Closed. She pushed through the door before he could lock it, letting the welcome bells usher her inside.

"Oh," said Sammy, zipping his eyes down the length of her dress. "I didn't know you were coming." Kathryn heard his words, but she didn't pay them any mind. She knew what she had come to say, what she had come to do.

"What do you see when you look at me?" she said. There was a buzz about her like a live wire. Sammy tilted his head, examined her.

"Uh, well, I don't—" he started, but she shushed him with a finger to his lips.

"Don't you dare answer," she said. "Not until you take the time to really see me." She wanted to catch a flicker in his eyes, some flame of epiphany. But he only looked confused, and maybe a little scared. Kate surveyed the store, making sure nobody else was in sight. Then she turned around and locked the dead bolt on the door. A sudden hush fell over the showroom—thick and palpable, like an audience going silent just before the feature picture.

"What are you doing?"

"Just come with me." She took his hand, guided him the length of the store. She reached behind the cash register and flicked off the lights, closing the two of them up in a pocket of shadows.

"What's gotten into you?" said Sammy. She turned into him, squeezing out the space between their bodies. Taking his other hand in hers, she pressed him against the counter. Her lips hovered inches from his. "Kate, have you been…drinking?"

Before she knew what was happening, her mouth was on his, their tongues pressing hard against each other. She had kissed boys before, but not like this—a craving pulling at the back of her throat so strong she thought she might consume him. Their bodies pulsed together, hands searching.

She thought she heard something in the corner of the show-room, but no—must have just been something falling off the counter beside the register. No matter—her body was moving without her now, thrusting forward. Just as she threw her head back, inviting his lips to her exposed throat, she heard another noise—shoes scuffling across the linoleum.

She looked up and gasped. The figure of a man stood at the back door, silhouetted against the fluorescent light coming from the hallway. He was motionless, perfectly quiet—*watching*. Kathryn pulled away from Sammy, flipping her dress back down to cover her thighs. Before she could react further, George Caldwell stepped forward, a triangle of light cutting across the length of his long, angular face.

26

Sometimes Kathryn hated her baby brother so much she thought she might split in two. The way he scratched his jagged finger-nails across her skin when she wasn't quick enough with the bottle. The way he'd spit up across her shoulder—as if aiming to miss the burp cloth. Even the way his tongue curled back in his throat when he cried. Everything the boy did was like a grain of sand caught in her eye. Most of the time she could beat back these feelings of contempt with an incantation of her will: *it's not his fault, it's not his fault.* But today—alone with the child in the quiet of the empty house—she gave herself over to the delicious horror of fantasy. *What if I left him in a basket at the fire station? What if I let the bathwater run too long? What if I locked myself in a bedroom upstairs and refused to come out? What if, what if, what if—*

Danny wouldn't stop screaming for anything. Kathryn pushed the stroller toward downtown, the baby's howls echo-ing off the brick storefronts. She was past the point of embar-rassment. *Yes, just look at us,* she thought, *the crazy Fairchild girl, unable to console her little brother, mother locked up again, father too detached to even care.* And what of it? Why should she be the one toting him around town instead of his actual mother? Of course, people thought of that, too. The only thing worse than being looked upon with scorn was being looked upon with pity.

By the time she made it to Blakely's Drugs on the round-about, her armpits were damp with sweat, and the summer humidity had flattened the curls from her hair. She pushed the stroller through the narrow aisles of the store back to the film counter, praying to God she wouldn't run into Sammy on his day off. Ever since the night at the shoe store, she couldn't push him from her mind. Every chance she got she would transport herself back to that night—to the taste of his salty-sweet lips on her tongue, the feel of his face under her hands—

"Well, she's back again!" boomed Larry at the film counter, pulling her out of fantasy and back into the cold light of the pharmacy. "Got a pickup today?" he asked, rifling through a filing cabinet of developed photographs. The baby was still screaming his head off, but it didn't seem to bother Larry. He beamed his usual smile—broad and sure.

"No, just dropping off," said Kathryn. She plunked down the little black canister of film Jack had hidden for her in the stem of the blue flower vase the week before. Just as Larry swiped it up from the counter, another voice sprang up from behind.

"Oh my word," said Margot Caldwell. "Can I? Please?" She approached with her arms outstretched, and before Kathryn had time to answer, the woman had scooped the baby into her arms. She jiggled him on her hip—and by God, the boy stopped crying.

Kathryn sat in a corner booth at Leon's Family Restaurant, watching across the table as Margot bounced Danny in her lap. She didn't feel much like socializing—especially not with Margot Caldwell. Every time she looked at the woman, she could think of nothing else but her husband—looming in the shadows of the shoe store, *watching*. But Margot was nothing if not persistent, offering three times back at the pharmacy to buy her lunch, so Kathryn finally gave in.

"I have a bit of a confession to make," said Margot. They had been exchanging pleasantries for a while, but now she seemed ready to get on with it. "I asked you to lunch because I have something I want to ask."

"Oh?" said Kathryn. Margot made googly eyes at Danny, trying to garner a smile from the boy while she gathered her words.

"Yes, well, I wondered if I could maybe…borrow Danny here from time to time." Kathryn looked at her brother, sitting contentedly in Margot's lap. A globule of drool hung from his bottom lip like a melting icicle.

"Borrow him?" She didn't quite know what Margot meant, but the thought of ridding herself of her brother every now and again was a delicious prospect.

"Well, babysit," said Margot. "I guess that sounds a little silly—a thirty-year-old woman asking to babysit your little brother. I wouldn't charge a thing, of course, and would talk to your father and your mother as well," she added quickly, her cheeks flushing red like she was embarrassed to have to say it aloud. "It just seems that I see you with him the most, so I thought I would start here. Maybe you could even just bring him around once in a while? To the parsonage or the church?"

"I suppose I could." Kathryn nodded—giving a little extra assurance to disarm the woman from whatever it was that was making her so anxious.

"I know it's a strange request," said Margot. "It's just that— we've wanted a baby for some time now." Her eyes had gone glassy. Kathryn looked away to save her the embarrassment. "I'm not sure it's going to happen for us. Not naturally, any-way." Kathryn didn't know what to say to something like that. She let Danny fill the silence with his gurgles and coos. "And

I'd so love to have a baby around, just a little—" said Margot, voice choking out before she could finish the thought.

"Yes, I understand," said Kathryn, though she didn't know if she did. Margot's chin quivered. The baby squirmed against her chest, working himself into another fit. Kate slid from her side of the booth and joined Margot across the table. She reached out to take the crying child.

"Oh, just a few more minutes," said Margot, pulling away, clutching Danny to her chest like the boy belonged to her. "You have no idea, Kate. You just have no idea."

27

1963

Three days later, Kathryn had just gotten Danny down for a nap when the phone rang.

"Kathryn! I'm so glad I caught you, are you busy tonight?"

"Margot?"

"Oh—yes. It's me," she said. "Sorry, got ahead of myself." Before Kate could answer, Margot pressed on: "Anyway, George is starting this new program over at the church. Weekly meetings for teenagers. You've heard of these youth groups starting up at other churches?"

"Yes," said Kathryn. "I suppose so."

"George thinks that's where the real ministry of the church belongs—with the youth. Invest in the future, that sort of thing."

"Okay," said Kathryn. She couldn't quite figure out what any of this had to do with her.

"Well, the first gathering is tonight. George is going to have a big bonfire out beside the parsonage—something fun and flashy to drum up interest. And after our chat the other day, I wondered if you might want to come."

"Oh, I don't know—"

"Please, Kate," said Margot, voice tight as a pressed spring. "Swing by for a little bit. And you can bring Danny with you—I'd be happy to watch him while the youth meeting is going on."

Kathryn said she'd think about it, though she had no real intention of going. But then the evening twilight crept up on her—dark and quiet and ever so lonely. There she was staring down another Friday night of babysitting while her dad enjoyed himself out on the porch—smoking his pipe, watching the bubblegum June dusk on the horizon like it was his only care in the world. It was in these moments when she best understood her mother, how the loneliness could creep in on you, how hard it was to simply *exist* in the dark.

She figured it might do her some good to get out of the house.

The night was cool and dry, so the small youth group gathered around the crackling fire, watching the orange flames lick the air. A dozen or so teens huddled together in small clusters, scuffing their shoes over white-headed dandelions, flicking desiccated sticks into the fire. Kate recognized just about all of them from the halls of Gray Station High—Jane Marshall and Shirley Culver, Steve Green, and Harold Stinson. But just like always, she repelled them like the wrong pole of a bar magnet, pushing them closer together and further from herself. She'd gotten good at pretending like she didn't notice—or even that she preferred to be alone. But still, she felt their sideways glances, their snickers and sneers like wet spitwads hitting her red cheeks. So much had changed since the senior prank, since she, for a single day, was not only normal but the coolest girl in school. She was back to being *the Fairchild girl*.

She stood opposite the rest of the group, staring into the flames, holding her hands before her like they needed warming—even in the mild June air. Before she knew it,

George was standing on her right side, like a lion protecting a cub.

He said a few words to the group and then had everyone join hands, making a big loop around the campfire. While everyone else bowed their heads and closed their eyes for a prayer, she studied the veins on the backside of George's hand, the dark, wispy hair curling over his knuckles. As the tenor of his voice sprang up with the rhythm of the prayer, his fingers twitched against her own. Looking at it was too much, but when she clenched her eyes, the image flitting across the reel of her mind was even worse: George Caldwell, standing in the shadows of the dark shoe store, *watching*.

"Amen," said George, giving her hand one final squeeze. She felt the burn of his palm long after she was released.

Later, they ate roasted hot dogs while George taught a Bible story—big and theatrical, the light of the flames slinging his god-sized shadow against the tree line of the woods. Kathryn watched him transform from the furtive little shoe clerk she had always known into something else—outsized and power-ful, a werewolf stepping into the moonlight. The story was a familiar one—about Abraham, how God promised him de-scendants as many as the stars in the sky.

"But Abraham was an old man," said George, pacing be-fore the flames, "and his wife, Sarah, had not born him a sin-gle child. How could God's promise be fulfilled?" He stopped now, planting his feet in the dusty earth. The teens were as silent as the still June air, enraptured in the rise and fall of his voice.

"Impossible, you might think," continued George, stretching his arms out wide. "And you wouldn't be alone. Abraham and Sarah thought it would be impossible, too." He surveyed each face around the circle. "But nothing in this wide world is im-possible for the God of all creation," he said. The fire popped and hissed, spitting red embers into the black sky. George settled his gaze onto Kathryn, searching her eyes as if they held the answer to a riddle. For the briefest of moments, he looked at her in that way he sometimes did at the shoe store when they were alone: small, lost, hungry. "The Bible tells us that all things work together for good to them that love God, to them who are called according to His purpose," he said. "You just have to listen for His still, small voice."

28

The day after the church bonfire, Kathryn collected Jack's pictures from the film counter at Blakely's Drugs and then drove the family Oldsmobile out to the country. She hadn't seen Jack in over a month, and she was starting to feel unmoored. Jack Chandler was the quiet part of her soul—the only person in this wide world who she could sit with for hours without saying a single word, more comfortable in his silence than she even was in her own. He was that rarest of human beings—one who knew how to get out of the way and let you exist without excuse. She'd never known another person who could do that so completely.

When she pulled into the dirt driveway, Jack sprang up from where he was sitting on the porch and took two big hops down the wooden stairs on his long, sinewy legs. He swung her into a hug and lifted her up, twirling her body like she was lighter than a handful of soapsuds. All that mechanic work had done wonders for his muscles, Kathryn thought. Her face flushed in the dry summer air as her mind wandered to thoughts of his hands on the small of her back.

"Hey, you," he said, taking the envelope of pictures from

her, sliding them into the pocket of his coveralls. Before she had a chance to respond, he took her by the hand, guiding her alongside the house like he used to do when they were children. He always had something or other he couldn't wait to show her—it was one of Kathryn's favorite things about coming to visit. At the back of the house, he put a finger to his lips to shush her, then he craned his head around to make sure his father wasn't watching. When he was satisfied the coast was clear, Jack swung open the heavy wooden doors to the root cellar and led Kathryn by the hand down the concrete steps.

"You won't have to smuggle my pictures for me much longer," he said, pulling the cord to an overhead light. When they were safely inside, he shut the doors overhead, trapping them in the silence of the concrete room. "It's almost finished." Kathryn stepped off the last step into the cool, dank room, feeling a rush of excitement at being back here underground, surrounded by rows of carrots, potatoes, jars of pickled vegetables. How many hours had she and Jack spent here in her childhood, hiding from imaginary enemies in their own private bunker?

"So?" said Jack, hands on his hips. "What do you think?" When Kathryn's eyes had adjusted, she saw that Jack had framed a new wall halfway into the cellar. Beyond the wooden beams was a long table stacked with ceramic trays. Strung up overhead was a wild-looking electric wire, curling its way to a single, amber-colored lightbulb. Kathryn puzzled over what she was seeing. "Oh, come on, Kate!" said Jack, his voice fluttering with joy. "I'm building a dark room." He took her hand once again, leading her through an opening in the wood where a door would hang. Kathryn watched him unstack the ceramic trays and lay them out on the table, his movements adazzle with energy and light.

"This one here will be for the developer," he said, adjusting the first tray. "And then the stop bath and the fixer." He spaced the trays symmetrically, gazing at them like he could already imagine the chemicals lapping up the sides of the ceramic.

"Oh, Jack," said Kate. "This is why you've been working all those hours at the garage."

"I'm nearly there," he said. "Just waiting on my next pay-check so I can buy an enlarger, and then I'll have everything I need." He looked around the room with wonder. No doubt he could picture the drying photographs strung up on clothes pins overhead. His joy was palpable, contagious.

"I can't believe your dad is letting you do all this," said Kathryn.

"What the old man don't know can't hurt him, right?" said Jack. "Besides, he can hardly hobble down these stairs with that wooden leg. I've thought it all out."

Later, they sat on the silty bank of the pond, flung off their shoes and socks, swirled the murky water with their outstretched toes. Jack leaned back against the clovered lawn, rested his el-bows inches from Kathryn's bare thighs. He clenched his eyes against the sunlight, and so Kathryn was free to regard him—the hard lines of strained biceps, the thick stubble of his two-day beard.

"Jack," she said, "what do you think the voice of God sounds like?" She couldn't stop thinking about what George Caldwell had said at the bonfire—*just listen for the still, small voice*. Some other person might have dismissed the question as crazy—but that wasn't Jack's way.

"Well," he said, thinking, "if there's a God, I reckon it don't have a voice at all."

"What do you mean?" asked Kathryn.

"More like a feeling," said Jack. He turned to her, leaning up on one elbow. "The tug and pull—down deep inside." Kath-ryn leaned her head back, folding her body into Jack's. She felt his hot breath float across her bare shoulder, and suddenly she was aware of their entangled bodies.

"Do you think I'm pretty?" she asked. Jack smiled, strung his fingers through the knotted curls of her sunset-red hair.

"Now, what kind of question is that, Freckles?" he said. Kathryn cringed at her childhood nickname. Jack was always trying to keep her at a distance one way or another. "There ain't a woman in this wide world half as pretty as you."

"Yeah?" said Kathryn, propping herself up, leaning her face inches from his. "Then why don't you prove it?" She closed her eyes and wet her lips, daring him. But after an eternity of time had passed—maybe five whole seconds—she knew it was no use. She opened her eyes to find him lying flat on his back. He was no more interested in her than he was one of those mules on the other side of the wire fence. She stood, casting her shadow across his face.

"Aren't you still seeing that guy in town?" asked Jack, watching as she brushed the dirt from her backside. "Sammy Something-or-other?"

"Maybe I am," said Kathryn. She wanted to hurt him, but she didn't know if that was possible. "I don't reckon it matters to you one way or the other, now does it?" She scooped her shoes from the ground and turned to leave.

"C'mon, Kate," he said, "Don't be like that."

"I'm not being like anything," she said, but she knew that was a lie. She was always *being like* something she wasn't—a mother, a woman, a normal teenage girl. She glanced over her shoulder, watching as Jack pinched the yellow head from a summer dandelion. What must it be like to know yourself so completely? To feel the thrumming of God in the ebb and flow of your insides? The summer weeds tickled her bare ankles as she made the long walk back to the car, alone.

When the sun finally tucked itself under the rolling westward hills, the projector at the Starlight Drive-In flickered to life, cutting its pale blue light through the balmy dusk. No matter how many times she watched a movie here, Kathryn always gazed at the sixty-foot screen with wonder—a gigantic canvas enchanted to life by the charm of dancing light. Pure magic. She sat next to Sammy Sawyer in the front of his brand-new Chevy Chevelle.

"That's our cue," said Sammy, handing the flask of bourbon back to Kathryn. He hooked the heavy metal speaker on the side of the car door, careful not to scratch the sky-blue paint. The sound crackled and spit before settling into the James Bond theme music, the stringy bass line thumping through the car. *Dr. No* was just about the dumbest movie title Kathryn had ever heard, but no matter—she didn't care about the film. She was here to get away from her thoughts, to unload the boulder of rejection she had carried home from Jack's house. She figured the easiest way to do that was to dump it into the lap of somebody else. No—it wasn't fair. But worrying about fairness only made you carry the burden that much longer. So as soon as she had returned from Jack's, she sat cross-legged on her bed back at the house on Poplar Street, took a swig from a can of PBR, and called up Sammy Sawyer.

"How about taking me to the drive-in tonight?" she said, her finger hooked into the looping pigtail of the phone cord.

"Well, I already saw the picture last week," said Sammy.

"That don't matter one bit. Can't you think of something fun we could do at the drive-in other than watch a movie?" Sammy went silent. Just for a second, she thought he might've dropped the phone.

"I'll pick you up at eight," he said, his voice cracking at the end.

Kissing Sammy Sawyer was both delicious and grotesque. It started well enough—the push and smack of his doughy lips, the tiny fissure broken by a pushing tongue, even the hungry pull of his teeth against her bottom lip. But after several minutes, every bit of skin from her chin to her nose was slippery with saliva. It was a messy business, kissing.

"Wait," she said, a firm hand on his chest. He pulled away like a scolded puppy.

"Right—sorry."

"No, I just need to get more comfortable." She untucked her blouse, lay back on the bench seat in the back of the car. Her plaid miniskirt crept up her thighs, and she didn't bother pulling it back down. Sammy's eyes went wild, but he didn't move—not yet.

"So, do you want to—" he said, but then—what was that sound? Laughter? From where? Before she knew what happened, something splashed against her outstretched legs.

"What the hell?" Sammy said, pushing up, slamming his head against the low ceiling of the Chevelle. Sticky soda dripped from his hair onto her bare thighs. The empty cup lay on the floor beside them. Kathryn sat up, trying to piece together what was happening. From the half-open front window, she could see the shadowy figures of two young boys running through the gravel away from the car, laughing, pointing back at their victims.

After Sammy unhooked the speaker from the car door and cranked up the window, he was in the back seat again, ready to pick up where they left off. But Kathryn was rattled.

"Maybe we should stop," she said, wiping a trail of sweat from her temple. Coming out of the heat of the moment now, she wondered: If those boys hadn't shown up, was she really going to go through with it?

"Oh, come on, Kate." Sammy leaned his head against the foggy window. He cracked his knuckles like they had looked at him the wrong way.

"Are you mad?"

"No—just confused. None of this was my idea, you know?" He snuck a quick glance at her, but then looked away. He was right, of course. She wished she had stayed with Jack at the fishing pond, content to wade through the shallow waters with her best friend.

PART THREE:

A STILL, SMALL VOICE

29

Kathryn Fairchild.

I write her name at the top of a new page in my notebook, the white space underneath as daunting as the first blank page of a new manuscript. I have just started to piece together Edith Fairchild's life—five pages of questions, fragmented ideas, the beginnings of a character sketch. But I know next to nothing about her daughter. On my way back to the Gray Station Public library, I can't help but resent Jonathan Aster all over again. Why didn't he tell me it was Kathryn who jumped? How could he possibly benefit from seeing me veer into dead ends? Maybe more importantly: What else is he still withholding, and why?

When I get to the library, I give a quick wave to Linda the Librarian and march straight to the microforms room *like a boss.* I quickly find the call number for the box of film I need and load the roll onto the machine. Scanning through the *Gray Station Gazette* archives, I find the article correction Gene Bartlett mentioned about the mix-up between the two Fairchild women; but it reveals nothing I don't already know. So I scroll over to the news for the next day—July 6, 1964—and find what I am looking for right away:

Kathryn Marie Fairchild
Kathryn Marie Fairchild, age 17, of Gray Station, KY, died
Saturday, July 4, 1964. Kathryn was born April 21, 1947, to
Edith and Norman Fairchild. She is survived by her parents, her
aunt and uncle, Clara and Raymond Clark, and her brother,
Danny Fairchild.

There isn't much heft to it, but at least there are a few names
I can track down. Still, one thing keeps bothering me: What
about the baby? I scan the other obituaries for the same day and
several days following, but there is nothing useful. I've assumed
all along that the woman in the picture was the child's mother,
but is this necessarily true? Kathryn Fairchild was seventeen
when she jumped, so it's certainly possible that she had a kid.
But if so, why wouldn't the newspaper report it?

I keep my eyes fixed on the screen, but my mind wanders.
Who was that baby? What did she look like? What was her
name? As if by instinct, my arms wrap themselves around my
belly, cradling the fetus inside. *Your baby is the size of a blueberry.*
She now has arm buds, which look like paddles.

Before my mind can catch up with my body, I fire off a text
to Ryan: I know something you don't want me to know. Call me.

30

1963

As the morning sun streaked through the slatted blinds of her bedroom at the church parsonage, Margot Caldwell lay in bed, gathering her flannel nightgown over her hips, letting the bottom hem rest just over her exposed belly button. George was methodical in his approach—no longer kissing her neck or smelling her bare skin. Years ago, he would have nuzzled his mouth and chin between her legs, breathed her in, tasted her as deeply as his pulsing tongue would allow. But now he rested back on his knees away from her body. With outstretched arms, he tugged on her plain white underwear until they came loose from her hips. She no longer worried if she didn't shower the night before. He wouldn't get close enough to notice.

Making no sound, he pushed himself inside her—the stick and tug of dry skin giving them both away. He clenched his eyes—this was his habit—and pulled his brows taut as if he were in great concentration. This thing that should be instinctual, animalistic, was as taxing on him as studying for his Sunday sermon. As he quickened his hips, the squeaking of the springs grew louder, louder still, until Margot could think of nothing else but the uneven rhythm of the bed. Then, with a shudder, he was finished.

Still, he stayed inside her, making sure not a single drop of life was spilled. It was always in this brief moment when he would finally look at her—when the hard work was over and the waiting would begin once again. After some time, he pulled himself out, slid a pillow under Margot, elevating her hips the way they had been told to do. Finally, he finished the ritual, laying his hands across her womb, reciting from *Psalm 128:*

"'Thy wife shall be as a fruitful vine by the sides of thine house: thy children like olive plants round about thy table.'"

"Amen," said Margot, and then George stood, leaving her in the darkness of the bedroom.

31

Back at the Little Yellow House, I check my phone for the millionth time to see if Ryan has answered my text. Still nothing. I need to keep myself busy, so I walk downstairs to the parlor to pay Mamaw for another week's stay. Instead, I find Quinn sitting on the couch *reading my book*.

"Oh my God, what?" she says, her face contorted. I must have been gawking at her.

"Nothing. I just—I don't want to know what you think."

"What I think about what?"

"The book. Whether you like it or whatever. I don't want to know."

"Okay, right. That's not weird at all." She's completely deadpan, and it takes me an embarrassing amount of time to register the sarcasm.

"I mean—I don't know," I say. "I don't read the comments, you know?"

"Whatever, man. I guess I won't tell you that I got it in the mail, like, an hour ago and I'm already eighty pages in."

I smile, and she smiles back, and yeah, it feels really good. But then I forget what to do with my hands—my normal reaction when someone starts talking about my writing. Before

I can open my mouth and say something super awkward, my phone buzzes.

I glance at the screen. Ryan. His first text since the night of my book launch: can u talk?

My pulse throbs in my temples. I feel faint.

"Um, are you—okay?" says Quinn.

"What? Yeah. Totally good." I slide onto the paisley couch next to her.

"You look all weird." She makes a face and scoots away. I read the text again and then look back at Quinn. I know I need to do this before I lose my nerve. I wish I could transport myself back to Brooklyn, to Myra.

"Hey, could you do me a favor?" I say.

"Bro, I just gushed over your book," says Quinn. "Don't get greedy."

"Seriously. I need to make a phone call. And I know I only just met you, but I need someone to just sit with me while I do it." She grabs something from the couch next to her, slides it into the book. "Please tell me you are not using a raw fettuccini noodle as a bookmark," I say.

"Don't judge me, bitch." She snaps off the top of the noodle, pops it into her mouth, and crunches.

We grab a few cookies from the server (Mamaw's snickerdoodles this time) and head upstairs to my room. Some young couple from Indiana just checked in to the room next to mine this morning, so I close the door for privacy.

"Okay, so…context," I say, pulling my phone from my back pocket. "I have to call someone. A guy."

"Yeah, you do!" says Quinn.

"Shut up. Just listen." She hisses at me, but then she sees my face drop. "So, anyway, I don't really want to go into much detail here. But I need you to just…be here? For moral support, make sure someone else is hearing what I'm hearing—he's been ghosting me for the last few weeks."

"Like, eavesdrop on your personal communications?" She sits next to me on the bed.

"Something like that."

"Julia," she says. She cranes her head around like she's checking that the coast is clear. "Did you...*kill somebody*?"

"What? Seriously, would you just—"

"Okay, fine," she says. "I mean, I was going to help you chop up the body or whatever, but yeah, never mind." I look up just in time to see her smile.

She picks up my phone, hands it to me.

"Look, I'm here, let's do this." Her voice is earnest and warm—like Myra's. I'm already on the verge of tears, but I make myself push ahead. I scroll through my contacts, hover my thumb over Ryan's name. I take a breath and close my eyes, trying to talk myself into it. Pretty soon I have no choice: Quinn reaches over, hits the call button, puts the phone on speaker. I want to fight her, but the line is ringing and I have to remind myself to breathe. And then—

"Jules," says Ryan. Hearing my name in his mouth sends vibrations through my core. I'm not prepared for this. "Julia? Are you there?"

"I'm here," I say.

"How have you been?" he starts, trying to stay casual, as though he hasn't been ignoring my texts for weeks. I can't find any words. But when I look at Quinn, I know that if I don't say something soon, she's going to start talking for me. That wouldn't go well.

"Where have you been?" I say—only four words, but they hold everything. Ryan is silent for a beat. I can picture him on the other end—his checkered Oxford shirt undone at the top two buttons, his three-day stubble trailing into his collar.

In Myra's words, *nobody works harder to look like crap than Ryan Alman.*

"Uh—mostly working? Living life. I've been booked up, Jules. Things have been—"

"No, that's not good enough." I can barely keep the shake from my voice. "You completely ghosted me, Ryan. And right after—"

"Look, I didn't think it was a big deal."

"*Not* a *big deal?* We don't see each other for, like, six years, and then we hook up? That feels like a pretty big deal to me."

"It's not like I planned for it to happen, Jules," he says. I throw the phone beside me on the bed. I want to say: *well, I didn't plan on getting pregnant, but here we are!* But I don't want him to know, not yet, not like this. "We just got carried away. I don't know what else to say." Quinn picks up my phone from the bed, holds it for me so I can clench my hands together like I'm squeezing a stress ball.

"Why did you finally text me back?" I say.

"What do you mean?"

"You ignored me for over a month. What changed?" I already know the answer, but I want to hear it from him.

"I don't really know, okay? But you sent that weird text, and it felt a little…threatening? I guess I just wanted to make sure that we're cool. You and me."

"Or maybe you just want to make sure I won't say anything?"

"Say anything to who?"

"I don't know, Ryan. Any ideas?"

"Oh, come on," he says. "Don't do this. We have a history, Jules. It's not like this is the first time—"

"This isn't about our history. It's about what happened early last month. And the full truth of your situation." He doesn't respond, but his silence tells me everything I need to know. An unexpected sob catches in my throat. Quinn puts a hand on my knee, which gives me just enough courage to choke it back down. I'm working out what to say next, but then Quinn coughs.

"Is that—" says Ryan, his voice catching. "Is there someone there with you?" Quinn covers her mouth, shoots me a look of apology. But I like hearing Ryan's paranoia. It gives me a delicious amount of power.

"And what if there is?" I say. "What if someone's sitting right here beside me? What would you say?"

"Look, Jules. We were both drunk—"

"That doesn't matter! We could have both been sober—the fact is, we slept together, and you weren't telling me the whole story."

"Let's not make a whole thing of this." He goes on talking, but I can no longer hear him. I have the sudden feeling I'm submerged in water. Something about his voice—the timbre, the inflection. The bleeding edges of a memory start to come to me, like a Polaroid developing into focus.

We're at the Sundowner, tucked away in the hazy light of the dead zone. I'm smiling, laughing. My fingers trace the contours of Ryan's biceps. I look at his left hand—no wedding ring. I kiss him. Then—the yellow light of the bathroom. I see myself, a simulacrum, pressed against the cold concrete wall. Ryan locks the door behind us. His hands roam up my skirt, my hands are at his belt. The muffled music from the bar thrums and pulses and he and I slip back into a familiar rhythm, moving together in sync like we used to so long ago, and for a moment I forget who he really is.

Quinn's hand brushes my knee, bringing me back into my body here in this moment, here in this soft, safe bed in this little house in Kentucky, a million miles from Brooklyn. Ryan's voice drones on through the phone, but I've had enough.

"Are you married?" I say. The line goes silent. A wave of humiliation washes over me. Quinn shakes her head—her cheeks flushed, her mouth hanging agape. I thought speak-

. ing the words would make me feel in control, but I only feel shame, regret. Hot tears bubble into my eyes.

"Maybe we should talk about this in person," says Ryan. "If we could just—"

I hang up, hold the phone against my chest, close to my thrumming heart, and realize I've known exactly who Ryan is all along—the man who broke my heart repeatedly for years, and now cheats on his wife. He is exactly that man, and he has forced on me—guilt, sorrow, shame—something that I never asked for.

32

In the dead of night, caught on the edge of a dream in her bed at the house on Poplar Street, Kathryn heard the *still, small voice.*

Or did she? A gentle thrum in the air—wispy and light, soft as the down feathers stuffed in her pillow. She sat up in bed, listening. At first, she thought the sound was coming through the open window, but that couldn't be it. The tepid breath of June had no voice—the air so still it barely ruffled the silk curtains covering the blinds. She titled her ear toward the door of her room, but was met only with the rhythmic ticking of the wall clock.

But then—she heard it again. A familiar hum, edging itself under the gap between her closed door and the hardwood floor. She thought of the sermon she heard growing up as a child—the moment when the Lord called out to Samuel in the night. The young boy had thought the voice belonged to his caretaker, Eli—but no, it was the voice of God Almighty. She tried to think of what Samuel had said in response to the Lord. Oh, yes—she remembered:

"Here I am," said Kathryn, just above a whisper. She sat perfectly still, waiting for a response, her heart fluttering wild in her chest like a housefly trying to escape a mason jar. But the voice didn't call again—not yet. So she crept toward the door, her zigzag steps aimed in just the right direction to keep the wooden floors from moaning underfoot. Gripping the brass knob, she pulled the door open just enough to glimpse into the hallway. The voice rose again, and suddenly she recognized—with both relief and disappointment—that the voice did not belong to God, but to her mother.

As the whispers carried down the hallway from the nursery, panic seized Kathryn's chest like a corset. She flung herself from her bedroom, no longer caring about the squeaking hardwood, and rushed down the hallway. When she pushed into the cracked nursery door, her eyes first went to Danny's crib—the crumpled blanket alone in the empty bed. Then she saw Edith, her back turned, facing the open window.

"Momma?" said Kathryn, her voice small, unsure. And then Edith turned, her body silhouetted against the cold white light of the moon outside. She held Danny in her arms, gazing down at the child as if she couldn't quite figure out what he was.

"Here I am," said Edith, never looking away from the sleeping baby.

Once, back when Kathryn was eight years old, Edith pulled her out of sleep in the small hours of the morning, wrapped her tiny shoulders in a warm blanket and took her on a stroll down Poplar Street toward downtown. Kathryn nearly screamed for her father—she had been told to do just that if Edith ever did anything that scared her—but she kept quiet. The truth was, she didn't think her mother was crazy. She certainly didn't think her mother was dangerous. Edith had never tried to hurt her, or anyone else for that matter. Though she couldn't articulate it at her young age, it seemed to Kathryn that the only thing her mother was guilty of was thinking differently than everyone else. All things considered, that didn't seem so bad.

What had they talked about on the way to the river that night? Memory was a fickle thing—constantly shifting like light in a mirror maze, reflecting both truth and illusion. They might have talked about the quiet storefronts along Main Street, gloomy and imperturbable in the early-morning light, like the faces of sleeping giants. Perhaps they regarded the people-sized sunflowers looming above the Eubanks' picket fence, brushing their outstretched fingers against the silk-soft petals. The only thing she knew for sure was this: at some point they had made it to the edge of the river, snuggling together on the rocky bank with their knees tucked under the blanket they now shared.

"It's magical," whispered Kathryn, her head nestled safely under her mother's arm. The breaking sun reached its blazing fingers over the edge of the river, lighting up the new train bridge in the distance.

"Magic, yes," said Edith. "The most beautiful kind of magic." A coal train approached from the Indiana side of the river, so far away they had yet to feel its rumble against the rocky earth. Kathryn didn't know what her mother meant, but she didn't have to ask. A mother knows the questions of her child's heart. "Some magic is just smoke and mirrors—nothing more than illusion," said Edith, stringing her fingers through the curls of Kathryn's flame-red hair, "but every once in a while you see something truly magical—something that turns you inside out, some beautiful thing that reminds you: this cruel and lonely life is worth living."

In the nursery, Kathryn sat cross-legged on the floor, watching as her mother rocked baby Danny. When was the last time they had been together like this? Comfortable and quiet, together in the same room. Kathryn wanted to call in her father, but she was scared it would break the balance they enjoyed—mother and daughter and son, as stable as an equilateral triangle.

"How are you getting along with your schoolwork?" asked Edith. The question caught Kathryn off guard.

"Well, it's June now," she said. Edith's face twisted, as if she couldn't possibly see the relevance of the answer. "I finished out the last quarter very well, I think," added Kathryn, though she knew that wasn't entirely true. As far as the county office knew, she had been homeschooling since baby Danny was born, but in reality, she rarely did more schooling than read a book or two from the public library each week.

"Education is so very important," said Edith. Danny was rooting his face across her now. "You're such a bright girl, Kate, but you have to keep your mind sharp." She lowered her nightgown and gave her breast to Danny. He mostly ate from the bottle these days, but still—the child latched onto the nipple and sucked deeply, as if trying to drink love.

"Yes, I know," started Kathryn, but Edith cut her off.

"No—I mean it," she said. "You need to be prepared to survive in this world." She contorted her face into a smile as if she were only making a joke. But Kathryn knew better. It was true: the world had not been kind to Edith Fairchild. The world hates what it doesn't understand. Kate watched Edith stroke the baby's face, tucking a wild curl of hair behind his ear.

"Momma," said Kathryn, "does God ever speak to you?" Edith looked up at Kathryn, searched her face.

"Oh, baby," she said. "Don't ask me that." She blinked through glassy eyes.

"But the voices you hear," said Kathryn. "Do you ever think—"

"Please," said Edith. "Don't." She shook her head, closed her eyes. Her chest heaved against Danny's face, but she held steady.

33

Alone in my rented room, Ryan's words echo through my thoughts. *I didn't think it was a big deal. We just got carried away. We have a history.* I desperately want to call Myra, even pull her name up on my phone before chickening out—twice. I just can't do it, not yet. She's been right about Ryan all along. She warned me not to invite him to the book launch, but I was feeling smug: we met as young writers, and now I was publishing a book. I know I shouldn't, but I can't help feeling ashamed, embarrassed. Like the whole thing was somehow my fault for not seeing the signs.

Oh, the signs: How far back do they go? The year we broke up? The first time we met in a poetry workshop sophomore year? Ryan was objectively the most talented poet in the class— and boy, did he know it. He feigned humility and surprise at every compliment he received—and it was convincing if you didn't know him well. But even when I learned to see through the facade, his charm was enough to keep me tethered to him. He'd write notes on my workshop manuscripts—little flour- ishes of praise that only occasionally touched on my writing itself. Myra was in the class, too—the only one in the room who was unaffected by his breezy nonchalance, the cool way he could undercut someone's work while making himself appear sensitive and noble. *I think I'm just too dense to really get what you're trying to do. There's nothing wrong with your prosody. I think I'm not smart enough to really get it, you know?*

The notes in class turned into notes after class, long walks through the quad and out onto Main Street, farther. I showed him the Poughkeepsie the other students didn't know—the secret spots my mom and I shared as longtime residents. After the first few weeks, the pace of our relationship was breakneck, unyielding—a tiger lily bursting orange-red from a single overnight rain, so intense, so vibrant that you know it can't last. Still, we were inseparable through senior year. To understand Ryan Alman is to understand what led to our breakup: he cheated on me the week after he proposed. The whisper network of our small campus let me know it wasn't the first time. And yet somehow, still, the night of the book launch—

Back in the moment, with a breath caught in my throat, I fire off a single text to Ryan: We need to talk about your wife.

34

With a pillow stuffed under her naked bottom, Margot Caldwell lay still in the master bedroom of the church parsonage, listening to the roar of the summer storm outside. The *plink-plunk* of tiny hailstones falling against the gutters outside was musical—so soothing that, in some other circumstance, it might have lulled her to sleep. She adjusted herself, trying to keep her hips elevated. It wasn't a pleasant thought, but sometimes she couldn't help it: How much semen had her husband deposited into her over the years? Perhaps enough to fill a case of pint-sized milk jars. And yet, what did they have to show for it? All that life, wasted. George returned from the bathroom. He loomed over her, bent at the waist, placed a hand just below her belly button.

"'Thy wife shall be as a fruitful vine by the sides of thine house,'" he quoted rhythmically, never looking at her face, "'thy children like olive plants round about thy table.'"

"Amen," said Margot. She waited for him to leave the room, and then she reached down to check the sheets under her raised bottom. Thank God—nothing had leaked out.

★ ★ ★

Ten days later, Margot walked through the front door into the cool parsonage, sweating from where she had been weeding the flowerbeds out front. Her back ached, and her stomach coiled and constricted. She went to the bathroom, and even before she sat down on the toilet, she knew. She emptied her bladder and then inserted a tampon, pulling back her fingers to reveal them spotted with blood.

She did not pray. How could she? All her prayers had been purged over the years, gathered into thunderheads in the sky above. Where had all those words rained down? Did they pour onto other women—the lucky ones—somewhere else in this godforsaken world?

She felt like curling up on the couch with the hot water bottle stretched across to ease the cramping, but there was no time for such idleness. George would be home from the shoe store in a few hours, and she had resolved to finally bring up the idea of adoption again. Over the past several months, Margot had manufactured opportunities to see little Danny Fairchild as often as she could—but it seemed like the more she saw him, the more she longed for a baby of her own. She didn't want a visitor. She wanted a child that stayed.

Margot had thawed out a nice chuck roast the day before, so she prepared it now with cut potatoes, carrots, and onions. She seasoned the whole pot with garlic, oregano, parsley, and just a bit of thyme. By the time she heard George's truck crunching through the gravel outside, the whole house smelled unctuous and buttery—an aroma so thick you could almost taste the air. She greeted him at the door, taking his suit coat and hat, offering him the only thing she had left to give: a smile, bright eyes, a tilt of the head.

They chatted about this and that over dinner, but as usual, it was mostly her doing the talking. George ate in that ravenous way only men were allowed, slicing off chunks of meat, smearing them across the plate to collect every morsel, gnawing through gristle with an open mouth. Margot had a few bites herself, but the gelatinous fat of the roast churned her stomach. When George had cleared his plate—pulling his fingers greedily through the last remnants of fallen salt—she offered him chocolate chip cookies and a cup of black coffee. She let him enjoy the dessert in quiet, but she could put it off no longer.

"We'll have to try again next month," she said. He looked up, stopped chewing long enough to process what she was telling him. A quiet resignation sank across his shoulders. This was always the way they talked about it—with a nod or a sigh, nothing more. The whole thing was a purpled bruise, too painful to touch anywhere but at the edges. But tonight, Margot knew she must push through the pain. She had to be brave.

"We simply have to keep praying," said George. "The Lord is testing our faith." Margot raised a mason jar of ice water to her lips, trying to keep the shake from her hands. How many times had they settled for prayer? She didn't dare ask: *What about the faithfulness of the Lord?* Hadn't she and George held up their end of the bargain?

"Yes, but maybe we should think about…" she said, pausing. What were the right words? How is the thing to be said? "Well, we should talk about…other ways." George went to take a bite of the cookie, but now he paused, dabbing his mouth with a cloth napkin.

"You want a backup plan?" asked George. "A *plan B*?"

"That's not what I meant."

"Why should the Lord honor our prayers if we don't truly believe He will answer them?" George did not look at her. He took up the cookie again, taking in nearly the whole thing in one ravenous bite. Margot felt the impulse to clear the plates, to leave George in his silence at the table as she normally did when they reached such an impasse. But she felt a stirring deep inside her. She might even say it was the Holy Spirit, though she dared not say it aloud.

"George, darling," said Margot. "Can't we at least consider—"

Before she could even say the word—*adoption*—George slammed his clenched fist against the table, rattling the silverware against the dishes. Margot sucked in a breath and held it. From outside, the shrill chirp of a barn swallow twittered through the open window, cutting through the thick silence of the kitchen. George wiped the sweat from his forehead with a cloth napkin, gathering himself.

"I'm sorry," he said. He stroked his hand down the length of his sweating mason jar, letting the condensation cool him. He rubbed his wet fingers against his reddened face, and when he was good and ready, he finally looked at her. "I just can't do that, Margot."

"That's how you feel right now," she said, trying to push hope into her voice. "But just think—there are so many children out there, George. Children who need homes. What if the Lord is asking us to—"

"No," said George, a warning coiled in his voice. "The Lord is asking no such thing."

"But don't you think—"

"I will say this once, and that will be the end of it," said George, pointing a finger in her direction. "If the Lord could bless Abraham and Sarah with a child, there's no reason he can't do the same for me." Margot caught eyes with him from across the table.

"For you?" she said.

"For us, Margot," said George. "You know what I mean." He flopped his napkin in the center of his plate, covering the remaining crumbles of the cookie. "I simply can't." He swiped a hand through the air, as if the gesture held his meaning. "I want my own child, Margot, *our* child. Flesh of my flesh. Bone of my bone."

"I know you do," said Margot resignedly. With her elbows on the table, she tucked her face into her open palms, waiting for the storm of grief to work itself out. George stood, softening toward her, and walked behind her chair. He placed his hands on her slender shoulders, bent over and kissed the crown of her head.

"'And all things, whatsoever you shall ask in prayer,'" he whispered, reciting the familiar scripture, "'you shall receive.'"

35

When I wake up, eyes crusted from a hard afternoon nap, it takes me several minutes to remember where I am. Soon enough I have my bearings and read Kathryn's obituary again with fresh eyes. This time, I'm struck by the last four words: *her brother, Danny Fairchild.* I've been thinking about the mystery baby so much that I didn't realize how huge this little detail about Kathryn's brother could be. The clip doesn't say how old Danny was when Kathryn died, but even if he was the older child, there is at least a decent chance he's still alive. The best I can figure, he's likely between sixty and eighty years old.

The last time I searched the internet (and the phone book) for any Fairchilds in the area, I came up empty-handed. But now that I am working with a first name, I figure it can't hurt to check again. Just as I reach for my laptop, the door to my room swings open. I jump, but then I see it's just Quinn—*barging into my room without knocking.*

"Uh, make yourself at home," I say. She flops next to me on the bed.

"Seems fair, considering this place really is, you know, my home."

"Yeah, but a knock would be nice." She doesn't seem to reg-

ister the comment. We both fall quiet, and I know she's thinking about the last time she was in this room with me.

"You wanna go get a drink?" says Quinn. Her face is sunken
into a pillow, her nose and lips smushed together like a cartoon
character who's just been punched.

"A drink? As in a *drink-drink*?"

"Um, yeah?"

"Okay, two things," I say. "Number one, you're eighteen years
old—"

"But that's, like, a hundred and twelve in cat years, so—"

"Most bars count human years these days." She turns over
onto her back and flips her middle fingers at the ceiling. "And
number two," I say, pausing to consider if this is something I
really want my new teenage friend here to know, "I'm just a
little bit…pregnant." The way she looks at me makes me feel
completely, totally naked.

"Oh." She roves her eyes over my belly as if trying to confirm. "Is it with…that guy? The one with the wife?" I nod, and
then we sit in silence, both of us trying to find a way forward.

"How about a coffee instead?" I say.

We walk four blocks to the downtown loop, clicking over
cobblestone sidewalks lined with sugar maples and river birches.
The facades of the connected storefronts are nearly uniform:
clay-red brick pocked with gray keystones, window-box flowers hanging from apartments above the shops. Quinn leads me
past Chuck's Hardware and Fine Gifts, Dreyer Brothers Furniture, Riverview Bakery—the kind of shops that look like
they've been around since the Fairchilds were walking these
streets in the 1950s. Quinn swings open the glass door of Spurl-
ing's Place, a funky little coffee shop/wine bar hybrid. I step inside, instantly reminded of some of the quirky stores Myra and
I frequent in Brooklyn. Quinn registers my look of surprise.

"What?" she says. "Did you expect a saloon or something?"

I have an impulse to defend myself, but maybe she's right. My ideas about Kentucky—or most any state in the South or Midwest—have been shaped by movies and political polls. In reality, after a week I feel fond of this little town in ways I never expected. Quinn flops her Hello Kitty purse atop the bar at the front like she owns the place. As soon as we climb onto a couple of stools, she's barking out an order.

"Two fingers of bourbon, neat!" she says. A big teddy-bear-looking dude approaches from behind the bar. He has a magnificently groomed beard and looks like he desperately needs an IPA.

"Nice try, Lindsey," he says. "Maybe in three years." He pours her a cup of black coffee.

Lindsey? Her real name is *Lindsey?* I can't make it fit with this little emo-punk teen sitting next to me.

"C'mon, Ben," she says. "You know what they say. Age is in the eye of the beholder—or some shit like that."

"I'm pretty sure that's beauty."

"Awwww, thanks!" she says.

"That's not—"

"Whatever, man." She gets up, skips to the end of the bar, right on up to an actual jukebox. "My friend from New York here wants this place to feel more *Kentucky*, so…" She pops in a few quarters, and suddenly Billy Ray Cyrus is crooning "Achy Breaky Heart" over the speakers.

"Ah, that's much better," I say.

"And what can I get for you, Miss New York?" says *Ben the Bearded Man.*

"Coffee for me, too," I say, but then I feel guilty and quickly add: "Decaf."

"Make it Irish?" he says, taunting Quinn. "You look to be of age."

"Bro," says Quinn, "she's preggers."

"She's what now?"

"Knocked up," says Quinn. I slap her on the arm, maybe a little too hard.

"Not cool, *Lindsey*," I say. Ben excuses himself to avoid the awkwardness. But he's a good sport and swings back by a moment later with the coffee.

"Sorry," she says. "But please don't call me that."

"Don't call you by your actual name?"

"It sounds weird coming from you." The coffee smells so good I almost forget it's decaf.

"Let's make a deal," I say. "I won't call you *Lindsey* if you don't tell any more complete strangers that I'm pregnant."

"Ben's not a stranger. I've known him forever." Before I can respond, she's bickering with Ben again. I don't know if she's just being her awkward self or if she's trying to flirt.

That's when I notice the guy sitting at the other end of the bar polishing off a negroni, and I can't help but think of Ryan—not because of his curly black hair or angular face, but his posture, in the way he takes up so much space with his spread elbows and outstretched legs. He holds up his empty rocks glass, motions toward Ben for another. The way he swivels in the chair tells me he's had one too many already. When you've worked in a bar for years like I have, you pick up on these things.

Ben grabs the gin and Campari, but then he reaches for a cocktail shaker and I can't help myself. "You're not seriously going to shake that negroni now, are you, Ben?" He looks at the shiny metal container and then back at me.

"I was thinking about it," he says.

"C'mon, man," I say. "Bartender 101. That drink is all booze. You gotta stir it." Ben gives me an embarrassed look. I almost feel bad for him, but then—

"But what if I like it shaken?" says the dude at the end of the bar. "Can't a guy get a drink the way he wants?" I take a sip of my coffee and shrug.

"That depends," I say. "Is the guy James Bond?"

* * *

I must be more tolerant of strangers down here because I've spent the last thirty minutes telling this guy all about the Fairchild case. Ever since I called out the bartender for his embarrassing mixing skills, *Mr. Shaken Negroni* over here can't seem to get enough of me. With all the stealth and confidence of a man who's four drinks into a Monday afternoon, he has gradually dragged himself over to the stool next to mine.

And yes: I'm aware he sees me as some sort of challenge—a chance to check off the *feisty girl from New York* box. But right now, I honestly don't care. Sometimes it just feels good to talk without a filter, to purge all these words building up inside me so somebody else can deal with them for a while. Myra is a bazillion miles away in Brooklyn, and Quinn is still trying to coax Ben into giving her some liquor. But there's always a drunk man in a bar willing to listen for as long as it takes.

"You must be one hell of a writer," he says, nursing another drink. His eyes are glossy and small. He smells like he slept in a Purell factory. "I mean, whoever it is that's paying you to come down here and run around Gray Station like this must think you're worth it."

"Maybe," I say, shrugging. I told him the book is on assignment, but I haven't mentioned who's paying me. Aster told me not to throw his name around. That's fine by me—one less thing I have to explain. "Honestly, though, writing the book isn't really the part I'm worried about. It's trying to find the story through all these dead-end leads. It's like I need to be a detective or something." He swivels in the stool, turning to me with a sly smile.

"Maybe you don't need to be a detective," he says, fumbling for something in his jacket pocket. "Maybe you just need to know one." He flashes his badge like it's a key to my bedroom.

"How long have you been waiting to whip that thing out?" As

soon as the words escape my mouth, I can hear my mom's voice in my head: *Phrasing, Julia!* He smiles, sliding the badge away.

"Name's Kyle," he says, extending his hand.

"Julia." He lets his hand linger in mine a beat too long, and I pull away. I wait for him to say something else, but he shrinks back—like he's disappointed I wasn't more excited about his little badge trick. "So tell me this, *Detective Kyle*," I say. "Why is one of Gray Station's finest day-drinking here in this little bar? Don't you have bad guys to catch?" His lips curl at the edges, but it's like he can't work himself into a proper smile. As he gulps down the last of his drink, I get the feeling that I'm toeing a line I better not cross.

"Alright, then, Julia," he says, ignoring my question. "If you won't let me buy you that drink, then at least let me do something else for you."

"And what might that be?"

"Introduce you to somebody who can blow your story wide-open."

"Okay, you've got my attention. Who are we talking about here?"

"My old man," he says. "Sammy Sawyer."

36

Kathryn didn't work much at the shoe store anymore, but when Norman asked her to come in to help with the annual summer sidewalk sale, she figured she'd give it a go. All the time she was spending at home with her baby brother was getting to be too much. She felt herself slipping further into that dark place—the slippery hands of some monster yanking her down into the sludge of despair, sometimes so black and deep she didn't know if she could find her way back out. Margot Caldwell had started taking Danny off her hands for a few hours each week, but it was never enough. This morning, Edith was back at the house on Poplar Street with the baby. Aunt Clara said she'd check on them in an hour or two.

Working the sidewalk sale meant Kathryn got to be outside hanging banners and organizing the sale tables—much better than being cooped up inside the store with Sammy. Ever since the night at the drive-in, she didn't know how to talk to him. And honestly, she was beginning to learn she might not have much to say to him anyway. Her whole relationship with Sammy had been bound up in a knot of nervous energy—a tension that pulled and contracted as she thought about the smell of his skin or the taste of his lips. But what did he offer her when the novelty of that feeling was spent? The truth was, she was just on the edge of being bored with Sammy—with the way he dismissed her until he had a craving, the way he looked at her as nothing more than a puzzle to be solved.

Plus, Sammy wasn't the only problem. There was the new awkwardness she felt around George Caldwell. Every time she was around him these days, she couldn't shake the feeling that he was always just about to corner her, to ask her about the voice of God or some other thing she wasn't prepared to understand. She looked through the plate glass windows of the storefront at him inside stocking shelves, the tail of his beige shirt ballooning sloppily from the back of his brown slacks. A scolded puppy—that's what George looked like: lonely and sad and a little scraggly if he went a day without shaving. As if pricked by some sixth sense that he was being watched, he snapped his eyes in Kathryn's direction. Caught in the awkwardness of the moment, she offered a slight smile, a wave of her hand. George took this as a cue and approached the door, sending the chime bells clanking against the glass as he swung out onto the sidewalk.

"Could you do me a favor?" he asked, jumping into the middle of a conversation they hadn't yet started. Kathryn nodded, waited for him to go on. He motioned across the street to O'Malley's Flower Shop. "Pick out a little bouquet for Margot and run it out to the parsonage. Would you do that for me?" He pulled his wallet from his back pocket without waiting for an answer. Kathryn looked at the half-open shoeboxes sprawled around her feet.

"But I'm working, George." He glanced down the empty sidewalk, flicked a hand toward the store showroom.

"It's slow this morning. Sam can handle the store. I'll keep an eye out here. Please?" Kathryn glanced at her watch, figured it would probably only take half an hour or so. A little time for herself might be nice.

"What's the occasion?" she asked. George fingered through the cash in his wallet.

"Nothing in particular," he said. "It's just—well, lately things have been hard for her. For us. Something colorful and pretty might just make her day."

Holding a petite bouquet of white-and-pink carnations, Kathryn strode across a line of sunken paving stones near the front of the yellow parsonage. Before she made it to the porch, movement from the backyard of the house caught her eye: Margot Caldwell digging through the dirt with a gardening trowel, potting a new azalea. Kathryn made her way down the side of the house, calling out before she got to Margot as not to scare her.

"Good morning!" said Kathryn. Despite her efforts, Margot still turned with a start.

"My goodness—Kate Fairchild!" The dark curls of her hair were spooled tightly under a green sun hat—the perfect complement to her sunburst orange blouse. Even when she was elbow-deep in mulch, Margot wore her beauty as naturally as Kathryn wore her freckles.

"Didn't mean to startle you," said Kathryn, extending the flowers toward the woman. "George wanted me to run these over to you." Margot bristled at the mention of George's name, but then she gathered herself.

"Oh, aren't these just lovely." She took the flowers, put them to her nose. She feigned a smile, but her eyes gave her away—red, watery, a little swollen.

"Margot, is everything okay?" said Kathryn, but before she could even finish, Margot was shaking her head, her chin quivering like another word could send her into a fresh crying spell. Everything seemed to go quiet around them. The usual sounds of the Kentucky countryside—rustling leaves, trilling warblers, creaking tree limbs—faded into a stillness as thick as finger Jell-O. After a moment, Margot stood, took Kathryn by the hand, and guided her to the far side of the yard between two tall hedges—right into a small garden tucked away from view. A wooden bench sat at the far end of a ten-by-ten plot of mulch. In the middle of the soil was a young American redbud—the brilliant lavender blooms just at eye level. At each corner of the dirt was a flat stone surrounded by impatiens—red and yellow and sunset orange. Margot sat on the bench and slid to the edge.

Kathryn regarded the tree, rubbed a twig of silky blossoms between her thumb and forefinger. "It's just lovely, isn't it?" asked Margot. Kathryn nodded, took a seat beside her. Margot removed her gardening gloves, draped them across her crossed legs.

"You want to know something strange?" she said. "I was only fifteen years old when George asked me to marry him." She eyed Kathryn up and down, and then a change came over her, as if she just realized something for the first time. "Younger than you are now."

"But I thought you didn't get married until after high school?" said Kathryn. George had a story he liked to tell—about watching Margot walk the graduation stage in her long black robe, and then exactly one week later watching her walk the aisle to him in her white wedding dress. At the end of telling the story, he always said, *What a difference a week can make.*

"That's right," said Margot, "but only because I made George wait." She tilted her head toward the cerulean sky, remembering. "If it was up to him, we would have been married right after my sweet sixteen party." Kathryn tried to picture Margot at sixteen. Did she feel as lost as Kate herself felt now? Did she ever want more for herself than to be the wife of a shoe clerk? The silent partner of a country preacher?

"We've had our fair share of ups and downs," continued

Margot, "but overall, I'd say we've been happy together. That we've carved out a place for each other. Hollowed out some bit of ourselves to make room for all the messy and lonely parts of this life." She rolled her thumb across the solitary diamond of her wedding ring, twisting the band halfway around her finger before bringing it back. "You have to do that in a marriage, you know—leave parts of yourself behind. Of course, you don't know it at first. Nobody ever tells you these things when you're a girl. But on your wedding day, it's like... How can I put it?" She closed her eyes, conjuring an image. "It's like you're given a paring knife—sharp and heavy and clean. And every year thereafter you cut a bit of yourself away. To make sure you don't take up too much space." A little house finch fluttered from a branch of the tree, landing in the rich, dark soil. It hopped across the edge of the raised bed, twittering as it went. Something in the bird's feathery little voice made Kathryn suddenly very sad.

"You know about the babies," said Margot, her voice cutting out at the end. "I suppose just about everyone around here does." She tilted her head back, trying to keep the teeming tears from streaking her cheeks. When she had gathered herself, she motioned toward the four stones in the mulch. *Memorial stones*, Kathryn thought. She suddenly felt the swell of Margot's grief—a cocoon big enough for them both. "There were more than four, of course," she said. "But these were the ones with names. The ones that stuck around long enough to be real."

"Oh," said Kathryn. She had known about the miscarriages all along, but they had never talked about them, not directly. People didn't speak of such things.

"I'm broken, Kate," said Margot, her chin trembling. "I'm not sure what it is, but my body simply won't carry a baby. It rejects them."

"I'm so sorry—"

"No, it's not for you to be sorry." Kate regarded the woman:

her pinstripe smile, the anxious squint of her eyes—a look caught on a tightrope stretched between hope and despair. "You letting me look after Danny these past few weeks—that's been such a blessing to me," said Margot. "But it's not enough. It will never be enough."

"Margot, I—"

"And George won't abide the idea of adoption. Says it's unnatural. Says a child must be his own flesh and blood."

"I wish I could help," said Kathryn.

"He just won't *hear* me," said Margot. She turned in to Kathryn, took both of her hands into her own. "But if you keep bringing Danny around—if George really has a chance to bond with a child—to feed him, bathe him, rock him to sleep—" she broke off, tears flowing freely now, forming rivulets along her jowls.

"Well, sure, I don't mind bringing Danny around, but I'm not sure what—"

Margot opened her mouth to speak, but her words had turned off like water from a bent hose. She blinked once, twice. She tilted her head to the side—studied Kathryn like she was the answer to a question that had not been asked.

"Kate, could you do something else for me? I want you to pray for me, Kate," she finally said. "Pray for me good and hard—every day. Could you do that for me?"

"Of course I'll pray for you, Margot," said Kathryn, softening. She didn't want to upset the woman any further, but she felt obligated to add: "But I'm not sure if my prayers will be any better. Surely there must be something else?" Margot shrugged, let out a little laugh, despite herself.

"If not prayer," she said, "then what?"

37

Sammy Sawyer. The name doesn't mean anything to me, but the bar is stifling and making me think too much about Ryan— so I leave Quinn behind and follow Kyle out into the daylight, watching him stumble through the door like a toddler trying to figure out his legs. Out on the sidewalk, he edges toward the street. I worry he may be heading for a car—but no, he just can't seem to keep himself in a straight line. I mean, I'm glad he's not looking to get behind a wheel, but I don't feel great about his ability to walk at this point, so—

"Why don't you just stay here while I go get my rental," I say. "It's just about four blocks that way." I point toward the river.

"And why would you do that, *Ju-li-a?*" he says, drawling out my name like it's a punchline to some joke that's been running in his head. "We're already here." He motions across the street, points to an awning overhanging the sidewalk. It's printed with a store name: Sawyer Shoes. He stumbles toward the street, and I hurry to catch up, putting my arm around his waist to steady him. He looks at my hand resting against his side.

"Well, alright, then," he says, smiling.

"Shut up," I snap. "I just want to make sure you don't die before I get the beat on this new lead. This better be worth it." I grip his shirt and pull back like I'm tugging the reins on a horse. A very inebriated horse. I let a few cars pass and then nudge him on, continuing across the street. You know—just a little jaywalk with a drunk police officer.

"So, I guess I should give you fair warning," says Kyle, talking slowly, every word an effort. He leans against the glass front of the store. When he slips off his sunglasses, he clenches his eyes hard against the light, like he thought the sun might have been bluffing. "My dad is not a pleasant person." I look him over, noticing for the first time the brown stain across his bleach-white shirt.

"Am I supposed to be surprised?"

"No, you don't understand. He really doesn't like talking about this stuff."

"About Kathryn Fairchild?"

"About any of it." He swoops his hands out wide. "About his past. About the Fairchild girl. About her dad." I pull out my phone and scan through my notes.

"Norman Fairchild?" I say, finding his name at the top of Kathryn's obituary. I've thought about Kathryn and Edith a good deal, but I haven't looked into the father. Kyle nods. I think he may say something, but he just gurgles out a wet belch. "Thanks for the primer," I say, pushing into the store. Kyle looks like he may collapse onto the sidewalk outside, but he trails in behind me.

This place is bigger than it looks from the outside, and surprisingly busy. Deep aisles stacked in shoeboxes create long corridors down the middle of the room, with people peppered up and down each row. Around every corner is a cardboard display for Keds or Dockers or London Fog.

Kyle fumbles his way ahead of me toward the cash register against the back wall, bumping past customers as he goes. I feel an apology rising in my throat each time, but I manage to choke it back down. *I'm not responsible for this man*, I say to myself—the mantra of every woman at some point in her life. When we finally make it to the end, an old bald man with a paunch belly stands from behind the register. His face is haggard—skin hanging loose over high cheekbones, like a chocolate bar left to soften in the sun. He pushes a smile onto his face, but speaks through clenched yellow teeth.

"Lord a-mighty, son," he says, just above a whisper. "You smell like you took a bath in a bourbon barrel." He nods and waves toward a woman and her child as they push out of the front door, triggering the electronic welcome chime.

"It's nice to see you, too, Dad," says Kyle. The old man starts to speak again, but there's a delay as he works his mouth around the words—like he has to chew them for a beat before he can get anything out. A purple vein bulges from his forehead. "I have a friend with me here who I think you're going to want to talk to," says Kyle, motioning to me. I take that as my cue.

"Julia White," I say, extending my hand. He doesn't take it.

"This is my father, Sammy Sawyer," says Kyle, speaking for the old man. I glance sideways at Kyle, trying to see a resemblance—but the age gap between father and son is noticeable. Kyle looks to be only a few years older than me—early thirties, maybe? But his dad is easily in his seventies.

"It's a pleasure, darling," says Sammy, still smiling for the benefit of the customers. "But I'm not much in the mood for talking."

"Really?" says Kyle. "Because she came all the way from New York to little ol' Gray Station." There's something in his voice—some bit of rancor directed at his dad that I don't have the context to understand. "She's writing a book." He turns toward me now, too, and that's when I see how similar they look—the slope of the jaw and narrow eyes, the pronounced chin and thick eyebrows. This old man could've been handsome at some point, but the years haven't been kind to him.

"Well, ain't that special," says the father, letting his smile slide. "Something you should be proud of, sweetheart." I'm just about to snap back but then—

"The book is about Kathryn Fairchild," says Kyle. A change comes over the old man. A slackening of his jaw. Slump of the shoulders. Kyle was right—I really need to talk to this guy.

"Alright," he says, willing a smile back onto his face. "Let's have us a little chat, then."

After the old man leads us through a skinny hallway behind the register, we come out into a claustrophobic, concrete-walled workroom stacked haphazardly with shoe inventory. In the corner is a small workbench that looks like it might have been used for cobbler work at some point. Kyle slouches against the wall to keep from falling over. His father collapses onto a wooden chair, his chest heaving from the short walk. I'm left standing between them, trying to figure out how to proceed. I slip my phone from my purse to take notes, but before I can ask a single question, the old man targets Kyle.

"You haven't embarrassed yourself enough already?" he says. "You gotta come in here all cork high and bottle deep?"

"Get off my ass, Dad," says Kyle. "This isn't even about me."

"You got that right. It's about this family business. It's about me protecting the only thing I have left." Kyle glares at him, shakes his head. It must have been too much movement, because now he closes his eyes and rests back against the concrete. He lets out a little laugh.

"Can't you see I'm trying to help you here?" he says. "She's writing a damn book, Dad. You could finally get some answers to all this stuff. You can get out from underneath it." I catch eyes with the old man, but then he looks away. He sucks a breath, then labors it with the force of a deflated balloon.

"Don't pay him any mind," he says to me, as if Kyle is no longer in the room. "When he gets this far into the bottle, you can trust the boy about as far as you can throw him." This seems to be my chance, so I go for it.

"So, you knew Kathryn Fairchild?" I say.

"Of course I did. This ain't New York. Everybody knows everybody in this town."

"Sure, I get that. But something tells me you knew her better than most. Otherwise, I don't think Kyle would have pulled me over here." He lets out a big belly laugh.

"Kyle pulled you over here because he's just drunk enough to think he can trade my history for the key to your bedroom. You have to be careful about who you trust around here, sweetheart." I look over at Kyle, and I think he might be passed out. If this is going to be worth my while, I need to make my move. I narrow my eyes and channel my inner *Myra*.

"Okay, so here's the thing," I say, taking two solid steps in his direction. "I've already heard enough to know you're part of this story I'm chasing down. So this is your one chance to tell me what you know—to spin it however you want." I'm standing over him now, looking down into his beady little eyes. "After that, I'm heading out that door over there and slinging the name *Sammy Sawyer* up and down every street in Gray Station until I find someone who's willing to talk. And like you said, in a place like this, everybody knows everybody, so—"

"Well, you're just a little firecracker, ain't you?" he says, flashing those yellow teeth. In one clean motion, I turn away, beat a path across the concrete floor. Just before I make it to the door, he gives in. "I worked for her old man," he says. "Started back when I was in high school."

"Okay. That's a start." I turn, but I keep one hand in the frame of the door, just to maintain my leverage.

"Right here in this shoe store." He looks around the little storage room as if he can see straight back through to the past. "I reckon you already know this place used to belong to Norman Fairchild?"

"Of course," I lie, never missing a beat.

"I bought it from him back in the late seventies—a couple of years after I got back from Nam. Working under Fairchild for all those years like I did—I knew the business inside and out. And the man was getting up in age with no family to take over, so me and him came to pretty good terms."

"But he had a son, right? Kathryn's obituary says she was survived by a brother." I scroll through my notes, looking for a name. "Danny Fairchild?" Sammy cocks his head to the side like he just can't figure me out.

"Honey, how long you been working this thing?" he says. "That boy hasn't been a Fairchild since a month or so after Kate died." I think back to those internet searches I did for Danny, which never yielded any results. "Norman adopted him out to some kin. Edith's sister, I believe it was. Couldn't manage the boy after what happened." I'm typing out notes as fast as I can, trying to make sure I don't miss anything.

"So, we're talking about—Clara Clark? Married to Raymond?" I check the photo of the obituary again.

"That's right. Far as I know, Danny still runs the little garage out there in the country. *Clark's Automotive*—something like that." Over against the wall, Kyle rolls over and groans. The man has a liquor bomb growing inside him, and I don't want to be around when it explodes.

"See?" I say, turning back to Sammy. "This isn't painful at all, now is it?" I give him a smile, trying to smooth out the tension.

"We ain't found our way to the painful part yet, doll," he says. His shoulders sag, as if pushed down by a heavy weight. "I'll warn you, though—there's no short version to this thing. Either we go through it from the beginning, or we don't do it at all." I grab a metal folding chair propped against the wall, pull it over in front of Sammy, and take a seat.

"Okay. I assume this is about Kathryn?"

"Well, yeah—that's part of it." Sammy shifts his weight in his chair. "And then there's the baby." I freeze in place, just for a second. Then I raise my phone.

"I need to record this," I say. I don't want to scare him off, but I'm not sure I'll be able to keep up with the notes, and I can't afford to miss anything here.

"Do what you have to do." He takes a breath—big and round, like he's about to submerge himself in water. Then he launches into the story, starting back to the first day he talked to Kathryn Fairchild, right here in the shoe store on Main Street.

38

Jack was out in the garage finishing up with a radiator on a Chevy Impala when he heard a truck crunching through the gravel outside. He'd been hoping he wouldn't have to mess with any new customers this morning. Mr. Clark was in town running some errands, so Jack was the only one in the garage. He loved pulling the guts out of a car—really doing anything that let him tinker and dismantle and build—but he sure could do without the business side of things. Truth be told, he could do without people, period.

The truck door slammed shut outside, so there was no getting around it. He wiped his greasy hands against his coveralls and went out into the cool morning air. When he caught sight of the man standing beside the Ranchero, some unnamed fear caught him in the chest, right below the sternum—almost strong enough to knock the wind out of him. In his early twenties, the man was clean-shaven, with a thick black swoop of rockabilly hair greased back away from his face. The way he leaned against the vehicle—one foot propped against the door, arms crossed loose over his chest—seemed to be posed and perfectly natural at the same time, like Elvis Presley done up on a poster for *Love Me Tender*.

"You the boss man?" he said, peering over his sunglasses.

"No, sir," said Jack, shifting his weight in the gravel. "But I reckon I can take care of you just the same."

"Okay, then," said the man, stepping forward. "Got a car that won't start." Jack looked past him at the baby blue Ranchero.

"Looks like it's running okay to me." He meant it as a joke, but it didn't seem to come out that way.

"Not this one, smart guy." The man smiled, and that made Jack feel better. "It's parked up a few miles toward town. Saw your sign out here and thought I might see about getting a tow."

"Well, yeah, we can do that," said Jack, feeling small. "It's just that I'm not allowed to work the truck just yet." He looked at his feet and then off in the distance—anywhere but at the man's face.

"Is that right?" said the man. He took a long step forward. Jack had to fight the impulse to turn and run. "How old are you, anyway?"

"Old enough," snapped Jack. He was wound up tight by some pulsing desire inside him. He scuffed his boot across the gravel.

"Easy now," said the man. "I was only teasing." He took another step forward—close enough now to reach out and touch Jack if he caught the urge to do so. After a torturous beat of silence, he reached in his back pocket and pulled out a card. "Just give me a call when you can see about that tow." Jack fingered the card, rubbing his calloused skin against the coarse paper. By the time he looked up, the man was back in the Ranchero, peeling out of the gravel and shooting down the winding highway, an apparition.

When Mr. Clark made it home that afternoon, Jack's insides were still knotted up like an old water hose. On his break, he crossed the open field, passed by the pond, edged into his house—careful not to let the hinge squeak on the front door. He tiptoed over the creaking floorboards in the entryway, but when he saw no sign of his father, he eased up a bit. In his bedroom, he closed the door, then reached down into the dark corner of his closet. Underneath an inconspicuous pile of clothes, his eager hands found what they were looking for: his brand-new Nikon F.

His dad would kill him if he knew he spent over two hundred dollars on a camera, but Jack couldn't help himself. Just holding the thing—the weight of it, the sleek metal body—was enough to make his palms sweat. Taking pictures was the one thing that made him feel whole, the one thing he could do right. Truth be told, there wasn't much in this world he was good at. He couldn't figure numbers all that well, and when he read a book for too long the words got all jumbled up so bad he could hardly see straight. But he could look through this viewfinder all day. It was magic—being able to frame something just the way you wanted, to change the world by adjusting the f-stop or the shutter speed. He'd always seen things different than most folks. Now he had a way to capture them that made sense.

Out behind the house, he saw his mother shelling peas next to the barbed wire fence, dropping the seeds into a bucket at her feet. Sitting a shadow-length away was his father, slumped over in a folding chair, a fifth of Jim Beam lying on the ground beside his outstretched arm. Jack made his way around the property and peeked out from the corner of the house—poking his head out just enough so he wouldn't be seen from behind the bricks. He couldn't afford any more film until payday, so every snap of the shutter had to count. With his old man's wooden leg stretched out into a streak of sunlight, Jack felt the prickling of his skin, the churning of his insides. He knew this might be the shot he was waiting for—he could always feel it coming just before the moment presented itself, like a sixth sense.

Stretched behind the acre of cornstalks in the distance, the setting sun fingered its golden light against cotton candy clouds. The moment was coming soon—you could miss it in a blink. He adjusted the aperture, peered through the viewfinder, focusing in on the harried face of his mother—worn, beautiful, hopeless. He let his finger hover over the shutter release, trembling with anticipation. "Not yet, Jack," he said to himself. "Not yet." But the moment would be here soon. All he had to do was wait.

Caleb Croxton—that was the name of the man with the baby-blue Ranchero. Three days had passed since he had come out to the garage asking for a tow, and Jack still hadn't told Mr. Clark. Why not? No logical reason at all, really. It was just that…for some reason he couldn't say, Jack wanted to keep the man for himself, a secret tucked away in his coverall pockets like the card with his name and phone number on it. Every now and again Jack would catch himself fingering the edges of the card, mouthing the name—*Caleb Croxton Caleb Croxton Caleb Croxton*—crunching through all those sharp consonants like a piece of hard candy.

He'd been practicing with the tow truck in the gravel lot—backing up, turning corners, hooking the winch on parked cars. So when Mr. Clark went into town again and left him in charge, he figured he was ready. It was always better to ask for forgiveness than permission—so he called and got directions to the dead car. Turned out, it was parked at one of those trailers just a stone's throw down Highway 41.

Before he left, he washed and shaved his face, combed some oil into his hair, doused his neck with Old Spice. When he arrived at the trailer, Caleb Croxton was leaning against the side of a mint green Oldsmobile, smoking a cigarette. There was something about the way his plain white T-shirt was tucked into his slim pair of Levi's that made Jack wish he had stayed back at the garage where it was safe.

"So the boss man finally let you handle that thing," said Caleb, motioning out to the tow truck. He blew a tight line of smoke in the air like he was aiming for a bull's-eye. Then he flicked the spent cigarette onto the ground—the butt smoldering at the edge of the grass. Jack had to fight the urge to go stomp it out himself.

"Well, not exactly," said Jack. "But what he don't know can't hurt him." He felt himself flexing his biceps as Caleb looked him over. Every part of him was wound tighter than the rubber core of a baseball.

"Oh, so you're some kind of bad boy?" said Caleb. He peered over the edge of his mirrored glasses. A long curl at the front of his rockabilly hair sliced a line between his gray eyes. "I bet that drives your girlfriend wild."

"What makes you think I have a girlfriend?" said Jack. Pinprick sweat glistened on his upper lip. The back of his neck burned in the hot sun.

"Oh, I don't know. You just got that look about you," he said. "Something about your eyes—all steely and dark. Girls eat that stuff up. Makes 'em wetter than an otter's pocket." Jack didn't quite know what to say to something like that. He shoved his hands into his pockets like he was looking for something. Caleb slipped a pack of Camels from his jeans, lit another one up. Jack watched him take a hard pull, and a craving opened up inside him—for a smoke or something else.

"I wouldn't know about that," said Jack. Caleb cocked his head, studied him through squinted eyes. "I can't say I've ever understood girls all that much." He swallowed hard. That was as close as he could get to saying it outright. He was toeing a line he'd never dared to cross, no matter how many times he had wanted to.

"No, I guess you wouldn't," said Caleb. He hit the cigarette again, and then the two men gave themselves over to the silence of the open country. The land stretched its limbs in every direction like a reposed god—knobby knee hills and armpit valleys, big enough to swallow them both up and never even feel the crunch of their bones. "You want to come inside?" asked Caleb.

How long did it last? Twenty seconds? Five minutes? An hour? Inside the dark trailer, Caleb Croxton pinched out the last of the light by pulling the heavy curtains, never taking his right index finger from the hook of Jack's belt loop. Lost in blackness, they were nothing but wet tongues and pulsing fingers, thrumming skin and slick chests. Was this what it felt like to be real? A hot throb of pleasure threatened to buckle Jack's knees, but then it was over before it ever had time to really get started.

Tires crunched through the gravel outside. The thumping of a car door.

"You gotta go," said Caleb, a voice lost in darkness. "That's my old lady."

39

Ever since I started tending bar at the age of twenty-five, drunk men have been an occupational hazard. Still, I don't know if any of them have ever ruined my day more than Kyle Sawyer. I've been sitting here in the shoe store listening to old Sammy peel back through his memories of the early sixties, and just when he's getting into the months leading up to Kathryn Fairchild's death, Kyle unfurls from his fetal position on the concrete floor and releases a chunky spray of vomit—right onto my feet.

"Well, now you've done it," says Sammy, standing from the chair, jumping away in case more puke is coming. And *of course* more is coming—but not from Kyle. It takes my first-trimester gut exactly ten seconds to start lurching, and then I'm like a firehouse blasting hot oatmeal. When all the retching is over, silence hangs like morning fog.

"Maybe we should take a break," says Sammy. He looks pale, as if he's on the verge of adding to the carnage puddled on the floor. I kick my soiled flats at Kyle one at a time—clipping him in the temple on the second try. "Grab yourself a new pair on the way out," says the old man. "And we'll try this thing again in a few days."

★ ★ ★

Later, I clean myself up back at the Little Yellow House and reset my stomach with some raw carrots (and, okay—a few chocolate chip cookies, whatever). Now that I'm alone with my own thoughts, all I can think about is Ryan and his wife and what I'm going to do about this baby occupying more space in my uterus with every passing day. So I do what I do best: chase a distraction, taking Highway 41 out to the edge of the county line. If what Sammy told me about Kathryn's brother was true—that he was still operating the little garage out here—this could be my best chance to connect with part of the Fairchild family.

I pass a field of dried cornstalks, and then the Kentucky country opens up wide in all directions like a landscape painting ready for a canvas. The sun has nearly hidden itself on the horizon now, bruising the sky across an open field. I slow the car as I come to a sign just at the edge of a little white farmhouse: Clark and Son Auto Repair. Bingo.

I park my Corolla in the gravel lot next to a Dodge Grand Caravan and a Ford Explorer—left overnight for repairs, I assume. As I get out and crunch through the rocks around the property, I see that the lights to the little office are off and the three garage doors on the metal building are all closed.

The little farmhouse at the edge of the property is too close not to be associated with the business, so I make my way across the sunken paving stones in the yard, feeling the brush of fall weeds against my legs. I knock on the door, but no luck. So I rummage through my purse for some paper—but of course all I have is an old napkin. I smooth it out and leave a note with my number, asking Danny to give me a call. After I slip the napkin behind the storm door, I step back from the porch and take some pictures on my phone for reference. Then I look across the field between me and a neighbor's house and see a gorgeous little pond catching the orange light of the dusk sky.

The beauty of it calls to me, so I walk closer, snapping some pictures of the landscape and little ranch house in the distance—figuring some of these photos might help in setting the mood for the book. When I'm halfway across the field, I hear a car pull to the shoulder of the road, stopping next to me. It's a state trooper. He gives a little *bloop* of the siren and turns his lights on for good measure.

"I was wondering when someone would be out here snooping around again," says the cop, pulling himself out of the vehicle and lumbering toward me. He's a big man with a low center of gravity—swinging his weight from side to side with every step. A bushy white mustache covers his upper lip like some cartoon sheriff. "It's been a few months since I've had to chase somebody off this property."

"I'm sorry?" I say. I look around me like he must be talking to someone else.

"You're lucky I was driving home and saw you before you made it up to the house," he says, his eyes gazing out to the little brick ranch fifty yards away. "Last time I had to charge a guy with breaking and entering."

"Sir, I'm a little lost here. I was just trying to track down the owner of that garage." I turn, nodding to the Clark property behind me.

"Yeah, alright," says the cop. He smiles, exposing crooked teeth the color of sawdust. "You go ahead and snap a picture or two. Get inspired, or whatever the hell it is you people always think you're doing. But if you go any closer to that house, I'll arrest you for trespassing on private property."

"Okay, can we just hit Rewind here?" I pull my ID from my purse. "I seriously have no idea what you're talking about. I'm in from New York, doing some research for a book—that's it. I'm just trying to track down the owner of the Clark auto place." He takes my ID, examines it. "Anyway, you can check me out with Detective Sawyer. He'll tell you what I'm doing."

"Detective Sawyer?" says the cop. "And who might that be, sweetheart?"

"Kyle Sawyer. Over at Gray Station PD." He hands me back my license and lets out a belly laugh.

"Kyle?" he says. "Shoot, if that boy's a detective, I guess that makes me chief of police." The October wind whips across my burning face. God, I'm so tired of feeling like an idiot.

"Okay, look—"

"Honey, I'm not looking to arrest you here," he says, cutting me off. "Looks like you've already been punished enough by Kyle Sawyer. But can I give you some friendly advice? You're better off heading back to New York than you are poking around this little house. The man has covered his tracks pretty well, and the Chandler family hasn't owned this place in thirty years." I peer out over the field to the little ranch house, trying to make some sort of sense of what this man is saying.

"There has to be some sort of mix-up here," I say. "I have no clue who you're talking about. I'm looking for Danny Clark, not the Chandler family."

"Oh, please," says the cop. "Every few months some amateur photographer shows up here like they're on some dadgum journey to Mecca. But there's nothing new to find here about Jonathan Aster than what people have been speculating about for three decades."

"Jonathan Aster?" I say, my breath catching in my throat. I haven't mentioned his name to a single person since I came to Gray Station. "How did you— What do you even mean?"

"C'mon," he says, dismissing me with a wave of his hand. "You think you're the first one to figure out that Aster grew up here? That his real name is Jack Chandler? Give me a break."

40

After the conversation with Margot out at the parsonage, Kathryn didn't go back to working the sidewalk sale. She was unsettled. She wanted a drink, but didn't have a way to get one, so she drove the family Oldsmobile out to the county line—heading straight toward the only person who could bring her comfort. She was sick and tired of other people's problems. How long had she been expected to care for her mother instead of the other way around? To practically raise her baby brother? To be the sole support for her father to keep him from crumbling? And now the Caldwells—to take on the responsibility of praying for Margot, for her dreams and wants. For as long as she could remember, nobody had ever actually asked her what she wanted to do with her life. What if she wanted to go to college, to leave Gray Station, to run somewhere far away where she could be something other than the daughter of the *crazy Fairchild woman* on Poplar Street?

When she neared Jack's house, she saw that the garage was open next door at Aunt Clara and Uncle Raymond's place, so she figured Jack was out there working on cars. She pulled into the gravel lot next to a baby blue Ford Ranchero. On her way into the garage, she crossed paths with a man who looked like he was headed to a James Dean look-alike contest. He flashed a smile as he passed and gave her a nod, lighting a cigarette on his way toward the Ranchero.

In the garage, she found Jack leaning against the side of a Chevy pickup, dragging on a cigarette of his own. The orange glow of the tip flared brilliantly as he inhaled.

"Hey, you," said Kathryn, startling Jack. His face was red as a fire truck. His hair was matted to his forehead with sweat.

"Jesus, Kate," he said, placing a hand over his heart. "Don't sneak up on me like that."

"Well, aren't you jumpy today." She tugged at the sides of her skirt and skipped playfully in his direction. She was making an effort to look cute, but it didn't seem Jack paid her much mind. As she got closer, she noticed a shake in his fingers as he took a pull on the cigarette. "What are you all worked up about?" asked Kathryn.

"Not worked up about nothing." Jack flicked the spent cigarette butt onto the concrete floor and stamped it out. "I'm just busy is all."

"Why don't you take a break?" said Kathryn. "Come sit with me down by the pond."

"I don't have time for that nonsense." Jack moved to the front of the pickup, popped the hood. Kathryn's breath caught in her throat. She opened her mouth to speak, but she couldn't find any words. Jack froze, steeling himself against the front bumper of the car. "I didn't mean that," he said. He picked up a nearby hand towel, rubbed some grease from his palms.

"I need you, Jack," said Kathryn. "Please." Jack closed the hood of the truck.

"To hell with the fishing pond," he said. "Let's go get us some ice cream."

★ ★ ★

About a mile down the highway toward Gray Station was Tuck's Gas and Sundries—a little country filling station known in three counties over for having the best hand-dipped ice cream in Western Kentucky. Jack had worked out a theory when they were kids: it was impossible to be mad at somebody else if you were both holding ice cream cones. He ordered them each a double-scoop of fresh strawberry, and they sat outside the store on a splintering picnic table under the shade of a giant black oak.

They didn't talk—not for a while. Sometimes you can just *be* with a person, nuzzling into the comfortable silence of shared space. She wanted to tell Jack all about the weird moment with Margot Caldwell at the parsonage, the swell of confusion she was always having about people constantly asking her favors and expecting things from her that no teenage girl should have to worry about. But now that she was here with him, feeling the warm breath of a June breeze swirling around them, she wasn't sure any of it would come out right. Besides, Jack seemed lost in his own thoughts.

"Listen, Freckles," he said, adjusting his weight on the bench. "I want to tell you something, but I'm not real sure how to say it." Kathryn pressed her tongue flat against the cold ice cream, twisting the cone in a perfect circle. Jack had a way of making big pronouncements like that, turning every little thing into something outsized and scary, so she didn't think much about it. But then she took a good look at him—the way he wore such a serious face, not even noticing the drip of melting ice cream inching toward his knuckles.

"Go on, then," she said.

"Well, it's just that—" he started, squinting into the sun. "I've had these feelings lately."

"What kind of feelings."

"I don't know—like, feelings you get when you like someone." He looked up, catching eyes with her just long enough to make her spine tingle.

"When you like someone?" she repeated. She hated the way she sounded so eager, like a child waiting for a lemon drop from the penny canisters at the drugstore. But she realized she'd been waiting for Jack to tell her this her whole life.

"Like, more than a friend," he said. Kathryn forgot she was holding an ice cream just long enough to feel the pointed edge of the sugar cone poke her thigh. She raised her arm back up lazily, letting the ice cream continue to melt.

"Okay," she said, willing him to go on.

"Sometimes it keeps me up all night long. This feeling— it's like it sucks the wind out of me until I can't breathe right."

"I think they call that love, Jack," said Kathryn. She heard her own voice, but it seemed she was outside of herself, watching this awkward redheaded girl toeing the edge of new love— a line she never thought she'd actually cross with Jack.

"I reckon it might be," he said, scuffing his work boot across the dusty ground. He put on a meager little smile, despite himself. "Whatever it is, it's not something I've ever known before." She thought of the barefoot boy she grew up with, gigging for frogs down in the murky pond. All those nights when they had chased fireflies over the cattails in the field, cupping them like glowing secrets, feeling the soft scuttle of their legs inside their palms. Hadn't their hearts been bent toward love even back then? Wasn't it always meant to be?

"Jack," she said, edging her bottom across the hard bench until her legs touched his. "I think I know what you're try- ing to say."

"No, Kate," he said. "You don't understand."

"I've always understood, Jack." Her whole life had led her right up to the edge of this moment. For the first time in years, she didn't want to disappear. She wanted to sit right here for the rest of her life eating strawberry ice cream with Jack Chandler.

"Listen to me," said Jack, shaking his head. "What I'm trying to say is, sometimes I get this type of feeling around—" He
paused, searching for words.

"Yes?"

"Around someone I reckon I'm not supposed to feel like that
about." Her heart was going wild now, pounding against her
chest like a chick trying to break free from an egg. She thought
she might explode if she didn't do something right then and
there, so she flipped her ice cream to the ground, took Jack's
face between her two trembling hands, and pulled him into
a kiss.

"Jesus, Kathryn," said Jack, springing away from her as if
he'd pressed his lips against an electric fence. "What the hell
are you doing?" He flung his cone to the ground, his melting
ice cream forming sad little rivulets into hers. Kathryn stood
to join him, reaching for his hand.

"I just thought—" she started, but then he pulled his hand
out of reach, backing away. "I don't understand, Jack."

"That's what I've been trying to tell you!" he shouted.
"You've never understood, Kate. And I guess you never will."
His words stuck in her flesh like cactus needles.

"I'm sorry," she said, mostly out of habit. But was it really
such an offense to love somebody? She eased back onto the
bench beneath her, feeling her legs give way. "I'll try to listen better."

"Just forget it," said Jack, wadding a sticky napkin into his
fist. "I need to get back to work anyway." As he turned, his
boots scuffed the dry earth, sending a plume of dust into the
air. Kathryn sat in silence, gathering the courage to follow him
to the truck.

41

"You want to guess where I am right now?" I say, my rental car idling in front of the old Chandler property.

"I've never been one for guessing games, Julia," says Aster. I picture him on the other end of the line—a neat bourbon in his hand, a stupid grin stretched across his face, his feet kicked up across what I assumed was a gigantic mahogany desk in his supposed Soho penthouse.

"I'm sitting in my car out in Nowhere, Kentucky. Highway 41. Right at the edge of Gray Station County."

"Oh?" says Aster. "That sounds rather pleasant. A nice break from the city, I would think." I try to listen for the edge of a Kentucky accent—elongated vowels, a guttural twang. But no, it's not there. I wonder how long it took him to choke the South out of his voice.

"Why are you doing this? How could you possibly benefit from not telling me that you're really Jack Chandler?" There's a beat of silence. For a second, I think Aster might be ready to stop toying with me, but then—

"Well, that would mean that I really am Jack Chandler," he says. "And I most certainly am not."

"Seriously? That's the card you're going to play? I spent the last thirty minutes doing a deep dive on Google. If you aren't Jack Chandler, there are a whole lot of confused people on the internet."

"Perhaps they are conflating the present with the past. I was born as Jack Chandler—that's true enough. But I became Jonathan Aster over fifty years ago."

"Oh, I see. We're playing with semantics now."

"It's not semantics, Julia. It's identity."

"Okay, fine—but the point is, you're keeping information from me. Doesn't that just get in the way of the story?"

"It might if the story was about Jack Chandler," he says. "Or about Jonathan Aster, for that matter. But it's not." I lean back against the headrest in my car, watching the night sky squeeze the last of the dusk light against the horizon. I've never been more lost in my entire life. "You're closer than you think, Julia," says Aster. "Please, don't give up now."

On the ride back to town, I wonder: Can that really be true? Am I really closer than I think? What have I actually discovered about the Fairchild case? Starting with the end of the story and working my way back, here's what I know:

On Independence Day of 1964, Kathryn Fairchild jumped to her death from the train bridge over the Ohio River, holding a baby that may or may not have been her child. Her mother, Edith Fairchild, was the *town crazy lady* (gross), and lots of people thought Kathryn was crazy by association. I also know Kathryn had some sort of relationship with Kyle Sawyer's dad, and apparently she was friends with Jonathan Aster—who used to be Jack Chandler. I know a bit about a handful of other people— Norman Fairchild (the dad), Danny (the brother), and Clara and Raymond Clark (the aunt and uncle).

All that's to say: I don't know much. Part of me wants to quit the whole thing, but I won't. I don't owe anything to Jonathan Aster, but I can't help feel like I owe something to Kathryn Fairchild herself. And I can't explain it, but I'm beginning to believe I'm right on the edge of something—circling some key that will unlock the rest of the story, some clue that I've already discovered but haven't figured out. Who else was Kathryn connected to in Gray Station? What did she hope for her life to become? Most importantly, why did she decide to step off that bridge?

42

Kathryn burned up the back roads of Gray Station County, "He's So Fine" by The Chiffons booming through the open windows of the Oldsmobile. She'd stolen a pack of Jack's menthols from his truck back at the garage, and now she sucked the smoke deep, her throat constricting, her lungs on fire. She guided the car with her free hand around the pinball curves of backcountry roads down by the river bottoms. How long had it been since she left Jack's house? Two hours? three?

It was funny—sometimes you didn't know what you were doing right up until you did the thing, like your mind was wandering off yonder while your soul was tethered to some purpose you couldn't fully understand. After the sun had tucked itself under the blanket of river to the west, Kathryn was surprised to look up just in time to see herself pulling the Oldsmobile into the parking lot of Riverside Baptist Church. There was no way to know for sure why she felt led to this place. George Caldwell might have said it was the *still, small voice of God* that guided her here, but she wasn't sure such a thing even existed. Either way, she took a final pull on the cigarette and swung herself out of the car, stretching her back from where it had gone stiff.

The front door was unlocked—as she figured it might be. A warm gust of summer-evening air followed her inside the dark and silent vestibule. She hadn't spent much time in the church, but it didn't take her long to get her bearings. The sanctuary was behind closed doors just up ahead, and off to the right was a hallway leading to the church office. Before she'd had time to close the door behind her, George Caldwell's shadow preceded the man himself out of the hallway.

"Kate?" he said, as if confirming she wasn't a ghost. He stopped at the edge of the foyer, silhouetted against the light coming from his office at the end of the hall. In the cover of darkness, George could have been anybody. She thought of Sammy Sawyer, of Jack, even her own father.

"Turn on the lights," said Kathryn, more forcefully than she had intended. "Please," she added. George did as he was told, flicking the switch on his right. They stood squinting at one another, their eyes adjusting. In the silence, the ticking wall clock beside the sanctuary door drew their attention. It was half past seven.

"Pleasant out there tonight," said George, glancing past Kate at the open front door. He was the type of man who talked about the weather when he didn't know what else to say. Uncle Raymond always said this showed weakness. "What brings you out to the church this evening?"

"I'd like to go into the sanctuary," said Kate.

"Well—okay," started George, but she was already ahead of him, swinging open the heavy oak door. The air in the sanctuary was thick and musky-sweet—floral and pungent, like roses grown in a tire factory. Wooden pews hemmed the room, facing a raised pulpit adorned with unlit candles. Multicolored sunlight streamed through stained glass, resting in broken patterns across the mauve carpet.

"My God," said Kate, caught somewhere between a curse and a prayer. "How beautiful." She spun in the aisle between the pews as if swimming in a sea of refracted light. George stood in the frame of the door, unmoved.

"When I was a little girl," she said, "Mom used to walk me over to church—our church, First Baptist there on the corner of Poplar and Main. The door was always left open through the week, so we'd just go in. People need prayer more on Monday than they ever will on Sunday—that's what Mom used to say."

"That's true enough," said George. He took a few steps into the sanctuary, tapping the back of each pew as he went.

"I never have cared much for church on Sundays," said Kathryn, climbing the stairs to the pulpit, tracing a finger across the back of one of the ornate chairs on the raised stage. "Too loud and busy—just like everywhere else. But during the week it's quiet, still. Almost sad—but the good kind of sad, you know?" She didn't wait for him to answer. She knew he didn't understand her. No one ever did. "Do you ever come in here to pray, George? By yourself?"

"Of course," he said.

"It's funny—all those times Mom took me over to First Baptist, I never once saw Revered Blackstone in the sanctuary praying. You'd think a preacher would wear this place out." She sat on the edge of the stage, the bottom hem of her dress resting just above her knees. She noticed George's furtive glance at her legs, but he averted his eyes just as quickly.

"One can pray anywhere, Kate," he said, rolling the sleeves of his beige dress shirt to his elbows. He swallowed hard, tugged at the starched collar around his throat.

"Maybe so," said Kathryn. "But truthfully, I've never been able to pray much myself. Not at church or anywhere else." George approached the stage where Kathryn sat.

"Did you want me to pray for you?" he said. "Is that why you're here?" She didn't answer. Why *was* she here? Before she could give it much thought, George had knelt beside her on the stage. He took her by the hand. For some reason she couldn't understand, she didn't pull away.

"Dear God," he said, clenching his eyes tight, as if each word required great concentration. The crease in his forehead was as deep as a mud trench at the river bottoms, and his eyes flicked back and forth behind his closed lids. "Dear God," he said again, working himself into it. "We come to you today…"

He went on with the words, using that familiar cadence of a preacher speaking into the void, crying out to the Great Something they all seemed to believe was attuned so completely to them and their small lives. What was it that made them think the Lord who breathed life into all creation would pay mind to a whisper of a sad little man in the sanctuary of a tiny country church? Perhaps the problem wasn't with the men themselves, but with the concept of God they preached. They seemed to think of God as some white-bearded king sitting on a throne, sifting through the ticker tape of men's complaints. But the God she believed in was made manifest in refractions of a rain puddle, the speckled-red burst of a tiger lily, the crunch of fallen magnolia leaves—in the voices she heard when she was alone and the world went quiet. If God was real, She wasn't some *great something* ruling from the clouds; She was the *every little thing* in this painful and beautiful struggle of life.

"Amen," said George, squeezing Kathryn's hand with a sweaty palm. He angled himself from his knees and faced away from her, sitting his bottom on the wooden platform. Pinching the bridge of his nose, he sucked in great drafts of air as if recovering from a fight. What must it be like to believe in something so fully and completely? For the first time in years, she felt the urge to pray herself. She had so much to say, so many words weighing her down like sunken pebbles in her gut, but she wasn't sure how to purge them. So instead of speaking to

God, she stood, planted her feet in the Berber carpet, and spoke to George Caldwell.

"I was six years old the first time I remember my mother being sent away," she said. "Of course, she had been down there at the asylum plenty of times before then—you know that better than most people, George. But the first time I saw my daddy fill her up with tranquilizers and cart her off was just after my sixth birthday." She closed her eyes, remembering. "I stayed at home there on Poplar Street, playing checkers with my aunt Clara. We sat on the floor of the living room for hours. Every time I would look out the window or ask about my mother, Aunt Clara would just get me to thinking about the game or some other thing. *Your mother just needs a little rest*, she'd say, and then she'd give me a peppermint from her pocket or sing a little song—anything to get my mind off Momma."

"She was trying to protect you," said George. Kathryn went on, ignoring the man.

"After that day, a little part of me knew that whatever it was that was wrong with Momma—well, it was something we were all supposed to be ashamed about. Some secret we had to carry with us in our back pocket. But it can't be a secret if everybody knows. Every single person in this town knows about *the crazy Fairchild woman*." George looked up just long enough to catch eyes with Kathryn, but he couldn't keep his resolve, wilting back down like a sprayed weed. "That's the worst part of it all. Everybody knows, but nobody talks about it. Only whispers and gossip and coded words, that's all you hear."

"I'm sorry, Kate," said George.

"I don't need you to be sorry," said Kathryn, though she knew deep down that maybe that was exactly what she needed—an apology, not just from George Caldwell, but from every person in Gray Station. For them to parade down Poplar Street, knock on her door one person at a time, say how sorry they were. Mrs. Eubank—for always stoking the fires of town gossip. Principal Newcomb from back in grade school—for using her mother's problems as a way to psychoanalyze Kate. Her classmates throughout the years—for all their laughter, their hatred, mostly their pity. It seemed every person in Gray Station had written a page in the mythological story of the Fairchild family—stitching their own projected fears and failures into a Frankenstein's monster made in their image, until Kate could see the monster herself when she looked in the mirror. Someday, they would all be sorry.

George angled his eyes up at her like a scolded child, big and sad, and Kathryn knew all at once why she had come to the church. She saw with a blinding flash of light what she had intended to say all along.

"Margot is unhappy," she said, thinking about Margot in the little memorial garden earlier that day. The question had lingered in her ever since she left Margot crying on the bench: *If not prayer, then what?*

"Kate," started George, furrowing his brow, "this isn't your business."

"She wants a baby more desperately than she wants air to breathe," said Kathryn.

"Yes, but—it's more complicated than you know."

"Maybe so. But there are solutions to—"

"God will provide, Kate," said George, a warning in his voice. He closed his eyes, reciting: "'The Lord is good unto them that wait for him.'" Kathryn stooped in front of him now, softening. *Wait.* She had heard it her whole life—the mantra of those who didn't have the courage to act. *Your mom will be alright, you just wait and see. You'll understand someday, you just wait and see. One day, when you're older, you just wait.* She thought about Jack rejecting her out at the ice cream shop. She thought about her teenage years slipping by as she gave her life away.

"You can't always just sit around and wait," she said. "Sometimes you have to take matters into your own hands."

43

I'm driving back toward Gray Station when I get a text from Myra: don't be mad.

So, yeah—I'm freaking out, but I can't text her back because this little country road is curvier than a pinball track, and I don't want to end up in a ditch. Before I can make it to a shoulder wide enough to pull off the road, my phone rings. I figure it must be Myra calling, but no—just some random number, which means there is a zero percent chance I'm going to answer. Just as I assume that it must be a spam call, I get a notification that I have a new voicemail.

I mean, who leaves a *voicemail*? When I listen to the message, my heart nearly stops.

"Yeah, hi—so, this is Morgan Springer-Alman. But I guess you already know that? I got some random DM from somebody named…Myra something? Anyway, yeah, she told me I need to check my husband's texts, and so I did, and here we are. Look, I have no idea who you are or really even what this is about. I'm guessing most of the texts have been deleted because there are only a few from last week. But they don't look good, and I just— Look, if there's something I should know, call me back on this number. Please?"

★ ★ ★

By the time I make it to Gray Station, I have three missed calls from Myra. I can't answer any of them. My chest feels like it's being crushed in vice grips. I'm not ready for this. I feel like I've lost control of the whole situation. My phone starts buzzing like a cheap massage chair, and I look down to see texts flying in from Myra, one after the other.

Mon, Oct 24
pls pls pls don't be mad Jules. I didn't mean to say anything before talking to you
(4:34 PM)

I was super drunk last night and i only barely remember looking at Morgan's profile
(4:35 PM)

and I guess I got pissed at Ryan and sent her a dm, I felt like she just had to know, none of this was fair
(4:36 PM)

I was hungover all morning and i didn't even remember sending it but i just checked my records and yup there it is
(4:38 PM)

I am so so sorry Jules don't hate me i hate myself so much right now
(4:40 PM)

I stare at Myra's last text for a solid minute like there has to be more, like this must be some kind of a joke. My eyes swell with fresh tears. I've spent so much time this past month thinking about how Ryan lied to me, how he ghosted me. I've thought constantly about this baby inside me that Ryan doesn't even know about. But not once have I really thought about what any of this might mean for Ryan's wife. A whole new shame washes over me—one that I'm not sure I'll ever fully understand. How can I feel so guilty for something that can't possibly be my fault? All at once, I know the Fairchild case will have to wait. I can't deal with this story in Kentucky until I confront my own in New York.

Back at the Little Yellow House, I settle up with Mamaw and pack my bags. Quinn is out, so I leave her a terse little note to say I have to handle something in New York. She deserves more, but I don't have anything more at the moment to give. I'm all set for the hour drive back to the airport, but then I look in the rearview mirror and see Kyle Sawyer walking toward my car, smoking a cigarette. And then I remember: I was supposed to meet with his dad again in a few days to find out what else he knows about the story. Crap. As Kyle approaches, I roll down the window but leave the car running. I need to make this quick.

"A little birdie told me I could find you here," he says, peering down at me with clear eyes. His hands are steady, his movements fluid. As much as I hate to admit it, the man isn't half-bad to look at when he's sober.

"What do you want?"

"Well, to apologize—that's the main thing."

"For what?"

"Oh, for being an asshole," he says. "I've made a bad habit of that lately."

"Alright. Is that it?" I put my hand on the gearshift, trying to signal him away. Instead, he leans over into the window.

"Actually, no. I thought I'd try to make it up to you. I've got some new intel for you about the Fairchild thing. Maybe we can go grab a bite to eat, go over some stuff."

"You have to be kidding me. Are you seriously trying to

spin this thing into a date?" He straightens up, scratches the underside of his chin.

"What? No. Is that what you think I'm doing here?" Something about the timbre of his voice makes me think he's telling the truth. I'm usually a pretty good judge of these things.

"Look, I'm a bartender," I say. "I have to assume guys are hitting on me."

"Fair enough."

"Plus, it's not like you've been on the up-and-up with me so far, *Detective Sawyer*." He gives me a smirk—like a toddler caught stealing a cookie.

"Yeah, about that," he says. "I'm not a detective. Never have been. Just a lowly street cop. But it sounds like you've figured that out by now." I'll give him this: it's nice to hear a confession without having to drag it out of someone. But maybe he knows that.

"So that's your move?" I say. "You lie to women and then come clean? You think it makes you some kind of hero?"

"Nope," he says, stepping back. "It makes me an asshole. But we've covered that already." He takes another drag on the cigarette.

"I don't mean to be rude," I say, putting the car in gear. "But I really need to go, so—"

"Just—hang on," he says. "Look, I'm going through a rough time right now, okay? That's just a fact, not an excuse. But this Fairchild thing means more to my old man than you know. I hope you'll give me a chance to help out." I take off my mirrored glasses so he can see my eyes.

"Okay, that's fair—and I definitely could use the help. But I need you to level with me from here on out. I mean, are you the lying, make-believe detective? Or are you the honest street cop?" He steps back, studies me for a moment—as if he's considering whether the question is a trap.

"Can't I be both?" he says.

"Oh, so now you're some kind of philosopher?"

"No, ma'am. All I'm saying is that we've all got a little of that in us—the need to slip out of ourselves once in a while. To be something we're not. Even fancy book writers from New York." I take a deep breath and sigh. I tell him I have to deal with something back home so I can't make the meeting with his father tomorrow, but I'll be back soon.

He nods, not questioning, not pressing—which is nice. He gives the top of the car a tap, then reaches into his wallet, pulls out a card with his number. "Just give me a holler when you want to talk," he says, and then he backs away, clearing my path away from the Little Yellow House, away from Gray Station, and back toward my own problems in New York.

44

Turns out, Caleb Croxton had a two-year-old son. He told Jack about the boy one evening after the two men had finished each other off there on the couch in Caleb's trailer. Jack was trying to put himself back together when the other man lit a cigarette, took a quick draw and handed it over—pinched between his thumb and forefinger like a joint. Jack savored a mouthful of smoke, watched Caleb grab his jeans from where they were crumpled on the hunter green carpet.

"You oughta know about something," he said, pulling his wallet from the back pocket of the jeans. He showed Jack a photo of a towheaded boy, the edges of the picture bent in from where he had handled it so often. "If this here is something we're gonna keep doing, you need to know that things are complicated on my end." Jack puzzled over the picture for a beat before he realized what Caleb was saying.

"Oh," said Jack. He'd known about the wife since that first time, and sure, it bothered him if he thought too long about it. But this here was something altogether different. A child wasn't something he could filter out. He said it again, the only word that made sense: "Oh."

"I know," said Caleb, pinching the cigarette from Jack's fingers.

A few weeks had gone by without Caleb reaching out, and even though Jack knew he should walk away from the whole thing, he just couldn't bring himself to do it. Even when he wasn't with Caleb, he could hardly think of anything else. The leathery smell of the cologne on his neck. The nearly translucent blond hairs along the small of his back. The hard triangle of muscle jutting from his hips down below his belt. Everything about Caleb Croxton was forbidden fruit—sweet, intoxicating, deadly.

Jack sat in his bedroom blowing smoke out of the open window, his telephone strung across the room next to him as far as the cord would allow. His old man would beat the piss out of him if he caught Jack smoking inside again, but no matter: he needed something to take the shake from his fingers while he waited on Caleb to call. His wife was taking the boy to visit her parents for the weekend, and the promise of two whole days with Caleb burned through Jack's insides like a double shot of Jim Beam. When the phone finally rang, Jack startled so hard he fumbled his cigarette. He gathered himself, answered the call on the second ring.

"Yeah?" he said, trying to sound casual.

"I'm not in a good place, Jack," said the voice on the other end. It took him a bit longer than it should have to realize it wasn't Caleb.

"I can't talk right now, Kate," he said, checking his watch.

"Well, that's just too bad," she snapped. "Because I'm going through something, and I need my best friend to act like he gives a damn." Jack pinched the bridge of his nose, thinking. Caleb could be calling right at that very second.

"How about we talk tomorrow," he said, only realizing after

the fact that he wouldn't be around the next day to answer her call. Just as well. Kate had always been needy, but lately it had gotten to be too much. "Kate?" he said. The line had gone quiet.

"I'm really low, Jack," she finally said. "It's bad this time."

"Kate, I—"

"And I need you to bring me out of it."

"Look, Freckles, if we could just—"

"Don't you dare call me that," said Kate. The line sputtered and crackled in Jack's ear, and then there was nothing between them but an expanse of silence. Some other day he would have said he was sorry. He might've driven into town to rescue Kate from her thoughts, let her say her piece as they walked along the winding edge of the river toward the train bridge. That was what you should do for your best friend. That was what Kate would've done for him.

"I'm sorry, Kate," he finally said. "I'll call you in a few days." He slid the phone back on its base, listening to the ticking of the Kentucky Wildcats clock on the wall beside his bed. Caleb Croxton would call soon, and then he'd feel better.

45

At the Sundowner in Brooklyn, I melt into Myra's hug as soon as I see her. I soak her in: the scent of her sweet pea skin, the tight curls of her hair brushing my fingers against her back. The tension in my chest releases like someone opened the valve on a pressure cooker.

"Do you hate me?" she says.

"Yes. I totally hate you. I hate you so much." I feel her face stretch into a smile against my chest.

"Just punch me in the face, Jules."

"Tempting, but I think I'll pass." I pull away, wipe my eyes.

"Come on. Right here, babe." She pushes out her chin. "It'll make us both feel better." I take her by the hand, lead her to a booth in the corner of the bar.

"God, I need a drink," I say.

"I mean, we're in a bar. I think we can make that happen."

"Yeah, but like—" I lean back, frame my belly with my hands like I'm doing the Vogue dance.

"Right," says Myra. "Hold on a sec." She scoots away, dips under the bar counter. Some guy demands a beer, but she ignores him. I watch her splash some club soda into a couple of glasses. A squeeze of a lime, a quick stir, and she's back in under thirty seconds. "Not exactly the real deal," she says. "But hope-fully it's close enough."

We both take a drink. Then we exchange glances across the table, each waiting for the other to go first. So much to say—but where to start?

"I need to do something," I say, "and you aren't going to like it."

"Um…okay?" She eyes her club soda. "Do I need to get some-thing stronger here?" I reach out, take her hands from across the table.

"I know you want me to go talk to Morgan."

"This isn't about what I want—"

"Just—listen." I hold out a hand to stop her. "Maybe I'll talk to her—I'm not sure yet. But I need to do something first."

"We're on your timeline, Jules."

"I have to talk to Ryan. In person." Myra doesn't move. She sucks a breath, holds it deep like she's not sure if the room has any more oxygen to give her.

"Okay," she finally says, deflating. "But is that a good idea?"

"I won't be alone with him."

"Well, yeah. But I mean—like, *emotionally*?" I shrug. It's the only response that makes sense.

"I don't feel like I have a choice. There's got to be some other explanation. At the very least, he needs to know about the baby."

"But does he though?" says Myra. "If you get an abortion, what difference does it make? Don't give him a chance to—"

"It's not right, Myra," I say, cutting her off—as if no other explanation is needed. "We dated for three years. We talked about forever. I need to give him a chance to do the right thing here."

"Jules—*the right thing?* What exactly does that look like at this point?" The room suddenly feels stifling. Myra must see the change come over me because she softens. "Listen, whatever you decide to do, I'm here. Full stop." I bite my lip to keep from crying.

"I'm glad to hear that," I say, checking my watch. "Because I texted him yesterday, and he should be—" I pause as I hear the welcome chime of the bar door. Myra follows my gaze, and there he is.

"Oh, honey," says Myra, looking away. "I hope you're ready for this."

"Hey...so good to—" starts Ryan, moving to give me a hug. He stops when he registers the look on my face. I don't speak. I study him—the elbow patches on his tweed jacket, his two-toned Brooks Brothers shirt, his faded jeans cuffed at the ankles. Mostly, I notice the platinum wedding ring on his left hand. He slides into the chair across the table. Myra eyes him from the bar like a hawk circling a field mouse.

"Look, let's just start with the most important part," he says. He pushes a strand of his long curly hair away from his eyes. He's composed, self-assured. "I'm so sorry, Jules." I take a breath. It's good to finally hear him apologize, but it feels like damage control at this point.

"Sorry for what, exactly?" I ask. Ryan cocks his head to the side like I've just spoken in German. He shrugs.

"For...all of it?"

"No—that's not good enough."

"C'mon, Julia," he says. "What do you want me to say here? I screwed up. Big-time. I'd take it back if I could." He pauses, then adds, "I think we both would, right?"

"What is that supposed to mean?"

"Nothing, I'm just saying that—"

"How was I supposed to know you would ghost me for a month? How was I supposed to know you were married? You made me into the *other woman* and I didn't even know about it!" He holds up a hand—either a sign of surrender or just a gesture to get me to shut up, I'm not really sure.

"I didn't come that night intending to…" he starts, trailing off before he has to say anything too specific. "But we were having fun, and the drinks were flowing, and—"

"You weren't wearing your wedding ring! You told me nothing about your life, nothing of substance. It was all vague and generic, so you wouldn't have to lie. But you certainly withheld information—some pretty relevant information, I might add." He opens his mouth to speak, then thinks better of it. He leans forward, noticing a few gawkers at the bar have taken notice of our conversation. He reaches for my hands, but I pull away just before our fingers touch, as if jolted from a static shock.

"Listen, Jules—"

"Your wife called me," I say. Ryan scratches the underside of his chin, fingernails scuffing against two-day stubble. Either he's actually not concerned with what I just told him, or he's one hell of an actor. I dated the man for three years, and I still have no idea how to read him.

"Yeah—I know," he says, glancing sharply at Myra. "Morgan told me." Hearing him speak his wife's name makes me queasy. "But I talked to her. We're going to be okay."

"What do you mean you *talked* to her? Did you tell her the truth? All of it?" Ryan shrugs, squirms in his seat.

"That's between me and my wife," he says. "And honestly, it doesn't matter."

"If you tell the truth? Uh, yeah—it absolutely matters, Ryan."

"No, I mean—it doesn't matter *to you* anymore," he says. "You don't get to insert yourself into my marriage. This doesn't concern you." My pulse throbs in my temples. I can feel hives vining up the back of my neck, red and splotchy.

"You have no idea how much this concerns me," I say. Instinctively, I place a hand across my belly, but Ryan doesn't seem to notice.

"You think you can just burn me to the ground and walk away," he says, "but this is my life, like I said, my marriage. I have responsibilities, Julia—and not just to her."

"*Responsibilities?* Seriously? How about having a responsibility to—"

"Look," he says, pulling his phone from his pocket. "It's not just about me. It's about him—this is about my family." He turns the phone for me to see his lockscreen.

A picture. Of a beautiful baby boy. Maybe two years old.

"So, yeah," he says. "I have responsibilities. I have a wife to think about, and a son. It's not just about me anymore." He slides his phone back into his pocket. "Look, Jules—you know me. We have a history together. Don't you think I still care about you?" It's framed as rhetorical, but we both know what the real answer is. "I wanted to come support you and your book—it was unbelievable, amazing stuff. I thought we could just catch up, be friends. But one thing led to another, and well, here we are. Let's just accept that what happened last month was a mistake, a lapse in judgment. We just move on, no harm, no foul. If we could…"

He keeps talking, but I can no longer hear him. My throat constricts. My pulse thrums in my fingertips. I feel myself sinking, the white noise of the bar coalescing into burble, pressure building in my ears. I cup my hands against my belly. *Your baby is the size of an olive.* I imagine the fetus, globular, bite-sized, floating in amniotic fluid like a dirty martini. I came here to tell him about the pregnancy, but I can't do it—not now, not like this.

Slowly, the sounds of the bar enter back into my consciousness, a discordant awakening of clinking bottles, drunken laughter, the splash of liquor into glasses. I look to Myra for strength, and she's coming my way.

"Are you okay, Jules?" says Ryan, reaching for my hands again. I want to pull them away, but I feel rubbery, weak. I can only watch as he brushes his fingers over my knuckles. "You don't look so good." I move my mouth to speak, but then Myra is there, kneeling beside me. She takes my hands away from Ryan, brushes the hair from my face.

"I'll take it from here," says Myra. "Now kindly get the hell out."

46

1963

At the Fairchild house on Poplar Street, Kathryn finally got baby Danny down for a nap in the nursery upstairs. She tiptoed from the room, but just as she reached the hallway, the hard-wood moaned underfoot, startling the boy, sending him back into another screaming fit. She'd been contending with the baby's colicky cries for going on two hours, and now this. A rush of hot tears bubbled in her eyes, but she tilted her head back and kept them in. She'd watched Aunt Clara do this when she was a child. It was a technique that took some time to perfect.

"Well, come on, then," she said, scooping the boy back into her arms. She might've made it calmly to the living room, but just as she approached the locked door beside the stairs, the boy screamed right into the curvature of her ear. She'd had enough. She couldn't take it anymore. She felt it deep inside: an unstitching—the shrink and pull of a body separating from soul—that was moving through her, clawing its way along her insides, itching at the seams.

Holding Danny tightly against her chest, she lunged for-ward, kicking the closed bedroom door. The frame creaked and moaned, but it didn't give. So she stepped back and kicked twice, three times. On the fourth try the lock broke free, splintering the frame as the door swung open. In the dark room, a box fan chopped away the noise outside. Her mother was a silent lump in the bed, unmoved.

The baby sucked deep for air, curled his tongue, howled. Kathryn pushed into the room, lay the screaming child at the foot of the bed like a guilt offering before the altar. She turned and left, unburdening herself. For once, her mother would be forced to deal with the child—or not. Either way, Kathryn couldn't do it anymore.

Kathryn sank further into herself. Something had gathered inside her—deep and dark, the sludge of spent motor oil sunken in her stomach. This must have been how it happened to her mother, she thought: over weeks, months, years—not in one moment, but in every moment. And then it was there all at once, peeling her into layers like the curled bark on a shedding birch tree, exposing the vulnerable, pulpy flesh underneath.

While Edith was emerging from her latest low spell, Kathryn was sinking into one of her own. She couldn't stomach being around other people. She could hardly manage being around herself. Most of all, she didn't want to be anywhere near the *still, small voice* of God. So on Sundays, Norman would get the baby dressed up in a cute little seersucker outfit and then hand the child to Edith. The three of them would walk the two blocks over to First Baptist, and for one day, they'd pretend to be a normal little family. Nobody asked about Kate. Well, nobody asked the Fairchilds about much of anything. They were a family to be watched from a distance.

Kathryn spent the hours alone rummaging through the liquor bottles in the dining room server. At first the drinking was nothing more than a curiosity, a way to pass the time. But then it turned to a balm—the only thing in this world she looked forward to each week. Soon it became the only way she could distract herself from the dark hole opening up inside her, one that threatened to swallow her up the way it had done her mother. She sucked down a shot or two from each bottle as not to raise suspicion, but over time the supply started getting low, so she'd add a splash of water to the vodka, a dash of cough syrup to the brandy.

But then one Sunday she was snooping through her mother's things in the master bathroom when a little orange bottle fell out of the mirror cabinet, scattering its contents of yellow-and-white capsules across the floor. Kate picked one up, squished it between her fingers. *Librium*, read the prescription label. She counted the pills as she scooped them back into the bottle—twenty-six in all. Nobody would ever notice if a couple went missing. So she rolled two pills against her tongue, swallowed them down with a splash of water from the sink.

47

"Can I get you a drink?" says Aster, leading me through a corridor in his penthouse large enough to swallow my entire apartment back in Crown Heights. "Sparkling water? Coffee? Tea?" I follow him through a set of ornate French doors into—I don't even know what. A living room? A parlor? A den? The furniture is stark white and completely impractical: egg-shaped chairs, an oblong leather bench, some kind of knee-height swing. Rich people are extravagantly stupid.

"Actually, a glass of wine sounds nice," I say. "Something red." Aster turns to me, flips his eyes toward my stomach and then back to my face.

"Of course," he says, masking his judgment. "Please, make yourself at home." He gestures toward the smattering of furniture as if I'm supposed to know what to do with it, and then he disappears through a door opposite from where we entered. I approach one of the egg chairs, but then I second-guess myself, wondering if I'm about to sit on some kind of art.

"Oh, my!" says a voice from behind. I'm not prepared for what I see when I turn around: a seventy-something balding man in a half-open lavender bathrobe. He clutches the neckline of the robe like a string of pearls. "Don't sneak up on me like that!" He sucks a breath like he might hyperventilate.

"I didn't," I say. "I mean, I was just standing here and—"

"Oh, I see you've met Charles," says Aster, swinging back through the door to my right.

"I guess so?"

"You might've warned me you were having company, Jonny," says the man in the bathrobe. He tightens the cloth belt around the robe as if he's strangling a wild animal. "This young lady almost saw more than she bargained for." Aster places two glasses of wine on a cylindrical serving table to my right. "Oh, did we open a bottle?" says Mr. Bathrobe.

"Charles," says Aster, ignoring the question, "I'd like you to meet Julia White. Julia, this is my husband, Charles."

"Oh!" says Charles. "She's the one you've been going on about." He reaches for a glass of wine, but Aster playfully slaps his hand. Charles recoils like he's been bitten by a snake.

"Help yourself to any of the bottles in the cellar, dear," says Aster. He grabs Charles on either side of the face, dismisses him with a kiss on the forehead.

"Okay, okay—I can take a hint," says Charles. He sashays across the carpet, but pauses right before he reaches the door, turns back to me. "Lovely to meet you, my dear," he says. "Aster can talk of almost no one else these days, and that's saying something." He exits, leaving a thick pocket of silence in his wake. I stand awkwardly beside the serving table, trying to figure out what to do with my hands.

"Sorry about this ridiculous furniture," says Aster. "This is Charles's doing, I'm afraid. Give him an inch and he'll take a mile." He shakes his head, but his coy smile makes it obvious: the man is in love. I pick up my wineglass, but I don't drink, not yet.

"I'm not making much headway down in Kentucky," I say. I take the sealed photograph from my purse, hold it out to him.

"And until I can be sure I can break this story, I can't keep holding on to this."

"Oh, don't worry about that picture," he says, waving me off. "It's just a print. The original is hanging in my private gallery."

"You jerk!" I say, though I don't really mean it. Of course he didn't give me the original. He would have to be an idiot to trust a stranger with it. I give him a playful nudge.

"Guilty as charged," he says, smiling. He looks fragile—like he's aged two years in the past two weeks. I raise the glass of wine to my lips, take a small sip. Aster looks away, as if giving me privacy.

"I can't have this baby," I say. I try to take another drink, but I can't seem to do it.

"Oh?"

"That's part of why I need to be here. I need to get this… taken care of. I need for it to be here, not down in Kentucky."

"You don't have to explain yourself to me, Julia."

"Of course I do. Or else you'll sit there quietly judging me." He opens his mouth to speak, likely to contradict me. But then he reconsiders.

"That must be difficult," he says. "Needing to explain yourself to perfect strangers." He doesn't say so, but I know he's speaking from experience.

"I'm sure you know how it is."

"How do you mean?"

"Growing up gay in the sixties—in Kentucky."

"Ah, yes," he says. "But that's the difference between you and me, dear. I never had the courage to explain myself. I just ran away." The room goes silent. I give Aster space to gather himself.

"And you've never been back? Not even to visit?" He shakes his head.

"I didn't just leave Kentucky behind. I left Jack Chandler. I left every part of who I was."

"Don't you ever wonder what the place is like all these years later? How it's changed?" He peers into his glass of wine as if trying to read tea leaves.

"Gray Station used to have Kate Fairchild," he says. "And now it doesn't. That's the only change that matters."

"You loved her, didn't you?" Aster clears his throat. He blinks through wet eyes.

"Let me show you something." He places his empty goblet beside my full glass on the serving table, and then leads me through the French doors and back into the winding corridor. Midway down the hallway, he pauses in front of an enormous portrait of him and Charles—the two men regally reclined, majestic, as though from the eighteenth century. Aster reaches to the upper-left corner of the gaudy gold frame (one that Charles picked out, to be sure), and presses a series of concealed buttons. Like something out of a James Bond movie, the paneled wall beside the portrait slides open, gasping with a mechanical *whoosh*.

"What's this, your secret lair?" I say.

"I'm a simple man," Aster says, winking. "But what's the point of being rich if you can't have a hidden passageway?" As he guides me into the room, amber light gradually rises on four stark-white walls of a private gallery. Centered on the far wall is the original photograph of Kathryn Fairchild jumping from the bridge. A small, gold-plated plaque announces the photograph's cryptic title: *Woman Saves Child*.

"Very few people have ever set foot in this room, Julia," says Aster, inviting me to gaze at the surrounding walls, all lined with photographs. "These pictures have never been exhibited. Never been up for sale. My most precious and personal work." I step quietly toward the wall on my left—a row of portraits, all of the same woman. It only takes me a moment before I realize what I'm seeing.

"Is this her?" I say, mesmerized by the photographs. Aster

doesn't respond, but he doesn't have to. I feel like I know her already. "My God—she's so beautiful." As I walk down the first wall and turn toward the second, I realize that I'm walking through a progression of Kathryn Fairchild's life. A freckle-faced tomboy. A gorgeous teen goddess. A haunted young woman.

I walk toward the final two pictures of Kathryn. One of her and Aster, back when he was still Jack Chandler. And one of her holding the baby girl. A wave of feelings hits me at once— regret and resignation, hope and joy: emotions normally distinct and separate coalescing into an amalgam of yearning. I study Kathryn Fairchild holding the baby, but all I can think about is my own mother.

"I wanted you to see her, Julia," says Aster, ten paces behind me. "The way I do."

PART FOUR:

EVERY LITTLE THING
1963–1964

48

1963

George had promised he would pray about adopting a baby—but that was three months ago now. He had come home from the church, eyes distant and dreamy, and talked about Kathryn Fairchild and the chat they had in the sanctuary. *You can't always wait for God*, he had mumbled. Cautiously, Margot had let herself fill up with hope. Three months on, that hope was seeping from her like sap from a sugar maple.

One night during the first week of autumn, she parked her Buick under the cover of the weeping willows at the corner of Elm and Poplar, two houses down from the Fairchild place. She sat there in the shadows, watching the glow from Edith's bedroom window. This wasn't the first time she had made such a trip. Sometimes she'd sit there in the car for hours. Often she'd bring along *The Common Sense Book of Baby and Child Care* to pass the time.

She wasn't quite sure why she did it. She knew it was an odd behavior—maybe even a bit unsettling. But for some reason she couldn't explain, she took great joy in being close to the Fairchild place, watching, imagining, pretending.

Sometimes she caught herself wondering: What if she could spin the Earth backward? How far back would she go? Before she lost the first baby? Before she got married? Before she ever met George Caldwell in Mrs. Field's arithmetic class at Gray Station Junior High? Sometimes she fantasized about going all the way back to before she was born—the *beforelife*, where she imagined eternity stretched in panorama around her bodyless soul like an endless field of wildflowers.

Edith carried baby Danny back and forth in front of the window, jiggling him up and down, patting his back. Margot couldn't hear the child's screams, but she could see them in his curling tongue, in his purpled face. That baby never seemed to be happy—and who could blame him? A child must have a mother's love—something that Edith Fairchild couldn't provide, not in any consistent way, not in her *condition*. She watched the woman lay Danny on the edge of the bed and step away—not a care in the world whether the child would roll off the bed, plummet to the floor. Edith placed her face in her hands, sobbing now.

As she watched, something bubbled up in Margot—some amalgamation of pity, fear, hatred. Yes, it was true: sometimes she hated Edith Fairchild. For the way she took her children for granted. For always being sad when she had every reason to be happy. Mostly she hated her because of the way Norman still looked at her after all these years of marriage—awestruck, enthralled, hungry. When was the last time George had looked at Margot that way? Had he ever?

Margot watched as Edith pulled the curtains to the bedroom window. She felt the weight of the book in her lap, looked down to read the passage she had underlined over five years ago: "Trust yourself. You know more than you think you do."

When Margot returned to the parsonage that night, George was lingering in his church office across the little asphalt park-

ing lot. He seemed always to be at the church these days—
praying, studying. The truth was, it mostly felt like he was
avoiding being home.

Margot brought a kitchen stool into the bedroom closet,
climbed atop, reached up to the back of the top wooden shelf.
She hadn't taken the box down in years, but she knew its contours when she felt it—the silk ribbon, the velvet cover. She
unwrapped the box, ran her hands over the sheer lace babydoll gown and matching panties—the playthings she'd bought
for George's pleasure on their one-year anniversary. The lin-
gerie had only embarrassed him then, but no matter—she was
his wife, his bride, his jewel. He could use a reminder of who
she was.

When he came home, she was ready. He was out there in
the kitchen for a good while—she heard his heavy footsteps,
the *plunk* of the refrigerator door, the skid of the kitchen stool
across the linoleum. She waited in the candlelit bedroom until
he pushed into the room and found her there—stretched out
atop the bedcovers, an offering. She made a show of opening
her legs, but he didn't seem affected.

"Oh," he said, loosening his tie on the way to the bathroom.
"I thought you might be asleep."

"I had other plans," she said. She shifted herself to his side
of the bed, moving into the flickering candlelight. He unbuttoned his shirt and pants, removed them without ever glancing
in her direction. He wadded the clothes, threw them toward the
hamper in the corner. The shirt missed, but he didn't bother to
pick it up. "Come over here," she said. He stood in the warm
light of the connected bathroom in his white briefs, his sagging
stomach pooched just over the elastic band like a scoop of ice
cream on a sugar cone.

"I've had a bit of a day, Margot," he said, hands on his hips.

"Well, let me help you unwind." She lifted herself from the

bed, moved toward him. "Let me be your wife, George." She locked eyes with him, reached her hands into the front of his underwear, fingering through the dense tuft of hair. He kept his hands at his sides as if unsure what to do with them. With her body pressed against his, she rocked her hand up and down. He was soft in her palm like a loose wad of warm yeast dough.

"I'm just tired is all," he said sheepishly. When he kissed her on the tip of her nose, she had half a mind to spit in his face.

"I need for you to want me, George," she said. Kneeling before him, she lowered his underwear, releasing his scent— damp and earthy, like the boggy muck of the river bottoms. She held her breath, put her mouth around him. In one clean motion, he reached under her armpit, jerked her up to her feet. Hot breath steamed from his mouth into her face.

"Don't," he said, as if that were the only word he could muster. She searched his face, trying to figure out who this man was.

"What is it that you want from me?" she said. George raised his hand to strike her, but Margot had already collapsed to her knees, weeping. He stood over her only for a moment, and then he retreated to the bathroom.

49

On Halloween, an early Kentucky winter brought a burst of blue-cold air and a rare swirl of snow flurries to Gray Station. Main Street was aflutter with tiny ghosts and goblins, mothers rushing to keep up with their children as they pattered from store to store to scoop up jujubes and Lemonheads, Tootsie Rolls and Candy Buttons. Kathryn stood outside of Fairchild Shoes—her green-and-white-checkered wool coat cinched around her sleek black catsuit costume—clutching a huge basket of homemade popcorn balls. She rarely made it out of the house for anything but school. With her mother leveling out a bit, Aunt Clara had convinced Kate she should go back to Gray Station High for her junior year. *Go be a normal girl for once in your life*, her aunt had said, and though she didn't mean any harm by it, the words hurt. Kathryn had never known what that word meant—*normal*—and being away from her peers all these months while she was tending to baby Danny had made her feel more isolated than ever. She didn't belong at school anymore, she thought, but she wasn't needed at home now either. Most days when she got back to the house on Poplar Street, she'd sneak a swig or two from a bottle in the liquor cabinet, and then she'd disappear into her bedroom upstairs.

Today, though, she was feeling alive. The Halloween festivities, the costumes, the revelry—these awakened a part of her that had lain dormant these past few months. For one day, she wasn't the only one pretending to be someone else. She hadn't had a drink all day, but she took a couple of the little yellow pills to help even her out. Behind her, the bells of the store door chimed against the glass.

"What in the world are you supposed to be?" she asked. Sammy Sawyer joined her on the sidewalk, blew into his hands to keep them warm. "Some kind of mobster?" He wore a fitted pinstripe suit and black tie, his hair coiffed into a tight combover.

"Oh, c'mon, Kate," he said. "Can't you see it?" Holding his arms out wide, he spun around, flashed a smile. *"Ask not what your country can do for you—"*

"Not even close," she said, shaking her head. She plunked a popcorn ball into the paper bag of a precious little witch on the sidewalk. "And you really need to work on that Boston accent." She nudged him with her elbow, and then they stood for a while in silence, figuring out a path forward. She and Sammy had fallen out of touch—tethered only by the impossibly distant memory of that sticky summer night in the back of his car at the drive-in movie. He kept himself busy these days—working full-time at the shoe store to pay for his night classes at the community college. The chasm between them hadn't bothered her much—but she had to admit it was nice to have the company.

"We're about to close up inside," he said, gesturing back to the store. "You need any help out here?"

"Nope. I think we have more important things to do, don't you, Mr. President?" she said, eyebrow cocked. He reached into the basket, grabbed a couple of popcorn balls.

"I'll have my secretary clear my schedule," he said.

★ ★ ★

Night fell. Flurries swelled into powdery flakes, coating Gray Station like sifted flour. With downtown clear of trick-or-treaters and the storefronts all closed, Kate and Sammy had Main Street to themselves. They linked arms, walked down the middle of the crystalline pavement. The satisfying crunch of untrodden snow. The sharp smell of winter air. Kathryn was already feathery and light, her senses dulled by two more pills she had taken after work. She unhooked her arm from Sammy's, galloped out ahead of him into the blowing snow.

"The cold!" she said. "And the snow! Have you ever seen snow like this in October?" The sudden arrival of winter thrilled her—unpredictable, unexpected. She walked the center line of the street as if balancing on a tightrope, her arms stretched out wide, her index fingers upturned toward the gunmetal sky.

"Well, I know a good way we can stay warm," said Sammy. Kate raised herself *en pointe*, twirling clumsily toward him. He caught her as she stumbled into his chest, strong hands circling her waist, resting against the small of her back.

"What did you have in mind?" she whispered, their lips so close she could taste his Doublemint gum. They lingered there for a moment, searching each other.

"Now, don't you start that again unless you mean it, Kate Fairchild." Sammy released his grip, stepped back just enough to where she could feel the cold come between them. "I was talking about this." He reached into his wool coat, pulled out a fifth of vodka. A rush of saliva swelled in Kate's mouth like Pavlov's dog at the sound of a bell.

The liquor ate her insides the way that it would, cutting through her throat and chest like molten glass. She put a hand to her mouth, coughed into the cold gray air. At the edge of the river, they skipped flat stones against the rippled surface, passing the bottle between them with numb hands. They didn't bother saying much—just went on drinking and throwing rocks and sometimes kissing.

"You think God ever regrets us?" said Kate. She'd been thinking about this question for a few minutes, but she just now found herself light enough to ask it.

"Regrets us?"

"Yeah, like—don't you think the world was better before we were here?" She paused, stretching her arms to the sides as far as she could reach, gesturing to the expanse of sky—big and wide and good in every direction. "Just look up there. How could we ever make that any better?" She felt the familiar pit in her stomach, the sinking, the darkness.

Sammy went to scoop up another rock, but then thought better of it. He took Kate by the hands. "Is everything okay, Kate?" She whipped her head toward him too fast, and it took her eyes a minute to catch up. This was her chance. The only thing she had wanted for these last few months of loneliness was for somebody to listen to her—to really *hear* her. She studied the snowflakes caught in Sammy's eyebrows, melting against the heat of his face. What could she possibly say to make him understand? She looked past him to the towering steel of the train bridge overhead. You could see for miles up there, she thought. God, how nice it would be to lift yourself out of this little rat-maze town, to see everything stretched out before you—tiny and malleable, like a clay-figure scene in a shoebox diorama.

"Follow me," she said, and then she was off, lumbering up the bank of the river.

Out ahead of Sammy, she stumbled across Main Street. The snow was piling up now—covering the circuitous tracks they had made in the street only minutes before.

"Kathryn, wait—" shouted Sammy, but she was already across the sidewalk, making her way uphill toward First Street.

By the time he had caught up with her, chest heaving against the ice-cold air, she was halfway up the access ladder. The cold metal rungs stung her bare red hands as she ascended, carefully at first and then with abandon, the world spinning into pinwheels around her like she was trapped in Van Gogh's *Starry Night*. She stopped only once—when Sammy clambered up the ladder below her, shaking the structure so badly she had to grip with both hands to hang on. But then all at once she was up there on top of the railbed, and *my God, the view*!

"Alright, then," said Sammy, pulling himself up beside her. "You've had your fun, now let's get off this thing before one of us gets killed."

"Oh, live a little," she said. They were only about twenty feet up—the land below them sloping gradually away before falling off into the river below. They were a good ten yards from the trestle of the bridge over the water. She hopped across a couple of wooden rail ties underfoot, testing out her balance.

"Come on, Kate. This isn't funny," said Sammy, his voice carried off in the blistering wind. The distance between them grew with each step she took. Before she knew it, she was standing at the edge of the first pier, the gaps between the wooden ties revealing the dark waters below. She lifted a foot, let it linger over the open hole.

"Don't you ever just need to feel something?" she said—maybe to Sammy, but he was too far away. She looked back, saw him clinging to the ladder thirty feet behind her. The snow cut across her face, blurring her vision. *Just a few steps more*, she thought, but then she found herself crossing tie after tie, approaching the second truss of the bridge over the open water. She couldn't stop herself, pulled by a force into the center of the bridge. A hot hiccup bubbled in her throat, the scorch of vomit threatening its way up.

"Kate!" yelled someone, somewhere, the voice nothing but a distant dream after waking. Caught in the dead center of the river, she saw the Indiana shore through the blowing snow, looming in the distance like the promised land. *What if I just kept going? What if I disappeared and never came back?* A mighty gust of wind pushed against her chest, nearly sending her between the rail ties. She stumbled, righted herself. She could have hunkered down, gripped the rail of the bridge—but no: she stood, arms dangling loosely at her sides as if she were standing on the Main Street sidewalk. She was utterly unafraid—unafraid to fall, unafraid of a coming train. With one foot on the rail of the bridge and the other stretched to the wooden tie, she looked south into Gray Station—colorless, soft with snow, quiet as a silent picture. Down there she knew nothing but fear, but up here she was untouchable. *It's just one step*, she thought, *and then poof! Abracadabra!*

Gripping the cold steel of the bridge, she leaned her body out toward the water just as far as her arms would allow—and then a bit farther. She closed her eyes, wondered what it would feel like to fly right up to the moment that the water swallowed her whole.

A voice in the wind—gravelly, distant. "Kathryn," it said. "Kate, damn it, wake up." She was outside of herself, coming back into the world in some other body. A blurry figure overhead—shadowed against a glare of bright white light. Her pulse thrummed behind her eyes.

"Daddy?" she said, adjusting to the light. A workbench to her right. Sweet stench of leather and shoe glue. The shoe store repair room was both familiar and foreign—like a dream of living in a house you've never been inside. Norman raised himself from his stooping position, loomed over her, hard and unmoving, like a giant marble statue. He reached down, snatched something from her chest—some makeshift blanket. She looked at her torso, her arms. Vomit stains across the black catsuit. Her lips were cracked, scaly as the sides of a river trout. Norman studied the fabric in his hands. A pinstripe jacket. The one Sammy Sawyer had worn the night before. He made a face—trying to place where he had seen it. "Daddy," Kathryn said again—the only word that didn't seem like it could give offense. Still, he warned her off with a shake of his head, his index finger pointed between her eyes like the scope of a gun.

"Go out the back door," he said. "We'll talk about this later."

The morning light screamed into her eyes on the walk home. It was past time for school, but she couldn't go, not like this. Her body ached all over—her legs, her shoulders. Too many pills. Too much booze. The night before was lost to her, nothing but thick fog in a dense wood. By the time she reached the front door of the house on Poplar Street, she was faint and needed to sit down. A cold sweat gathered across her brow. Last night came to her in broken pieces, a kaleidoscope of memory. Standing atop the train bridge—rusted steel, a broken wooden rail tie. Pillowy snow drifting along the bank. Sammy Sawyer—sweat-slick chest and bourbon breath. Where was he? When did he leave her?

Inside the house, she eased herself up the stairs into the bathroom. She turned on the shower and then undressed, pulling off her skintight costume and then her underclothes, a rank odor pluming into the air. She flung her panties onto the floor, but then something caught her eye—a stain across the white fabric, pulpy, red. She picked up the underwear, pulling them apart, studying the dried blood.

She turned, raised one foot up onto the countertop of the vanity, examining herself in the mirror. She pushed aside a thick tuft of pubic hair, winced as she discovered how tender she was to the touch. Her labia was swollen, discolored. She sat on the toilet and emptied her bladder—the urine stinging on the way out like pinprick needles. She wiped, found only a trace of crusted blood.

★ ★ ★

She lay in bed all afternoon, her throbbing head underneath a pillow. Sleep wouldn't come. She called Sammy's house, but when his mother answered she lost her resolve and hung up. Her stomach lurched—whether from hunger or nausea, she couldn't be sure. In the kitchen, she found her mother feeding Danny homemade applesauce. Edith looked content, even happy. Kathryn sucked deep, trying to swallow what she knew she couldn't contain.

"Oh, baby," said Edith, leaving the boy fidgeting in the high-chair. She pulled Kathryn into her chest, crushed her with the force of a mother's love. "What is it?" Kate gave herself over to the flood of grief, let herself cry into Edith's cardigan. How many times had she longed to be held like this?

"I think I might've done something," said Kathryn. She clenched her eyes, tried with all her might to conjure some image of the night before. Flesh pressed against flesh. Sharp spike of pain. Hot breath against her neck. Edith stroked her hair, pulled away just enough to look her in the face.

"Honey," she said, "you're shaking." She placed a cool hand against Kathryn's forehead, as if checking for a fever. "You wait right here," she said, and then she was off, bounding up the stairs with more energy than Kate had ever seen her use. The baby screwed up his face, working himself into a fit. Kathryn studied his reddened cheeks, his downturned lips. Right in that moment, she hated him more than anything in the whole world.

"I know I shouldn't do this," said Edith, springing back into the kitchen. "But I tell you, I've just never known anything to work so well for me." She took Kathryn's hand, opened it up like the cup of a blooming rose. She placed two little yellow pills into her palm. "You just let these work their magic, and then we'll talk." Kathryn swallowed the pills, knowing they would never be enough.

50

Norman couldn't seem to think straight, not after finding Kate
the way he did. What had gotten into that girl? Always seemed
to be looking for something without quite knowing what it
was. He could hardly blame her. Sometimes he thought about
her and her mother and even that baby at home and he couldn't
help but want to rip himself apart.

He tried to busy himself by resoling that pair of horsebit loaf-
ers dropped off the day before. But then he got to pulling on
the leather and he couldn't get his head right. His hands were
shaking something fierce. That jacket he had pulled off Kate
kept taunting him—outstretched on the floor next to the workbench like a body at a crime scene. Finally, he remembered
who was wearing it for Halloween: Sammy Sawyer. He bolted
from the bench and headed for the showroom, where he found
George restocking tennis shoes. When Norman called his name,
George startled as if caught pocketing money from the register.

"Good gracious," said George, hand across his chest. "You
snuck up on me." Norman puzzled over that one for a minute, but there didn't seem much point in taking it any further.

"Well, anyway, I'm headed out for a bit," said Norman. "Need some air." George clasped his hands, tilted his head to the side in that way he did when he was speaking to a parishioner.

"Anything I can do for you?" he said. Norman regarded his creased forehead, his squinting eyes.

"Just stock the shelves, George," he said. "That's what I've hired you to do."

In the Northridge subdivision over on the east end of town, Norman pulled the Oldsmobile into the Sawyer driveway. Nice little brick ranch. Spiffy. Truth be told, he'd never cared much for the Sawyers. The kind of people who allow a grown son to live there at home two years after he graduated high school— well, he just couldn't understand people like that. He'd always tried to give the boy the benefit of the doubt, but some things couldn't be overlooked. Sure, he was taking a business course or two out at the college, but he sure didn't seem to be in a hurry to get on with his life. A man with no ambition—that was what Sammy was. What did the boy plan to do—clerk at the shoe store for the next thirty years?

"Oh, Mr. Fairchild," said Sammy, standing in the frame of the door. He looked like he'd just rolled out of bed—unshaven, hair matted to one side of his head like an ill-fitted wig. Norman checked his watch. Already a quarter till noon. "What can I do for—" started Sammy, but then he noticed the jacket clenched in Norman's hand.

"Thought we might have a talk," said Norman. Sammy squinted against the sun, thinking.

"Look," he finally said, hands held out in front of him as if to show he wasn't wielding a weapon. "I didn't know what else to do." Norman cocked his head to the side.

"And what was it, exactly, that you did?"

"Well, to be honest, I'm not clear on all the details myself."

Norman clenched a fist, and Sammy noticed. "It wasn't like that, sir."

"Help me to see what it was like, then," said Norman. "Because all I know right now is that I found my sixteen-year-old daughter passed out on a concrete floor with this draped across her body." He slung the jacket across the boy's shoulder. "That doesn't sit too well with me."

"She was drunk, you understand?" said Sammy. "And she had these pills, too."

"That so?"

"She was out of her mind, Mr. Fairchild. I'd never seen her like that before. She kept going on and on about—" He stopped, waived a hand through the air.

"About what?"

"I don't know. All kinds of stuff. Mostly about God."

"What's that supposed to mean?" asked Norman. The boy shrugged, shook his head.

"Like I said—she was talking out of her mind. She was already drunk, and she just kept drinking. And those pills, too. I couldn't take her home like that, you understand. And I couldn't bring her here with me, either."

"So you just left her there? That was your solution?"

"I was pretty drunk myself, I'm sorry to say. It seemed like the safest thing to do." Norman ran a hand along the underside of his chin, considering.

"And so that's all that happened, son? You had some drinks, left her to sleep it off?" Sammy furrowed his brow.

"Well, yeah," he said. "I covered her up with my jacket and locked the door on my way out. That's all there is to it."

51

Walking home from the Clark garage, Jack saw Aunt Peggy's teal Volkswagen Beetle parked in the driveway at the farmhouse. He went into a sprint, tearing across the field between the properties like a lost dog who'd found his way home.

"Aunt Peg?" he called when he walked in, and there she was—setting out the good plates along the oak table in the dining room. She spun around, her paisley dress bursting with flowers, psychedelic orange and green, like she was wearing her soul on the outside.

"Get over here, you," she said, pulling Jack into her chest. She smelled of sweet pea and lavender, same as always. Sure, she may have been his **aunt**, but Peggy was more like a big sister—a full twenty years younger than Jack's old man, and only six years older than Jack himself.

"I didn't know you were coming," said Jack, holding her hands.

"Can't make it for Thanksgiving next week, so I figured I'd pop in for a day or two now." She went back to the table, placing the silverware just so. "Told your dad about it weeks ago, but you know how he is." As if on cue, the man clunked through the screen porch and into the dining room. He lumbered toward them—stumbling on account of either the wooden leg or the bourbon, Jack never could be sure.

"Well, don't go all quiet on my account," said the old man. "Y'all was in here going on about what an old sonofabitch I am, so get on with it." With his breath lingering in the air, the slightest spark could have set them all ablaze. Jack flicked his eyes back and forth from his aunt to his father, measuring them both. Peggy was unflinching, as always. The bravest person in this whole wide world, that was what she was.

"Sit yourself down and drink a tall glass of water, Clyde," she said, pointing at him with the business end of a butter knife. "You sober yourself up and I just might let you have some of that Honey Baked ham I have cooking." Jack smiled at the twang in Aunt Peg's voice. Didn't matter how long she lived up there in New York, she'd always be a little bit Kentucky. She was the only person Jack knew who belonged everywhere all at once—like one of those wooden nesting dolls: a container of multiple selves, separate parts of the same whole. He thought of Caleb Croxton—his wife, his baby, the salty-sweet taste of his neck.

"Alright, then," said Clyde, easing into the chair at the end of the table. "You best fetch me a glass of water."

Dinner went okay, but then Clyde started in on another bottle of bourbon. It was a marvel—the way the man could suck down liquor like it wasn't nothing but sweet tea. Jack's mom was in the kitchen working through a heap of dirty dishes, so Jack sat with Aunt Peggy, listening to her go on about what she'd been doing in New York. Parties, galleries, nightclubs—there always seemed to be some kind of excitement in her life. To Jack, that kind of existence seemed as foreign as China. Aunt Peggy had been up there for going on a decade now—found a way to get into NYU, and then decided to stay and make a way for herself. How a person could do such a thing was a mystery to Jack. He glanced out the window as Peggy talked, looking out over the Western Kentucky hills—hemming in his little life like the seam of a quilt.

Clyde sat at the head of the table, drinking. You'd think he was on the verge of passing out, but Jack knew better. The man had drunk himself just to the point of meanness—still three or four shots away from when you'd really have to worry.

"I showed some of your photographs to Charles," said Aunt Peg, dabbing her fingers through the crumbs of her apple pie.

"Yeah?" said Jack, trying to sound casual. He glanced at his father, but he didn't seem to be paying attention. Charles was some guy Aunt Peg had kept in touch with from her college days. Some up-and-coming bigshot in the art world, that was what she wrote in her letters. Jack had sent her some photographs, hoping she'd pass them along. He didn't figure much would come of it, but still.

"Says you got yourself some real talent," said Peggy. "Says he might be able to get you into a show in SoHo." She cocked her eyebrow, shrugged as if this was no big deal. Jack didn't know SoHo from Timbuktu, but he still felt like he might burst inside.

"What's that mean, exactly," said Clyde, leaning forward, taking up every bit of space around him. "A show."

"I was talking to my nephew," said Aunt Peggy. "This doesn't concern you." Clyde leaned back, edging up off the hardwood floor. Jack watched the rock of the chair—tilting farther, farther still. One solid shove would send the old man spilling back, maybe crack his head wide-open on that curio cabinet behind him.

"Come on, Jack," she said. "Let's go to your room. We don't need an audience."

Once they got out of earshot, Jack grabbed Peggy by the hand, led her straight past his bedroom door and out the back of the house. Down into the cellar they went, Jack bounding down ahead of her two steps at a time.

"Your friend really said all that?" said Jack, holding the door open for Peggy. She was still halfway up the stairs, taking her time not to slip on the rain-slick concrete. "About a show and everything?" When Peggy finally reached the landing, she looked at Jack in the face—her expression caught on the edge of sadness.

"He's not my friend exactly," she said. "But yes—he thinks you really could be something special." She brushed a hand through Jack's hair, then stepped past him into the cellar. He was behind her now, watching as she took in the scene: a flutter of photographs around the room—some displayed in crudely homemade frames, others drying on clothespins stretched over-head. The space was a wonderwork of depth and light, sad-ness and hope: pictures of landscapes and people, sunsets and flowers. But there was one photograph that enraptured Peggy, drawing her like a moth to a flame.

"Oh, Jack," she said, taking the framed piece from the top shelf. "Who is she?" Peggy turned the frame around, revealing the saddest picture Jack had ever taken: Kate Fairchild focused in the foreground, holding that baby brother of hers against her chest. Edith Fairchild loomed in the background—just a blur of a woman, distant, out of focus, empty. Jacked had snapped the picture months ago, but he'd never shown it to Kate. She would've complained about her unkempt hair, her puffy eyes. But it was true: that picture captured everything there was to know about Kathryn Fairchild. Every time he looked at it, he felt like he could split in two.

"She's just so…" started Peggy, searching the photograph as if it held what she wanted to say. She stroked Kate's image with a careful finger, reaching through time and space. What word could she use? Lonely? Desperate? Beautiful? Whatever it was, she never could get it out. Instead, she put a hand to her mouth, overcome.

"Now, what's this all about?" asked Jack, moving to her. He took the photograph from her fingers, pulled her into him. The way she leaned her head back to try to keep the tears from falling made her look like Kate. Her freckles, the slope of her jaw, even the way she swooped her hands through the air while talking. If it weren't for Peggy's coal-black hair, you might think the two women were sisters.

"I don't know," said Peggy. "I'm always bursting into tears these days. I can't figure it out. Seems like everything sets me off." She stared at the photograph again, her eyes trained not on Kate Fairchild, but on the baby in her arms. "I just feel so alone all the time."

"But you're always going on about your friends up there," said Jack.

"And you believe me?" She tilted her head as if looking at a child—naive, hopeless. "Honey, New York is the loneliest place in this whole wide world." She paused, staring off in the distance somewhere, transported through the cellar and over the Kentucky hills. "It's like—how can I put it? Like you're surrounded by everybody and always completely alone at the same time. All these parties and whatnot—it's like I'm the only one there, Jack. A crush of bodies and not a single soul."

"You could always move back down here," said Jack.

"Oh, honey. You know this town is no place for a woman like me." Peggy looked at him, a change coming over her face like she'd found a flashlight inside a black cave. "But you could move up to New York with me," she said. Jack stepped back as if shoved.

"New York?" he said, sounding out the words like something foreign, syllables with no meaning. "You can't be serious."

"Dead serious. You'd be so happy there, Jack. We both would."

"C'mon, Aunt Peg. I wouldn't know what to do with my-self in New York. All that concrete. All those people. That's just not me."

"Oh, but I think it is," she said. "There's all kinds of folks in the city, Jack. Folks that think with their hearts like you do. Folks with the same feelings." She touched Jack's chest, let her palm linger against his thumping heart. "People like me. People like you."

"What are you saying?" said Jack. He forced a laugh, but it came out wrong.

"You know exactly what I'm talking about," she said. "There's more than one kind of normal up there, Jack." He thought about Caleb Croxton—his lips, the curve of his back. How long had Peggy known? Probably before he knew it about himself. That was just who she was. "It'd be good for you. Get you out from underneath that sorry ass father of yours." She spun around, swooping a hand overhead. "And all this, Jack—just think of what moving could mean for your art."

"Yeah," he said, trying hard to imagine an impossibly different life than he had ever known. "Just think."

52

Christmas was usually Kate's favorite day of the year, and not on account of the presents. Some of her favorite childhood memories involved sitting around the dinner table out at Aunt Clara and Uncle Raymond's house for a big Christmas dinner, passing steaming bowls of sweet corn and green bean casserole, yeast rolls and hot mashed potatoes. Then there were the pies. Apple crumble. Pecan. Cherry so tart it made your ears tingle. Her favorite part was that, for one day, they could all play make-believe that the Fairchild family was just like any other. They laughed, teased each other, played dominoes and gin rummy. Her mother always seemed to be home for Christmas. As much as the woman was in and out of the state hospital down south, Kathryn couldn't remember a single year when Edith wasn't there with the rest of them. Like some sort of magical pill, the spirit of the season always seemed to level her out.

But Christmas of 1963 was altogether different. For one thing, President Kennedy had been shot just the month before, and everybody was struggling to work their way back into normal life. But Kathryn knew her *normal* was never going to be the same—for another reason entirely. She'd managed to put this thing from her mind for much of the morning, but there she was mixing a sweet potato casserole in the hot kitchen when she started to feel faint. It was too much—all those boiling pots and steaming dishes, the men bumping through her and Aunt Clara to steal an olive or cracker from the pickle tray, the flour-dusted apron cinched around her waist. If she didn't get some air soon, she knew she might just turn her stomach inside out right there on the yellow linoleum floor.

She pushed through the porch door into the punchy December wind, never even bothering to grab her coat on the way out. Standing there in her sleeveless dress, she watched her steaming breath escape in plumes into the icy air. Sweat had gathered in the hair by her temples, and now it felt like icicles might form along her ears.

"Hey, you," said Jack, leaning against the side of the house, smoking a cigarette.

"Don't sneak up on me like that," said Kathryn, startling. Jack flicked his ash onto a frozen puddle by his feet.

"I've been standing here for five minutes," he said. "So I reckon I'm not the one doing the sneaking." He flashed a smile, revealing those big, crooked eyeteeth of his.

"Didn't think you'd make it this year," said Kate. She hugged her arms around her chest, feeling the cold now.

"When have I ever missed a Fairchild Christmas meal?"

"When have you ever missed a free meal, period?" Kate raised an eyebrow, getting the laugh out of Jack she was after. Their friendship had been stretched thin these last few months, but still: she loved him more than any single person on this planet. "There's something I need to say to you," she whispered, careful not to let her voice carry through the screen door. "And I need for you not to judge me for it."

"I've never judged you for a single thing in your whole life,

Kate," he said matter-of-factly. "Besides, I need to talk to you, too. But you go first." He took a hard drag on the cigarette.

"Okay, then—I'm just going to say it."

"Alright."

"Here goes."

"Okay."

"I think I'm pregnant, Jack." As soon as the words were out of her mouth, it seemed like the air went still around her. Everything was quiet and fuzzy—like she had dived eight feet into that pond across the field. Jack's face contorted and slackened, like his brain couldn't process the words. "Well, say something," said Kate. She wished Jack had the courage to come give her a hug, but he stayed there next to the house, thinking.

"Okay," he said. He flicked the spent cigarette onto the concrete porch, stamped it out with the toe of his boot.

"That's all you have to say?" she asked.

"I'm still working through it."

"Well, work faster. I've kept this whole thing bottled up since Halloween and I can't keep it in any longer."

"Halloween?" said Jack. "You told me you were with Sammy Sawyer that night." She nodded, took a step closer. God, why wouldn't he just wrap her up in his arms? "So, he's the one…" he said. He trailed off before he said anything too definite. That was just the way Jack talked about hard things.

"I reckon he is," said Kathryn.

"You *reckon*? You mean to say it could be someone else?"

"No, it's him," she said. "It has to be him." She stared off beyond Jack, her soul transported back to that night. The tears came all at once, pouring out like water from a busted pipe. Jack pulled her into his chest, squeezed her till she could hardly breathe.

"Okay, Kate. Okay," he said, releasing her just enough. "You know I'm here, no matter what. But you're going to have to help me understand this one."

"I just can't remember," she said, choking out words between sobs. "We were drinking down by the river, and then I was up on the train bridge, and then—" She broke off, burying her head into Jack's wool coat. "I swear to God, Jack—I don't remember anything else." They stood that way for a while—hugging, rocking back and forth there on the porch. A minute or so into it, Uncle Raymond poked his head through the screen door. When he saw them intertwined like they were, he grunted like a little English bulldog and went back in the house.

"And you're sure?" said Jack, picking right back up from where they left off, as if no time had passed at all. "I mean, you're positive that it happened?" Kate tried to speak, but she couldn't get the words out. She thought back to the morning after—her dad standing over her in the hard fluorescent light of the shoe store repair room. The blood in her underwear. The swelling between her legs.

"I can't get it to make sense any other way," she said, dabbing the dripping mascara from her eyes. "And now I'm late." Jack rubbed his palm in circles on her back, and then she felt him tense up. He was breathing heavy, building into something.

"That son of a bitch," he said, just above a whisper.

"It wasn't like that," said Kate.

"Really?" said Jack. "Because it sounds like he got you drunk, waited until you passed out, and then—"

"No!" Kate shouted, cutting him off. "That's not him, Jack. Sammy Sawyer might be a lot of things, but he wouldn't do that."

"Then how else do you explain it?" said Jack. "What does he say happened?" Kate pulled away. At his side, Jack's fists clenched in and out. She'd seen him like this a handful of times before. She figured he was about two steps away from jumping in his pickup truck, driving into town, beating the daylights out of Sammy Sawyer.

"I don't know," she finally said, shrinking into herself.

"Oh, Kate," said Jack. "Don't tell me you haven't told him."

"I haven't talked to him about anything at all," she said, so softly her voice barely survived in the air between them. "I've been at school, and I can't go to the shoe store—I just can't—and then in the evenings Sammy's got his night classes, and—" She cut herself off from making more excuses, because she knew they were exactly that. Jack paced across the splintering wood of the front porch, stopped at the edge, made his way back.

"Well, maybe I'll go see him right now," he said. He made a motion toward the steps, but Kate caught his arm.

"Just stop it, Jack," she said. "I don't need a hero. I just need for you to listen to me." She worried that Jack might slink away like a wounded puppy, scamper off toward his truck and go on anyway. That was what most men would've done—she'd learned this over the years. But that wasn't Jack's way. The fire slowly drained from his eyes to where he could see her clearly. He nodded, led her over to the wrought-iron porch rocker.

"Okay, then," he said, sitting, inviting her to join him. "Let's talk, Kate. I'm not going anywhere."

53

The day before New Year's Eve, Kathryn was finally ready. She marched through the front doors of Fairchild Shoes on Main Street. Sammy Sawyer was near the front of the store, fitting a young boy for a pair of wingtip dress shoes. She paused only long enough to smooth the front of her pleated dress.

"I need to talk to you," she announced. She stood before him just as she had rehearsed it the night before: hands calmly at her sides, feet shoulder-width apart. If she focused on controlling her body, she wouldn't have to think too much about how this whole thing made her insides feel like they were going to explode.

"Uh, hey there, Kate," said Sammy, shooting an apologetic glance at the child's mother. "Give me a few minutes to finish up here and then—"

"No, this can't wait," she said. "George can take over for you." She never even looked in the man's direction—just pointed a finger over to where he sat behind the cash register. George stood, flicking his eyes back and forth between them.

He busied his hands, stacking carbon copy receipt books into a neat little pile.

"Yes, of course," said George, his voice hesitant, like that of a scolded child. "Happy to help."

Back in the repair room, Kathryn and Sammy were alone. She'd been avoiding this place since the night it happened, but she knew this conversation had to take place right here. She looked around to get her bearings—rows of metal shelving for shoe storage, bins of leather and tools, her father's wooden workbench. She finally let her gaze linger on the cold concrete floor—right in the corner where she had woken up that morning after Halloween night.

"How've you been, Kate?" said Sammy. He stood a good ten feet away, regarding her with suspicion. Despite everything, he didn't look nervous. It must be nice to go through life like that, Kathryn thought.

"Were you ever going to talk to me about it?" she asked.

"Well, I just—" Sammy crossed his arms and then uncrossed them, trying to figure out how to stand. Watching him shift and shimmy like that made Kathryn breathe a bit easier. "After your old man came out to the house and everything, I just didn't feel good about going to see you."

"My dad?" said Kathryn. "What are you talking about?" She thought back to the night after it happened—how she had stayed up in bed for the rest of the day and into the evening, waiting for her father to come home and interrogate her. But it never happened. When Norman finally dragged himself home after nightfall, he ate his dinner at the kitchen table, alone. He had a beer in the living room recliner, and then another. Then he went upstairs, right past her open bedroom door, and went to bed.

"I thought he was warning me away," said Sammy, waving a hand through the air. "Stood right there at my front door giving me the third degree. Looked like he might sock me in the face, to be honest."

"Well, what did he say?" Kathryn couldn't figure out if she was embarrassed or proud. Her daddy had stood up for her. That meant something.

"He just kept asking me about what happened."

"And?"

"And I told him." Sammy took a step in Kate's direction. She wanted to shrink away, but she stood her ground. "Look, I never meant to leave you like that. You gotta believe me."

"Leave me? That's why you think I'm upset? Because you left me here?" Sammy squinted at her, tilted his head.

"Well, yeah," he said. "What else is there to be upset about?" Kate shook her head in disbelief. Was he really going to make her say it? She'd never thought of Sammy as a coward, but as she studied him there a body-length away from her, hands stuffed into his pockets, she couldn't think of another word that would fit.

"I'm pregnant," she said. She focused her gaze on the constellation of freckles across the bridge of Sammy's nose. She couldn't manage to look him in the eye, but she didn't want him to know it. As the words fell over him, his posture changed.

"But—we didn't—" he said, faltering. "I got you settled in over there. Covered you up with my jacket. And then I left." He scanned his eyes across the concrete as if he was searching for a missing puzzle piece that had dropped to the floor.

"I need you to listen to me," said Kathryn, taking a methodical step in his direction. "I can accept the fact that we were drunk and did something stupid. I can even forgive you for not knowing I was too far gone to stop it from happening." She placed a hand across her churning stomach, as if to protect the baby growing inside. "But it happened, and we're in this together now." Sammy stood in silence, mouth agape. He looked at the ceiling, down at his shoes, behind his shoulder at the closed repair room door.

"Kate, I swear to God—"

"Don't," she said, pointing a finger at him like the scope of a rifle. "This is something you've got to own, Sammy. There's no other way." They stood that way for a solid minute, searching each other. When it was clear there was nothing more to say, Kathryn walked out the back door, leaving him alone.

Was it possible? Could she really be losing her mind? She hadn't been to the doctor yet—no blood work to confirm what she knew had to be true. She could think of nothing else for the next three days. She had these dreams at night—a faceless man looming over her, the weight of his body crushing her against the cold concrete floor. In one of the dreams, the storeroom smoked and crackled in a blaze of fire—burning through the ceiling, the cardboard storage boxes, blue-white flames licking at her bare legs. Still, the faceless man didn't budge, grunting and contorting until he had finished what he came for.

A week later, Sammy called. She closed the door to her room, sitting on her bed atop the thick comforter Aunt Clara had quilted, her legs tucked under her bottom.

"I've been thinking about everything," said Sammy, skipping the pleasantries.

"Okay," she said. She wrapped the phone cord around her index finger.

"I don't remember it happening, Kate. I've wracked my brain here, and still—nothing."

"Sammy, just—"

"No, wait. Just let me explain." Kathryn bit her lip. "Just 'cause I don't remember something don't mean it didn't happen. I've gone over this thing a million times, and if you're really pregnant—" He paused, as if he needed her confirmation before going on.

"Yes," she said, holding back a sob. She still hadn't gotten her period and it had been two months now.

"Well, then, it must be like you say. You've never lied to me about anything before. I believe you, Kate. Whether or not I remember it happening doesn't matter." Kathryn's eyes burned with fresh tears. She knew he was a good man. She just knew it.

"Thank you," she said—so low she wasn't sure if he heard her.

"And I want you to know something else. Everything is going to be alright here. For you and the baby both." She could picture him on the other end: holding the base of the phone against his hip, dragging the cord with him as he paced back and forth in front of the curio cabinet in his bedroom—filled with all those track trophies he had accumulated in high school. "I don't have a whole lot, Kate. But what I have is yours. And the baby's. It's all ours, from here on out. You hear me?"

"I hear you," she said. She lay back in her bed, placing a careful hand across her belly. Sammy had gone silent now, but she knew he was still there. He was working up to something.

"Kate?" he said finally, a wobble in his voice. "I think we should get married." She closed her eyes, listened to the fall of frozen chestnuts from the tree beyond her frosted window.

"Okay," she said softly.

54

In the middle of a rented room at the Riverview Motel, Jack stood in just his white briefs with his camera strapped around his neck. Caleb Croxton was reposed on the bed, his sweat-slick chest awash in the daylight seeping in from under the pulled curtain.

"C'mon, now," said Caleb, grabbing his menthols from the bedside table. "We've talked about this." But Jack couldn't help it—he went on, adjusting the shutter speed, snapping picture after picture. It happened every time after they were together: a fleeting moment where Caleb wore his soul on the outside—a quiet sadness in his distant stare, desperation folded into the worry lines that creased his forehead. "I'm serious now. Cut that out."

"Just one more," said Jack, taking the shot. He eased the camera onto the nightstand and then slipped the cigarette from Caleb's fingers, and said. "Don't mind if I do." He took a slow drag, savoring the taste, the view, the thrill of being here in this seedy motel with a married man at one o'clock in the afternoon.

"You've got a whole damn pack of smokes over there in your

jeans, and here you are stealing one of mine." Caleb made a playful swipe at the cigarette, but then settled back onto the pillow, watching Jack, studying his lips, his fingers.

"This one tastes better." Jack crawled atop the bed, straddling Caleb's naked body. He leaned down, his lips hovering inches away from Caleb's.

"Well, don't be a tease about it," said Caleb. He moved up for a kiss, but Jack held him down. That was something Caleb liked—to be toyed with, told what to do. Jack had learned this over these past few months. And something else: if he withheld himself just enough, he could unearth a desire in Caleb Croxton as deep and dark as the bituminous coal from the mine under those Western Kentucky hills.

"One condition," said Jack, tasting the shared breath between them.

"Look here," said Caleb. "I already got what I came for. You need to learn how to negotiate." They traded smiles, but then the moment lingered, and Jack felt the pressure. It was now or never, so he figured he'd better get on with it.

"Come with me to New York," he said. Caleb snickered.

"Real funny," he said. "That's rich."

"I'm serious. My aunt wants me to move to the city. She thinks I could have a future there with my art." He'd been putting Aunt Peggy off for months, figuring there was no way he could leave Kentucky now that he'd found this new world with Caleb Croxton. The two of them had been sneaking off together two or three times a week for a while now, growing desperate, impatient. He couldn't help but wonder: What if he didn't have to choose? What if he could have every little thing he'd always wanted in this life?

"Your *art*?" said Caleb, his lips upturning into a wry half smile.

"You know what I mean—my photographs." Jack lifted himself from Caleb's chest. "Aunt Peggy says there could be a life for me up there." Caleb pulled another cigarette from the pack, losing interest in the one Jack still had clenched between his fingers.

"Well, as long as Aunt Peggy thinks so." He lit the cigarette, burned through a quarter of it in one pull. Standing there next to the bed, the light from under the shade cutting across his bare legs, Jack suddenly felt exposed. He grabbed his jeans from where he had draped them across the sitting chair in the corner, tugged them on.

"Don't be like that," he said.

"I'm being the only way I know how to be," said Caleb. "Don't fool yourself, Jack."

"What's that supposed to mean?" Jack hurried to get his belt buckled, feeling the burn of Caleb's stare.

"Maybe you need to be reminded what this thing is between you and me. And what it's not." Jack glanced at the radial clock on the nightstand just long enough to realize he was going to be late getting back over to the garage.

"I know what this is," he said, pulling on his shirt. "Don't you worry yourself about that."

"I'm not sure you do. Else you wouldn't have asked me such a ridiculous question." Jack stepped into his boots and fastened his watch.

"You can't blame me for thinking about the future," he said, easing onto the edge of the bed. "About how things could be for us." He reached to touch Caleb's naked thigh, but the man slapped his hand away, put a finger right in Jack's face.

"You're just a damn naive kid," said Caleb, letting out a humorless laugh. Jack flexed his hand, feeling the sting.

"Maybe so," he said, grabbing his wallet from the table. "But at least I'm not a coward." When he turned to leave, Caleb sprang up from the bed like a rattlesnake coming out of coil. He grabbed Jack by the wrist.

"A coward?" he said. "That's what you think I am?"

"Look, if you could just see—"

"The world don't like people like me and you, Jack," snapped Caleb. "Don't matter if it's in New York City or *Middle-of-nowhere*, Kentucky." He released Jack's arm, settled back onto the bed. "I'm a married man with a beautiful baby boy. It don't take courage to run away from that. It takes courage to stay."

Jack was turning the knob when Caleb said: "Jack? I'll call you tomorrow."

"Okay, then," said Jack. He cracked the door just enough to make sure nobody was around, and then he stepped out into the blinding daylight.

When Jack arrived back at the garage, Kate Fairchild was sitting on the porch swing of the Clark farmhouse. He checked his watch. Seeing as he was already a half hour late, he figured five more minutes couldn't hurt. He pulled his truck through the gravel drive, sending a cloud of dust into the air toward Kate.

"You haven't even tried to talk me out of it," she said.

"What's that, now?" He sat next to her on the swing, so close together their elbows were touching.

"The baby. Getting married to Sammy Sawyer." She kicked off the porch with her bare feet just hard enough to set them in motion. "Aren't you going to tell me it's a mistake?"

"Is it a mistake?" he said. "I reckon you're a better judge of that than I am." She dragged her foot against the porch, bringing them to a stop. She turned to him, tucking her knees to her chest.

"I never dreamed in a million years my life would go this way, Jack," she said. "But Sammy—he's an okay guy. He's sweet enough. He'll take good care of me."

"Well, that don't sound half bad to me." Kate tilted her head, smiled the saddest smile Jack had ever seen. He moved to grab his camera, but then thought better of it.

"Don't you see, Jack?" she said. "It was always supposed to be you." She leaned in close to his face, her lips inches from his own. He thought she might try to kiss him again. Right there in that moment, still reeling from the stuff Caleb Croxton had said back in the motel, he thought he just might let her do it. But then she pulled away at the last moment.

"But this here changes everything," she said, cupping her little baby bump between her hands, gazing down at it like she could see through her dress and skin, straight through to the tiny human growing inside. "It's a wonder how something so small can feel so big." Jack had an impulse to comfort her, but he never was one to talk when he didn't know the right words. He kicked back against the porch to send them swinging again.

"Don't do it, Kate," he finally said. He wasn't completely sure he had said it out loud until she raised her head from his shoulder.

"You're just saying that now because—"

"No, I'm serious. Don't marry him unless you mean it. You can't take something like that back." He thought of Caleb Croxton standing up at the front of a church on his wedding day, looking at his bride, knowing.

"But the baby."

"I know," said Jack, though he wasn't sure he did. "But there are other options. You've got people here who love you, who will take care of you. Both of you."

"People?" she said.

"Well, yeah." He pictured Caleb back at the hotel now, stretched out on the bed, burning through cigarettes. "I love you, Kate. You know that." She smiled a pitiful smile.

"I need someone who's going to love me the right way. If nothing else, that's something Sammy can give me." Up in the big black oak tree overshadowing the porch, a pair of squirrels scurried across a bough. They looked so happy—relishing the fragrant spring air.

"Okay, then," said Jack. "But just do me one favor."

"What's that?"

"Make sure you can love him back."

55

The morning Sammy Sawyer tried to quit his job at the shoe store, Norman was running late. Edith had woken up in one of her low spells, and after trying to reason with her through the locked bedroom door for the better part of the morning, Norman gave up and called Clara.

"I'll call the doctor later today," he said into the telephone. "But I need someone to take care of the boy." Danny was content with a pile of Lincoln Logs on the living room floor, but that wouldn't last but another few minutes. "Clara?"

"I'm here," she said. "I'll send Kate." Norman leaned against the door frame, bracing himself with an open palm.

"I'd rather you didn't, Clara," he said.

"Well, that's what I'm offering. I've got things to do here. Kate's free as a bird." Kate had been staying with Clara and Ray ever since…ever since Norman found out. Three months later, he still hadn't told anyone other than family about the pregnancy. They still had time to figure this out—but that clock was ticking louder each day. He checked his watch. It was already going on ten o'clock. He gave it some thought, figured he didn't have much choice. And anyway, she'd only be out in the open as she walked from the car up to the house. Still—you just never could tell when Mrs. Eubank would be watching.

"Put her in a loose dress," he finally said.

"I won't be putting her in anything," said Clara. "She's a grown woman."

"Okay, then." He thwacked the phone on the base. "Okay, then," he said again, this time to himself.

When Norman walked into the showroom there at the store, George was sweeping the entryway.

"Quiet this morning," said Norman. He checked his watch again. Maybe he should've just stayed home after all.

"Yeah, looks like it," said George. Norman gave the man a hard look—really saw him for the first time in weeks. His hair was getting long now to where a stray curl hung down near his eyes. And something else: he looked greasy, unkempt. His forehead had a sheen to it like he'd decided to forego showers for the better part of a week.

"You've lost some weight," said Norman, thinking out loud. "Everything okay?"

"Me?" said George, looking up from the broom for the first time since Norman came in. "Oh, yeah. Shipshape." He smiled with his mouth, but not his eyes. "Anyway, you might want to go talk to the Sawyer boy."

Back in the repair room, Sammy was sitting at the workbench drinking a Coca-Cola.

"Good, you're here," he said, swiping some cracker crumbs off his pants just as soon as Norman walked through the door.

"Taking a break?" said Norman, hands on his hips. He glanced down at the Coke gripped in Sammy's hand just long enough to make sure the boy noticed.

"Well, no," said Sammy. "Just waiting for you to come in so I could tell you in person."

"What's that now?"

"I've gotta quit this job," said Sammy.

"Quit your job."

"That's right."

"Right before you marry my daughter." Sammy stood now, nearly a head taller than Norman. He screwed up his face like he was trying to solve a long division problem in his head.

"Didn't she tell you?" he said. "Kate's called it off."

"No, I don't believe that's right," said Norman, his words coming out before he even had a chance to think them over. "We've planned it all out. The two of you are getting married. And she'll have the baby. And you'll keep on working here and take over for me someday." Norman looked up to see George Caldwell standing in the door frame. The man looked downright ill.

"A baby?" said George, enunciating the word like it held magic.

"You back here hunting for a pair of shoes?" said Norman, swinging an arm wildly toward the boxes stacked along the wall.

"Well, no, I just—"

"Then I reckon this doesn't concern you." He closed his eyes and sucked a breath. He always seemed to lash out at George, and he wasn't quite sure why. He figured he better apologize, but by the time he opened his eyes again the man had disappeared.

"I'm telling you, Mr. Fairchild," said Sammy. "She called me up last night. Said she'd been wearing a wedding dress all day and just couldn't picture a future with me. Said she didn't love me like that." His chin got to quivering. Norman had to look away.

"Love?" he said. "What in God's name does love have to do

with anything?" He thought about Edith locked away in that room upstairs back on Poplar Street. Something black seeped through his chest, spreading like ink dripping into water. "You've got a duty here, Sam. You and Kathryn both." Something out in the hallway caught his eye—some movement, some shadow flitting across the wall just beyond the open door. He lowered his voice, leaned in toward the boy. He thought he might reach out and touch his shoulder, but no—that would be too much. "You'll learn to love each other. That's how this thing will have to work."

"I already love her with everything I am, sir," said Sammy, stuffing his hands in his pockets. "So I can't keep coming in here every day being reminded that she don't want me."

"Never mind that," said Norman. Kate was back there at the house right that very second—rocking the boy, making googly eyes, feeding him. He couldn't think about it too long or he got to feeling light-headed. "I'll talk to her," he said.

"All due respect, Mr. Fairchild," said Sammy, shifting his weight. "It can't be like that."

"Excuse me?"

"You know how Kate is," said Sammy, smiling now. "You telling her what to do is just going to send her running the other way."

"Well," said Norman, shrugging a little. He didn't have much more to say about that.

"She's something else," said Sammy.

"Yeah," said Norman. "She sure is." As they stood that way together, thinking about Kate, something occurred to Norman for the first time: it wouldn't be half-bad having Sammy Sawyer as a son-in-law.

56

An hour later, George Caldwell took an early lunch and drove out to the parsonage. He cranked down the window, letting the blossom of spring air overtake the cab of the truck. His mind was a mason jar filled with flies: thoughts racing every which way with no way to escape. The girl was pregnant. He needed to talk to Margot. But first, he had to stop at the church.

After unlocking the dead bolt and the doorknob to his church office, he tidied his belongings and folded up the little cot in the corner where he had been sleeping these past months. He gathered the shirts hanging from the windowsill, the dirty clothes stuffed in the bottom drawer of his desk. Before he left, he brushed his teeth and washed his face in the men's bathroom next to the sanctuary.

In the parsonage, Margot was running the sweeper in the nursery—a chore she completed with the regularity of a monk going to vespers, even if they presently had no use for the room. When George walked in, she stood the sweeper upright and smoothed her dress, regarding him as just another thing to be swept clean from the room. Brand-new lime-green curtains fluttered against the breeze from the open window.

"Those are nice," said George, even though he thought they clashed with the striped paint on the walls. Margot glanced at the curtains and then back at George—standing there with his hands full of clothes and knickknacks he'd been keeping at the church. "I want to come home, Margot," he said. As soon as the words were out, he wished he'd have said them differently. So much regret was balled up inside him he didn't quite know how to start untangling it.

"Your name is on the deed," said Margot. "Who am I to say you shouldn't live here?" She gave a little shrug, but a breath caught in her throat, giving her away. George unloaded his belongings onto the empty rocker in the corner.

"I've been awful these past few months," he said, coming to her, taking her hands from where they were still gripped around the sweeper. "But things can be different now."

"Different."

"That's right."

"And how is that?"

"Kate Fairchild—" said George. "She's pregnant." Margot looked at him, her face contorting as she processed the words.

"Kate Fairchild?" she stammered, shaking her head. "How did she— But who—"

"The Sawyer boy. I heard Norman talking to him about it this morning." He looked away, but only for a moment. "It must've been months ago now. They've been hiding Kate out there in the country at her aunt's place. Biding time until her and Sammy can get married."

"Yes, but—" Margot started, bracing herself against the railing of the crib. "What does any of this have to do with us?"

"Listen to me now," said George, going over it again in his head. What he said next had to be just perfect. He had one chance to get this right. He touched her cheek, her ear. She didn't pull away. "Kate's told the boy she can't marry him. That she doesn't love him. If we offer to take the baby, just think how much it would help her. This could be good for all of us." A shadow of memory loomed over George. *Thy wife shall be as a fruitful vine by the sides of thine house: thy children like olive plants round about thy table.* "This could be our answer, Margot." He lay his head in her lap like a child needing comfort from his mother. Margot relented, twirling a long curl of hair around her index finger.

"Oh, George," she said. "I'm so ashamed of what's happened to us over these last few months." A sob caught in her throat, but when George pulled back, she was smiling. "This is the path the Lord had for us all along. Can't you see?"

"Yes," said George, though he wasn't quite sure which part he was agreeing with. "The Lord works in mysterious ways." Margot fell into his arms, weeping. When she pulled away, she looked around the room in wonder—the yellow stripes on the wall, the cherry crib and matching chest. George knew she was picturing a future that was not yet written—its pages filled with secrets she could never know. "Yes," he said again. And then he worked the words into his mouth, the ones he had rehearsed all morning. "I've heard the still, small voice, Margot. This is the will of God."

57

And who was to say he was wrong? As far as George was concerned, the scriptures were clear on the point: *all things work together for good to them that love God, to them who are the called according to His purpose.* As many times as he'd gone over it—revisiting the murky memories of that Halloween night in his mind—he never could bring himself to feel entirely at fault.

Margot was the one who had taunted him. Complaining of a headache, she had stayed back at the parsonage, leaving him alone to chaperone the youth at the fall festival at the church. Once the last teens had cleared out, George walked through the ice-slick parking lot and into the parsonage to find her sitting there in the middle of the living room floor—dressed up like some schoolgirl from a peepshow fantasy.

"What are you doing?" he had said, regarding her babydoll slip, her knee-high stockings. An empty wine bottle lay on the coffee table beside her.

"Thought you might like a surprise." Margot lumbered half-way to her feet. After a moment of valiant effort, she lay back down on the carpet, letting the slip ride up her exposed upper thighs.

"You're embarrassing yourself," said George, looking away. "Get up and go put yourself together." But the woman did no such thing. Instead, she undulated her body against the carpet like a dog tending to an itch.

"What do you see when you look at me, George?" She raised her bottom into the air now, angling herself on all fours. The dry skin of George's lip pulled against his front teeth.

"You're my wife, Margot," he said, but she ignored him. Her eyes were closed. She was there and not there—transported to some quiet fold of memory he could reach for but never quite touch.

"A broken body," she said. "That's what you see. Admit it."

"Listen to me—"

"You haven't made love to me in two months." Margot gripped the ledge of the coffee table and pulled herself up, standing on wobbly legs like a newborn calf. She tilted her head to the side like something had dawned on her for the first time.

"Let's get you cleaned up." He took her by the crook of the arm, but she pulled away.

"I've never been enough for you, have I?" she said, floating her wine-soaked breath across his face. "Admit it."

"That's enough!" said George. His hands pulsed at his sides. Never in his life had he struck a woman. Odd that he should think of that now.

"Oh, George," said Margot, collapsing to her knees before him. "Oh, George. What's happened to us?" Shaking with grief, she opened her mouth for a wail that refused to emerge.

He could have held her right then, comforted her. He could have apologized—for all the nights he had left her alone, all the time he spent retreating into himself. But the shame that had cocooned his reason for years had trapped him again. If he couldn't give Margot a child, he could give her nothing. The packed suitcases tucked away on her side of the closet—he had seen them. This was the fulcrum of their marriage.

Without saying a word, he left her there on the carpet in the middle of the living room floor, crying, moaning. He drove out into the black night, flicking his windshield wipers against the plink of sleet. The church was no refuge for him now—it would consume him whole like the great fish had swallowed Jonah. So he kept right on driving down the pinball curves of River Road, taking pulls from a bottle of lukewarm whiskey, feeling like Adam hiding from God after eating the fruit in the Garden of Eden. By the time he made it into downtown Gray Station, powdery snow was sifting into drifts along the sidewalks and medians. With blue moonlight refracting brilliantly against the crystalline glaze, Main Street glowed as if it were midday.

That was when he saw them—Kathryn Fairchild and the Sawyer boy, dancing through the empty street. He didn't recognize Sammy at first—but the girl, he'd know her anywhere. Her fire-flame hair twirled around her as she lifted herself *en pointe*, a ballerina, spinning, floating. Nowhere to go, he parked the car a block away under the cover of a magnolia tree.

And then he watched. They passed a bottle between them, sucking the liquor down, stumbling, laughing. Kate put a hand to her chest only once, fighting through the burn. But then she tilted the bottle to her lips again and again. The cab of the truck was getting cold, the windshield frosting, Kate Fairchild's slender figure blurred in the distance like an unfocused photograph. He thought about cranking the engine, but no—that would only attract attention. He liked watching from the shadows.

Ten minutes later, the snow was really blowing in. Nearly out of sight, Kate and Sammy traversed the bank down by the river. When George felt like they were far enough away not to hear the creak of the door, he pushed himself out of the truck.

A pervasive stillness hovered in the air, the snow dampening the noise as if the ground was covered in cotton. He trailed behind the teens, watched them skip rocks, along the river's edge, laugh, hold each other, even kiss. A bulge of desire swelled inside him, lodging itself just below his thrumming heart.

(How long did he stay that way, watching, waiting? How many times did he tell himself to get back to the truck and go home to Margot? Vicissitudes of memory—lapping against the soul like the murky water of the Ohio.)

But then she was clambering up on the bridge, stumbling, clinging to the frozen steel arches with her bare hands. Sammy was behind her, barely off the access ladder, hugging the deck like a comfort blanket. George didn't call her name. He didn't wave her down. She leaned her body out over the water, even stretching one arm into the icy wind.

And what would he do if she fell? Watch her lifeless body swallowed by the black water? Would he tell anyone he was there? No—that didn't seem likely. He had never been that kind of man.

Immobile, George watched Sammy coax Kathryn down off the bridge. Then he wiped the snow from his windshield and tucked himself back into the truck, out of view. He blew a hot breath into his purpled hands, gave them a shake to get the blood flowing. Checking his watch, he saw that it was going on eleven o'clock.

(In the recesses of his fantasy life—the simulacrum of his existence that he would believe real in due time, even conjure in memory—this was the exact moment he decided to drive back to the parsonage. This was when he started the journey that would have him finding Margot soaking in the bath, trying to sober up. This was when he joined her, whispering *I'm sorry I'm sorry I'm sorry*, pulling her into the bedroom and making love to her for the sake of the act itself, never mind the hope of a child. All this happened and nothing else.)

But in the real world, he sat stoically in the truck, rubbing his hands together to create friction, watching Sammy Sawyer unlock the front door of the shoe store. The boy guided Kathryn Fairchild through the door and into the dark showroom, a leading hand against the small of her back. George looked at his own hands, red, tingling with sensation, almost as if he had been the one touching the girl. For five minutes he waited there in the cold cab, breathing in and out, waiting for something—but what? Some mimeograph of human connection—some way for him to have what Sammy and Kathryn had, a light touch, an ease. He closed his eyes, trying to remember: a life uncomplicated by marriage, unhindered by the desperate need to have a child. The whiskey ate his words, his reason. All that remained was some unnamed yearning, something he couldn't speak but could feel, the drumbeat of sin, pounding and pulsing.

When Sammy Sawyer emerged back into the cold night, he was alone, no longer wearing his jacket. George watched him walk in the opposite direction to his car. The boy scraped the windshield clear of snow, and then he was off, making fresh tire tracks down Main Street and out of downtown. George reached for the keys in his pocket, the metal still cold from when he had been outside. The key to the truck sat snuggly against the key to the shoe store. There was a right choice and a wrong choice—he knew this. But by the time he figured out which was which, he was already out of the truck, crunching through the ankle-high snow.

Cold blue light refracted from the ice outside, allowed George to see, however faintly, clear through the showroom back to the cash register. The room was empty. He took two steps forward and then thought better of it, turning around, flipping the dead bolt with a satisfying *thunk*. He gave the world outside one final look. The street was desolate.

"Kate?" he said. "Kate, are you there?" If she answered, he figured it was all the better. He was only checking on her after all. It was the decent thing to do.

But she didn't answer. So he pressed on, feeling through the dark hallway behind the register, his soft footfalls against the tile floor measured and precise. He ran a finger on the wall next to him as the light died away, guiding himself to the closed door of the repair room—a barrier he had to push through, a choice.

Inside, all was pitch-black. He heard the rustling of clothes against the floor in the corner of the room. The light switch was on the wall, inches from his hand. He knew this, but he wasn't ready for the light, not yet. Perhaps it would be seen outside. Why did this matter?

"Kate?" he said, nearly a whisper. He was there to check on her, to protect her. Nodding in affirmation to the thought, he pressed on, listening. The labored exhalation of his own breath. The stick of saliva caked at the corners of his mouth. Nothing else. He edged his way forward—hands held out in front of him like Frankenstein's monster. When he bumped the corner of Norman's workbench, he remembered the flashlight tucked away in the top drawer. Light he could control—a beam in one direction. Gripping the handle, he pulled, the scrape of the metal drawer screeching against the frame.

He froze. The girl stirred, but she said nothing.

His searching hand found the flashlight, and then with a click, he saw her illuminated there in the warm amber light, her body curled atop a pallet of old blankets, covered with stray fabric and Sammy Sawyer's jacket. She raised her head, shielding herself from the light, a hand to her eyes.

"Sammy, you're back," she said, drawling out her words, the liquor exaggerating her accent. George kept the flashlight at eye level, his body hidden in the cloak of darkness cast behind the light. "Come over here," she said, flopping her free hand beside her on the pallet once, twice. "Come keep me warm." She laughed aloud—maybe remembering some joke George had never heard. She wasn't talking to him.

"Kathryn," he said. His voice sounded distant, strange, as if it belonged to someone else. The girl seemed to think so, too. She thwacked the pallet beside her again, pulled her feet toward her bottom, raising her knees into the air.

"You've wanted this for so long," she said, slurring. A hole of desire ripped through George. He tried to pray it away, but that was no use.

"What do you want?" he said, not sure what she was saying.

"I know you've always wanted me."

But surely she recognized him now? Surely she knew that Sammy was gone? "Kate—is this what you want?" He wasn't trying to conceal his voice now. She could tell him to leave, and that would put an end to all this. But then—

"Yes," said Kathryn. One word, everything and nothing. George thought of Margot back home, taunting him, scolding him. And he turned back, clicking off the flashlight.

PART FIVE:

WOMAN SAVES CHILD

58

"You didn't do it?" says Myra. I can picture her back at our apartment in Crown Heights leaning on the balcony rail, her morning coffee steaming into the October wind.

"I know I should've told you," I say. "But I had to decide this on my own."

"Jules—you know I'm on your side."

"I know, but—"

"But what?"

"You think I'm making the wrong choice, right?"

"I *know* you're making the wrong choice."

"And that's why I didn't say anything. I don't want you to try talking me out of this, Myra." I sit near my gate at JFK, waiting for my seven o'clock flight back to Kentucky. It's been two days since I saw Aster's private gallery. Every time I close my eyes, I see Kathryn Fairchild looking back at me. There's something hauntingly familiar about her—the almond dip of her eyes, the curve of her upper lip. Viewing those photographs made her real. I am part of her world now. She is part of mine.

"You can't wait much longer, Jules," says Myra.

I suck in a mouthful of air and force myself to say it: "I want to keep the baby." I clench my eyes, imagining the look Myra is giving me through the phone. She lets the line go silent. "Myra? Are you there?"

"I'm here, babe," she says. Then, more silence.

"I know you think it's a bad idea. And you're probably right. But the truth is, I only decided to have the abortion after I saw Ryan in the bar. It was based on raw emotion."

"Either way, it was the right choice."

"Maybe. Probably. But I just keep thinking that—I don't know. It feels like the decision was more about Ryan than it was about me or the baby. And he already thinks he can—" I stop, choking down an unexpected sob. "It's just, I don't want him to have that kind of power over me. This is my choice, not his."

"I get that," says Myra. "But, like—let's think this through. Are you ready to raise a real live human being on your own? There's no trial period here, Jules. No return policy if you don't like it. And don't you want to get your career started first?"

"Come on, Myra. Don't give me that false choice bullshit. My mom didn't have to choose. She raised me on her own. Got three degrees in the process. Landed her dream job at Vassar."

"Yeah, and that's an amazing story. But your mom had it all planned out. I mean, she went to a sperm bank. That's not exactly the same thing as making a rash decision to—"

"Jesus, Myra—I'm not making a rash decision." I surprise myself by the anger in my voice. I take a deep breath. "It's not like I've committed to anything here. That's the whole point, right? I'm giving myself more time to choose. Isn't that a good thing?"

"Maybe. But you're getting close to the second trimester. The longer you wait—"

"I know," I say. *Your baby is the size of a strawberry. She now has fingernails.*

"And I know you don't want to talk about it, but—"

"Myra, don't."

"You really need to tell his wife," she says. "You can't let him get away with this. In his own words, he has a *responsibility* here."

"I know. But I'd have to tell him first, I'd have to at least try to get him to understand the situation, give him the chance to do the right thing. I mean—they have a kid, Myra. What if I'm just doing more harm than good?"

"Oh my God—Jules, you can't be serious. He's in your head, babe."

"Yeah, but—"

"I mean, we can't even be sure Ryan *really* has a kid at all, can we? He lies about literally everything."

"Oh, c'mon. You don't think he would—"

"I do," she says. "I absolutely do." I close my eyes, seeing the little boy in Ryan's photograph. I can't stop thinking about him. My baby's half brother—if he exists.

"I have to go," I say. "I'll call you when I get there."

When I knock on the front door of the Little Yellow House on the River, I have the oddest sensation that I've returned home to some other life—like I've existed forever in parallel universes, and my two selves are just now intersecting. I smile when Quinn opens the door. I've genuinely missed her. Unfortunately, the feeling doesn't seem to be mutual.

"Sign here," she says, plunking an ink pen on the guest registry. She leaves the door wide-open, flips her purple-tipped hair in my face as she walks away.

"Well, *hello* to you, too." I lug my suitcase into the foyer, kicking the door closed behind me. The scent of snickerdoodles wafts through the air.

"Whatever," she says. She plops down on the couch in the adjacent parlor. I swoosh my signature across the page.

"Okay—did I miss something here? You seem really pissed."

She lifts a throw pillow from the couch, looks at me like she might chuck it at my face.

"You just left without even saying goodbye or anything," she says. "Not cool, bro." I walk into the parlor, sit on the edge of the couch. A billion excuses run through my mind. But I know none of them would matter as much as a simple apology.

"I'm sorry," I say. "It was a crappy thing to do. You didn't deserve it." She stares at the TV, completely uninterested in anything I have to say. I open my arms, lean forward.

"Dude—what are you doing?"

"I thought I'd give you a hug," I say. "I mean, we just had a nineties sitcom moment, so—"

"I still hate you and I don't forgive you," she says. I can't tell if she's being serious or deadpan. I'm not even entirely certain she knows herself.

"Fair enough," I say, giving her knee a playful slap. "But if you change your mind on that hug, you know where to find me." I grab my suitcase, make my way toward the stairs.

"There's an envelope in your room," says Quinn, never looking at me. "Something Kyle Sawyer dropped off for you a few days ago."

Up in my room, I put away my clothes in the dresser, then open the manila envelope marked with my name. Inside, I find a photocopy of an old article from the *Gray Station Gazette* with a sticky note attached to the front: *Found this in a box of my dad's old keepsakes. He didn't want to talk about it, but I figured it might be useful. Happened right around the time Kate Fairchild died.—K.S.*

Above the article is a striking photograph: a church building engulfed in fire, flames licking from the windows upward toward the steeple. The date printed on the paper is July 10, 1964—less than a week after Kate Fairchild died.

Church Fire Apparent Suicide, Police Say
By Edward Culver

GRAY STATION—A fire at Riverside Baptist Church has claimed the life of a local pastor, Reverend George Caldwell, who was found dead in his church office after the flames were extinguished.

The fire was started in the late evening hours on July 9 and was extinguished in the early morning hours of July 10. According to local authorities, the incident is suspected to be an act of arson. "There is clear evidence of an accelerant," said Fire Chief Rob Glintmore, noting the presence of an empty gasoline can recovered from the scene.

The matter is also being investigated as an apparent suicide. According to a statement released from the sheriff's office, the point of origin for the fire was in the church office, the same location where the pastor's body was found. Furthermore, according to Police Chief Larry Reynolds, "There is no evidence that anyone else was at the scene of the fire."

I read the article twice through, trying to figure out how it could be related to Kathryn Fairchild. Maybe she was a member of the church? I'm not sure what to do with the information just yet, but it feels like a lead I should follow.

First things first: I sink my head into the feather-soft pillow of this now-familiar room, in this now-familiar Kentucky town. I will myself into the ecstasy of sleep—the only place I can escape the incessant worry about the life growing inside me.

59

1964

Caleb Croxton hadn't called for an entire week. Jack didn't think much of it the first two days, but soon thereafter he got to where he could think of nothing else. They'd worked out a scheme when they started this thing months ago—Caleb would call on Jack's lunch break, letting the phone ring once if they could meet up, twice if they couldn't. After the talk of New York back in the motel, Jack figured he might get a few two-ring days while Caleb gathered his thoughts. He didn't blame him for that. But the phone didn't ring at all that first day, then the second. A full week later, the silence was palpable—like seeing a flash of lightning beyond the hills and waiting for a clap of thunder that never came.

It wouldn't hurt to take a quick drive down Highway 41 to Caleb's trailer. Jack wasn't allowed to call on account of the wife—she was nearly always home. (Yes, she had a name, Sharon, but Jack didn't like to think about this too much.) On the first pass by the gravel driveway, he didn't even slow down—keeping his head forward as he drove by as not to raise suspicion if the woman happened to be outside. He stole a glance as he approached, eyeing her tan Buick Electra parked right where it always was on the left side of the trailer. With the car facing the road like it was, the headlights and grill made a face at Jack as he passed, watching, judging. He drove on, turning around at the Johnson pick-and-pull lot two miles down the road. He had a cigarette on his way back, blowing the smoke through his cracked window.

And then he went again—three times, four, five—retracing the same stretch of road, past the same trailer, staring down the same Buick Electra. Before he knew it, his lunch break was over. He'd eaten nothing but smoke from a half dozen cigarettes, but he wasn't hungry.

After work, he was back at it. But this time, the Buick Electra was gone—replaced by that familiar blue Ranchero he'd come to love. So Caleb was alone there in the trailer. Jack idled his truck right in the middle of the highway, debating with himself. Maybe he should just drive back home, call the man on the telephone. Couldn't be any harm in it—Caleb was the only one home to answer. Surely he wouldn't take exception to a thing like that. Jack checked the rearview mirror for cars, the highway stretching out behind him, disappearing around a bend in the road some two miles back.

Then again, if he wasn't going to go through with it, what was the point of all this driving he'd been doing? Kate was always going on about how he couldn't make any decisions. He thought about this for a second or two, and then he cut the wheel hard to the right, pulled in behind Caleb's Ranchero, nearly kissing the back bumper. He swung himself from the truck before he had time to second-guess himself, sending the hinges squealing as he shut the door. Running a hand through his oily hair, he gave himself a once-over in the reflection of the truck's window. God, he looked awful. His three-day beard was wiry, uneven—like someone ripped out a swatch of pubic hair and glued it to his face. He brushed a hand against his filthy coveralls, as if it would make a difference.

"Can I help you?" called a voice from behind. Jack turned to see Sharon Croxton standing in the open front door of the trailer, wrangling the baby boy in her arms like a slippery football. Jack opened his mouth to speak, but—what was there to say? He peered back inside his truck as if the answer was sitting behind the wheel. "You looking for Caleb?" she said.

"Caleb?" echoed Jack, sounding like a damn parrot.

"Caleb Croxton. My husband." The baby had a handful of the woman's hair. In some other life, it might've made for a good photograph. Jack swallowed hard.

"Caleb Croxton," he said, screwing up his face like he was thinking on the name. "I think that might be right." He scratched the underside of his chin.

"About the car?"

"Yes, that's right," he said. The woman was looking at his coveralls now. This could work. "Is it this one here?" he said, gesturing to the Ranchero.

"Well, no. The Buick. Caleb took off with it an hour or so ago. Said he needed to see somebody about a—well, something or other." She flipped a hand through the air.

"I see," said Jack. Sharon cocked her head to the side, made a face.

"You look awfully familiar. Have I seen you around?" Jack's tongue stuck against the roof of his mouth.

"No, I don't think—" He made a strange little gesture over his shoulder. "Well, I work just up the road there. Over at the Clark garage." He looked down at his coveralls like they were some sort of explanation.

"Huh, that's funny."

"How's that?"

"Well, it's just that—don't take this the wrong way," she

said, shifting the baby to the other hip. "Caleb said he didn't do business with the Clark place anymore."

"Oh?"

"Something about one of the guys over there. Said he didn't get a good feeling about him." Jack must've looked as hurt as he felt, as the woman was quick to add: "I think he must've meant the old man. Ray, I think."

"Well, I best be getting on," said Jack. "I'll give him a call in a bit—your husband." Why did he feel the need to add those two words? He reached for the door handle of the truck but missed.

"Hold on now. He should be back any minute." That was precisely what Jack was afraid of. He turned to the truck, but it was too late: he could already hear the Electra pulling around the bend in the road.

Caleb stopped the Buick twenty yards before the driveway, looking at Jack and Sharon standing there chatting outside the house like old friends.

"What on earth are you doing?" said Sharon, mouthing the words for Jack's benefit, as Caleb was too far off to hear. She waved him in with her arms, laughing. "He looks like he's seen a ghost."

"I shouldn't have come out like this," said Jack. "I should've just called." Caleb pulled forward, keeping his gaze fixed straight ahead as he drove past Jack. He parked next to the Ranchero. The baby put a hand to his mouth, rubbing his stubby fingers against his pink gums.

"That's right," said the woman, cooing at the child. "Daddy's home. Say *Da-da*? Say *Da-da*?" Jack felt the prickle of sweat on the back of his neck. Caleb pulled himself from the Ranchero, looked back at Jack to get a gauge on the situation.

"Mr. Croxton?" said Jack, giving a little wave. He tried to smile, but his face felt like it couldn't move right. Caleb said nothing—turning his attention to his wife and then back to Jack, still trying to get his bearings.

"He's from the Clark garage," said Sharon.

"You called about the car?" added Jack quickly. A little pretext couldn't hurt. The baby giggled, a globule of drool clinging to his bottom lip.

"Honey, why don't you take the boy inside," said Caleb, never even turning around. He narrowed his eyes at Jack. "Let us get this car situation squared away and I'll be right in." Jack watched the woman—the sink of her shoulders, the downturned face. She was used to being dismissed. A sharp pain lodged itself in Jack's chest, right under his heart. As soon as Sharon disappeared into the trailer, Jack went into damage control.

"Look, I didn't mean—"

"The hell do you think you're doing?" snapped Caleb. He took three big steps forward, boot prints sinking into the gravel. Jack put his hands in front of him. He'd been walloped upside the head by his old man more times than he could count. He knew the look of a man just before it happened.

"Please, just listen to me," started Jack, but Caleb warned him off, holding up a single finger. The man looked over his shoulder at the lighted front window of the trailer. Inside, at the edge of the pulled curtain, Sharon stood with the baby, watching.

"You've come into my real world, Jack." When he turned back around, Caleb's eyes were glassy. The anger was gone—replaced by that more primal emotion: fear. "Can't you see what you've done?" Jack wanted to move closer, but he didn't think that was something he ought to do.

"We can fix this. We've got a story here. I came to see about your car—that's it." Caleb shook his head.

"You're going to come over here and shake my hand," he said. "Then you're going to get in that truck of yours, and you're never going to come back."

"Well, let's just think about this."

"There's nothing to think about. I'll figure out what to tell my wife. But that's going to be it." Jack fiddled with his truck keys. Anything to delay.

"Okay. You can give me a call when this settles down."

"No, you don't understand," said Caleb. "This is the end of it. All of it."

"You can't mean that."

"Come over here and shake my hand," said Caleb. "And then get the hell out of my life."

60

I call Kyle Sawyer's cell phone once more with the same result as the previous six times: straight to voicemail. He's probably passed out drunk in an alley somewhere. And then he's going to wake up and see a bazillion missed calls from me. I fire off a quick text just so he won't get the wrong idea: sorry for blowing up your phone. Just trying to get your thoughts on this crazy church fire story.

Just as I hit Send, my phone buzzes in my hand. It's some random number, but the Gray Station area code gives me just enough courage to do something I haven't done in my entire life: answer an unknown call.

"Hello?" I say, as if answering a question.

"Yeah, I'm trying to reach, uh—Ms. White."

"I'm pretty sure that's me," I say, though I genuinely don't remember ever being called "Ms." anything in my life. The line goes quiet for a moment. The caller clears his voice, raspy and dry—like he's ten cigarettes into a two-pack-a-day habit.

"Okay, yeah. Well, this is Daniel Clark." I expect him to go on, but he doesn't.

"Um, okay?" I literally can't think of anything else to say.

"You left a note on my front door. Wanted to talk about

some project." I wrack my brain trying to think of who this guy could possibly be, but I come up with nothing.

"I'm sorry," I say. "I just can't quite place who you are."

"Well, I'm Daniel Clark."

"Yeah, I heard that the first time. It's just—"

"Kate Fairchild's brother."

Thirty minutes later, I'm standing in the gravel lot outside of Clark and Son Auto Repair at the edge of the county line. Danny Clark looms in front of the first bay of the garage in grease-streaked coveralls. His body belies his age—sharp and sinewy, a testament to a life of physical labor.

"Okay, then," he says, cigarette dangling from his bottom lip. He glances at his watch, cocks an eyebrow. He looks like a man who wants nothing more than to get back into the garage and rip the guts from a car, so I get right to it.

"I'm doing some research on Kathryn Fairchild. Writing a book about what happened to her in 1964."

"Yeah, I've heard," he says. "What do you want with me?"

"Well, I can't know Kate's full story without speaking to you."

"And why is that, now?"

"You're her brother," I say, as if no other explanation is needed.

"In a manner of speaking."

"What does that mean? You're either her brother or you're not." Danny wipes his filthy hands on an equally filthy rag. It's not clear which way the grease is being transferred.

"Ma'am, I've not been a Fairchild since I was adopted out to Clara and Raymond Clark in 1964. Kathryn jumped from that bridge when I wasn't even two years old. So, yes—I'm her brother. In a manner of speaking." I want to spout off some cliché about blood being thicker than water because I think he might relate. But I think about the baby growing inside me.

Ryan Alman is the father—*in a manner of speaking*. I decide not to press the issue any further.

"Okay," I say. "I suppose you don't have much to add for me, then."

"I didn't say that," says Danny. "Look, I didn't know my sister. But I grew up under her cloud all the same. She was always around—pulling at the edge of my aunt Clara's voice. I saw her in my mother's blank stare every time I went down to the hospital for a visit. I felt her in the way my old man couldn't ever look me in the eye when we'd visit for holidays. You don't have to know a person to *know* a person." I open my mouth to speak, but I find that I've lost my voice. I remember what my mom used to say about a painting—that they can be studied with not only the eyes, but with the soul—a portal through time, a conversation with all who have looked before, a shared experience with the dead painter themselves.

"I understand exactly what you mean," I manage to say. "I wonder if you can share any particular memories about how Kathryn shaped your own life. Or maybe you have some keepsakes from her past that might be helpful for me to see."

"I might," says Danny. "But you'll forgive me if I'm not sure how much I want to share with you." He flicks his spent cigarette onto the gravel, smashes it like a pesky bug underfoot.

"Don't you want your sister's story to be told?"

"Sure I do," he says. "I just need to know you're the right person to tell it."

"Okay. How can I prove myself to you?"

"Let me think on it," he says, "and maybe I'll give you a call."

61

Kathryn walked beside her mother along the perimeter of Town Square Park, pushing Danny in the baby carriage. Same as ever, the people of Gray Station gawked at them as they passed on the sidewalk—the crazy Fairchild woman and her unwed, pregnant daughter. But Kate had made the conscious decision that such things could no longer bother her. She had called off the wedding with Sammy Sawyer a month before, and she refused to hide herself away out in the country at Aunt Clara's place. These choices had consequences—she knew this. But she also knew her choices weren't only about where she lived or whom she would marry. She was choosing a whole new life, replete with possibility, raw and beautiful and terrifying. In less than three months, she would bring a baby into this world. That wasn't the same thing as being a mother—she was careful to make that distinction. She had started thinking about adoption. That was what her parents wanted her to do. Sammy, too. She wasn't ready to decide just yet, but she'd promised to give it some thought.

"Kate?" said a voice from behind—one that Kathryn recognized immediately. She and Edith turned in unison, finding Margot Caldwell standing an arm's length away, her hands clasped behind her canary yellow sundress like she was palming some secret. Kathryn hadn't spoken with the woman in months. She could still see Margot sitting in the little memorial garden at the parsonage, desperate, defeated. But here in the park, standing in the muted glow of the overcast spring sky, she looked like her old self: striking, confident, like an image of Audrey Hepburn ripped from the cover of *Elle* magazine.

"Well, Margot Caldwell!" said Edith, reaching forward, gripping the woman's hands. Kathryn allowed space for her mother. This was the way she put people at ease—feigned enthusiasm, forced eye contact, physical touch—compensating for whatever impression she had to overcome. Kate was starting to learn these techniques, too. Edith's episodes had been far less frequent, and she'd been out of the hospital for going on a year. Still—people had their ideas.

"You're a hard woman to track down," said Margot, speaking to Kate, ignoring Edith like she was nothing but an obstacle to maneuver around. Kathryn remained silent, unsure as to whether Margot Caldwell was worth the expenditure of her effort.

"Well, she's been off visiting her aunt Clara," said Edith. She feigned a smile, but it wasn't clear whether Margot noticed. The woman's eyes fixed on Kate's belly—her facial expression caught in the liminal space between hope and despair. Kathryn had an impulse to cover herself up, but she fought it. She stepped from behind the carriage, flipped her cardigan open, putting herself on display—for Margot, for anyone else who cared to look.

"Is there something I can help you with?" said Kate. Margot faltered, unsure what to say—or maybe how to say it. The burbling water of the park fountain pushed away the silence. Some other time, it might've been nice to just sit there on the grass next to the fountain, look up at the passing cotton-candy clouds.

"I wonder if we could go find somewhere quiet and have a little talk," said Margot. "Just the two of us." Kathryn shifted on her feet, feeling the weight of her growing baby.

"Seems quiet enough right here," she said. "And anything you have to say to me, you can say in front of my mother." Margot crossed her arms and then uncrossed them, figuring out the right way to stand.

"You know George and I—" She paused, her breath catching her throat. "We just think so much of the two of you. And Norman, too. You Fairchilds—you all have really been like family to us over the years." A friendly gust of wind swirled around them, setting Margot's black curls to tickling her cheeks. She didn't bother to push them behind her ears.

"Isn't that nice—" started Edith, trying to fill the void of silence that bubbled up between them. Kathryn put a gentle hand at her elbow, shook her head.

"Let's let Margot finish, Momma," said Kathryn. "Seems like she's got quite a bit to say." And the truth was—whatever it was, Kate wanted to hear it. For a while there it seemed the Caldwells wanted more from her than she could give. Margot seemed to think Kate could be a part of fixing her marriage. George wanted to put the pressure of God on her—his calling, his *still, small voice*. It wasn't the only reason, but the whole business with George and Margot had helped to send her spiraling down all these months.

"Well, I suppose I'll just say it." She took off her kid gloves, folding them in her hands. "I want to adopt this baby, Kate," she said, her eyes lingering on Kathryn's midsection. If any other woman had come to her with this kind of brazen request, Kathryn would have been taken aback. But she knew Margot. This day was always coming. "George and I—you know how desperate—"

"I know," said Kate. She looked at her mother—a smile on Edith's face, but her brow furrowed, like she couldn't quite comprehend what was happening.

"Kathryn," said the woman, stepping forward. She made as if to reach for Kate's hands, but then propriety made her reconsider. "I'm not a perfect woman. But I would love this baby as much as any mother has ever loved a child." Her chin contracted and dimpled. "And you, sweet girl—you've got your whole life ahead of you. You could go to college. Have a career. Start a family—when you're ready for it." Kathryn shifted her weight. Edith hooked her arm into the crook of her elbow. A mother can always tell when she's needed. "And of course," continued Margot, "you could still see the baby."

Despite herself—despite all the bottled-up resentment she had felt for the Caldwells all these months—Kathryn answered in the only way that felt right in that moment: "I'll think about it."

62

Back at the Little Yellow House, I find Quinn sitting cross-legged on the parlor sofa eating peanut M&M's. I watch her pop a blue candy into her mouth, bite off the shell and chocolate, and then spit the peanut into a serving dish on the coffee table.

"You know, they do make regular M&M's," I say. "Like, ones without peanuts. Seems like it would save you a lot of work." She proceeds to suck the shell from a red candy, spit the peanut into the same dish.

"Yeah, but that would defeat the purpose."

"Which is?"

"I save these up," she says, gesturing to the bowl of peanuts, "and then when we have a guest I hate, I set out the bowl and watch them eat my spit." She pops another candy into her mouth, turns to me. She holds the bowl in my direction. "Want some?"

"I think I'll pass, thanks."

"Whatever. I'm bored."

"Perfect. You can come with me to Sawyer Shoes."

"That sounds thrilling."

"I'm trying to track down Kyle about that thing he left for me," I say, "but he won't answer his phone."

"Kyle doesn't even work there, genius."

"No, but his dad does, moron."

"Sorry, but I'm busy." She spits another peanut into the bowl.

"Oh, right. Preparing slobber candy."

"Some of us have to work for a living."

"Come on," I say. "It'll only take an hour, tops."

"Will you buy me a pair of shoes?"

"No."

"Distract Sammy while I steal some?"

"Not a chance."

She eyes the bowl of peanuts, then looks up at me. "Eat three of these and I'll go."

"You're disgusting," I say, walking out the door.

Quinn catches up with me halfway down the block. I smile at her, nudge her with my elbow.

"Whatever, man," she says, scowling. "I just needed some fresh air." We walk the rest of the way to Main Street in a comfortable silence. In the cool October air, with the crunch of fallen magnolia leaves underfoot, an epiphany: if I raise this baby, I want them to be exactly like Quinn. I look at her for a bit too long, and she notices—so she pushes her hair in front of her face like Cousin Itt and lags three steps behind me.

In Sawyer Shoes, Quinn wanders down one of the aisles, but I head straight to the back register. I expect to see Sammy, but I find Kyle instead.

"Well, isn't this a happy coincidence," I say. Kyle looks up, smiles. His white dress shirt is unbuttoned at the top, coarse chest hair matted against tan skin. I try not to look.

"Didn't know when I'd see you around these parts again," he says.

"Well, now I'm back."

"Glad to hear it," he says. I put my hands on the counter, maybe too close to Kyle's.

"Why are you here, anyway? Shouldn't you be out writing speeding tickets or busting meth heads or something?" He straightens a stack of receipts by the register. Something tells me he isn't in the mood for my jokes.

"I figured you'd have already heard by now. Small town and everything."

"Heard what?"

"That I'm—" he says, breaking off. "Well, I'm not exactly a cop at the moment."

"Ah, I see—first you're a detective, then you're a cop, and now you're— What's below a cop?"

"What? No, I didn't— I mean, I am a cop, just not right now."

"Well, that clears it up."

"I'm on *administrative leave*," he says, hooking his fingers into air quotes. "Which literally means they pay me not to work."

"Must be nice."

"No, it's really not," he says. "And honestly, I don't want to talk about this anymore. Can we skip to the part where you tell me why you're here?" His voice is sharp. I get the feeling I'm toeing a line I better not cross.

"Help me understand this." I slip the article about the church fire from my purse. "What does this have to do with Kathryn Fairchild?"

"Maybe nothing," he says, shrugging. "That pastor who died—what's his name?"

"Caldwell." I glance at the article to double-check.

"Right. George Caldwell. He used to clerk at this shoe store with my dad. Back when Fairchild owned the place."

"Okay—so he had a connection to the Fairchild family at least."

"Yeah, but it feels like there's more to it than that. After you left last week, I went digging through my dad's basement. Found an old box full of stuff about Kathryn. Old letters, pictures, ticket stubs—that sort of thing. And right in the middle of it all was that piece about Caldwell." I scan back through the article as he's talking, trying to find some connection.

"Well, the fire happened about a week after Kathryn died," I say. "Maybe your dad just stored it together for no other reason."

"Maybe. But if there's one thing my old man is good at, it's keeping clear inventory." He sweeps his hand around, as if the shoe store itself proves his point.

"Well, then, I think I'll ask him about it."

"Good luck with that," says Kyle. "He's fallen off a cliff since you talked with him last week. He's not sleeping. Won't talk about anything. Didn't even open the store for two days, which is why I'm here."

"Oh," I say. "I'm sorry. I didn't realize it would affect him so much."

"Yeah. This whole thing is still raw for him after all these years."

"See, that's what I don't understand. Why does he care so much? I mean, I get that he was close to Kathryn, but it's been over fifty years." Kyle smirks, shakes his head.

"Come on, Julia," he says. "I thought you were some kind of researcher. Haven't you put it together yet?"

"Put what together?"

"It's not just about Kathryn. It's about the baby." He raises an eyebrow.

"Oh…" I say, processing. "Your dad is the baby's—" Kyle holds out a hand to stop me from saying the word.

"If you talk to my old man," he says, "you didn't hear that from me."

63

When it came right down to it, Norman figured there was no other choice. Kate wasn't going to marry the Sawyer boy—she had made that clear. So be it. The only responsible thing now was to get the baby adopted. The paperwork was stacked nice and neat in the middle of the kitchen table, a few pages dog-eared from where Norman had tried to thumb through all the gobbledygook written up by Bill Marshall at his law office on Oak Street. Bill said it was all pretty straightforward—so long as either party didn't change their mind. Norman knew the Caldwells were as sure as the night follows day. He wasn't so convinced about Kathryn.

"This'll brighten the mood a bit," said Clara, sliding a strawberry Jell-O pie onto the table beside the paperwork. "We don't need it to feel so big and serious in here when Kate comes in." Norman nodded as Clara took a seat next to him. He was awfully grateful she had come. Clara just had a way about her. She could make a person feel at ease even when the air was thick and weighty with tension. That was something Norman had never quite been able to figure out. Edith was there, too—

sitting stoically across the table, eyes fixed on the contract or the strawberry pie, you couldn't quite be sure which.

"This is the right thing to do," Edith said—though the way her voice turned up at the end made it sound like she was asking a question. Norman cleared his throat. Okay, then—they were ready. Now the only thing to do was wait for the girl to come home from her afternoon errands.

Soon enough, the front door creaked across the jamb, announcing Kathryn's entrance. Clara stood to greet her at the entryway between the foyer and the kitchen. "Aunt Clara?" said Kate, wiping a bead of sweat from where it had gathered on her forehead.

"Come in and rest yourself," said Clara, taking her by the arm, guiding her into the kitchen. Kathryn eyed her mother and father, the strawberry pie, the stack of papers.

"What's all this?" she said—though the timbre of her voice made it clear she had already figured it out.

"Have a seat and I'll fix you a slice of pie," said Clara. Norman adjusted himself in the wooden chair. Edith did not move.

"I don't want pie," said Kathryn. She spoke to the whole room, but mostly to Norman: "I told you I wasn't ready yet."

"Come now, have a seat," said Clara, easing Kathryn into a chair next to Edith. "We just want to help you figure this out, that's all."

"Daddy, I told you!" said Kathryn, ignoring her aunt. "I need more time to think about this." The way she said *Daddy* made Norman's mouth run dry. God, how ashamed he felt that he hadn't protected her from all this. That was his job. Where had he gone wrong? He looked at Edith as if she might hold the answer—but the woman was there and not there, her mind transported somewhere far away from the house on Poplar Street. *Come back*, he wanted to say. *I can't do this on my own.*

"Listen now, Kate." Norman reached for her hand, but she pulled away. "The truth is, we don't know how much time you have left to make this decision." He regarded his little girl across the table—the swell of her belly, the hurt in her eyes. "The timing on these things—it's not always so predictable." In a transient moment, the shadow of memory: the day Kathryn was born—barely eight months into gestation, the broken water in the middle of the night, Edith on all fours on the bathroom linoleum, laboring. Norman swallowed hard.

"I'm not signing anything," said Kathryn. "Not today." She folded her arms on the table, hid her face in the crook of her elbow.

"We didn't expect you to, darling," said Clara, placing a cautious hand against the girl's shoulders. "The papers have to be signed in front of the lawyer anyway."

"We just wanted to talk you through it," said Norman. "To get you used to the idea. You know that Sammy is on board, he fully supports this already." Kathryn sat up, swooped her arms around the bulge of her belly like if she let go the baby would fall right out.

"I don't know if I can," she said, regarding the contract as if it were a coiled snake.

"I know it's hard," said Clara, "but it's the right thing to do. For you and Sammy, for the baby—for the Caldwells." For the first time since Kate had come into the room, Edith turned her head. She opened her mouth as if to speak, but nothing came out.

"Yes, Kate," said Norman. "If nothing else, think about George and Margot. You could be a real answer to their prayers." Kathryn thwacked an open palm against the surface of the table.

"I'm not an answer to anyone's prayers!" she said. "I'm not an answer to anything!" She stood, scooped up the collated papers. For a moment, Norman thought she would rip them right in two. Instead, she took a breath, turned and walked back out of the house.

★ ★ ★

The next day, Norman trudged home from the shoe store through the sticky air of early June dusk. He hung his coat and hat on the rack beside the door, then walked into the kitchen to scrounge up some dinner. Instead, he found the adoption contract stacked neatly in the center of the table, the edges of the pages curled upward like a worn paperback novel. He flipped to the last page and saw her notarized signature there, right below Sammy Sawyer's: *Kathryn Marie Fairchild*, the swooping calligraphy sad and sure, just like his precious daughter.

64

"Please tell me you paid for those," I say, gesturing toward the new black pumps on Quinn's feet. She skips ahead of me on the sidewalk, showing them off.

"Does it matter?"

"If you just committed a felony? Yeah, I think it matters, Quinn."

"Misdemeanor, actually. Anything under five hundred bucks is—"

"Are you serious right now?"

"God, Julia—chill out." She rolls her eyes, pulls a wadded receipt from her pocket, slaps it into my hand. "You've got to admit, though—it would have been pretty badass if I lifted these shoes with a cop sitting behind the register. Goals, right?"

"I mean, can you call him a cop if they took his badge?" I say. "I can't figure that guy out. He's so full of himself." I expect Quinn to back me up, but she grows somber.

"You should really go easy on Kyle," she says. "He's been through hell."

"How would I know anything about that?"

"Yeah, well—maybe you should learn about it before you

slam him." As we round the corner beside the Little Yellow House, a gust of cold wind takes my breath away.

"Okay," I say. "Enlighten me."

"Well, for starters—his wife died a couple of months ago," says Quinn.

"Oh, God—I had no idea he was married. What happened?"

"Crashed her car into a tree out near the county line. Kyle was on duty. He was the first one on the scene." The image of my mom's dead body flits before my eyes. Limp body, slackened face. I try not to blink.

"They took his badge because his wife died?" We climb the two steps to the porch of the Little Yellow House, but I don't want to go inside. My cheeks are flushed. I feel faint.

"No, they took his badge because he broke some dude's face in half. Left him in a coma for almost a week. Nearly killed him."

"Yikes," I say. "What was that about?" Quinn squints against the sun, shakes her head.

"That's Kyle's story to tell, not mine," she says. "But seriously—go easy on him."

In my room upstairs, I try to add to my notes about the Fairchild case—but my thoughts are scrambled from what Quinn just told me about Kyle. I think back to my interactions with him, wonder if I should've recognized the signs of grief, if I should've given him the benefit of the doubt. I feel a fluttering inside my belly—probably just indigestion, but it's enough to make me swell with a fresh grief of my own.

I lie back on the bed and pick up my phone. I want to call my mom, to tell her about the baby. To cry with her. To let her tell me it's all going to work out even if it's not. When she was crashing against the waves of her own storm, she was still always my buoy. That's what a mother does. I rest my hand across my mole-hill baby bump. Could I ever offer that kind of love? With a clarity I haven't felt in months, I know what I need to do—for my baby's sake, if not for my own.

I send a text to Ryan: I need to tell you something very important. This is bigger than you.

I need to occupy my brain while I wait for Ryan to respond, so I head back to the library. Now that I know Sammy Sawyer played such a big role in the story, I write out everything I know about him, including the bombshell Kyle dropped on me back at the shoe store—that he was the father of Kathryn's baby. I had started to suspect that maybe Aster was the father, based only on how emotionally tied up he seems. But with this new lead, I know I need to hear what Sammy has to say.

In the meantime, I turn my attention back to the newspaper article about the church fire, hoping I can find some sort of lead about the pastor. I scroll through some microfilm archives to find George Caldwell's obituary, but it doesn't tell me anything terribly useful. No kids to track down, no mention of any siblings. It does give me his wife's name—Margot—but a Google search for her doesn't yield any leads worth following. Just as I'm about to give up—

"Well, hello there, Ms. New York," says a voice from behind. I turn to see the Linda the Librarian—the sweet woman who first pointed me to the microfilm room a couple of weeks back. "How's the research coming along?" I look at her and then back at the microfilm machine.

"Not great, actually," I say. A part of me wants to keep up the big-time-researcher-from-New York persona and tell her that everything is wonderful. But honestly, I just don't have the energy to be that person anymore.

"Oh, no!" she says with a dramatic flourish. "Well, tell me how I can help." She grabs the bifocals hanging from a chain around her neck, slips them onto her nose, leans in close to the microfilm reader like she's trying to find the last edge in a pile of puzzle pieces. It is at this precise moment that I realize that Linda the Librarian might just be old enough to be able to help me out here.

"You wouldn't happen to know anything about this, would you?" I say, pulling a photocopy of the newspaper article from my purse. Linda tilts her head upward and peers down at the paper through her bifocals. She reads, moving her lips as she goes. If the article were longer, I suspect she would lick her fingers before turning the page.

"Oh, yes. Reverend Caldwell," she says. "I was a teenager at the time. Didn't know him well, but I went to his youth group meetings on occasion."

"At Riverside Baptist? The church that burned down?"

"Yes. Little country church just past the county line." She hands the article back to me, cleans the lenses of her bifocals on her paisley sweater. "So tragic. And right after the thing with the Fairchild girl, too."

"The timing does seem curious, doesn't it?" I say. "I'm trying to see if there is some kind of connection."

"Between the pastor and the Fairchild girl?"

"Right."

"Well, yes—I'm fairly certain there was." I try not to look too eager as I pull out my notebook. (I've graduated from napkin notes, thank you very much.)

"Anything you can tell me would be super helpful."

"Well, don't quote me on this," she says, scrunching up her face. "But if memory serves, they had an arrangement about the child."

"The child? You mean the one that Kathryn—"

"Yes," she says, willing me not to finish the sentence. "Caldwell's wife—I can't remember her name—"

"Margot?"

"Sounds right. Anyway, that poor woman couldn't seem to have a baby on her own. The whole town knew about her miscarriages—" I nod, listening as she goes on about Margot Caldwell, but I can only think of my mother—how she wanted to be a mom so desperately but never had any interest in having a partner. How she tried artificial insemination without success. How she had to go through three rounds of IVF treatments to finally bring me into this world. When people used to say that I was a miracle baby, she would scoff and quickly correct them: she's no miracle. She's a scientific wonder.

"I'm sorry, honey," says Linda, bringing me back out of myself. "Did I upset you?" I feel the tears pooling in my eyes. I blink them away.

"No, I've upset myself," I say. "I have a bad habit of that. But you've actually been very helpful."

"Well, you'll need to confirm everything with a more reliable source than an old librarian," she says, winking. She puts a hand on my shoulder, and I find it's not weird.

"Ah, yes—reliable sources," I say. "I seem to be running out of those. Any ideas?"

"Well, I figure you might start with Margot herself."

"Wait—Margot Caldwell? She's still alive?"

"I believe so. But she's not Caldwell anymore. Got remarried a few years after George—well, after all that mess."

"Do you know her name now? Or where she lives."

"Afraid not," she says. "But I'm a librarian. We have ways of finding information."

65

Kathryn lay awake into the night, watching the shadows play across her lamplit bedroom: fluttering leaves of the sugar maple outside, swooping black across her white ceiling. She had signed the papers. The decision was over, but she felt no relief. She needed to talk to Jack more than ever, but over the last two days, he flat-out refused to return her calls. And now she faced the truth of it: her best friend had abandoned her. He'd been emotionally absent for weeks, and now it seemed he was on the verge of disappearing from her life altogether.

She tossed and turned through a sleepless night, and by the time the morning sunlight streamed through her slatted blinds, her sadness had burned itself into white-hot anger. She gave herself a quick look in her vanity mirror—her frizzy hair like half-eaten fluffs of cotton candy, her puffy eyes crusted with day-old mascara—but she didn't bother to fix her face or even change from her nightgown. It was clear that Jack couldn't be bothered with her no matter what she looked like, so why waste her time? On her way out the front door, she was startled to see her mother standing by the bay window in the living room, cradling Danny against her hip. She wore a dark blue pinstripe dress and powder blue kerchief—her hair curled and makeup done like a model waiting on a photoshoot for the new Sears catalog. She smiled at the child, and then stared out into the pink glow of the dawning sky.

When Kathryn arrived at the Clark garage, Uncle Raymond was elbow-deep in a Ford pickup.

"Where's Jack?" she said. Uncle Raymond peeked from around the raised hood of the truck, a cigarette dangling from his mouth.

"Holy mother of Jesus," he said, giving her the once-over. "You sleepwalk all the way over here, girl?"

"I need to talk to Jack," said Kathryn. She ran a hand through the thick pouf of her hair, as if that would do any good.

"I ain't seen him this morning," said Uncle Raymond. He checked his watch, made a face. "Why don't you go get his hind end out of bed, tell him he was supposed to be here half an hour ago." Kathryn breathed deep, sucking in the sharp, oil-sweet scent of the garage. Uncle Raymond started in on the truck again, but when she turned to leave, he glanced up.

"Hey," he said, eyes creased at the corners like slackened cellophane. "Want to do some magic this weekend?" A hot rush of tears surged into her eyes, but she blinked them away. Uncle Ray was a good man. She wanted him to come to her, to pull her close, to wrap her up and protect her like he used to do when she was a kid. She wanted to tell him everything she'd been going through—with Jack, with Sammy Sawyer, with George and Margot Caldwell. But there was a hole in the middle of all that sadness that she couldn't explain—to him or anyone else. She thought of her mother back at the house on Poplar Street, the dark pit of silence where she so often lived. We all speak the language of our own lonely grief.

"Not unless you can make me disappear," she said, forcing a smile.

★ ★ ★

She didn't dare knock on Jack's front door—you never could tell what kind of state his father would be in. She slipped around to the back of the farmhouse, rapped her knuckles on his bedroom window. The room was dark against the bright morning light. All she could see inside were Jack's fingers pulling apart the blinds as he peeked through.

"Go away, Kate," he said, his voice muffled through the single-pane window. She had stored up everything she wanted to say to him, but she had left all those words back at the home. All she had left was this:

"What have I done? What could I have possibly done to deserve losing you?"

Moments later, she heard him unlatch the window lock—an invitation. Kathryn clambered inside the room, a protective hand tucked around her swelling belly. Jack had slid back under the cover of his bed, hiding from her view.

"This isn't about you," he said, pulling the blanket over his head. An unexpected laugh bubbled out of Kate. She put her hand to her mouth as if trying to catch it.

"When has anything ever been about me, Jack? I've never been of much concern to anyone in this wide world except you. And now—"

"You just don't understand," he said. "I'm not who you think I am."

"Bullshit," she said, the word lingered in the air between them, sharp and satisfying. Jack was the one who taught her the wonder of curse words—the power they held, the feeling they gave you. She stood looking over the lump of his body under the bedcover, trying to remember why he was worth all this. "I know exactly who you are. You're the boy who taught me to gig frogs and catch fireflies. The one who taught me to weave wreathes out of wildflowers. You're the boy who sees magic and captures it with a camera. Who sees beauty and goodness in every little thing around you." She sat on the edge of the bed beside him, ran her hands through his tangled hair—the only part of him exposed from under the cover. "You're the boy who stole my heart without ever realizing you have it, Jack Chandler."

"Kate, I just—"

"Don't talk over me," she said, her voice calm and controlled. "I came over here to have my say. You owe me that much."

"Alright, then," he said. "I'm listening."

"I'm done fighting for you," she said. "I'm done with this all being one way. I've got too many burdens to pack around, and your indifference can't be one of them." Jack shifted in the bed. Slowly, like the parting of a theater curtain, he lowered the blanket from his face.

"I'm so sorry, Kate," he said. Her eyes widened as the streaming sunlight settled across his swollen eyes, his puffy cheeks. He'd been crying—and likely for a long while. Despite all her pent-up anger, Kate felt herself soften. She didn't want to hurt Jack, no matter how he made her feel.

"Oh, Jack," she said. "What happened?"

"I let someone see me for who I really am," he said. His lips twitched—maybe the start of a smile or the tremble of a cry. She touched his brow with careful fingers. He took her hand, gently led it away from his face. "I'm moving to New York, Kate," he said.

"What? Jack, no—"

"I've been trying to find a way to tell you."

"No, you can't leave me," said Kate. She thought about the baby, the adoption papers, the Caldwells. She needed his support. She wasn't sure she could do this without him.

"I'm no good for this place," said Jack, glancing out the window. "And it sure as hell isn't good for me."

"But I need you, Jack," said Kate, cupping her hands around her belly. The baby kicked, as if to protest. "What am I supposed to do without you?" Jack leaned over to his nightstand, withdrew a small key from the drawer. Kate knew what it was: the key to the cellar door.

"I'm never going to love you, Kate," he said. "Not in the way you need to be loved." He placed the key into her hand, the metal cool against her hot palm.

Kate, alone in the cellar. All around her was a crisscross of clothesline, with photos hanging from pins like Sunday wash drying in the summer air. She regarded the picture closest to her: a man she didn't recognize, reposed against white bed-sheets, a cigarette dangling from his lip. And then there was another: the same man, shirtless, rockabilly hair fussed atop his head, a two-day beard strewn across his face.

And another: close on the man's face, his creased eyes peering through the photograph to some distant memory.

And another: a feathery bunch of wild aster flowers fore-grounded on a hotel table, the man a blur in the background, cigarette smoke pluming from his parted lips.

And another, and another, and another.

Kate moved through the room, lingering over each photo-graph, tears swelling in her eyes. "Oh, Jack," she said aloud. "Oh, my sweet Jack."

66

The next morning, I wake up and check my phone—still no word from Ryan. I wash my face and brush my teeth to give myself time to gain a little courage. Then I dial his number—but it goes straight to voicemail. My phone vibrates a minute later, and I panic until I look at the caller ID and see that it's Myra—calling to video chat. When I swipe to answer, my entire screen is filled with nothing but her eyeball.

"Gross, Myra," I say. She pulls back where I can see her entire face. Her eyes are watering, but she's laughing.

"Sorry—felt a lash in the corner of my eye right when the phone was ringing."

"So you wanted to share that with me?"

"Shut up. I was using the camera as a mirror." She wipes a tear away, stretching her mouth open in that weird way you do when you're trying to get something out of your eye. "Anyway—just checking in. Seeing if you're okay."

"I don't know," I say. "But…I think something weird is going on?"

"What do you mean?"

"First, you have to promise to let me say the whole thing. Like, you can't interrupt me or tell me I'm wrong." Myra pinches her thumb and forefinger together, swipes like she's zipping her lips.

"Okay, I decided to tell Ryan about the baby—no matter what, for better or worse. So I texted him a super cryptic message—the kind you can't *not* respond to, you know? But it's been a whole day and he still hasn't texted back." Myra looks on with a poker face—trying her best to keep her mouth shut. "You don't have to literally stay silent, Myra."

"Oh, thank God," she says, letting out a big breath. "Have you tried to call him?"

"Yeah, just did. But it goes straight to voicemail."

"Weird."

"Right?"

"Hang on," she says. "Check your texts again. Does Ryan have his read receipts turned on?" I swipe to switch widgets and open my texts.

"He used to," I say. "But there's nothing there this time. Like, not even a *delivered* notification." I swipe back into the call so I can see Myra's face. Right before she says it, the obvious dawns on me.

"Oh—" she says. "I think he's blocked you."

"Right, of course he has." My stomach sinks. I should've expected it after we met at the Sundowner. But now I don't know what to do—Myra could call him, I suppose. Unless he's already blocked her number too?

"You know what this means, right?" says Myra. I can tell where this is going. I can already see it in her eyes.

"Stop," I say. "I don't have the bandwidth for this right now."

"Just hear me out."

"Myra, no—I'm not ready for that. Just let me hide from my feelings in Kentucky, okay? Things are actually going pretty well here and—"

"If Ryan has you blocked, it's the logical next step. You've got to talk to her, Jules." I pull the phone away from my face, think about chucking it across the room. "Come back on-screen, babe," says Myra.

"What am I even supposed to say to her? Really, I've been thinking about this. I call Morgan and—what? Tell her I screwed her husband? What good does that do?"

"Jules—"

"No, let me finish. Who's to say she'll even believe me? She doesn't know me. It's my word against his."

"I mean—it's kind of obvious which one of you is telling the truth." She makes a face, angles her eyes toward my belly. I grab a blanket from the bed and pull it tightly around me, feeling exposed. "And if she still doesn't believe you, there's always a paternity test," she says, "it's not an immediate solution but it would still—"

"Myra, stop," I say. "You know I love you, but this is not what I need right now." She takes a breath, shakes her head.

"Sorry—you're right. You're totally right. Full stop." Myra zips her lips again. I wish she could understand: I feel guilty, culpable. My brain tells me I did nothing wrong—he wasn't wearing a ring, and he certainly didn't try to put me off in any way. But my heart still sinks every time I think about fessing up to Morgan. Good or bad, she's living inside an illusion right now that everything is okay. Just because Ryan is making my life extremely difficult doesn't mean I have to make hers any more so. But I don't say any of this to Myra. I can't rationalize these feelings, and I don't have the energy to try.

"I'll let you know when I'm ready," I say. "If I ever am."

67

The wavy heat of summer had settled over Gray Station. It was all Kathryn could do to waddle up the stairs at the house on Poplar Street so she could pull the old rocker beside the window air conditioner in Danny's room. She propped her bare feet up against the unit—one foot at a time so that she didn't squish her cartoonish belly like an accordion—and let the cold air work its way up her legs and under her dress, billowing the fabric like a parachute. She imagined she must look awfully silly—but some things you just couldn't bring yourself to care about when you were nearly eight months pregnant in the middle of an early Kentucky heatwave.

As miserable as she felt, she didn't want the baby to come— not yet. She'd gotten Jack to promise he wouldn't run off to New York until she delivered the child. She couldn't ask him to stay forever—but one more month sounded reasonable. Three days after Kathryn saw all those pictures of the man hanging in the cellar, she took Jack out to the pond, guiding him by the hand through the cattails like she used to do when they were kids.

"I'm sorry, Kate," he had said. She had brought him to the

pond to apologize, but he spoke up first. They rolled up their pants above the knees, swished their feet through the cool water.

"We don't get to choose who we are," she said—and she meant it. But honestly, she did want him to feel sorry. She wanted to go back to the illusion that somehow, someday she and Jack would end up together. This was the hope that had buoyed her entire life. That was a hard thing to give up, even if it was the right thing to do.

"I should've told you. You're my best friend." He took her by the hand. "Shoot, you're my only friend." The baby stretched itself inside Kate. Sometimes she still wished she were keeping the child. It'd be nice not to feel so alone.

"Who is he?" she said. Jack's fingers twitched against her own.

"I'm not sure that matters anymore," he said. "Just some guy who doesn't love me." Kate leaned into him, rested her head against his shoulder.

"I know a guy just like that," she said. She was trying to make a joke, but the words came out sad and fragile, maybe even a little mean. She stepped out of the pond and sat down on the edge of the water, her feet already drying in the hot sun. Crawling on the grass beside her was a perfect little ladybug—cherry red with coal black spots, a tiny creature plucked from a children's book. She picked it up, felt the scuttle of its dust-mote legs across her tender palm. Whirring its wings, the ladybug lifted itself into the summer sky. *The little things are the only things*, she remembered.

Kate's body hadn't felt right for going on two days—cold sweats and splitting headaches, nausea and dizziness—but she just chalked it up to the heat. The mercury bubbled to 101 degrees—the hottest day on record for June in Gray Station, that was what the paper said. And now the little window air conditioner just couldn't keep up, sputtering and gasping until it finally gave out. Kate braced herself against the chair and heaved herself to her feet, the world spinning in pinwheels around her. She just needed air—that was all. A walk might do her some good.

Out on the sidewalk, Kate fanned herself with the June issue of *Seventeen* magazine, an issue she hadn't even bothered to read. Its pronouncements on the cover—"SUMMER BEAUTY in the sun under the stars," "Just for fun FASIONS," "AM I RE-ALLY IN LOVE?"—all struck her as particularly juvenile. Now that she was *actually* seventeen years old, she was coming to realize how much she had aged out of the magazine. No matter: the glossy pages made for a good fan, and that alone was worth the cover price.

Her stomach churned as she plunked down the sidewalk, her paper-thin dress clinging to her sweaty thighs like Glad Wrap. She left the house with the intent to just take a quick stroll to the town square and back, but less than a block down the street she was already winded. Her pulse thrummed in her temples, her mouth chalky and dry.

She paused, hands on her hips, her chest going tight. Somewhere in the distance, the ringing of a church bell, the laughter of a child. Above her, a hot breeze pushed through the stiff leaves of a magnolia tree. The ground swelled and shifted beneath her feet, the undulating pavement buckling her knees. By the time she decided to sit down, she found she was already on the concrete.

"Kate?" said a voice—carried off in the distance on the wings of the hot summer wind. "Honey, can you hear me?" Mrs. Eubank's face came into focus for only a moment. Kate tried to speak, but her mouth didn't seem to work right. She listened to the *whoosh* of her own exhaling breath, the patter of footsteps as the neighbors gathered around to see about the commotion. Then she closed her eyes. *Abracadabra!* And she felt herself disappear.

68

When I open the door of my room at the Little Yellow House, I nearly trip into an enormous, thigh-high cardboard box in the hallway. There is an unmarked enveloped taped to the top, and a sticky note from Quinn: *I carried this heavy-ass box up the stairs while you slept in. You owe me donuts.*

I drag the box inside my room and shut the door. From the envelope on top, I withdraw a formal letter in swooping calligraphy, written by Danny Clark:

Dear Ms. White,
To tell you the truth, I didn't expect to be contacting you again. As you might realize, my family has been something of a spectacle around these parts for going on sixty years. When people speak the Fairchild name, they do it in pity or disgust—neither of which I'm terribly interested in. You can understand why I might be hesitant about a New Yorker coming in to poke the hive.
I asked after you around town and came across your book and was able to get my hands on a copy and read it—well, part of it, anyway. I'm still working through it. At any rate, in those pages I see the way you've treated the people in your life with dignity and respect. I even feel like I know your mother—not just a char-

*acter of the woman, but the woman herself. Her hopes and fears.
Her loves and losses. I wouldn't mind if someone wrote a book
like that about my sister.*

*I'm not sure I can tell you anything directly that would be
much use, but I reckon you'll find plenty of interest in the contents of this box. These are some of Kathryn's keepsakes. Dad
gave them to Aunt Clara, and she handed them along to me before she passed away. All that's to say—I hope you'll treat this
box with the same respect our family has given it for the past six
decades. It contains a life, more or less.*

Take care,
Daniel Clark

Folding the letter carefully back into the envelope, I picture
Danny Clark sitting on the wooden porch swing at his little
farmhouse, reading my book. He is no longer just a stranger
in Kentucky who can help me with the Fairchild case—he's
someone who knows my mother's story, who's seen her the
way I wanted the world to see her. And for the first time, I understand what Aster is really asking me to do: to give Kathryn
Fairchild a voice. To make sure her story didn't die with her
in the depths of the Ohio River. For nearly two months, my
mind has been a demolition derby of memory and anxiety and
shame and denial: webs of inextricable grief tugging and pulling inside me until everything I feel is inseparable. But right
now, at least for this moment, none of that matters. I have a job
to do. I have a story to tell.

I open the box, gently folding each flap of the cardboard,
handling each item inside as carefully as if it belonged to my
mother. Over the next hour, I catalog the contents, taking pictures and organizing into clear categories: photographs, draw-
ings and other artwork, diaries and notes, and—a small library
of magic books? Magic history, illustrated guides, step-by-step

illusion instructions. All the disappearing acts are underlined and marked as if scripture.

Through the afternoon and into the evening, I fall into the well of Kathryn Fairchild's story headlong. I dive deeper and deeper, and I don't want to come up for air. Every time I examine an item in the box, Kathryn becomes more real to me, materializing out of the ether, a soul made manifest in words and images and art. I learn the most from the pages in her diaries: she loved her mother fiercely—and yet she was terrified of becoming her. She was full of courage and independence, but she was crushingly lonely. She adored magic and literature and—more than anything in the whole world—Jack Chandler. Every other entry seems to be about Jack. Catching frogs with him beside the pond at Aunt Clara's house. Posing for photographs in an old pole barn behind the Chandler property. Jack was her only companion—even her savior in many ways. Before I even realize what I'm doing, I've dialed Jonathan Aster's phone number. He doesn't answer, which is just as well. At the tone, I leave a voicemail.

"Mr. Aster, I wanted—" I say, but then I pause, unsure of exactly what I could tell him that would express what I was feeling going through Kathryn's old keepsakes. In the end, there is only one thing to say: "She just loved you so much." I linger on the line for another moment, but then I realize no other words will do.

Later, after a makeshift dinner of Mamaw's cookies and a half bag of granola I found crumpled in my suitcase, I read Kathryn's diaries into the night. After a while, I notice broad cycles in her writing—lightness into dark, joy into sadness—a pendulum swinging over the course of days or weeks. Even on the happy days, there seems to be an underlying sorrow—something so familiar to my own life that sometimes it feels as if I'm reading my own thoughts.

Page after page, I progress through Kathryn's life. As she moves into the middle of her teenage years, I expect more to be written about Sammy Sawyer. There are entries here and there, with a predominant spike just after she met Sammy her freshman year of high school. But overall, she has surprisingly little to say about the man who would eventually become the father of her baby.

Another surprise: after only a few mentions early in the journals, George Caldwell seems to occupy an inordinate amount of page space. At first there were intermittent notes about George and Margot—their presence at a dinner party, their struggles with infertility, George's work at the shoe store and then at the church. But then a shift occurs after Kathryn writes about a church youth group meeting she attended. Mentions of the Caldwells flicker over the pages like wildfires. Little by little, thoughts of George himself seem to consume Kathryn.

At first I read with puzzlement, and then with disgust, and finally with horror. She's piecing together what happened on Halloween night 1963. At some point it becomes clear, even before I read the words on the page. I fall through the rest of the entries like a skydiver without a parachute: I know the inevitable end, but there isn't anything I can do to stop it.

69

Streaks of fluorescent light. Sharp stench of rubbing alcohol. An assault on the senses from every direction. Where was she? Stiff vinyl sheets. Spikes of pain. Swirling color.

"Honey, I need you to keep real still for me," said someone. The voice came from everywhere and nowhere. Kathryn tried to tilt her head to the right to find the source, but a firm hand caught her at the temples, leveled her face. "Easy there," said the voice again, firmer this time. "Somebody hold her still. She's starting to seize again." Her head throbbed. Fuzzy memories formed like a photograph dipped into developer. The sidewalk on Poplar Street. Mrs. Eubank.

"Where—" she said, but then her words gave way to sputtered breath.

Her mother came to her—dazzling white dress, hair curled and coiffed like Doris Day on an album cover. Kathryn felt her body contract and shrink—down, down, down, back to her infant self, curled into Edith's rocking arms.

"Ten tiny fingers," said her mother, counting each one with a pinch. "Perfect."

Perfect. Perfect. The little things are the only things.

Kathryn's tiny body stretched and yawned itself through time until she was a grown woman, now holding a baby of her own. She sat in the middle of the empty sanctuary of Riverside Baptist Church, stroking the child's head.

But the child's face! A wrinkled smudge, no eyes, no lips.

"Is this what you want?" asked a voice. She looked up to see George Caldwell looming over her, god-sized, hair matted with sweat. "Is this what you want?" he repeated.

She closed her eyes, awoke on a concrete floor in a dark room. Fairchild shoes. The repair room. She mumbled, tried to form words.

Is this what you want? Is this what you want? Is this what you want?

"Sammy?" she said. His shadow covered her completely. And then the weight of his body pressed onto her. "The baby!" she cried, but she looked down to see the infant had disappeared—back through the funnel of time, back into nothingness.

"Is this what you want?" asked Sammy—but it wasn't Sammy's voice. His face contorted and morphed into George Caldwell's.

Hot breath against her cheek. A spike of pain between her legs.

When she opened her eyes, she was back at the house on Poplar Street, examining her bloody underwear in the harsh light of the bathroom vanity, pulpy and red. Behind her: Sammy Sawyer, his reflection distorted in the fog of the mirror. He moved his lips, voice crackling as if distorted through a telephone line.

"Just because I don't remember doesn't mean it didn't happen," he said. She turned to face him, but he was gone. In his place stood George Caldwell—sitting on the edge of the porcelain bathtub, sweating drops of blood like Christ at the Garden of Gethsemane.

"Pray with me, Kate," he said. He took her by the hand, bowed his head. "Dear God. Dear God. Dear God."

The cadence of his voice lulled her further into sleep. When she opened her eyes, she was sitting in the middle of the memorial garden at the Caldwell parsonage. Margot paced before her, holding the faceless baby against her chest.

"Perfect," she said. "Just perfect." Back and forth she went. Kathryn looked down at her hands—found that she was holding a pen and a clipboard. She heard the voice of Aunt Clara: "It's the right thing to do. For you, for the baby—for the Caldwells."

Back in the hospital, the room was silent. Kathryn stirred herself into consciousness, examined the IV needle stuck in the backside of her hand. She wiggled her toes, bent her knees, coming back to herself one part at a time. Pain knifed through her abdomen.

"The baby," she said, though she wasn't sure the words made it into the air.

"You just rest now, sweetheart," said a voice.

"Where's the baby?" A hand touched her elbow. Kate recoiled like a snake. She squinted against the light to see Norman standing over her.

"The hard part's all over," he said. "But now you just need to rest, get your strength back."

"I want—" Kate started, every word an effort, "the baby."

"Everything's fine. The nurses are taking care of her." Norman eased himself onto the edge of the hospital bed. "She'll be ready to go home with the Caldwells soon enough." Kathryn tried to process the words.

"He can't have the baby," said Kathryn. Norman stroked the hair from her eyes.

"Just try to sleep," he said, dismissive.

"George can't have the baby." Her voice was louder now, more assured. She tried to sit up, couldn't get her weight off her elbows.

"It's for the best, Kate. We've talked about this."

"No! You don't understand!" She thrashed her legs about. She gripped Norman's collar, tried to pull herself up.

"Easy now. You're not well. You just need—"

"It was George!" she said. "On Halloween. George—" She wanted to finish, but what were the words? Her hands we flailing about now. She pushed with all her strength against her father.

"Nurse!" he said, fighting back against her.

"It was George!" she said again. Two nurses rushed in from the hallway, pinning Kathryn against the bed. Swirling lights. Tinnitus in her ears. She thrashed about like a bluegill on the pebbled shores of the Ohio.

"Okay now," said one of the nurses. She produced a syringe. "Okay now," she said again, and then the light faded to black.

70

When I get to the end of the diaries, I keep searching for another page—something to tell me the story doesn't end here. But there are no more pages. There is no happy ending. Kathryn Fairchild was raped by George Caldwell. Seventeen and pregnant. No evidence. No one to believe her. No way to prove Caldwell was the father.

I lie back in bed, resting my hand across my bare stomach. The ceiling fan whirs above me, the steady *chop chop chop* sending me into a sort of trance. Something is coming to me, some feeling, some longing. But what is it? A prickling of my soul, nearly imperceptible—the scuttle of a ladybug across your open palm. And then I recognize the feeling washing over me: pure, unadulterated fury. My insides burn, a powder keg in the gut.

My head is spinning with stuff I need to deal with back in New York, but my work here in Kentucky isn't done. I call Sammy Sawyer's phone again, but it goes to voicemail as usual. He hasn't been working at the shoe store for the past week, but I need to get out of the house anyway, so I take a stroll down Main Street, watching the swirl of fallen leaves play in the autumn air. An odd sense of nostalgia hits me—for this little Kentucky town. I'm going to miss so much about Gray Station.

Inside Sawyer Shoes, I'm surprised to find Sammy sitting behind the register, staring blankly at an open copy of the *Gray Station Gazette*. The store is vacant except for me and the old man. By the time he looks up and sees me approaching, he doesn't have time to scurry off to the back.

"Now, I just want you to know something," he says, hand in front of him as if warning me not to come any closer. "I've thought on this thing a lot. Matter of fact, I don't think I've thought of anything else since we spoke last week."

"Mr. Sawyer—"

"It's just too hard, Julia." He blinks through watery eyes, and I feel the threat of tears in my own. "It's been near sixty years, but it don't get any easier." He pulls out a drawer from under the register, withdraws a plain white envelope, holds it in my direction. "I can't talk about it. But I've written it all down in here." I take the envelope, pulling just a bit to fight the resistance of his grip. It's heavier than I would've thought—maybe fifteen or twenty pages folded tightly under the seal.

"She was such a lovely person," I say. "I can see why you miss her so much." He nods, folds his purpled hands across his stomach.

"I just wish I could've said something. Some way I might've talked her down. At least the baby—" he says, breaking off.

"Actually, that's what I've come to talk to you about. The baby."

"I would've done right by the child," he says. "I know we agreed that the Caldwells would raise her, but I would've done everything in my power—"

"Mr. Sawyer," I say, trying to will out the rest of the words. "The baby wasn't—"

Behind me, welcome chimes clank against the glass door. A young mother trails in behind two scurrying kids, and instantly, the silence of the empty store bursts with voices and laughter.

"Be right with you," says Sammy, smiling and waving at the young family. Just like that, my resolve is broken. I just can't bring myself to tell him—not here, not with an audience. I think about how crushed I was to read Kathryn's notes about George Caldwell. I can't imagine how much harder it will be on Sammy Sawyer. He deserves to know, and he will.

"I'll tell you what," I say, holding up the thick envelope. "I'll give this a read and send you a letter of my own."

71

Margot couldn't stop marveling at the perfect baby girl. Despite being born four weeks premature, the child had only been kept in the hospital for five days after birth. As far as the doctors were concerned, she was as healthy as a full-term infant. All the books told Margot she should rest when the baby slept— but how could she pull herself away from this miracle child? How strange it was to hold this tiny human being against her chest, this weight she had carried with her for nearly a decade, now made manifest in blood and bone. She had worried that the child might feel foreign to her—but as soon as she touched the girl for the first time, that fear had slipped away. That was a week ago. This was her new life. Time melted away pleasantly like the drip of an icicle.

She eased the child into the crib, but she didn't leave the room. Sometimes she sat in the rocker opposite the sleeping baby, watching, cherishing. She tried not to think of Kathryn Fairchild, but sometimes she couldn't help it. She heard the rumors. That the girl wanted the baby back. That she had slipped over the edge of madness like her mother. It was such a shame, but still: her lawyer told her there wasn't a thing to worry about. The baby was right where she belonged. This was the will of God. There was no other explanation.

The porch door slapped against the wooden frame, startling Margot from her thoughts. George had been out mowing the small parsonage lawn, and now he dragged in the sharp stench of cut grass. He leaned against the frame of the nursey door, his bare chest gleaming with sweat.

"How is it?" he said, nodding toward the crib.

"It?" snapped Margot, keeping her voice just above a whisper.

"The child. You know what I meant."

"Your daughter has a name, George." She rolled it against her tongue. *Elizabeth. Betty.* Oh, how many times had she written those names in her journal, her hand dipping across the page with swoops and curls.

"You think I don't know that?" said George. Margot sucked a breath, beat away the impulse to challenge him. He was disappointed that the child was a girl, she sensed. It was only natural for a man to want to raise a boy.

"You want to know something magical?" said Margot. She sprang from the chair, invited George to join her by the crib with a flick of her wrist. "Look at the bridge of her nose. The curve of her ear."

"Yes," said George. "She's beautiful." Margot regarded her husband. Even with his long hair curling between his eyes, it was plain as day.

"You don't understand," she said, nodding back toward the sleeping child. "She looks just like you, George."

"Oh, I don't…" stammered George. His eyes grew wide, then narrowed again as he studied the baby. "But that's not possible."

"Don't you see?" said Margot. "This is the fingerprint of God. This is confirmation that this child is right where she belongs." George reached a hand toward the child, but stopped just short of touching her doll-sized hands.

"Well," he said, his voice catching in his throat. "Praise the Lord."

The night was humid, the air heavy with the gathering storm outside. A whisper of wind fluttered through the cracked bedroom window. Margot stretched awake to the sound of fat raindrops pattering against the sill. She glanced at the ticking clock on the wall just as the first clap of thunder rumbled against the thirsty countryside. It was just past three o'clock in the morning. The house was silent, still. The baby hadn't cried in hours.

The floorboard moaned under Margot's steps as she crossed the room. She shut the window with a thump, but George never stirred, his hot breath bellowing into the air above him. Margot felt her way through the dark hallway, fingertips against the wall to guide her steps. She paused outside the nursery door, listening. A clap of thunder boomed outside, so she pushed into the room, ready to comfort the baby. But then—

The green curtains fluttering in the cool wind. The blow of raindrops against the nursery carpet. The window open wide. Still, the baby didn't cry. Lightning crashed in the distance, a blue-white burst of light flooding the room. Margot's eyes turned to the empty crib.

"Betty?" she said, voice low and controlled, as if the child could answer back. She looked to the floor, back to the empty crib, again at the open window.

"George," she whispered, her mind spinning. The baby. The window. The crib. "George!" she said, and then she was on the floor, wailing.

72

I sit on a bench in Town Square Park. Sunlight fights through a copse of oak trees, resting in broken patterns across Sammy Sawyer's letter in my open hands. In shaky scrawl, the letter recounts Sammy's years with Kathryn Fairchild—from their first meeting in the showroom of Fairchild Shoes all the way through the night he saw her jump from the bridge with the baby in her arms. A baby he still believes to be his own child. A guilty throb pulses inside me. He deserves to know the truth. But how is such a thing to be said? How do you change a person's entire history and then just walk away? Maybe more importantly: Would knowing that the baby wasn't his make his memories of Kate more painful, or less?

These questions will have to wait. Right now, something more pressing to address: my phone rings beside me. I answer the random number because apparently that's who I am now.

"Hello?"

"Well, hello there, Ms. New York," says the woman on the other end. Based on the greeting, I could be talking to literally every single person I've met in Gray Station.

"Can I help you?" I say.

"Actually, I was hoping that I could help you," says the

woman. "This is Linda from the library. I've got some information on Margot Caldwell."

"I need a favor." I pace the steps in front of the Gray Station
Public Library, trying to dodge the snappy gusts of crisp air.

"I expect nothing less," says Kyle on the other end of the
line. I want to tell him I'm sorry about his wife, but I think
that would just be awkward for the both of us. Better to play
it safe and just get down to business.

"I need you to do some detective sleuthing. Track down a
name."

"No can do," he says. "I'm not a detective. You already called
me out on that one."

"Come on. I just need an address."

"That right?"

"Margot Abbott. Former wife of George Caldwell." Linda
the Librarian was able to get me Margot's last name, but she
couldn't find an address. Google searches didn't help.

"And what do I get in return?" says Kyle. There's a catch in
his voice. I can't tell if he's sleepy or drunk.

"Full redemption." I'm trying to be snarky, but when the
line goes quiet, I realize I came off too strong.

"So, you want me to do some detective work to make up
for not being a detective?"

"Are you going to help me or not?"

"I'll see what I can do."

73

1964

Wet, cold, blue—the baby howled.

Kathryn held the child tight against her chest, steering the Oldsmobile with her free hand through backcountry Kentucky. The car's wipers couldn't keep up with the pouring rain, but still: she drove with abandon, taking the pinball curves at break-neck speed, putting as much distance between her and the Caldwell place as she could.

But where was she going? Where could she hide?

She had to take the child—there was no other choice. The lawyers wouldn't listen. Her father wouldn't fight for her. Her mother was gone, gone, gone—back in the asylum, a disease to be quarantined. Her first trip back there in over a year couldn't have come at a worse time.

No matter what, George Caldwell could not have this baby. *Don't close your eyes. Don't remember. Drive.*

Two hours east, she could no longer ignore the screams of the child. She pulled the car to the shoulder, lay the baby on the bench seat, mixed the evaporated milk. She hadn't sterilized the bottle, but she couldn't worry about that now. One thing at a time. The baby drank in great drafts, her tiny cheeks sinking and pulling. Kathryn felt the child's lips as if the bottle's rubber nipple were her own. A yearning opened inside her, deep, foreign, unnamed.

She looked at the open bag in the back seat. A handful of cloth diapers. A smattering of bloomers, pajamas, shirts. An open box of Carnation milk powder. A gust of wind rattled the windows. The child pulled away from the bottle, content at last.

The rain chased her eastward. Somewhere outside of Lexington, she stopped at a filling station. She covered the sleeping baby with a blanket, tucking her from view. She didn't dare get out of the car, even though her bladder felt like it might burst. The story was probably on the radio by now. Maybe her face had been on the TV news. She tucked her red hair up under the cover of her hood while the attendant ducked through the pouring rain. She cranked the window just enough to slip him three dollars.

"Put in as much as this will get me," she said, looking ahead. The tip of the man's cigarette burned bright against the dark sky. He stood at the window for an eternity, watching as if she were an animal in a terrarium. "Keep a dime for yourself," she added, cranking the window back to the top. The man regarded her through the glass, pulled hard on the cigarette. He glanced in the back seat of the Oldsmobile. Finally, he slouched toward the pump, filled the car.

Five miles down the road, Kathryn veered onto a gravel easement. She left the Oldsmobile in the pouring rain and urinated into a ditch. Back in the car, she cleared her eyes of any tears, and drove on.

By morning light, she was near the border of West Virginia. But why? What could lie beyond the state line that would make anything better? She tuned the AM radio dial through the crackle and pop of static, but she couldn't get a signal. How many people already knew? Was there a search party?

On the shoulder of the road, Kathryn changed the baby's soiled diaper, wiping her red, puffy bottom with featherlight strokes. She searched the bag for rash ointment but came up empty—just one more thing she forgot in the frenzy to get out of town. As she fed the child, she thought of something else: she had no food for herself. Her own hunger was an afterthought. Contracting, grumbling, her stomach complained. Her head felt bubbly—from lack of sleep or food, probably both.

Driving in daylight was risky. Every car she passed on the highway was a threat. Worse were the pedestrians gawking from the sidewalk of every nondescript town she passed through. In the middle of the afternoon, she found a quiet park on the outskirts of a little city in central West Virginia. She tucked the Oldsmobile under the cover of a towering black oak and crawled into the back seat with the child. The hot breath of summer slithered in through the cracked windows. The baby was a warm stone against her sternum, the weight a comfort atop her thrumming heart.

"Abracadabra," she whispered. Then she closed her eyes, and waited for the world to disappear.

Hours later, sticky with sweat, Kathryn woke to the cries of the child. She sat up with a great deal of effort, cradling the baby's head. The parking lot around her was still empty. Across the horizon, the pink glow of bubblegum dusk ushered in the night. After the baby was clean, Kathryn prepared another bottle. The box of evaporated milk already felt light.

In the cover of darkness, she puttered the car around the town until she happened upon a little drive-in restaurant. Flashy neon sign. Loud music pumping from speakers attached to the building. She parked the Oldsmobile at the edge of the lot, giving herself room to stake out the place before committing to anything. A good number of cars flanked the pavement on both sides of the building. Beside the ordering window, a group of teens huddle together, smoking cigarettes, laughing, posturing.

Kathryn's stomach burned with hunger. If she had to take a risk, this was the place to do it. With so many people around, she might be able to slip by without drawing attention. She rolled a blanket next to the sleeping baby so she wouldn't fall off the bench seat. Then she took a breath, pulled the hood of her light jacket over her greasy hair, and walked toward the ordering window. About twenty feet away, she noticed the pretty girl in psychedelic hip-huggers standing in the center of the group of teens—the tip of a compass measuring out the circle of boys around her. The girl tilted her head, laughed. Her bright eyes were as big as half-dollar coins.

"Hey, doll," said one of the boys. Kate looked up to see his shaded eyes trace the length of her body. *Never trust a man who wears sunglasses at night*—that was what Uncle Ray had always said. The rest of the boys spread out behind Sunglasses like a flying V of migrating birds. Kathryn looked away, tried to push forward as if she didn't know they were looking at her. "You deaf or something?" said Sunglasses. The hip-hugger girl stood beside him with her arms crossed, smacking on a wad of bubblegum.

"Get a clue," said Kathryn, pulling courage from somewhere deep inside. Sunglasses smiled. His gaggle of friends snickered behind him.

"Oh, don't hurt my feelings like that. We were just trying to be friendly." When he took a step forward, Kathryn froze. The others formed a loose circle around her. The hip-hugger girl stepped into the center with Kathryn, took her by the hand.

"Don't worry about him." She flipped her hand as if swatting a fly. "He's just a big ol' softy."

"What's your name, doll?" asked Sunglasses. Kate glanced past him toward the Oldsmobile at the edge of the parking lot. Music pulsed and pounded through the night air. The scent of frying hamburger nearly made her knees buckle.

"Please," she said, head swimming. "Just leave me alone." The circle of boys tightened around her. Sunglasses stepped forward, so close Kate could smell his Old Spice cologne—so sharp it felt like someone was needlepointing her nostrils. The boy cocked his head to the side, studied the hood of Kate's jacket.

"Why you all covered up like that? Let's have a look." He reached for the hood, but Kate slapped his hand hard as if swatting a fly. The flock of friends gasped and fidgeted. The boy lowered his sunglasses just enough for Kate to see his black eyes.

"Just let her be," said the hip-hugger girl. She squeezed Kathryn's arm, but Kate jerked away. She elbowed her way through the boys, but Sunglasses followed close behind.

"Don't run off now. We were just getting friendly."

"Stay away," she called back, but Sunglasses crunched through the gravel after her.

"Knock it off, Mikey," said the hip-hugger girl, hurrying to catch up. "You've had your fun, now let her go." She grabbed Sunglasses by the elbow. He regarded her hand in the crook of his arm as if it were a wasp that had just stung him. The rest of the boys were watching the scene like a drive-in movie, so Sunglasses had no other choice: he clenched his jaw, flung his arm wildly away, sending the hip-hugger girl onto the gravel.

"Jeez Louise," he said, glaring at Kate, then turning back to his gaggle of friends. "Can't a guy have fun anymore?" He walked away, leaving the girl on the ground. Kate was nearly to the car. She glanced at the baby—still asleep on the bench seat—and then back at the hip-hugger girl.

"Are you okay?" she asked, kneeling. The girl wiped a hand across her snotty nose. The boys were twenty yards away, smoking and laughing as before. They had already forgotten the two girls existed.

"I'm sorry about all that," said the girl. She picked gravel from a tear in her jeans.

"It's not your fault." Kate reached out a hand. The girl took it, let Kate pull her up.

"Maybe not, but—" She paused, searching. She looked toward the sky as if the right words might be hidden in the clouds. "Why is it like this?" she said, blinking against wet eyes. Kate knew what she meant, even if she couldn't articulate it. The two girls were tethered by some invisible thread—same as all women. A great well of sadness opened inside Kate, so dark and deep the gravity of it could have swallowed both girls at once. Without warning, the hip-hugger girl lunged forward, squeezed Kate into a hug like they were childhood best friends. Some other time Kate might have pushed the girl away, but the hug felt good and right. She wrapped her arms around the girl's back, felt the warmth of another body—one that wanted nothing in return but to be reminded that it wasn't alone.

When the girl stepped back, her hand brushed across Kate's hood, pulling it away, revealing the curls of Kate's flame-red hair. The girl looked at Kate, narrowed her eyes.

"Oh my—" she said. Kate covered herself once again, but it was too late. "You're that girl, aren't you? The one on the news!" Kate stumbled backward toward the Oldsmobile, fumbling with the keys as the girl followed close behind. Just as Kate had gotten in the car and shut the door, the girl saw the baby.

"Please—" mouthed Kate behind the window. But it was no use.

"Somebody stop her!" she called out. "She's the one who stole that baby!" In the distance, the boys came rushing toward the car like a stampede of wild horses. The girl pulled on the locked car door, pounded her fists against the windows. By the time Kate fired the engine, the boys had circled the car. They jerked the door handles, tried to pry their fingers at the edges

of the windows. "Call the police!" the girl shouted back toward the restaurant.

Kate turned on the headlights, revved the engine—but the
boys wouldn't relent. They pulled and slapped and pounded.
Sunglasses stood in front of the car in the glow of headlights,
his palms on the top of the hood like he was holding the car
in place.

The baby howled, scratched her cheeks with her fingernails. The car rocked back and forth like they were caught in
an earthquake. Kate had no other choice, so she put the car
into Drive. When they heard the gears shift, some of the boys
backed away—but not Sunglasses. The smile grew across his
face broader and broader, right up until the moment the front
bumper rammed against his thighs.

The hip-hugger girl shrieked, but Kate drove on, acceler-
ating as she made a doughnut in the gravel lot, slinging rocks
every which way. The boy in the sunglasses clung to the hood
like a moth stuck to a spider's web, but his grip eventually gave
way, sending him tumbling off the car and onto the gravel. Kate
placed a hand against the baby's heaving chest, pressed down on
the accelerator and peeled away into the black of night.

74

I've found myself on a road trip headed southeast of Lexington. Kyle sits in the passenger seat of my rented Corolla, gorging himself on a bag of Combos, cracker crumbs littering his shirt like he's a toddler who hasn't quite figured out how to eat. He insisted that he go with me, so I dragged along Quinn so I wouldn't feel like I'm on a date with a dude who just lost his wife and is helping me investigate this story. I glance in the rearview mirror and see Quinn passed out in the back seat, head tilted and mouth open, like she's waiting for someone to toss her a piece of popcorn.

"So how did you find her?" I say. Kyle sucks powdered cheese off his fingers.

"A magician never reveals his tricks," he says.

"Good thing you aren't a magician, then." He slurps down a gulp from a twenty-ounce Coke, looks at the bottle like he's mad at it for not being a beer. "You find her in some police database or something?"

"Some *police database*?" he says, mocking me. "Yes. Absolutely. I found her in the supersecret police database of domestic octogenarians without criminal records."

I turn my head in his direction for a moment to make sure

he sees the full arc of my eye roll. He crunches lazily through another Combo.

"I just went over to the church and asked around."

"The church where Caldwell used to pastor? The one that burned down?"

"Yep. They rebuilt a few years after it happened. Nice little country church. Figured they might know something about former clergy. Talked to one of the pastors—Brother Jim, I think he called himself. He knew where to find Margot."

"Look at you!" I say, slapping him on the arm. "That's some A-plus cop sleuthing right there."

"Yeah, well, being on desk duty this is the most I could do." I swipe my hand through the air, trying to lighten the mood.

"What's that old saying? You can take the badge from the cop, but you can't take the cop out of the—wait, no, I don't think that works." I smile, but Kyle grows quiet. I glance in the back seat to make sure Quinn is still asleep, and then I turn down the volume on the radio. "Hey—I just want you to know I'm so sorry about your wife." He crumples the empty bag of Combos, brushes a hand down his shirt.

"Yeah, me, too," he says.

"We absolutely don't have to talk about it. But I wanted to say that—well, I made some pretty stupid assumptions about you. And I'm sorry."

"Easy to do. I was a drunk guy in a bar. I was a cliché. I invited assumptions." The cruise control pulls us across the highway, hills dipping and cresting like waves on the horizon. I want to say something more, but I fight the urge. "Guess you also heard why they took my badge?" says Kyle. I instinctively glance at Quinn in the rearview mirror, and he notices. "I'm not usually a violent person." He looks out the window as if he's trying to distract himself from the memory.

"You don't owe me any explanations," I say. But he goes on anyway, talking more to himself than to me.

"The guy was an old buddy of mine, actually. We were out drinking. But honestly, I don't think the alcohol mattered a bit. He was spouting off some rumor that had been going around about my wife. That Sarah—" He breaks off, gathers his words. "That she did it on purpose. That she was aiming for that tree like an arrow at a bull's-eye."

"Oh, Kyle, I'm so sorry," I say.

"I don't even remember what happened after that. I just saw red, and the next thing I know I'm being pulled off him like I'm some kind of rabid animal. His face was all—" Kyle gestures over his own eyes and nose, as if he can't put the image into words. "He didn't deserve that."

"Probably not," I say quietly. "But he should've known better than to talk about your wife like that. I know what it is to grieve someone so close. He had no right."

"It wasn't just him though. The whole town was talking. He was just the first one man enough to say it to my face. That was the worst part—the secrecy of it all. The gossip. Like they thought it would be better for me if they just passed stories around behind my back." I hear a rustling in the back seat, turn my head to see Quinn sitting up, wide-awake. She bites her lip as she listens. "Nobody knows how to talk about this shit. We don't have the words. And when you can't talk about it, sometimes the only thing to do is to run your car into a tree."

"It was an accident," I say. "You have a right to that version of the story. It's yours. Nobody can take it away."

"Maybe so. But I was the first one on the scene," says Kyle. "There were no skid marks on the road, no indication that she lost control." I turn off the radio completely now, trapping us in a pocket of silence.

75

Norman didn't worry much that first day. The girl would come to her senses. Despite everything, she had a good head on her shoulders. But then one day seeped into the next like an open wound bleeding through a bandage. The police weren't much help. There were reports Kate was meandering around West Virginia, but nothing was confirmed.

Truth be told, this was all information Norman preferred to keep to himself. He couldn't figure why it had to be plastered all over the radio broadcasts. Even the TV news had got ahold of the story, sniffing out ratings like a shark going after a chum bucket. *Gray Station Girl Kidnaps Baby. Teen Mother on the Run.* They didn't know Kate like he did. Everything would be okay.

Still, he couldn't avoid it any longer: he had to tell Edith. Better she heard it from him than from one of the nurses—or even worse, the evening news. She'd been down at the state hospital for the past month. This spell was worse than usual— that was what the doctors said. They couldn't get her to talk. Couldn't get her to eat much of anything.

Norman sat in the visiting area, picking at the seafoam-green upholstery on the chair. They pushed Edith into the room in a wheelchair—her limp arms hanging over the rests, her head pointed straight down like her chin was sewn to her sternum. Norman gave the nurse a quiet nod, waited for her to leave before he let himself breathe. He took Edith by the hands, folding them together into her lap, his big hands covering her tiny ones like an oyster protecting a pearl. She didn't move, and he couldn't bring himself to talk, so they sat like that for a long time, just being together. Sometimes that was the only thing you could do.

"Well," he finally said, "I better get on with it." She didn't move—her neck still crooked like a question mark, eyes pointed at her bare feet. He studied the top of her head, noted the line of thinning hair down her center part. This was the woman he married. The woman he still loved. "It's about Kathryn," he said. Edith's fingers twitched at the mention of the girl's name. She made no other movement. "She's got herself into a mess." He felt a sob climbing his throat, but he choked it down the way he'd always been taught to do. Through broken sentences, he told her how Kathryn had snuck into the Caldwell place and taken the baby. He told her everything he knew—that she was probably somewhere in West Virginia, that the police were tracking her down. Edith made an effort to raise her head, but it seemed she just couldn't get there.

"Kate," she managed to say, but that was it—as if the girl's name was the only word that mattered. That was how it had always been for Edith.

"Something happened to her after the baby came," said Norman. He'd been puzzling it out for days but couldn't quite make sense of it. "Changed her mind about giving the baby to the Caldwells." He told her about Kate in the hospital that day—her delusions, the mumbled words. How she kept crying out, saying George Caldwell couldn't have her child. She was out of her mind, of course—claiming George was the father. Norman knew better. They all did. The doctors called it a psychotic break—*considering the family history*, they said. And they said something else, too: even if she changed her mind about giving up the child, it was clear she wasn't fit. The lawyers agreed. Nothing to be done. He told all of this to Edith. He had no intention of making her feel responsible, but she deserved to know the whole truth.

Norman went on for over an hour—saying more words in sixty minutes than he likely had said in the past sixty days. When his voice was all dried up, he figured it was time to leave. But when he went to stand, Edith gripped his hand against hers. She raised her head for the first time all morning.

"Do you believe her?" she asked. Her voice was soft, but clear.

"Believe her?" echoed Norman, as if the words were nothing more than a random string of syllables.

"Our girl doesn't lie," said Edith.

"Of course not," said Norman. "That's never been a question."

"Then what? She's crazy?"

"No, that's not what—"

"Psychotic?"

"Hold on now—"

"Like me?"

76

Kyle, Quinn, and I careen through the Knobs of Central Kentucky, each of us folded into a pocket of our own silence. My mind runs north to Brooklyn, but my body accelerates east toward Margot Abbott—the last major piece of the Fairchild story. Across the dips and curves of asphalt, I distract myself with what I know about the case, the questions left unanswered. How much did Margot know? Did she protect her husband, even after the rape?

Fifty miles south of Lexington, my GPS leads me onto a winding gravel driveway. A puff of dust billows around the open gate of a wooden ranch fence. We bump and gash around a bend to find a blue-sided farmhouse, fluffy white clouds framing the roofline in the distance like a *happy little* Bob Ross painting. Quinn sits up in the back seat, her sleep-hair plumed like she's ready to belt an eighties power-ballad. I just love her so much.

"Wake me up when you're done," she groans. Kyle and I leave Quinn behind to sleep in the car. We cross over sunken walking stones onto the front porch of the farmhouse and ring the doorbell—which makes the sound of a cow's moo (because of course it does). The door swings open to reveal a sinewy woman in a flower-print apron. Her hands are dusted in fine white powder—maybe flour.

"We don't want any," she says, slamming the door in our faces. I turn to Kyle, give him a look. He smirks, as if to say *What did you expect?* I go to knock again, but just before my knuckles reach the wood, the door flings open. The woman doubles over, laughing.

"I'm sorry," she says, trying to rein herself back in. "I've always wanted to do that." She snorts, wipes her nose with the back of her hand. I can't figure her age exactly, but there are clues: the irony gray roots of her hair, the sunspotted cheeks, the crow's-feet at the creases of her eyes. Still, she looks far too young to be Margot Abbott. "Lord a-mercy, you should have seen the look on your faces!" The woman screws up her nose, crosses her eyes.

"I'm so confused right now," I say—though I'm not sure if I'm talking to myself or to Kyle. He only smiles and nods. He knows her type, apparently.

"Oh, I'm just foolin' with you, honey," says the woman, swiping a powdered hand through the air. "You not from around here?"

"Not exactly."

"Let me guess—Ohio? Michigan? Gotta be somewhere up north. You got that look."

"New York," I say with a sigh.

"New York?" She steps backward like I spat in her face. "Darling, are you lost?" For just a second, I would like nothing more than to cuss this woman out on her own front porch. Kyle must notice the look in my eye, so he intercedes.

"I'm Kyle, and this here is Julia," he says, sticking his hand right into the woman's powdery palm without thinking twice. "You've got yourself a beautiful place out here." He cranes his head, taking in the view. He sucks a breath as if drinking the country air.

"We like it alright," says the woman, wiping her hands down the front of her apron. "What can I do you for?"

"Well, Julia here is doing some research for a book she's writing."

"Ooh, fancy," says the woman. But the way she looks at me tells me she does not, in fact, think it is *fancy* at all.

"And we're here trying to track down a piece of the story."

"Okay, then," says the woman. "Just make sure you get my good side." She raises a hand into the air, strikes a pose. Kyle smiles because—what else can you do?

"Actually, we're hoping to talk to…" He pauses, looking to me for the name.

"Margot Abbott," I say. "Formerly Caldwell. Used to live in Gray Station."

"Oh," she says, searching my face like a TSA agent at the airport. A look of recognition falls over her—like she's been anticipating this day for years. "Well, you best come in."

77

The whiz and pop of bottle rockets echoed against the parsonage. Margot stood at the bay window, watching the teens who had gathered themselves in the church parking lot. One after another, they lit cherry bombs and sparklers, firecrackers and Roman candles. Independence Day. Freedom from what? Freedom from whom? The world spun forward as it did, celebrating the holiday while she was trapped in her own psychological hell. She blamed herself. She blamed the Fairchild girl. Mostly, she blamed God.

"The police should've called by now," she said. The hysterics had gone from her voice. All her raw emotion had been spent up; what was left was a bottomless pit of quiet despair. She had reached a place of detached curiosity, observing her feelings as they occurred to her. So much loss over the years had taught her this skill.

"They'll call when they have information," said George. "The best thing we can do now is pray." He sat at the table in the adjoining kitchen staring at his open Bible. That was his answer for everything it seemed—prayer and devotion and utter inaction. It was impossible to believe she had ever been the same way. An unexpected burst of laughter burbled inside Margot. She caught it in her throat just before it could escape into the air.

She checked her watch—nearly eight o'clock at night. She imagined Police Chief Reynolds sitting comfortably on his back porch, stuffing his face with hot dogs, watching his kids swipe sparklers through the night air. Just when she'd made up her mind to call him, the telephone rang in the kitchen. George regarded the phone suspiciously, as if he couldn't quite figure out what it was. Margot rushed past him, pulled the receiver from the wall. She sucked a deep breath and held the phone to her ear.

It was not Chief Reynolds.

She had to park three blocks into the residential section of Main Street, as the roundabout and town square were closed off to traffic for the fireworks display. The phone call had been short:

If you want the baby, meet me by the river.

That was it. No specific location. No specific time. Kathryn had hung up before Margot could press for details, the dial tone droning like a cardiac flatline. She hurried along the sidewalk toward downtown, nudging through the forest of bodies at the entrance of Town Square Park. Hay bales flanked the sides of the street, funneling people in one direction toward the lawn by the river.

Margot climbed atop one of the hay bales to see over the crush of bodies. The streetlights would be cut soon to prepare for the city fireworks on the river, so she had to act fast. But how? What could she do? She felt at once close to her baby and miles away—the same feeling she got when she thought about God these days.

"Where are you, baby girl?" she whispered. The child couldn't answer, of course, so she did the only thing she could think of, not knowing if it would work: she prayed.

Thirty minutes later, Margot still hadn't found Kathryn or the baby. She had walked the length of the river's edge by the downtown access road, and she had forced herself through the tiny rivulets of walking space between all the blankets strewn across the park lawn. On the verge of fresh tears, she wondered if it was even Kathryn on the phone at all. Perhaps it was just a prank—some teen girl answering a dare to impress her friends.

By the edge of the park, two police officers stood surveying the crowd. She didn't know whether she should ask them for help or not. Would more people be able to find the girl faster? Would they just scare her off? In the end, she didn't have time to make the decision. The streetlights clicked off in unison, and the crowd erupted into applause. The first fireworks boomed from a barge on the river like gunshot.

For ten minutes, Margot never looked to the sky, but continued to survey the crowd with every burst of light. Faces flashed blue and yellow, orange and red—but none of them belonged to Kathryn Fairchild.

But then, a scream.

"Oh my God!" said a voice.

"What is she doing?" said another.

"Is she holding— Is that a baby?"

Margot followed their outstretched fingers, their stares, their shrieks. By the time she looked to the train bridge, Kathryn Fairchild was plunging to the black waters below, holding the precious baby girl.

78

In the kitchen of the farmhouse, the flour-hands lady goes back to kneading an enormous mound of yeast dough on a Formica countertop. I look down an adjacent hallway, but the rest of the house is dark. Pushing and pulling, the woman works the dough in silence. Kyle and I stand by, watching her like she's the host of a cable cooking show on mute.

"Gotta get this bread set soon," she finally says. Then she plunks the dough into a stainless-steel mixing bowl, covers it with a kitchen towel.

"Take your time," says Kyle—completely sincere, not a hint of sarcasm in his voice. The woman rinses her hands, pats them dry. Then she turns to us as if picking up a conversation we never actually started.

"I assume this is about George Caldwell," she says, eyes downcast. "And the whole mess with the Fairchild girl." I pull my notebook from my purse.

"So—you're Margot's daughter?"

"Jenny Abbott," says the woman, flicking me a little wave.

"And George Caldwell was your—"

"George Caldwell wasn't a damn thing to me." She places a hand across her chest, heaves a breath. "Don't get me worked up now, or I'm gonna need me a baby aspirin." She pours a glass of water from the kitchen tap, chugs it down in one gigantic gulp. "I apologize," she says. "It's just that—Caldwell was not a good man."

"Yes. I understand," I say.

"After he—" she begins, considering her words. "After the fire in that church, my mother moved away. Settled down here. Eventually married my father." Jenny stares past me, transported back through time to a place that existed long before she did, a place she only knows through the invisible thread of memory passed from one generation to the next. "All that stuff in Gray Station—it was a lifetime ago for my mother. But it still lives inside her." Jenny brushes by, but before she leads us into the dark hallway, she turns back toward Kyle. "You best stay here. Mother doesn't do too well with strange men." Kyle gives her a nod, takes a seat at the kitchen table.

At the end of the hallway, the woman pushes into a bedroom dimly lit by the amber glow of a bedside lamp. The stench of urine hangs thick in the air, sharp, acrid. Margot Abbott lies at a forty-five-degree angle in a hospital bed, eyes affixed to the sickly blue glow of a silent television set. Her head trembles back and forth like a broken windup doll.

"Momma," says Jenny, taking Margot by the hand, "this here is Julia. She wants to talk about—" She turns back to me. "Well, I'll let you do the rest. She doesn't speak much these days, but she can hear you just fine." She places a hand on my shoulder—a warning or consolation, I can't be sure. And then she moves behind me, leaving me face-to-face with a woman I've known only through newspaper articles and diary entries, a soul made manifest.

"Margot?" I say, testing out my voice. "Mind if I ask you some questions?" I sit on a footstool near the edge of the bed. Other than an occasional blink of the eyes and twitch of the neck, the woman doesn't move. "I wonder if you could tell me anything about your life back in Gray Station. Back when you were married to George Caldwell." At the mention of Caldwell's name, Margot tilts her head to the side. She looks at me for the first time since I entered the room, regarding me like a map without a legend. Slowly, a change comes over her—some flash of recognition.

"Kate?" she whispers, searching my face. Worry lines trench across her forehead.

"I'm Julia," I say—probably a little too loudly. "But yes—I'd love to talk about Kathryn Fairchild."

"Oh, sweet Kathryn," says Margot. She raises a trembling hand to my cheek, brushes a strand of hair from my eyes.

"No, I'm not—"

"I'm so sorry, darling," she says. "I didn't know. I didn't know."

"Momma," says Jenny, leaning toward her mother. "This here is Julia. She's from New York."

"'Thy wife shall be as a fruitful vine,'" says Margot, tears bubbling in her eyes, "'thy children like the olive plants round about thy table.'"

"I don't think this is going to work," I say, looking back to Jenny. "I don't want to cause any harm here." Before I can step away, Margot places a hand on my wrist. When I look up and catch eyes with her, the fog seems to lift from her mind.

"Forgive me," she says. "Please." I fight the urge to speak. Right in this moment, I want to become Kathryn Fairchild, to take Margot by the hand and tell her I forgive her—to let the woman live her final days inside the illusion that she had made peace with the past. But that forgiveness is not mine to give. So I do the only thing I can: turn away, leaving Margot at the mercy of her conscience.

"Okay—okay, Mom," says Jenny. She places her hands on

either side of Margot's face, leans her head back onto the pillow. "Just rest now. No need to get upset."

Back in the kitchen, Kyle checks his watch. "Well, that didn't last long," he says.

"I'm afraid you're just too late," says Jenny. "She is always so confused these days." My mind flashes back to my own mother weeks before she took her life—the way she would stare blankly at the wall, lost in a haze of morphine or hydrocodone. My heart swells with pity for Margot, though I'm not sure how much she deserves it.

"Before we go," I say, "I wonder if you could help me understand more about George Caldwell's suicide." From my purse, I pull the photocopy of the article about the church fire. Jenny glances at the paper.

"Oh, honey," she says, head cocked to the side. "That man didn't kill himself."

"But I thought—" I say, looking at the newspaper article. *Suspected arson. Apparent suicide. Active investigation.*

"Let me fetch you something that might help you understand," says Jenny.

"What's that?" I say.

"A letter sent to my mother after the fire." She makes her way back down the darkened hallway, and then calls back to add: "From Edith Fairchild."

79

1964

Edith watched from the parking lot as the fire consumed the church building. Flames slipped from the windows like flicking tongues, licked heavenward, orange-white against the gray night sky. What was it about fire that was so satisfying? Power and beauty—all-consuming, deadly, magnificent. Her precious Kathryn had been a flame—her ash still smoldering inside Edith six days after the girl had jumped from the train bridge.

Norman had not been able to tell her. Head in his hands, he had sat in the plastic chair near her hospital bed, broken. She couldn't blame him, at least not for that. The nurse with the kind eyes turned on the evening news. Edith watched as the reporter read the words from the teleprompter, detached, uninterested, as if reading from a Betty Crocker recipe.

Teenage girl. Desperate. Suicide. Baby. Kidnap. Words tethered by other words, syllables and sounds, nothing more. Edith could not digest the news. Instead, she held it deep inside her, each word a distinct part of the same whole, a bag of marbles sunken in her stomach. How could something so shocking be so predictable? Could you mourn for that which you always knew

would come to pass? How did Kathryn find the courage that
Edith never could? These questions would linger in her for the
remaining thirty-two years of her life.

But for now, she watched the warped siding of the church
begin its collapse into itself, the flames so hot she felt the sear
on her face.

At the hospital two days prior, Edith received a white envelope marked with no return address. The orderly woman
with the crooked teeth knew that Edith had a habit of letting
mail stay unopened on her nightstand, so she suggested she
could open the mail, perhaps read the contents aloud. Maybe
it was important. Perhaps it would lift Edith's spirits. When
Edith didn't respond, the orderly took it upon herself to slide
her index finger under the seal, open the flap with a satisfying
swoosh. And there it was: a letter written in the dead girl's own
hand, the crackling voice of a ghost coming through from the
Other Side.

"Mrs. Fairchild," said the orderly. Her dry lips smacked as
she spoke. "I think you need to see this, honey." Still, Edith
didn't move. So the orderly added three words that she knew
would elicit a response: "It's from Kate." Edith sprang to life as
if she were a coin-operated pony. She took the letter from the
woman's hand and read. Her eyes flicked back and forth over
the words, resting on the shape of each letter. The birdwing's-
swoop of an *M*. The pigtail curl of a *J*. She ran her fingers
across the page, traversing time, ink wet against the paper, her
darling girl's fingers pushing against the other side of the leaf.
What a wonder—to know someone through the dance of her
pen. The grief was almost too great to bear.

Still, she read all ten pages. And then she read again. She read
the words over and over, retracing each syllable, hearing each
utterance in the unmistakable voice of Kathryn Marie. Before

long: a spark of something in the gut, the flame fed with each pass through the letter. By the end of the day, the fire inside her could not be contained.

She was released from the hospital to attend the memorial service. Arrangements were made for her to spend the night at home and return to the facility the next day, a zoo animal on loan. She sat stoically in the hard pew during the service, face veiled, gloved hands tucked into her lap. She was hugged by people she didn't know. They whispered words she couldn't understand.

Later that night, when Norman retreated into the shower, she drove the Oldsmobile along the river to the outskirts of Gray Station, squealing to a stop in the gravel lot of Riverside Baptist Church. Her body moved mechanically, muscle memory and adrenaline, while her mind fluttered off in the ethereal space between the living and the dead—at once a fingertip's length from her perfect girl, yet still an eternity away.

She carried the five-gallon jug of gasoline along the sidewalk, arms nearly as heavy as her heart. Soft yellow light glowed from a single window in the church building—Caldwell's office. For a moment, she was paralyzed by the beauty: silver moonlight breaking through magnolia leaves, painting the little country church blue. She opened her eyes wide, recited from memory: "'Every good gift and every perfect gift is from above, and cometh down from the Father of lights.'" But then she felt the weight of the gas can in her hand and remembered why she had come. She entered the front doors of the church and made her way down the dark hallway toward the light.

George Caldwell looked up from behind the mahogany desk, open books strewn across the surface like fallen leaves on a lake. The thick curls of his hair were matted to his sweaty temples. His suspenders undone and his shirt untucked, the man looked in Edith's direction, not *at* her but *through* her—as if he couldn't quite register the presence of another human being. Edith studied him—this man who had sat at her dinner table, who had laid hands on her in prayer. Her fingers twitched against the gas jug.

"Edith," said George, his voice ticking up at the end as if he were asking a question. He regarded the can of gasoline in her grip like it was a shrunken head. She followed his gaze. His look was not one of fear, but of resignation.

"Do you remember the first time we met, George?" She moved her arms upward, sloshing the liquid in the can. He reached out, touched the pages of the open Bible in front of him, as if they held the answer to her question. After placing the can onto the Berber carpet, Edith took a seat across from George at the desk. The office was the antithesis of the sterile-white blankness of the hospital: cluttered and musky, the smell of sweaty T-shirts stuffed in a laundry hamper.

"I can't—" he said. Whether he intended to continue talking was of no relevance.

"That day you came into the store for your first shift, I took one look at you and told Norman he should find someone else." She caught eyes with George, held him in her stare. "I couldn't put my finger on it, but there was just something about you. Some weakness I couldn't place. Some shiver of recognition—something that told me the kind of man you truly were."

"Edith, please—"

"It was supposed to be temporary—your job, that is. I was pregnant with Kathryn. Just about to burst, really." She folded her hands over her stomach as if she expected to feel the kick of a fetus. "I told Norman something was off about you. Something I couldn't name but could feel. But you know how Norman is—always looking for the best in people. He said you were just wet behind the ears. You needed direction. Lost your father in the war and needed some help finding yourself." George shifted, the chair complaining under his weight. "Just a few months, he said. Until things get settled with the baby."

"I've always been grateful—"

"But then something broke inside me," said Edith. "Like someone pulled the plug to my soul. Like I was detached from feeling anything at all. A blankness, a nothingness—that's what it was. Drifting through empty space." She was looking beyond him now, through the church walls, back through time. She felt the weight of baby Kathryn in her arms. "Norman would ask me what was wrong, and he meant it. He's a good man. But try as I might, I couldn't answer him. Words fluttered up inside me. *Sadness. Depression. Anger. Loneliness.* But truthfully, there was not a word for what I felt." She closed her eyes, remembering. "It's temporary, they said. You'll feel like yourself again soon. But there never was a bottom to it, George. You just keep sinking and sinking, no way to pull yourself back up. The worst part is when you lose the light altogether—like you've dived to the endless depth of the ocean but can't ever reach sand. You've lost all sense of yourself, no reference point, no way to orient to anything around you. No up or down or sideways. Every direction is the same."

"That sounds awful," said George, but Edith wasn't interested in his sympathy.

"And then the voices started," she said. "Well, that's what they call them—*voices.* That word never felt quite right to me. They aren't really *voices* as much as perceptions. Urges. Longings you can't explain. They started me on the pills then. A little white one for this, a little green one for that. Pills to help balance out the other pills. The doctors said it would go away. But all these years later, I can't ever seem to crawl out from under it." George cleared his throat as if preparing to speak, but she wasn't quite ready for that. "How can I explain it? It's like—after Kathryn was born, there was a vacuum inside me. I've never been able to fill up that space."

"I'm sorry," said George, "about Kate." Edith felt her pupils dilate. Blood rushed to her face. Hearing her name in this man's mouth—after what he had done. It was too much.

"You're *sorry*? What on earth am I to do with an apology?" She sat upright in the chair, stifling the rage climbing her throat. "She was the only one in this world who understood me. The only one who felt what I feel. Who knew what it is to die a little every night just to wake up and have to live another day." For the first time since she heard the news of Kate's death, hot tears rushed Edith's eyes. She didn't fight them. "And you took her away from me, George." Purging the words into the air gave her strength. George shook his head from side to side.

"Edith, I—" said George, faltering. "You think I wanted her to jump? With my child in her arms?" He blinked through tears. "This is a loss we share. You and me and Norman and—" He began to choke out Margot's name, but he couldn't quite get there. "There's enough grief to go around." Edith stood, towering over the man slouched in his chair.

"No," she said. "You don't get to grieve. Not after what you've done."

"What are you talking about?" said George. Edith didn't respond with words—she had none left. Instead, she pulled Kathryn's letter from where she had kept it in her bra—right next to her heart. She held it before him, just out of reach.

"It's all in here. The whole story. From the very beginning up through the night when you…" The words stuck in her mouth like phlegm. She forced herself to say it. Some words had to be said. "When you raped my daughter." The color drained from George's face. His eyes were glued to the letter as if she were wielding a weapon. She expected him to deny it right away, so she wasn't surprised when he opened his mouth to speak. But then a change came over the man—a slackening in his shoulders, drawn lips. A resignation, it seemed.

"I'm so…" he began. But what could come next? *Sorry. Ashamed. Broken*. No word could suffice. No regret would be enough. She knew this all along. That was why she brought the gasoline. She lifted the can, unscrewed the lid.

"Forgive me, Reverend," said Edith, "but I've never been one to believe in a literal hell." She tipped the can, poured a steady stream across the desk, soaking the books, papers, pens. "Fire and brimstone and eternal damnation—that never seemed quite right to me." She moved around the desk behind George and then back in front, pouring a perfect circle of fuel around him. "God is love—that's what John wrote. And to my mind, *Love* could never stand by and watch as someone burned for all eternity." She lifted the can, pouring the remaining liquid atop George's head. He never moved. When the can was empty, she leaned in close to his face, her nostrils stinging from the fumes. "But I'm not God, George Caldwell."

She reached into her dress pocket, withdrew a book of matches. She broke off a single match, but she didn't strike it. Instead, she placed it into George's open palm. Her only mercy was letting him do the act himself. She would wait outside until she saw the flames.

Standing at the edge of the parking lot, Edith watched the glow of the blaze, flames flickering in the reflection of her eyes. Far off in the distance, the wail of sirens—her cue to leave. She turned to face the parsonage—its dark windows on either side of the front door like the vacant eyes of a soulless face. She knew Margot wasn't inside. She'd been staying with her mother outside of town ever since the death of the child. She didn't feel anger toward Margot, only pity. She would mail her a copy of the letter the next day. It was only right that she know the truth.

80

Leaving Gray Station is harder than I thought it would be. But I have all the information I need to write Kathryn's story, and I need to close a chapter of my own. I've said my goodbyes (properly to Quinn this time), but I can't help but feel I'm leaving part of myself here in this little Western Kentucky town, maybe a part of me that always existed here, one that I never knew I had. On the flight home to New York, I read the letter Edith Fairchild sent to Margot Caldwell—the one written by Kathryn the night before she jumped from the bridge. This is it: the last document I need to piece the full story together. I'll have to fill in the gaps, of course—same as I did with the book about my mother. The story will be real and imagined, history and myth. But I suppose that's what all writers do. We don't tell the facts; we tell the truth.

Aster opens the door to his penthouse, welcomes me into his home with a sad smile and a nod. He knows the work is done. Kathryn's story can finally be told.

For the next hour, we drink coffee and eat Charles's homemade madeleines (not quite of the same quality as Mamaw's snickerdoodles, but still delicious). We talk about the shape of the book. We debate the way the story should be told. Who gets to have a voice, and why. I go over all my notes and research with Aster, filling him in on parts of the story he never knew, parts he had long forgotten. The hardest part is talking about George Caldwell. It's a shame to have to write about such a vile man, but there seems to be no other way.

"I suspected," says Aster, eyes wet with tears. "But I had no way to know for sure." He studies the black coffee in his cup as if it holds the secrets of the past. "She deserved so much more. And sometimes, selfishly, I think of how different my life would have been if Kate Fairchild had been a part of it all these years."

"It seems she affected a lot of people that way," I say, thinking about Sammy Sawyer in particular. "The whole story is so tragic. It's going to be a tough book to write—in more ways than one."

"I warned you about that," says Aster, trying on a smile.

"I mean, at least there is some sort of justice."

"What's that?"

"The church fire. And Edith Fairchild finding her voice. That's worth something."

"Yes, indeed," says Aster. "That letter Kate wrote is remarkable. Irrefutable. I can hear her voice when I read it."

"But I wish there was something else, you know? Like, some way to reach back through time. Some way to make Kate's story less—I don't know. Less final?" Aster looks at me, tilts his head.

"Well, there's always the story of the baby," he says. I give him a look.

"Well, yeah—that's what I mean. It's all so sad. So absolute."

"What if I said it isn't?" He places the coffee cup on a saucer, reaches for my hands. "What if I said there was one more secret to be discovered."

"But I talked to everyone," I say. "I've strung together the whole story. What secret could be left?" Aster's hands tremble in my own. I can't be sure if he's overcome with emotion, or if the shake is just the natural condition of a man his age.

"A secret that I alone know. A truth that you weren't ready to hear until you discovered the rest of the story."

"Yeah? And what truth is that?"

"The baby," says Aster. "She didn't die."

81

Kathryn was running out of time. Seventy-two hours after she left Gray Station, she and the child had shared the last of the milk powder. The baby was red with fever—the result of drinking from a dirty bottle or something else, no way to know for sure. With the car parked on a nondescript residential road in rural West Virginia, she fed the child, watching the sink and pull of her tiny cheeks.

Delirious from hunger and exhaustion, Kathryn slipped into the liminal space between consciousness and sleep, wading through a waking dream like the murky waters of the river bottoms. She felt as if she were splitting into two selves: the girl snuggled with a feverish baby in West Virginia, and the *Other Kathryn* running through the clearing beside Jack's pond. The wildflowers and tall grass of the open field flicked against her calves; the morning wind brushed through her hair. Her open arms outstretched like a propeller, she spun through the grass, eyes to the clouds, ethereal, light.

When she stopped spinning, she turned to see Uncle Raymond standing beside her. He smiled his smile, took her hand, pointed the way to a wooden stage on the other side of the pond.

"Are you ready?" he whispered, winking the way that he does. He wore a tuxedo, lighting-white shirt against midnight-black jacket. She turned her eyes to her own shimmering dress—silver sequins dancing wildly, flashes of sunlight caught by a thousand mirrors. She climbed two wooden steps onto the stage, and there stood a magic box of just her height—the door flung open to receive her like a casket receives a corpse. When she turned back to face Uncle Raymond, he was gone—his body morphed into that of her mother.

"You've waited for this your whole life, baby girl," said Edith. "This is your chance." Kathryn studied the box, ran her hand along the smooth grain.

"But it's all just a trick," she said. "There's nowhere else but here." Still, she stepped into the box, the wood so snug she had to turn around and back in, squeezing her shoulders against the sides. The interior smelled of lavender and honeysuckle—as if her mother had been sleeping inside and left her scent behind. "Do you know the magic word?" said Kathryn. Someone else has to say the magic word. She knew the rules.

"Oh, honey," said Edith, smiling the saddest smile that ever existed. "If I knew the magic word, I would have said it years ago." Thunderheads gathered in the distance. The wind exhaled, bending tall weeds in front of Kathryn like supplicants bowing before a god. She closed her eyes only for an instance, and then her mother was gone, scattered away like dandelion fluff in the wind. She was alone again. Always terribly alone. Who would say the magic word? Who could make her disappear?

But then she heard a familiar sound coming from the edge of the platform.

The cry of a newborn baby.

Kathryn worked herself from the box, scooped up the child,

felt her bird-bone weight in her hands. She turned back to the magic box—still standing there in the center of the stage like a portal to another world. And then it hit her. She was no longer alone.

Maybe it was the child who needed to disappear. If Kate couldn't save herself, she could at least save this precious baby. And for the first time in her life, Kathryn knew what to do.

She had to act fast. She wrote the letter for her mother and mailed it from West Virginia, figuring it would take at least three days to reach the state hospital. She also wrote a note for Jack, then called him from a pay phone in Eastern Kentucky to make arrangements. She didn't tell him everything, of course—he'd only try to stop her, and that wouldn't be good for anyone. By the time she made it back to Gray Station, the night sky had already descended, and nearly the whole town was gathered at the riverfront for the fireworks display. She had no problem driving the Oldsmobile through town undetected; for all anyone knew, she was still in West Virginia.

She parked the car in the alleyway between the storefronts—back where only the business owners and their staff parked during weekday business hours—and used her key to let herself and the baby through the back door of Fairchild Shoes. She made sure to bring the extra blankets from the back seat of the car. A magician always has the right props.

She waited in the dark for Jack to arrive, bouncing the baby on her hip. For the first time in weeks, she caught herself smiling. She thought that when the time came she would be anxious, sad, even scared. But now that her mind had been made up, a sense of euphoria coursed through her. Despite everything, she knew that the baby she coddled in her arms would never suffer the way she had. She would never need to swim in the depths where the light never touches. The child looked at Kathryn—her mother—with wonderment. She did not cry.

★ ★ ★

With the baby tucked into the crook of her arm, Kathryn paced the darkened showroom of Fairchild Shoes on Main Street, waiting for Jack to arrive. She had made the phone call to the Caldwell house, kept it short to squeeze the emotion from her voice. "If you want the baby, meet me by the river." Margot had to see it happen. There was no other way to be sure the plan would work.

"Oh, Kate," said Jack as he squeezed through the back door. He nearly crushed the baby between them as he pulled her into a hug. His arms around her felt good and right, same as always. "I thought I might never—"

"No time for that," she interrupted. She pulled away, keeping her eyes fixed on Jack's forehead so she didn't have to look into his glossy eyes. She glanced at his truck in the parking lot outside, saw that the bed was piled with his belongings—all covered by a tarp and secured with a rope, a perfect metaphor for Jack's whole life. When she called him from West Virginia, she told him he had to be ready to go to New York, that he had to leave that very night, after the fireworks—no questions, no exceptions. Anyone else would have balked, but not Jack.

"All packed up?" she asked. Despite the evidence, she still needed to hear the confirmation from him. She had only one shot at this.

"Ready as I'll ever be," he said. "And you?" He tucked a strand of her hair behind her ear, featherlight strokes against her temple. He was as familiar to her as anyone in the world— he, her best friend, the one she loved the most. This was how she would remember him: camera around his neck, crooked smile, wrinkles at the corners of his eyes.

She knew what Jack would assume—that she was running away from Gray Station again, this time with him to New York. And if she were honest, she would like nothing more. But what then? A life always on the run? Police following her like hunters tracking wild game? Of trying to claw her way out from the darkness? No, a life in hiding was no life at all. They would never give up. The lawyers had already deemed her unfit to raise her own child. If they caught her, the baby would be given to George Caldwell. That was not an option.

"I just need to take care of something first," she said—not lying exactly, but not telling the full truth either. Jack deserved the life waiting for him in New York—a life where he could exist as the person he was created to be. "Here—take this stuff to the truck, would you?" She nodded toward the diaper bag and few remaining provisions left over from the last few days. Jack went to scoop up the bag, but a rush of tears hit Kate's eyes, and she couldn't help it: she lay the baby on a soft pallet of blankets and rushed to Jack, wrapping her arms around his neck, breathing him in.

"Hey, what's wrong—" he murmured, but she shushed him with a finger to his lips.

"You would do anything for me, right?" she said.

"Have you ever doubted it?" He smiled, and she smiled back, despite everything.

"You're the best person I've ever known, Jack Chandler."

"Well, I won't argue with you," he said, giving her a wink. "But we can talk about that later. Let's get on the road." He grabbed the diaper bag and supplies from the concrete floor. "Be right back," he said, and then he popped out the door into the darkness. Kate wanted to call back to him—to tell him she was sorry, to tell him how much she loved him. But after all these years, he surely already knew.

The remarkable thing about a magic trick was this: you know it's just an illusion, but you choose to believe it anyway. The willing suspension of disbelief. The hope of the impossible. As Kathryn cut through the alley toward River Street and climbed the access ladder of the train bridge, she remembered:

People create the truth they want to believe. The magician just helps them to see that truth.

Rung by rung, she climbed with one arm—holding the baby-sized wad of blankets against her chest. *Show them where to focus, and then—hocus-pocus!* Leaving her life below her with each rising step, she never thought about the journey back down. She didn't think about death or pain. She had nothing to fear. Instead, she imagined the spectacle: the pop and boom of fireworks, curtains of light, an unexpected show of courage, faith, and love.

Pure magic.

By now, Jack had surely discovered the note she had left for him on top of the baby. She pictured him reading slowly at first, then frantically. He would rush out, try to stop her—but it would be too late. Later—months later, even years, throughout his remaining life—he would read the note over and again. He would know she made the right choice. Someday, he might even forgive her.

When she pulled herself onto the rail ties, she thought of the other letter she had written: the one addressed to her mother, the one carefully and precisely recounting the full story of what George Caldwell had done to her—from all the stolen glances and unseemly comments to the very night he forced her to carry his child in Fairchild Shoes. After this was all said and done, someone needed to know the full story. Kathryn knew she could not convince anyone else. But her mother would never doubt her. And she would understand why she had to do this.

Between each tie, she walked deliberately to the center of the bridge. The blast of the fireworks echoed off the steel, reverberated against her chest. When she was parallel with the barge on the river, she heard the first cry from down below.

Oh my God!

Look!

Somebody stop her!

What is she holding?
Is that a baby?

Leaning out over the open water of the Ohio, she gripped the metal frame of the bridge in one hand, squeezed the swaddled blankets against her chest. The fireworks clapped and thundered in the sky above, but the only sound she heard was the exhalation of her own breath. Watching somewhere down below was Margot Caldwell. She would tell the police that Kathryn jumped with her baby. They would find the swaddling clothes, search the river for days. Eventually, they would have to make up an explanation. The baby was swept away in the current. *When people experience something they can't explain, they tell themselves a story.*

With the crowd working into a frenzy below, she scanned her eyes over Main Street. Standing beside the door of Fairchild Shoes was sweet Jack Chandler, his camera in hand. Into the hot summer air, Kate whispered the magic word. She released her grip from the bridge, and just like that—*poof!*—she made her daughter disappear.

82

My dearest Jack,
I don't need you to save me. Besides, by the time you read this,
it will be too late. This isn't your fault. None of this could ever
be your fault. You are the kindest, most loving soul on this whole
earth. I've loved you forever, and that will never change.

You need to do something for me. I'm not asking so much as
I'm telling you. I don't have any other choice. You need to take my
baby girl to New York. As far as the rest of the world will know,
this baby won't exist. She'll disappear. Poof. Abracadabra—just
like magic. I'm not asking you to raise her. But I need you to
find a home for her—a home where she can grow and thrive. A
home far, far away from Gray Station. One where she'll never
hear the name George Caldwell. I don't know how you'll do it,
but I know you'll find a way. As for the rest of the trick—well,
you just leave that to me.

I can't tell you the full story. There's no time for that now, and
you don't deserve the burden. But perhaps I'll get that chance in
some future life. I know you'll do this for me because you love
me. And because you're the only one I can trust.

One other thing: don't ever tell her. Don't let this baby know about me. Let her live inside the biggest illusion of all: that her precious, perfect life really is what it seems.

Love you always,
Kate

I stand with Aster in the middle of his private gallery, inches away from *Woman Saves Child*, the framed photograph of Kathryn Fairchild falling into the black Ohio River. Even now, the picture deceives me: where my mind knows there are only wadded blankets, my eyes see a baby swaddled in Kate's arms. A magic trick, indeed—one sixty years in the making. Aster takes the letter from my hands, places it back from where he retrieved it: an envelope affixed to the back of the picture frame.

"Abracadabra," he says, voice trembling. "Kathryn Fairchild's story wasn't so final after all. Her beautiful baby girl grew up in New York. And then—" he pauses, taking time to regain his words "—that beautiful baby girl had a daughter of her own." I look at Aster, my brain catching up with what my heart already knows. Questions swirl inside me, but I don't have the words to ask them.

"I took the child to New York," he continues. "I didn't look back. I didn't think twice. I already knew where I would take her before I even left Kentucky. My aunt desperately wanted a child, but she wasn't allowed to adopt. Her name was Peggy White. But of course, you knew her as—"

"Grandma Margaret," I say. Aster only nods.

"The baby was your mother. Mary Kathryn White." I hear his words, but I can't process them, not yet. My knees give out, so I sit right where I am on the hardwood floor of Aster's gallery. He kneels beside me, gingerly, easing himself down in a way that shows his age.

"All these years, I've honored Kate's wishes in that letter," says Aster. "When Peggy took Mary in as her own, I knew I couldn't be involved in her life anymore—not directly. I was a part of the world Kate wanted her baby to leave behind. Gray Station was buried too deeply inside of me. So, Peggy and I lived mostly separate lives. She moved upstate, raised your mother. I kept in touch from afar. Sent money whenever they needed it. I made sure Mary had the chance to go to art school." He goes on, connecting the dots of my own history in ways I've never known. "Later, after Peggy died and your mother was teaching at Vassar, I introduced myself to her. Gave a few guest lectures in her classes. Even met you when you were just this high." He extends a hand only a couple of feet in the air. For the first time, I hear the Kentucky accent in his voice.

"I kept my word to Kathryn," he says. "I never told her about the past. For better or worse, Mary lived the illusion of her life until the day she died. But you—" he says, voice breaking. "When I read your book about you and your mother—I just couldn't take this to my grave. I couldn't let you live in an illusion—" He can't finish the sentence, and he doesn't have to. I move to him, wrap my arms around his neck.

"Thank you," I say—the right words, but ones that feel insufficient. Aster gives my back a squeeze, and then pulls away to look me in the face.

"This is your story, Julia," he says. "It's always been your story."

Later, I stroll the sidewalks of Brooklyn—my body in New York, but my soul still tethered to Western Kentucky. I place a hand across my swelling belly, trying to imagine the branches of my baby's family tree. I am here in this moment; I choose to exist in the liminal space between a past I never knew and a future I can't predict. I'll make sense of the world the only way I know how: I'll write a story.

But first, there is one thing I must do. I take my phone from my purse and dial Myra. As the line rings, I turn to see the Brooklyn Bridge looming behind me. I think of Kathryn

Fairchild—my maternal grandmother, the woman who made my mom disappear. I imagine myself standing on the bed of the bridge, wind ripping across my face. Could I jump to save my baby? Could I jump to save myself? In some ways, I feel I'm on that precipice even now.

"Where are you?" says Myra, snapping me from my trance. I shield my eyes, look two blocks ahead to the Sundowner. I see Myra standing in front of the door, scanning the sidewalk for my face.

"I'm here," I say, giving her a wave. "I'm right here."

83

1964

When Jack came back inside the store, he didn't notice the baby. He didn't notice the letter. What he noticed was Kate's *absence*. At once, he knew she was gone—and not just for the moment.

"Kate?" he said, just to break the stillness of the air around him. He felt the weight of the camera hanging from his neck. He'd brought it in to take a final shot of Kate in this place—one that was so precious and full of memory for her, one that she'd want to take with her to New York. A feeling was snaking its way through him—a grief he couldn't yet name, a mourning he couldn't fully know.

From the corner of the room, the baby cried—little arms flailing around her in jerks and stops like she was falling, falling, falling. Jack moved to pick up the child from the pallet of blankets, but he stopped when he saw the note on top of her—perfectly creased with his name swooped across the front. He opened the note and scanned the page as if deciphering a code.

I don't need you to save me.
You need to do something.
I can't tell you the full story.

One other thing: don't ever tell her.

He read, and then he read again—mouthing the words to himself, anything to help him comprehend. He had to take the baby. He had to find Kate. How could he do either? He stood paralyzed, regarding the child, looking at her face for the first time. The upturned nose and milk-white skin. The perfect mountain-peak dip of her upper lip. She was a portal into the past, a portrait of his precious best friend—back when she was still her own person, before she learned to give herself away, piece by piece by piece. How long did he stand there, studying the child?

The baby screamed, bringing Jack back to himself. "I'll be right back, I promise," he said—though he couldn't be sure if he was speaking to the child or Kate. Then he was moving, running toward the front door of the shoe store, pushing out onto the empty Main Street sidewalk. In the distance, the boom and crackle of fireworks over the river—bursts of orange and white against the bruised night sky. The crowd had gathered on River Road, but here a block away, he had a straight-line view of the bridge.

That was when he saw her—swinging one foot over the parapet, and then the other, heels against the ledge. A flash of light. A boom reverberating against his chest. What was she holding against her body? He had seen the child lying against the blankets in the shoe store only moments before, but still— for a fleeting moment, he was convinced.

Should he call out? Scream her name? He was helpless—just as she knew he would be. How could he go on without her? *I don't need you to save me*, she had written. But who would save him?

He raised his camera—it was all he could think to do. One last shot. One more memory.

A block away, the crowd gasped and pointed. He steadied his hands, found her in the viewfinder. The fireworks boomed on, building into the finale. But all he heard was the *whoosh* of his spent breath. The thrumming of his heart. The staccato snap of the shutter as his camera worked its magic.

EPILOGUE

As I step onto the raised platform at the front of the art gallery in Manhattan, I gaze at the bustling crowd and wonder: *What of this moment will I remember a year from now? Five years? Twenty?* On my right: a table stacked with copies of my new book, *Woman Saves Child*. On my left: Aster's photograph of the same title, veiled in a red satin cloth, waiting to be shown to the public for the first time. My heels scuff against the wooden platform, silenced by the *click-clack-click* of camera shutters from the press. I step to the podium, fight the temptation to tap the mic with my trembling index finger.

"Good evening. My name is Julia White." I move my head away from the microphone, shocked by the reverberation of my voice. "With the exception of the handful of friends I dragged in, I have no delusions that any of you have come tonight to hear me speak. However, Jonathan Aster has given me the stage first, so if you want to see his photograph, you're just going to have to wait." Burbles of laughter scatter through the crowd. I scan the faces in the front row, lingering over each one. Danny Clark and Kyle Sawyer. Harley Quinn. Myra. Morgan Springer and her impossibly handsome son, Connor. And of course—

squirming in Myra's arms, trying to wriggle her way to freedom, my perfect three-year-old daughter: Katie Marie.

"This is not my first book. Maybe you know this. Probably not. Four years ago, I published the story—part real, part imagined—about growing up as my mother's daughter. That may sound like an odd way to describe myself, but only if you didn't know my mother. In the unlikely event that you have heard of Mary White, you likely knew her as an art historian—well respected in her field, though not necessarily celebrated. Certainly not well-known. But I knew her as the hero she was. I knew her as a woman who loved her only child with an indescribable desperation. A woman who was never interested in having a partner, but who managed to juggle the pressures of a career in academia and a life as a mother with grace and ease." I instinctively look to my daughter in Myra's lap. I look away just as quickly, swallowing a swell of grief.

"When the cancer came," I continue, glancing at my notes for guidance, "I watched my mother's body, ravaged with disease, melt into itself—loose skin draped over sharp angles and jutting bones. But as much as her body changed, her spirit never did. Even when she…" I say, pausing, wondering if such things should be spoken here. Yes, of course—where else would they be? "Even when she took her life, she did so with dignity. She left this earth on her terms." She told me as much in her note. Who was I to say she was wrong? I look back to Aster. He gives me a quiet nod.

"Growing up, I never knew where my mother got it—her strength, her resolve, her character. But now, thanks to Jonathan Aster, that mystery has been solved." I flip quickly through my notes. There is so much left to say, but I'm not sure I can make it through the rest of it. "So, without further ado, I'd like to turn the stage over to Mr. Aster, so he can introduce you to the source of my mother's strength—my maternal grandmother, Kathryn Fairchild."

Uproarious applause erupts as Aster makes his way center-stage. He moves slowly, deliberately, allowing me time to disappear down the side steps, tucked out of view. He's aged these past three years—his lean body more stooped than before, the plume of silver hair thinner at the crown of his head. But he's still just as dignified as ever, carrying himself with the same natural grace and charm as the day I met him at the Sundowner nearly four years ago.

Just as Aster begins to speak, Katie wriggles free from Myra, patters around to the side of the stage where I am standing. Myra tries to reach for her, but then gives up, mouthing an apology from her seat in the front row. I smile, wave her off. The crowd is too engrossed in Aster's remarks to worry about me or my little girl.

"Mommy!" says Katie, just loudly enough for me to shush her against my chest as I pick her up. I need this: to feel the weight of her body, to breathe in her sweet-pea skin. The hook of her nose, the curvature of her ears—these are constant reminders of her father—a man she knows from a distance, a man she calls *Daddy* without fully understanding the weight of what it means. I grew up without a father. I'm doing my best to make sure she doesn't have to do the same.

I look back to where Katie was sitting, see the empty chair, and wonder: what would my mother say if she were here today? What would she think of Aster's photograph—a picture where she exists only as illusion? How would she feel about Danny Clark sitting two seats away—the uncle she never knew she had, from a town she never knew existed? Katie wriggles in my arms, the weight of her body pushing against the grief inside me.

Laughter rings throughout the audience—a reaction to some joke Aster has just made. But I don't pay him any attention. I study Quinn in the front row—a girl bursting into womanhood like a dogwood blooming from a spring rain. She's *Aunt Quinn* to Katie, which is so delicious I can hardly stand it.

I turn my gaze to Morgan Springer. (She dropped the *Alman* two years ago—after I finally returned her call and told her my side of the story, after she finally confronted Ryan and forced on him the responsibility he wasn't willing to accept, after she finally divorced him.) She wears a thin smile—warm, unsure, a little sad—as she loops a finger through a curl in Connor's hair. The boy is five years old now. Katie can't pronounce his name yet, try as she might, but it doesn't matter. Most of the time she just calls him *big brother*, which makes my heart swell to bursting every time I hear it—for so many reasons intertwined and inseparable, a knot that will never be untangled.

And then there's Kyle Sawyer—back in New York for the fifth time this year, the unlikeliest of souvenirs from my time in Gray Station. I'm not sure what we are to each other, not really. We've never felt a need to define it. But he's been a part of Katie's life from the start, and that counts for something. We don't talk much about Kyle's wife—the *accident* or anything else. We almost never talk about Ryan. I suspect someday these things will get easier, but we haven't found that place yet.

With a swoop of his hand and a flourish in his voice, Aster unveils the photograph to gasps and sighs of the audience. Katie turns her head to see the commotion, flailing herself about in my arms like a butterfly wresting itself from a cocoon. She follows the gaze of the crowd, lets her eyes settle on the photograph in the center of the stage—the first time she's seen the image, I realize.

"Who is that, Mommy?" she says, pointing her stub of an index finger toward Kathryn Fairchild. I open my mouth to speak, forming the name on the tip of my tongue before swallowing it back down. I think of all the ways I could answer, none of which would hold the full truth—especially to a three-year-old.

"She is," I say, measuring out the words, "the woman who

saved your grandmother." A fleeting look passes over Katie's face—one lost between confusion and satisfaction. Either way, she nestles her head into my shoulder. She will know the story of Kathryn Fairchild—her great-grandmother. She will grow up rooted both in New York and in Western Kentucky. But that will come later. For now, we have each other.

"Okay, baby girl," I say, shifting her to my other hip. "Let's go sign some books."

★ ★ ★ ★ ★

ACKNOWLEDGMENTS

I am profoundly grateful to the many people in my life whose support, encouragement, guidance, expertise, friendship, and love have paved the way for me to write this novel. Despite my better judgment, I'm going to name some of those people below—knowing that I will exclude others due to my own faulty memory or oversight.

Thank you to my agent, Danielle Bukowski, for a second chance, saintly patience, and steadfast belief in me and my work; to my editor, Meredith Clark, for seeing what this novel was—and then seeing what it could be; to all the other publishing professionals who had a direct hand in shaping the book—whether in copyediting, sensitivity reading, design, marketing, sales, publicity, or any other way—for your expertise and beautiful work.

I extend my sincerest gratitude to my former teachers, professors, advisers, and mentors—both those living and now gone—especially those who had the most direct influence on my writing: Annette Allen, Brad Watson, Michael Williams, Paul Griner, Shelley Salamensky, Sena Jeter Naslund, Jody Lisberger, K. L. Cook, Kirby Gann, Mary Yukari Waters, Neela Vaswani, Roy Hoffman, Rachel Harper, Beth Kemper, Bob Doty, Bill Neal,

Sarah Sims, Mary Jane Chaffee, Laura Williams, and Janelle Conn.

My love and thanks also go to my friends and former classmates at Spalding University and the University of Louisville—many of whom had the unfortunate task of reading my earliest pages—for your long-suffering and grace. There are too many of you to list, but I owe a special debt of gratitude to my current and former inner writing circle, early readers, and writing group friends from the distant past: Dave Harrity, Keith Nixon, Nadeem Zaman, Angela Jackson-Brown, Emily Bonden, Adriena Dame, Kristi Combs, Bruce Smith, Savannah Sipple, Mindy Beth Miller, Chris Harold, and Laura Levin.

Likewise, thank you to the administration of Campbellsville University for the trust you've placed in me and my career, and to my faculty colleagues in the English department and beyond.

More broadly, thank you to members of the Woodland Creatures, The Porch, and Vineyard Campbellsville for your encouragement during the writing process, the daily joy you bring into my life, and for simply being the lovely humans you are.

Finally, my deepest love and appreciation go to my family near and far, starting with the two who gave me life: my mother, Veda, and my late father, Terrye. Above all, I'm especially grateful to Rochelle, Ari, Elin, Avey, and Finn, whose love and support sustain me every day. You've created space for me to work on this craft—work that could never promise anything in return. This is the definition of selfless love. I will never deserve you, but I'm so thankful I have you.